Passion Unleashed

"Come to me, darling. . . ."

Her body throbbed with his pressure. His firm, passionate flesh within her brought her to ecstasy, her fingers biting savagely into his shoulders.

But a part of her remained detached, and watching: *Enjoy him. This joy will not last. You must not let yourself be conquered by a physical craving. You cannot trust him.*

Perhaps, in some dreadful way, she was not the Catherine Earnshaw to her beloved Heathcliff. She had so much wanted that role when she first knew him. Perhaps she was only another Isabella Linton, the besotted girl Heathcliff had used and despised.

Despised? That couldn't be true, she would sense that. Surely he loved her a little.

He seemed to prove that tonight. Or was it only sexual satisfaction that he sought when his lips brushed so sensuously over her breasts or her abdomen and between her thighs. . . . She wanted to scream with the ecstasy of his touch, but she did not scream. She remembered his sister, separated from them only by the hallway and the bedroom door, slightly ajar.

She caressed his hair and then her hands moved over his body, his thighs and loins. Her tantalizing hands lingered over his erection, his need for her. Maybe in this way she could bring him to love her as she so desperately loved him.

Hours later, when she was lying there staring at the high ceiling, Jason sleeping beside her, she felt his hand move suddenly. She remained motionless, pretending also to sleep. His hand found her thigh and rested on it. The heat of his flesh seemed to burn through her gown.

DARK WINDS

ALSO BY VIRGINIA COFFMAN

VIRGINIA COFFMAN

DARK WINDS

PaperJacks LTD.

TORONTO   NEW YORK

PaperJacks

DARK WINDS

PaperJacks LTD.

330 Steelcase Rd. E., Markham, Ontario L3R 2M1
210 Fifth Avenue, New York, N.Y. 10010

Published by arrangement with Arbor House
Arbor House edition published 1985
PaperJacks edition published March 1986

Cover design: Brant Cowie/Artplus Ltd.

Cover illustration: Wes Lowe

This is a work of fiction in its entirety. Any resemblance to actual people, places or events is purely coincidental.

For Jay, the original brain of the enterprise, and for Donnie and Johnny, its heart, with my deepest thanks and much love

PART ONE

ONE

The letter lay on the side table of the entry hall for an hour that evening before either the servants or Miss Wentworth noticed it. In fact, if a careless housemaid hadn't knocked over the silver plate, with its usual assortment of calling cards, the letter might have gone unnoticed until morning.

The housemaid stacked the cards neatly back on the elegant, polished plate but curiosity got the better of her and she unfolded the letter.

She was still trying to read it when her mistress, young Cecily Wentworth, snatched it from her. "Get on upstairs and see if Mama requires anything. Then turn down the beds. Lay a warming pan to my and our guests' beds. And, Biddy—"

The girl turned nervously.

"—you know better than to read other people's mail."

It was a compliment to assume Biddy could read at all, but the girl murmured, "Aye, mum," and hurried up the stairs. She paused at the top of the staircase, smiling to herself at how eagerly her golden-haired young mistress was reading the letter. Addressed to Cecily's fiancé, Jason Bourne, it had been written by Miss Wentworth's future sister-in-law, Maria Bourne. But as far as Cecily was concerned, any scandal that tainted Jason's family was her business. After all, she had a reputation to maintain. A hopeful suitor had once called her the Purest Young Lady in Leeds and she was proud of this title.

She sat down on the bottom step of the stairs and continued reading.

Dearest Jason,
You have always been my own dear brother and looked after me; so be good to me and understand. I have gone to my lover. You and the others were so innocent or so indifferent to my needs, you have no notion there was a lover, but he taught me to want him when he was in Leeds during the Tory Party's spring meetings. Every woman needs a man who can make her feel immortal, loved!

He isn't dark and masterful like you, Jason, but delicate and gentle. He has a young daughter and he adores her as he will adore me. He is completely selfless. He has told me he will not marry me until he is able to stand for Parliament, but I will not ask him to wait, as that may be years away.

I have been told that he takes the London coach tomorrow morning, and I am going with him. We will be married in London.

Ask Mother to forgive me. I know you yourself will, though I doubt that your empty-headed little Betrothed will ever speak to me again. Forgive me for running away from you. Just remember how happy I will be when I am Mrs. Everett Hinton.

Your Maria

"Empty-headed, am I?" Miss Wentworth murmured, and then reread the last lines and felt vindicated. So the uppity Maria Bourne expected to marry Everett Hinton. Much good that dream would do the poor wench.

Meanwhile, there was the problem of Jason. He was not a man

to be fobbed off with excuses. The letter must be put in his hands the minute he returned with her father from the Tory debate tonight. And that would mean scandal. It might even mean violence, to a man of Bourne's passionate temper and strong family loyalties. And since Jason and Maria had been spending the week at Leeds in the Wentworths' house, Jason was sure to blame Cecily's family for the lack of supervision over the impossible young Maria Bourne.

It was all so unfair. Cecily Wentworth was notorious among her admirers for her sweet disposition, her flawless deportment, and her innocence. Cecily's mother could hardly be responsible. The dear soul was an invalid confined to her bed-sitting room. How could Cecily or her mother possibly suspect what Maria Bourne was up to? Ultimately, the problem was Jason Bourne himself.

While many Yorkshire females were struck by Jason Bourne's deep voice, his luminous, heavy-lidded black eyes, to Cecily it was his mouth, often voluptuous, that made her uneasy.

And there was much more to Jason Bourne, as Cecily was discovering. Even the most confident men would think twice before angering this man, with his tall, powerful physique and the air of authority that he had acquired after his father's early death. Cecily found such qualities ungentlemanly. She preferred delicacy in all matters.

As a Yorkshire mill owner and the master of Bourne Hall, a spacious house on the Yorkshire moors, Jason was considered a satisfactory husband for the popular Miss Wentworth. Certainly no scandal would attach itself to his name.

But having read Maria's letter, Cecily saw that her sister-in-law could very well bring imminent shame upon Jason as well as the Wentworths. Walking the floor of the stuffy, overfurnished parlor, she waited uneasily through the evening for Jason's and her father's return from their political meetings.

When she heard the Wentworth butler unbolt the front door close to midnight, Cecily rustled out into the narrow entry hall, posing prettily in her ruffled, yellow Lyons silk gown with its huge leg-of-mutton sleeves. For the two men who entered, she presented the ultimate image of fragile femininity.

Humphrey Wentworth was still arguing with his future son-in-law, but the sight of the prettily demure girl at the top of the stairs prompted the two men to disguise their differences with more genteel talk of the recent ascension of little eighteen-year-old Princess Victoria to Britain's throne.

One of the difficulties in dealing with young Bourne, his Tory neighbors agreed, was Bourne's stubborn concern for the rights of mill workers thrown out of their lifetime jobs by the mechanization of the Yorkshire mills. He could not get it through his head that this problem was of no concern to the mill owners. It was simply among the blemishes of an imperfect universe.

Wentworth was glad to step inside his comfortable house just beyond the smoky, polluted heart of Leeds, far from the filthy River Aire, which ran through the city collecting all the ordure and detritus of a town that had become a northern metropolis almost overnight, thanks to the industrial revolution sweeping over Britain.

Cecily embraced her father lovingly, and permitted Jason to kiss her hand (or the air an inch above it). She handed the folded letter to him, and murmured, "I'm so dreadfully sorry, dear."

Jason's dark brows raised but he did not answer. Piqued by his indifference to her well-meant sympathy, Cecily added, "I am afraid she has put herself quite beyond the line of what is acceptable among"—his piercing eyes reduced her last words to a whisper—"among decent women."

Jason read the letter quickly, then lowered the thin, ink-stained sheet. There was no point in concealing the news from Humphrey Wentworth. His dutiful daughter would certainly tell him. It was one of her many suffocating virtues, as he had begun to discover.

"Sir, are you acquainted with a man named"—he glanced at the sheet—"Everett Hinton? The name sounds local."

Wentworth had already judged from his daughter's expression that the matter was grave. "Matter of fact, I've met the fellow. So have you. At party meetings. Born somewhere in the north of the shire, but he's a London fob, through and through. Very pretty sort. Fair hair. Weak mouth. Keeps coming up here hoping we'll invite him to stand for office. Not a chance of that, I say."

Cecily put in, "He was here to dinner in the spring. He

14

showed us a charming miniature of his daughter. About ten years old, I thought."

"He talked a good deal about her. Why, Jason? Hope the fellow hasn't borrowed money from you."

"Worse, sir. Maria is running away to marry him."

Wentworth was so aghast he dropped his walking stick, but the shock of its crash on the flagstone floor was nothing compared to the shocked look on his face. "My dear boy, then you must stop her. The fellow is very much married already. Frenchwoman she is, with a tidy little fortune. He's not going to abandon that. Not our indolent friend Master Hinton."

Jason Bourne closed his eyes for a moment, imagining Maria's despair when she discovered the truth . . . his little sister whose passions ran deep and violent, whose need for love was so great.

Seconds later he took Wentworth's wrist in such a tight grip that the portly older man winced.

"Sir, where does he lodge when he is here, in Leeds?"

Neither Wentworth nor Cecily was sure, but she thought it might be Trimmer Street, a select area in which there were a number of "private hotels" that took in respectable moneyed men.

When Cecily caught up with him, Jason Bourne was already striding toward the front entry door. The Wentworth butler, all ears, waited to usher him out, but Cecily murmured earnestly, "Jason, do take care. This could become a scandal. And for Maria's sake, we wouldn't want that to happen, would we?"

He looked at her oddly, as if he had never seen her before. Then he walked out without a word to her.

She felt deeply hurt. At the time of their betrothal, after every young lady Cecily knew had set her cap for Jason, she had thought herself the most fortunate of women. But that triumph had eroded during the last three months. She didn't understand half the things he talked about. She never knew what he thought. She often suspected he found her ways amusing—and who enjoyed being laughed at? Worst of all, when he did take her in his arms to kiss her, his ardor alarmed her. Now there was this unflagging loyalty to a girl entirely lost to shame.

She turned back to her father, who put an arm around her comfortingly. He assured her with a touch of smugness, "I doubt that my little golden Cecily would ever behave in the fashion of Miss Bourne."

"Never, Papa!" she vowed, looking heavenward.

It was late that September evening when Everett Hinton returned to his lodgings. He walked the distance, a ten-minute stroll, reflecting on what a waste the political meeting had been. In spite of his wife's pressures, Everett Hinton was not a politician. He would be glad enough to leave Yorkshire tomorrow morning, headed for home and the more civilized pleasures of London.

He turned the corner, passed the peak-roofed apothecary's shop, and crossed the cobbled street to his lodging house, which he had taken because it was far from his usual haunts on Trimmer Street and unknown to most of his acquaintances.

There on the steps crouched Maria Bourne. Damn that persistent, tiresome girl!

Hinton could hardly fail to recognize her, even though the murky air blurred the moonlight, lingering in the narrow streets of the industrial city. She wore the same provincial brown spencer with the ruffled bonnet that she had worn the day she first came to his more elegant lodgings during his visit to Leeds the previous spring.

He tried to recall whether he had noticed then that she was all arms and legs, tall for a female, a trifle awkward, with little to commend her except her age. She was the only female under twenty who was present at several of the Tory social affairs.

It was at this time that he had enjoyed the virginal sweetness of the girl, the awkward shyness that seemed flattering. Nor could he deny the pleasure of her eager body during those days. In fact, he had seldom experienced more passion in anyone so young.

He had met Maria at a benefit ball in aid of those millhands thrown out of their jobs due to the mechanization of the Yorkshire woolen mills. Thanks to the Bourne family and a few others, the Tory Party was belatedly displaying its sympathy.

Everett Hinton had little interest in the mill workers. He was proud of the fact that he had never worked a day in his life. For a gentleman like himself (as his mother had often pointed out), life was to savor and enjoy. His knowledge of Maria's older brother, Jason, and their mother—both partisans of the millhands' cause—was scant. He regarded them as traitors to their class, but there was no doubt the Bournes were an asset to the Tories in the north.

Young Maria shared Hinton's impatience with the problems of starving mill workers. She was sympathetic (who was not?), but as she had confessed to Hinton during their first meeting, "I'm young. I'm alive. And politics is so boring. Even our language is different."

That had attracted him after the assaults on his ears of dozens of broad Yorkshire dialects. This pale, ladylike young female was clearly educated, a fact that spoke well for her family. Then she had said, "I wish I might go somewhere and laugh and love and forget the mills for just a day."

"Or a week," he had joked.

"A fortnight."

"A year, then," and they had both laughed.

After that, they were friends. She realized that neither her brother nor her mother would approve of their friendship. The mother, Amy Bourne, was quiet and small, and blond like her daughter, a woman who had a taste for literature, music, and other pleasures unsuitable to a country wife. No danger from that little ultracivilized creature.

Maria's brother, Jason, was another matter. A powerful young man with eyes as black as midnight and a broad, high-boned face, he made his presence felt with few words. He was, in Everett Hinton's view, a born troublemaker, arguing the rights of men who had once marched on the Bourne Woolen Mills with pikes and guns, for all the world like a revolutionary French mob.

Everett Hinton could not forget the remark of a Tory friend, "Yorkshiremen make loyal friends and allies, but if you cross them, beware. Do not confuse them with those London dandies fluttering around the new queen."

That might be, but Hinton still remembered how eager, and yet how shy, Maria had been that first afternoon when she surrendered to his genteel seduction. She had told her brother and her mother that she was visiting a school girlfriend. Invaluable

17

friend! How useful, during those exciting afternoons that followed!

In his mind he could still hear her young voice, guttural with passion, whispering, "I adore you. You aren't like my people. What smooth flesh! It sets my loins on fire."

For a fortnight that spring Maria Bourne, in her journey from shy virginity to warm sexual desire, had set his own loins on fire. But enough was enough. She had ceased to amuse him almost before he was ready to leave for his London home at the end of May.

Perhaps he had been too gentle when he explained to her at their parting that they must never meet again.

"My dear," he had told her earnestly, "your reputation means everything to me. I saw the way my landlord looked at you with those mean little eyes of his yesterday. I will not have you soiled in the world's eyes by his suspicions. Merely because you gave me the most precious gift you can bestow. Until I can offer you the position you desire, as the wife of an M.P., I am going to send you home—"

Naturally, this had panicked her. "No, oh, please, no . . ."

But he remained firm. "At sixteen you are too young to be bound by a memory. At Bourne Hall you will be safe from foul looks and gossip. These beautiful days were all too short, my dear. They will remain with us forever. But take care. That scowling brother of yours must never know. To him our love would appear improper. He might do violence to you."

"Not Jason," she said. "He loves me."

Everett Hinton had put his palm softly over her mouth, and said, "He would certainly murder me. I know the temperament of fellows like your brother. Do you know what my friends say about Jason Bourne? He thinks he is the lord of those blasted moors he's so fond of. And when he sets those fierce eyes on a man, it gives you the feeling that there will be pistols at twenty paces."

There was a certain truth to his words. She had pressed close to his body, hugging him. He remembered feeling her heart race with her passion for him.

"If anything happened to you, my darling, I couldn't bear it," she whispered. "I never really lived before I met you. Let me go with you to London. . . . Or let me follow you. I'll be your servant, luv. Your slave. Only let me share just a tiny corner of your life."

What a calamity that would be!

Above all things, Nicolette must not hear of this girl. It was his French wife who held his purse strings, most of those strings leading to Paris banks. It was her money being poured into the coffers of the Tory Party. And at this moment Nicolette was probably carrying on a flirtation in London with Thomas Etheredge, or one of those other towering bowls of Tory pudding, hoping to influence their votes. A Tory vote, she thought, would ensure the protection of her tidy fortune.

But the same Nicolette had given him that mischievous, gray-eyed little charmer, his ten-year-old daughter, Rachel. She was worth more to him than . . . If any hint of his liaison with Maria Bourne came out, Nicolette would be certain to put barriers between him and Rachel. Even though the law gave him control of his wife's estates, as was natural, Nicolette and her French advisers managed to keep him financially dependent on her. If he made trouble, she would hurry across the Channel, taking his adorable daughter with her.

When he and Maria Bourne parted in May, he had tenderly blotted her tears and muffled her sobs against his breast. He sent her on her way to the school friend's house after one gentle kiss. That was to be the end of it. Further entanglement might reach Nicolette's ears, or those of Maria's deadly brother. Maria had understood. About Jason, at all events. Thank God she knew nothing of Nicolette.

Tonight, four months later, she was a nuisance, if not an outright danger. He pulled himself together, straightening his shoulders in their carefully padded, fawn-colored greatcoat. He stepped out across the street with the heavy skirts of his coat swinging.

Maria Bourne raised her head. The cold northern moonlight, glazed by the smoke-filled air, illuminated her face inside the bonnet, reminding him of the young lady he had found briefly entrancing: her stiffly reined sensuality, her faded hair and nervous eyes, her tight lips that softened so easily. But the more he looked at those lips, the more he saw an uncomfortable resemblance to the determined mouth of that ogre, her brother.

Maria Bourne's small mouth opened now in a hesitant smile. "Found you out, didn't I?"

Her speech sounded slurred. Had she been drinking? Most unlike the frigidly correct Miss Bourne he had known. Gently, gently, he reminded himself . . . don't let her guess your outrage at this, this invasion!

He watched her eyes following him. Like most of his female acquaintances, she admired his slender form and graceful movements. He was proud of them himself and very much aware of the appearance he made as he reached the bottom step of his lodgings only an arm's length below her. He put out one gloved hand. "My dear," he cooed. And then, when she had absorbed the kindness in his greeting, "Don't tell me you've waited here in this abominable cold. This is no place for you."

She brightened perceptibly, showing the latent desire that had first attracted him. "How handsome you look! 'Zactly as I remembered. I wanted . . . make sure . . . seeing you, Everett."

Everett. The intimacy of his name on those drunken lips disturbed him as much as her condition. "Come in. We must talk."

With a sweeping, exaggerated gesture, she went through the open doorway under his arm, and then waited.

"Don't stop here. Up the stairs," he murmured, hoping Mrs. Gantry, the lodger on the ground floor who owned the building, was tucked in for the night. He didn't want her to hear this ridiculous scene.

Maria Bourne hesitated on the narrow staircase. "Who lives there?"

"Mrs. Gantry." He was forced to nudge her on. "Above stairs, and to your right."

She continued. "Is she . . . well favored?"

"Handsome, I'd say."

She wrinkled her nose. "Handsome. Shouldn't think she'd be a rival." She looked back at him, her mouth smiling but her eyes worried. "Have you ever made love to her?"

"To Adelaide Gantry?" He gave a snort of laughter. "Good Lord, no! Not in my style."

"S'good."

He unlocked the aging timber-beamed door beyond the newel post. She slipped inside and he followed with little joy. He bolted the door quickly and then realized too late that this action had been misunderstood. Maria looked pathetically pleased—anticipating, no doubt, a night of love.

He didn't remove his greatcoat. "Aren't you afraid your family will find out that you are here?"

Unsteady on her feet, she caught herself. "Oh, no. Jason's at a silly meeting. Went with"—she giggled—"went with Wentworth. Slyboots, stout little Wentworth. He likes to put his hand on my knee. I hate him. I retired early. I wanted to avoid that dreadful Cecily." She wandered around the room, examining the faded and inadequate furnishings, glancing in at the bedchamber beyond and then back to him; her head lolled sideways and back in a pathetic attempt at sensuality.

Hinton steeled his jaw. "Maria, it is very late, and I will be taking the London coach early tomorrow. Nearly two days' rocking along in that odious contraption, crushed between eaters of onions and fish and God knows what-all."

Her lower lip quivered slightly. Then she closed her upper lip over it. Her thin cheeks had lost all their color. "Oh, Everett, take me along. I promise I'll be the best wife you ever had. Mother to your girl, Rachel." She reached out to him, clawing at his hands. "I don't care if you never get into Parliament. Don't make me wait. I want, I need, to marry you now, luv."

He recoiled. "Please do not call me 'luv.' You know I detest these provincial accents."

She tried to retrieve her former light mood. "Did I say that? Must be the brandy. Never drank it, till . . . Needed it tonight for—courage. Stole old Wentworth's brandy. Serves him proper . . . Don't you miss me, even a little? I've got to marry you. I need you, Everett, my whole life . . ."

Her voice began to rise. Panic. All the things he loathed. He shook off her long groping fingers. "And do not call me by my Christian name."

She swung around so fast her bonnet fell back over one ear. Her thin, fine hair was arranged in sausage curls that bounced around like the wig of a rag doll, a style extremely unflattering to her admittedly intellectual features. How could he have ever wasted his time on this repulsive child?

"Well, what am I to call you then?" she demanded. "You will not have 'luv.' You refuse your own name. What have I done?"

A sudden fear wrenched his stomach. "My God! Are you in the family way?" he asked her in a failing voice.

But she was at least honest about that. "Oh, I wish I was," she whined in a voice as shrill as a fishwife's. Next would come hysteria. He moved to the liquor-scarred old gaming table between the long, narrow windows. He took the whiskey decanter and poured an inch of whiskey into the glass for himself, but she snatched it up and bolted the scotch in one startling gesture, then held the glass out to him. She was staring at him with disturbing intensity.

He forced himself to remain calm despite her dangerous excitement. It would be just like her to run home and complain of him to her precious brother.

"The girl I knew never drank, my dear."

She was ashamed. If he wasn't careful, she would break out in tears. "Nobody knows. Not even Jason. Darling, I haven't been . . . loved. Not since you left. Life's been so—so cold."

He tried once more. "It was for your sake that we parted. You are a young woman on the threshold of life, scarcely older than my daughter. You deserve a husband and family. One of your own kind. These good Yorkshire people."

She didn't seem to be listening—she was removing her spencer. She wore a frilled muslin gown with huge upper sleeves, absurd for the season. Gad's life! She must have thought it was provocative. Six months ago it might have been. But her breasts were small, her clavicle and bones prominent, and the display simply looked pitiful in the light of the two lamps Mrs. Gantry had left burning for him on the mantel.

He reminded her, "You really shouldn't be here. You know that. Remember our good-byes last June? How we said it was for the sake of—of—" What the devil had been his excuse? What reason would penetrate her drunken little head?

She tried again, starting to touch him, then hesitating. The gesture reminded him of their first sexual encounter.

"We were well s-suited, you and me, Everett. You taught me all the j-joys of the flesh. Darling . . ." She began to unfasten the

22

neck of her gown, and he caught glimpses of her pale flesh. She reached for his reluctant hand, drawing his fingers to the slight mound of left breast. The sensation aroused nothing in him but embarrassment. He longed to cover her, to keep her from humiliating herself.

With what she doubtless thought was a sensuous, teasing gesture, Maria lowered the muslin collar and camisole still farther to reveal the unexpectedly large ruddy nipple of her breast. She pressed his fingers crushingly to its surface. He could almost feel its throbbing with her desire for him and withdrew his hand quickly. Memory began to creep into his own body. He didn't want to start that up all over again.

Her voice, garbled by liquor, grew plaintive. "Everett, don't you remember how it was, that first—"

"I cannot take you with me. You must understand, my dear. There are reasons. Sound reasons."

Maria straightened up, readjusting her clothes. With a sigh of relief, Hinton crossed the room to open the door for her. But she instead reached for the whiskey decanter. Good God! She was taking it into the darkened bedroom. If she drank any more, she'd be out cold. Then how would he get her out of here?

She called to him across the intervening space. "Luv, . . . take me with you. I'll be such a good wife. Not like that dreadful Cecily and my poor brother. I'll be good for you. And your little girl. . . . Luv?"

He shuddered. Even as his body hardened with the first stirrings of desire he thought of the disaster that would follow if he brought Maria to London. He must not get involved with her again. And here, heaven sent, was his escape. He would hurry out while she slept off the liquor.

He snatched up his portmanteau and the carpetbag, thankful that he had been careful not to bring his valet on these political trips. He wanted no witnesses who might tell tales to his wife. With a bag in either hand he rushed out of the room toward the front door.

He almost fell over the carpetbag Maria must have brought with her. She had left it on the top step. He halted his panic-stricken flight, afraid Mrs. Gantry might be peeking out the front windows. He proceeded down the steps with dignity.

A minute afterward, he heard the clatter of footsteps after him and knew Maria Bourne was determined to go with him. She tripped on the carpetbag but caught herself, barely maneuvering the steep staircase. Luckily, the street was deserted. He prayed that she would awaken to the impropriety of her behavior. But she was too far gone.

"Everett, . . . you did love me. You said I would be your wife. I could be a companion to your Rachel." Her voice twisted painfully. "I'm young. I'm only six years older than she is. Take me with you." She caught his sleeve and clung to it.

"Miss Bourne . . ."

"Call me Maria, luv. Why are you being so deliberately cruel? You said one day we would be together forever. You know you did."

"Please, my dear, do go home!"

It was no use. She kept clawing at him like an animal. Revolted by her touch, her loss of pride, he lashed out instinctively, elbowing her sharply aside.

As she fell, she seemed to dissolve into the smoky air. A piercing scream of pain shivered through his bones.

When he looked back, he saw her crumpled in a spreading heap of skirts stained with the filth of the street. She was groaning. She cradled her left arm and rocked back and forth in her agony.

He knew if he helped her, she would begin to plead again, to claw at him, and he would never escape her. In a panic he looked around. No one in sight, but someone was sure to come by presently to help the poor creature.

He hoisted his bags and began to run.

Her flesh burned—she didn't realize that it was the cold—her muslin skirt and two petticoats were crumpled up above her knees, her legs exposed to any passerby as if she were a common trollop. The pain across her left shoulder and her upper arm came in suffocating waves that cut her breath and made her gasp. Her mind, blurred with pain, wandered to other moments of such agony.

Once, when her pet black lamb, Moogin, was lost on Kilbride Moor, she wandered all night looking for him. Terrified that he might have fallen into a pothole, she had stumbled and twisted her ankle. There had been pain then. But Jason had found her, his strong arms had carried her back across the endless maze of sheep trails. She remembered how roughly he scolded her for going out alone in the dark, but no one could have held her with more tender care.

And then, when they came back to Bourne Hall, Maria saw her beloved Moogin standing silhouetted against the bright red sunrise, chewing away at the grass that grew around the York stone wall of the front yard.

Curiously enough, it was only then that Maria was able to cry.

Now she heard herself groaning, the sound cutting through the smoky air. Two men passed across the far end of the square. The murmur of voices made her raise her head, but even that movement was excruciating. They looked her way, exchanged a few words, and laughed. Doubtless, they thought she was some drunken whore.

I've got to get out of the street, she told herself. *If someone could find a horse and carriage for me . . .*

But how could she go back to the Wentworth house? The mere thought of Cecily Wentworth's disdainful glance nauseated her. She dropped her head, huddled over the cobblestones, and vomited.

Long seconds afterward, her flesh finally numb from the cold, she found herself floating off into a pleasant darkness as her heartbeat thumped deafeningly in her ears.

She was brought to by her own shriek of agony and found herself lifted up from the street. She had been wrapped in a man's greatcoat. She knew who had saved her. The only man who would care enough to come looking for her was her brother, Jason. She muttered sleepily, "Moogin came home. Didn't fall in a pot—a pothole."

"That's right, luv. Moogin's safe. And so are you."

"Shoulder hurts."

"I know. Anywhere else?"

She considered. "Shoulder. Bones broken I think. And arm."

She felt his hands. The hard pressure under her bosom and under her knees made her wince. But that small added pain was not as disturbing as the leashed anger in his voice. "Did he do this to you?"

25

"He wanted to go. Said I disgusted him."

"Did he see what had happened to you?"

"Yes, but he was afraid. Afraid his precious daughter would know about me. His daughter!" Finally, she began to weep again, now that her world had ended. "I wanted to be her friend. Jason, I did!"

She felt his anguish, his pain numbing her own as he lifted her into the closed carriage waiting with its bored, patient horse and the curious old coachman looking down at them from his box.

On the agonizing, jolted ride to the Wentworth house Jason demanded, "Would you really have gone to London with him?"

She tried to blot out the pain by concentrating on his question. "He said we would be married." It could have been a glorious dream. Why had he deliberately hurt her like that?

As if reading her mind, Jason said abruptly, "He *is* married. To a woman with money. He would never rid himself of her."

The words hurt more than the physical wounds of Everett Hinton's betrayal. So, he had lied from the first. Everett Hinton had used her as contemptuously as he would have used a common whore on the river bank.

"Don't tell Mother."

"She will know. She knows everything that happens to us."

This was true.

"I hate him."

"I know. I'll pay him for what he has done. Don't think about it."

"*I hate him!*"

Her brother's arms were gentle around her, as she had known they would be, but the racking pain shot through her shoulder and arm. She cried out, trying to stifle the sound against the rough coat in which her brother had wrapped her.

Presently, the pain faded with consciousness. She barely heard her brother's anguished vow: "He'll suffer, as he made you suffer. I promise you that. I'll break more than his own damned shoulder—I'll break his neck if I must."

Even at this hour Everett Hinton was not the first to reach the coach yard of the inn that now dignified itself by the title of "hotel." A drunken, somewhat effete older gentleman of fifty-odd years introduced himself. "Branscomb, my dear fellow. Lord Branscomb. Saw you at the meeting tonight. Or was it last night? Shouldn't be traveling in this rackety style but lost a packet during our Tory business. Gaming, you know. My besetting sin. And that incredible clown, Jason Bourne, actually proposes that we turn our pockets out for his precious mill workers! Who is to turn out his pockets for us, I should like to know?"

Hinton was relieved when the fellow shut up and went to sleep in his greatcoat with the collars pulled up around his florid face. But afterward, as Hinton sat in the ancient coaching inn, praying for time to pass, he wished the peer had gone on talking. Anything to take his mind off his own deep thoughts.

Toward dawn he dozed off. Presently, a half-dozen travelers entered the waiting parlor, chattering loudly. They were continuing the journey south and immediately assumed the air of long-established residents. The heady aroma of boiled onions and bad liquor assailed Hinton from all sides. He closed his eyes and tried to sleep again.

He dreamed of darkness and pursuit. He was the pursued, the treacherous bogs of Yorkshire's West Riding everywhere around him. Cold terror crept into his veins. His eyes snapped open.

And in the heavy gray light he knew his nightmare existed. He stared up at Jason Bourne's tall figure in its many-caped greatcoat as it moved toward him across the uneven surface of the floor. No gentleman would appear at such an hour without his hat, but here was this repugnant sheep farmer with all his coarse black hair blown about by the wind, like the commonest laborer. Hinton could not fail to read the menace in the man's dark eyes as Bourne hovered over him now.

How had Jason found him? Could he have tracked Maria down? The landlord in Trimmer Street must have given him Hinton's new address. And Maria knew he intended to take the London coach this morning.

Hinton sprang up, shrinking away from Jason. "Look here, sir. I was—there were others. The girl lies. Lies!"

"Lies, is it? She says you left her helpless in the street with her arm and shoulder broken!"

Despising himself for being intimidated by this brute, Hinton stammered, "Not I, sir. There were others. Many . . . others."

"You sniveling little cur!" The creature had him by the throat. Those eyes burned. Hinton fancied he felt the searing pain of them but it was only Jason's hands at his neck, shaking him.

Others in the parlor crowded around. One or two men tried ineffectually to separate them. Several went for reinforcements.

Jason slapped Hinton fiercely across the face with the flat of his hand and hurled him away. He fell hard against the wall. Not content with this brutality, Bourne picked him up, hit him again, and once more he struck the wall.

In a burst of pain Hinton became aware that the witnesses, unaware of the true cause of this shocking, unprovoked attack, were fussing over him, the women especially sympathetic. "The poor lamb. See how he bleeds."

"Aye. Here's me kerchief. Fresh to me neck only yesterday, it was. His head, pure cracked. Bust 'is arm, too, belike."

Then a man's indignant voice, high-pitched and querulous, cried, "How dare you! Did you see that, everyone? He attacked me as well." It was that man, Branscomb, seizing upon the perfect opportunity to rid himself and others of the tiresome Tory firebrand. Branscomb had attempted to defend Hinton. But the brutish Yorkshireman quickly put him down. Branscomb could barely speak in his imperious, slightly drunken way. "These young moor-born ruffians! Think they're the lords of creation. Attacked us merely for our politics, sir, and so I shall testify. He'll be made to suffer. We all saw his attack. Unprovoked, sir. You've our word on it. Has he not, my friends? Hold that ruffian fast for trial, you lads."

The response went far to soothe Hinton's varied injuries. He certainly had enough witnesses. Already, Jason Bourne was being challenged by half a dozen of Hinton's prospective "witnesses" as he made his way out of the inn. Even Bourne's strength was vulnerable to the force of that onslaught.

Luckily, no one understood Bourne's reference to Maria. The man would never dare use his sister's ruin in his defense. It would serve no purpose except to give him a stronger motive, and would announce her shame to the world.

Hinton closed his eyes again, comforted by the fussing ministrations of the women around him. If the trial was well managed, he could have this brute shut away for murderous assault on a gentleman. Who knew how many years Jason Bourne would serve in prison, or the hulks?

God knows, the creature has earned it, he thought, gingerly feeling his aching head for wounds.

All would be well, after all, as long as his little Rachel never learned the real cause of this wretched brawl. Once Lord Branscomb laid their testimony before the local magistrates, Hinton would take care never to return to his native Yorkshire until he was under the sod and couldn't help it.

And there were more like Maria Bourne's kind to be found. Only last month he had met a very comely brunette in Plymouth. Her husband was the mate of a barkentine whose voyages took him away fourteen months at a time. No awkward interruptions there, and small likelihood that Nicolette or his little Rachel would hear of it.

TWO

Yorkshire to London via the Scotland Express, May 1850

The southbound Scotland Express hurtled out of the night into one more dimly lit Yorkshire railway station. The young lady in the first-class carriage closed her novel on her forefinger and looked out the window.

Lively and curious by nature, Rachel Hinton Etheredge found the passengers at each station intriguing and, to her metropolitan eyes, excitingly primitive. In defense of this view, which was reinforced by the romantic novel she had been reading on the journey, she reminded herself that one could hardly confuse these rugged faces, or their sturdy bodies and unfashionable clothing, with any of her London friends.

Nearly a dozen passengers stood on the platform by her window. Most of them seemed to find her as exotic as she regarded them. The richness of her green silk bonnet and the glimpse of her gloved hands probably struck them as out of place in a city like Leeds, which even Rachel recognized as the steamy heart of the industrial north. Though it was long after nightfall, the air was still thick with smoke and other pollutants.

None of the passengers waiting on the platform seemed aware of the foulness of their environment. Most of them were men of business, bound for London and the great world. They looked sober, preoccupied, portmanteaus either in hand or on the platform beside them.

After her annual pilgrimage to the birthplace of her father, Everett Hinton, Rachel Etheredge had packed her own portmanteau with a suitable Yorkshire romance, this one titled *Wuthering Heights*, and embarked on the journey down to London. Intending to read in the comfort of the railway car, she was instead distracted by the activity of arriving passengers.

Two countrywomen especially interested Rachel. They carried napkin-covered baskets of food: she imagined Scottish pasties, fresh bread, fruits, gingerbread parkin, probably some of that delicious York ham, and, of course, strong black tea.

Rachel smiled through the window glass at the two stout, comfortable women who looked puzzled, then exchanged glances and smiled back at her. Rachel was sorry when they headed for the third-class carriages.

Little Miss Hesper Fridd, now dozing beside Rachel in the carriage, was not the most lively or entertaining companion, though she had served in that capacity once Rachel no longer needed a governess. In spite of the little woman's less than dazzling personality, Rachel valued Hesper Fridd beyond any treasure. In her quiet way, Miss Fridd had comforted the lonely girl through all the losses of her young life. First, there had been Everett Hinton, her careless but devoted father, who died when Rachel was fourteen. Then, after three years, the loss of both her mother, Nicolette, and her stepfather, Sir Thomas Etheredge, in the collision of their Channel packet. Between them, Sir Thomas and Nicolette had left Rachel one of London's most sought-after heiresses. But that inheritance could not provide the friendship and loyal companionship she always sought. She was not a girl who enjoyed solitude, and a mischievous trick played in her childhood had left her terrified of huge, open spaces. Nature was the enemy when Rachel found herself alone.

Hesper Fridd stirred and shivered. Rachel smiled to herself, feeling a bit guilty. Mischievous by nature—a quality she inherited from her French mother—Rachel had been teasing Miss Fridd earlier about the harrowing dangers that awaited them along these shimmering tracks. Rachel had not forgotten to include the stations that suddenly loomed up and then vanished in the dark blue of the long northern twilight.

Little Miss Hesper Fridd, as amiable and obliging as a docile cow, had believed every word of Rachel's tall tales and was almost afraid to close her eyes. "My dear Rachel, we must remain upon our guard. A young lady like yourself, I mean to say, an heiress—one never knows." She had straightened in her seat and leaned over to pat Rachel's silk-covered arm. "But I intend to stand by you, at all costs."

As always, Rachel had been amused and appreciative. But by this time darkness shrouded the scene, and the forbidding landscape outside the windows began to meld into blackest night.

"Thank you, Friddy. Now, go to sleep. I'll wake you if I need you."

"Well, dear, if you say so." Miss Fridd had adjusted herself against the stiff cushion. Gradually, her head, with graying curls crushed by her pink bonnet, began to nod, and she slept. Rachel took out *Wuthering Heights*.

Rachel considered it especially appropriate to begin this sensuous story of love and hate on her return from Yorkshire, since it was obvious that only a Yorkshireman could write such a romantic and terrifying book.

Ignoring the depths that lurked beneath the love story of Catherine Earnshaw and the gypsy Heathcliff, Rachel thought the book soundly written for women like herself.

Her mother had been far too practical to understand how an otherwise sensible daughter of hers could be so romantic. "Rachel," she used to scold, "you are so bad as your Papa. Always, you see sex in things."

Rachel had pricked up her ears at that; Nicolette backtracked rapidly. "It is your fortune, the fortune I leave you, that will give you the life you enjoy so much. Do not be fooled by bodily desires. Look at your father."

Poor Papa was certainly an example. Everett Hinton had been shot dead in 1841 when he and a sailor's wife in Plymouth were surprised by the woman's outraged husband . . . "Surprised in the creature's bed," Rachel had heard from one of her school friends at the Select Female Academy of Richmond, Surrey.

A sad story, but very romantic!

Nicolette Hinton's mourning had been brief. There was faithful Thomas Etheredge waiting to marry Mama and raise her daughter as his own. But though Rachel obligingly took Sir Thomas's name, a part of her always thought tenderly of Papa. It wasn't his fault that the ladies found him irresistible.

Curiously enough, her occasional visits to his gravestone near the Westmoreland border had shown her that the elegant golden-haired Everett Hinton was nothing like a typical Yorkshireman. Much as she loved Papa, Rachel's personal tastes ran to darker males, like *Jane Eyre*'s Mr. Rochester or that new favorite she was enjoying tonight, the shadowy gypsy, Heathcliff in *Wuthering Heights*. Her pulse throbbed at the thought of that muscular body entwined about hers. . . .

Heavens! She was surprised by her own ability to imagine such intense passion. *What a shocking idea!*

She looked around, but Miss Fridd still slept. Fortunately, no one could read Rachel's thoughts. She caught her reflection in the windowpane and smiled at the lively gray eyes looking back at her. Unhappiness was so dreary. She tried very hard to enjoy life on her own terms—a philosophy her fortune made surprisingly easy.

Rachel was twenty years old when her mother and Sir Thomas died. In some respects the tragedy left her more mature than her age. Her mother's careful rearing had left Rachel only a trifle spoiled. Now, at twenty-three, she could judge for herself the wisdom of numerous long-faced advisers and, of course, Hesper Fridd. She had already discovered that to many casual acquaintances, and some suitors, her charm was greatly enhanced by her fortune.

Abandoning the view from the train window, she returned to her book and read: "Is Mr. Heathcliff a man? If so, is he mad? And if not, is he a devil?" She drew a deep pleasurable breath.

Suddenly, there was a click. The track-side door opened and a shadow crossed her page. A tall gentleman stepped into the carriage. Still haunted by her mental image of the novelist's

Heathcliff, Rachel was astonished to see the hero-villain himself, in all his dark, romantic glory, stride past her and Miss Fridd. He took the far corner seat facing them, and kicked his carpetbag behind his feet. He snapped open the folds of the *Yorkshire Post* and, without looking at either Rachel or Miss Fridd, calmly began to read.

Such a prosaic end to a fascinating moment! She was angered by her own susceptibility. Surely, she was much too old to be moved by surface appearances!

Rachel raised her book and tried to concentrate again on the words. But curiosity was one of her greater sins and she continued to watch the new passenger over the top of her book.

He was far from young—she assessed his age as thirty-five, or older—but she was adjusting her ideas about mature men. Unlike so many gentlemen of Rachel's acquaintance, this one was clean-shaven, a fact that made him conspicuous in itself. For Rachel, it added to his attraction. His features were naked to her observation, and she felt guilty studying him so closely. He had large, heavy-lidded black eyes, a strong nose, and a mouth that intrigued her. Forbidding, perhaps. As cruel as Heathcliff's? She suspected a great deal of passion was concealed in its wide curves.

He raised his head and stared back at her. The flickering railway-carriage lights accentuated his prominent cheekbones as well as his rumpled black hair. The light did nothing to soften his features. He certainly had no use for ladies in rich green silk and elegant bonnets. She shifted her gaze.

Returning to her book, fully conscious of the stranger's stare through eyes that appeared to be half-closed, she reflected that Heathcliff might be romantic but he must have been difficult to live with. She giggled nervously at the thought and sensed the stranger's annoyance. He must have heard her. He returned to his paper and apparently dismissed her from his mind.

Pride came to her rescue. She raised her chin. Then she tried to read. Presently, she fell asleep.

They arrived at Nottingham Station some time after dawn. Miss Fridd was awake and looking eagerly out the window into the gray light beyond the platform. "My dear," Friddy whispered, "I do so enjoy passing through Robin Hood country. Such a delightful creature, I always thought."

Rachel laughed, then remembered that their dour companion might be sleeping. She covered her mouth, glancing furtively toward where he sat in the far corner of their carriage. To her surprise, though his grim visage did not thaw, there was a glint of humor in his eyes as they looked at Hesper Fridd.

Somewhat piqued, Rachel realized that Friddy was making a conquest. It went further. Miss Fridd dropped one little wheat-colored mitt and the gentleman leaned over at once, his long fingers touching the mitt just as Rachel reached for it. She retreated awkwardly and the gentleman returned the mitt to Friddy, who, flustered with pleasure, received a smile that did much to soften his stern face.

"And are you always fond of forest thieves like Robin Hood, ma'am?"

Miss Fridd looked helplessly at Rachel, who feigned concentration on her novel. The poor woman murmured, "Well, sir, not precisely. That is, today, only when they are dead. I mean—"

"I understand. I share your fondness for Robin Hood." He smiled again and settled into his seat with his head back, as if he were tired, or thinking deep, unpleasant thoughts.

When he closed his eyes, Rachel resumed her study of him. He did not look like a man whose life had been easy. His clothes proclaimed the gentleman, but it was clear that some time in his past he had worked at manual labor. His well-shaped hands were hard and calloused, with a number of healed scars. Another white scar trailed upward above the collar of his open greatcoat, ominously near his jugular vein. Where had he spent his life? In what dangerous company? All this went far to explain the man's somber look and unpleasant disposition.

"Such a gentleman!" Friddy whispered. "So polite, so kind. He quite overwhelmed my aversion to speaking to strangers."

"I rather expect that is his usual method," Rachel muttered, trying not to sound sour. To her horror the gentleman opened his eyes at that moment and looked over at her. She had finally said something that amused him. All the same, she could not

35

help feeling that he despised her. She was both angry and dismayed.

Nor did matters improve when the train reached London. Rachel told herself she was delighted that the Yorkshireman's attentions were exclusively paid to Miss Fridd. Nobody deserved them more, and they showed his gentlemanly qualities. He ushered the little governess down to the platform, bowed to her, wished her well, and went his way. At the same time, a stout, officious woman, her great skirts swinging as she moved to meet a passenger, pushed Rachel to one side and almost knocked her down.

The Etheredge family solicitor, Sir Bayard Lorimer, met the two ladies and escorted them home to Berkeley Square in his carriage. He was the father of Rachel's favorite friend and confidante, Miss Clare Lorimer.

"*Le pauvre cheri* was born old," her mother used to say of Bayard Lorimer, though she had invariably relied upon him. Spare and distinguished, he had neat silvery side-whiskers and a fatherly manner to match that concealed a sharp judicial mind. Another important asset was his ability to handle young heiresses. He had two children of his own but spent considerably more time extricating Rachel from the various mishaps that befell her, thanks to her impetuosity, her self-sufficient and over-generous nature, and the fact that he had always secretly loved her mother.

He did not outwardly disapprove of Rachel's visit to her father's grave in Yorkshire, though he had considered Everett Hinton a very frail reed, unworthy of his favorite client, Nicolette.

As the open carriage rattled over the London cobblestones, he asked, "I trust you enjoyed your journey, Rachel. Nothing untoward?"

Rachel agreed regretfully that nothing untoward had occurred. "Dull, dear Sir Bayard. Not a single exciting thing happened. We kept hoping there would be a minor disaster on the railway line, but here we are."

Since they were approaching the square, she began to pull off her carefully fitted long gloves. "At all events, we are home again and slaves to propriety once more. We shall sit very properly in my drawing room and wait for royal invitations from Windsor. If any. Think how exciting that should be! Especially the waiting."

"Oh, Rachel," Miss Fridd protested. "Don't—I pray you—don't wish for disasters. It is frightfully bad luck."

But Friddy had no sense of humor. She was still protesting when Sir Bayard handed them up the steps to the narrow, elegant house facing on Berkeley Square. It had been chosen by Nicolette DuVaux on the day of her betrothal to the handsome Everett Hinton. The house possessed all the qualities that Rachel associated with her mother.

It had been an excellent investment. Beautiful not only for its carefully chosen objects—the paintings, statues, bric-a-brac, as well as the polished ebony, rosewood, and sandalwood furniture, much of it carried to England from China and the Hawaiian Kingdom. The interior of the house, with two stories above the street floor, its kitchen and utility areas below the street, still bore the touches of Rachel's stunning, iron-willed mother.

Perhaps it was that exceedingly feminine atmosphere that so often drove Papa away. Not that he was excessively masculine. As Rachel remembered him, he hadn't been the least like the north countrymen she saw in the past fortnight, but judging by his conduct toward his daughter, she could well imagine how kind and gentle her father had been to the ladies who loved him.

Lorimer stopped in the narrow vestibule of the house. The hall was cold and formal, with its delicate Regency chairs and the portrait of stout George IV. Its greatest ornament was the slender white and gold staircase, so flattering to wide-skirted gowns and splendid uniforms of all the Etheredge guests who had graced the upper-floor ballroom in her stepfather's time.

Lorimer said, "Rachel, I believe we have an acquaintance in common, a young gentleman who has gone into trade. The publishing business."

Surprised and then hopeful, Rachel agreed. "George Smith, of Smith, Elder. Perfectly respectable, I assure you."

"Yes, yes. And done very well, from all accounts. I believe he owes much of his present success to that scandalous *Jane Eyre* novel."

"Scandalous? Really, Sir Bayard, you are showing your age. I'll wager your children don't think it's scandalous. Clare and I have both read it twice. Even Desmond thinks it's—tolerable." Her persistent suitor, the solicitor's handsome flaxen-haired son and heir, had never been known to open a book since he left Cambridge. "Why? Have you seen Mr. George Smith recently?"

The publisher's luck in discovering a sensational and shocking novel had awarded him great success in less than five years.

Sir Bayard was rambling. "Saw him yesterday, matter of fact. Young Smith had a curious message for you. He and his mother will attend the Italian Opera at Covent Garden tomorrow evening. They will be escorting the person you discussed. . . ." The solicitor stroked his side-whiskers. "He said you would understand."

The hazy autumn day began to brighten. While Miss Fridd gave their luggage to the Etheredge housekeeper's fourteen-year-old son-in-training, Rachel walked back to the door with Lorimer. "I do understand, and I thank you. My stepfather invested in Smith, Elder, and I have been interested in their success with *Jane Eyre* and one or two others. I'm mildly curious about *Jane Eyre*'s author, Currer Bell. His newest novel, *Shirley*, is presently on the market. But tomorrow night I mean to meet this person who writes so romantically. And successfully."

"He?" Sir Bayard echoed. "I've heard Currer Bell is a female. Lives in the north, what's more."

But Rachel refused to believe this. "No woman could create such masculine characters as Edward Rochester and Heathcliff. If Currer Bell did actually write *Wuthering Heights*. There seems to be some doubt."

The solicitor smiled at her enthusiasm but felt obliged to add, "The other books, *Wuthering Heights* and *Agnes Grey*, I believe, were written by Miss Bell's sisters." He cleared his throat politely. "At all events, that's the story at Smith, Elder."

This was crushing news, but Rachel decided not to dwell on the disappointment and to attend the Italian Opera at Covent Garden anyway.

"Sir Bayard, I shall ask Clare and Desmond if they will make a party of it. Please promise Desmond that he may flirt with all the pretty creatures he can find; he may even bring them refreshments between the acts. We would never accuse him of deserting us."

Sir Bayard looked pained at this aspersion upon his light-hearted son who had an insatiable eye for a likely female. He reminded Rachel, "If he might be certain he has caught your affections, he would soon lose interest in other women."

Knowing better, she smiled but refused to be drawn in. He took Rachel's hand briefly, bowed to Miss Fridd, and was gone.

THREE

Assuming that Sir Bayard Lorimer's information was correct, Rachel took great pains in dressing to compete with the famous Currer Bell. She knew that the author, whether male or female, would be certain to interest the select audience of the Italian Opera House at Covent Garden.

Clare Lorimer agreed to attend as Rachel's guest so that the two young ladies could speculate about the unknown celebrity to their hearts' content. Her brother, Desmond, had accepted Rachel's invitation to escort them, as she very well knew he would after his sister's hintings that he wished to further his pursuit of Clare's friend.

Lanky, tow-headed Desmond Lorimer, who seemed still to be all legs, as he had been in childhood, was born with a greater gift for making friends than for earning a livelihood. He was supported by his stern-faced but amiable father and by a small inheritance from his doting mother. Having found it remarkably easy to gain whatever he wanted in life, he had discovered by the age of twenty-four that only those objects that were withheld from him were worth having.

Rachel was one of those unattainables. How could she be expected to moon over a boy who had pulled her hair and left her hopelessly lost during a picnic in the New Forest? A boy who had sent a milk cow to scare her as she stumbled to the Lorimer estate across a trackless meadow? To this day she found it unnerving to face great green stretches of heath and common.

Desmond naturally found it boring to escort a mere sister to the opera, but he had convinced himself that he loved the unreachable Rachel Etheredge. Or Rachel Hinton, as she was born. He had always admired Rachel's father, especially his reputation with females, and Desmond did not approve of abandoning one's father's name, even to oblige an overbearing mother. Desmond hoped to emulate the dashing Everett Hinton and was well on the way to succeeding with just about every female he encountered. Except the amused Rachel, who knew all his tricks.

Rachel took pains with her toilette that night. The white gown bore twenty yards of little flounces on the underskirt exhibited at the front of the silk gown under yards of tulle. The daringly low neckline was emphasized by the tiny artificial flowers and revealed all of her shoulders, as well as most of her well-developed bosom.

She had a moment's misgivings over the display of her breasts and wondered if, when she curtsied, she would expose herself improperly. But other young ladies risked it, and Rachel felt that at the age of twenty-three, when most women her age and class were long since married, she should be permitted a daring décolletage.

Her mother's maid, Brigitte, had always felt superior to her present young mistress, but at times like this, the tall haughty Frenchwoman was invaluable. Since Rachel's light-chestnut hair was thick and curly, little needed to be done except to pile it into place and skewer it loosely and to frame her face with two tiny white roses.

The roses were natural, as was most of Rachel's coloring; Brigitte merely added a touch of kohl to her lashes and a faint rubbing of powdered paper over her nose. Rachel brightened her cheeks with red paper and bit color into her sensuous, mischievous mouth.

She herself, knowing the Frenchwoman's reluctance, made the best of Hesper Fridd's modest looks, tinting her faded cheeks and mouth, bringing out the charm of her bouncing gray curls. The middle-aged woman's gown suited her years. It was of changeable lavender-gray silk, generously dotted with knots of lavender ribbons.

Once the Etheredge carriage horses had come to a halt before Sir Bayard's town house just off Grosvenor Square, both ladies emerged, splendidly dressed.

Blond Clare Lorimer, two years Rachel's junior, was one of those people whose presence usually added to the gaiety and nonsense of a party. Neither beautiful nor clever, she was nevertheless a great deal more popular than the cleverest of her contemporaries. Rachel had more than once defended Clare to Desmond: "You say she isn't clever, but the fact that men don't find her so may be the cleverest thing about her."

He admitted with a grin, "They certainly do *find* her. The house is forever filled with the tiresome rattles. One of them could discuss nothing but the flight of King What's-His-Name in France and the return of the Republic. As if any of that mattered. The real question is, Will the quality of French brandy be weakened?"

Rachel had raised her eyes skyward in exasperation. Nor did it help when he added hurriedly, "But I wouldn't for the world burden you with that deep twaddle. I want to talk about things you like. In your little world."

Rachel had not appreciated this left-handed compliment, and Des, the Fool, as his loving sister dubbed him, was forced to back out of yet another conversational trap he had galloped into.

The girls embraced, in spite of Miss Fridd's nervous comments about the exposed angle of their low-cut gowns. Rachel embraced Desmond as well, disentangling herself before he could take advantage of the opportunity offered. He gallantly helped the ladies back into the carriage.

Dressed in trousers far too tight for the current mode, Desmond sat opposite Rachel, with his dress coat spread open and his legs parted. Suspecting he was trying to advertise an excessive masculinity between his long limbs, she refused to look in that direction. Very likely, in the fashion of some dandies who were whispered about, he had stuffed his garments with a cloth bag and silver tissue, to make her and other ladies think that what Rachel and Clare referred to as his "manhood" was exceptionally well proportioned. The idea might have excited her in someone else, but she knew Desmond too well. On him it was simply annoying.

He made light conversation, showering Rachel with compliments, but with unerring bad luck managed to time his remarks just as the horses clip-clopped over the cobblestones into a hopeless tangle of carts, pedestrians, bellowing vegetable vendors, and elegant carriages headed toward or from Covent Garden.

When they reached the opera house portico beyond the market, he invited Rachel to a future show at a well-known music hall famed for its daring French dancers, but she begged to be excused due to a prior engagement.

"But I haven't given you the date," he protested as he maneuvered her around abandoned crates of cabbage, turnips, and squash at the Covent Garden market. She gave him an apologetic look, explaining that without exception, every evening of the next fortnight was taken up by "some tiresome engagement or other."

Coming along in their wake and assisted by the timely arrival of one of her own beaux, Clare called out some sisterly advice: "Try late June. London will be a dead bore, and Rachel will be glad to see even you, Des."

Rachel tried to soothe him, but she did so abstractedly. She was anxious to see all the new gowns, the dashing males, and the general splendor of the Italian Opera House on a gala night.

Sir Thomas Etheredge had always occupied a box at the opera, and Rachel kept up the tradition. It was somewhat removed from the proscenium, and the Etheredge guests were forced to crane their necks to catch a glimpse of the royal family. But as Sir Thomas had once remarked to his stepdaughter, "We are far down in the aristocratic hierarchy. If it were not for our purchasing power, we would be the merest bourgeois family. Always remember that, Rachel. Mere possession of a fortune does not bring us nearer the Royal Enclosure."

The opera was *The Barber of Seville*, which was, as Desmond complained, impossible to sleep through. He was already gesturing to friends in boxes across the theater's pit.

Rachel, amused, commiserated with him while looking around for the publisher's box in the hope of seeing young George Smith and his guest. The opera house always suited her taste for the romantic, with its great chandelier dazzling the beholder, golden-banded ceiling displays, and rich crimson plush everywhere.

It was not until the second-act intermission that her purpose in visiting the opera was satisfied. The two young women and Miss Fridd strolled over the rich crimson carpets while their escorts piled high their several plates with pâtés, cakes, and glasses of champagne. Clare was momentarily enthralled with her latest admirer, Roderick Dinnes-Evans, who had either tried Desmond's stuffing trick or was, as Clare whispered with rolling eyes, "exceedingly well gifted."

"Did you notice?" she added after exchanging a knowing look with Rachel.

Miss Fridd gasped. But Rachel had similar thoughts. She had caught herself wondering about the matter with the gentleman in the railway carriage, and worrying for fear that such obvious masculinity was his sole attraction in her eyes. But it had nothing to do with Dinnes-Evans or her old playmate Desmond.

She shrugged. "Too obvious. I saw someone on my northern trip who . . . Never mind."

Clare was instantly alert. "Rachel, tell! Who did you see? Where? Not at your papa's grave, surely!"

"No, no. Nothing like that."

But before she could further betray herself and her most private feelings she saw the publisher George Smith approaching. He was accompanied by two women: his mother, a stout, genteel lady with a pleasant smile, and another female, a tiny woman who peered about her nearsightedly through small spectacles. The tiny woman must be the governess to the publisher's youngest sister, but where was the Lioness?

The "governess" did not look comfortable in this festive silken crowd. Her high-necked, poorly styled tarlatan gown did nothing for her. The puce color was far from flattering. Nor did her manner help her. She seemed to be critically observing everything in the hubbub around her. None of the clothing or behavior went unnoticed by those nearsighted, pale eyes. The strength of her intensity made Rachel uncomfortable.

The two groups met and introductions were made. George Smith, tall, distinguished, with beautiful manners, appeared a trifle uneasy.

"Miss Charlotte Brontë, may I present Miss Rachel Etheredge? Sir Thomas Etheredge was a dear friend and business associate of mine." He said nothing about Miss Brontë's identity.

Rachel was astounded. It seemed incredible that the sensuous and passionate *Jane Eyre* could have been penned by this strange little woman. But a close study of Miss Brontë modified some of Rachel's first misconceptions. There were those dangerous, observant eyes, and quite possibly some of that intensity was the strong sexual passion of a plain woman.

While Miss Brontë listened attentively to a dissection of the opera performances between George Smith and Clare, Rachel's eyes wandered questioningly to George's mother. Mrs. Smith nodded, with a small, tight smile.

Rachel tried not to be disappointed. She had visualized quite a different prototype for the mysterious Currer Bell. She would like to have discussed the book with its author and especially to have asked about *Wuthering Heights,* supposedly written by Ellis Bell, but something in Miss Brontë's face, a kind of pregnant stillness, suggested that this was not the time. Though she had an unworldly look, Rachel perceived in her countenance a great deal of firm conviction.

In fact, Miss Brontë seemed to be very like the proud, intelligent heroine of her novel, with few outward qualities to attract the casual observer, yet possessing a fiery passion within.

While Mrs. Smith and Rachel dallied over the plates brought to them by their escorts, the older woman remarked with amusement, "You are disappointed. Confess it. You hoped *Jane Eyre*'s creator would be quite different."

"Not at all. I—" She broke down and grimaced. "Yes. I was a fool. I think I expected someone rather like her hero. Or the hero created by the person who calls himself Ellis Bell."

Mrs. Smith lowered her voice, though the babble in the luxurious corridor around them made it impossible to be overheard. "Another disappointment for you, I fear. It is extremely secret. The lady was adamant that her identity should not be known."

"Lady?"

"Sister to Miss Brontë. Now regrettably deceased. It is my personal opinion that both young ladies took their heroes from the same physical model. A gentleman acquaintance in their own West Riding. That is, the moor country of Yorkshire." Rachel was hanging upon her every word, but Mrs. Smith broke off suddenly. "Enough of that. I mustn't be caught gossiping. My son would be cross as two sticks. You know how men are. But Miss Brontë chanced to see that very man yesterday, near my son's Cornhill offices." Mrs. Smith hesitated. "Miss Brontë is very close-mouthed, but George believes that the man in question inspired something of the physical aspect of the characters she and her sisters created."

"Does Mr. Smith know the man?"

"Yes, indeed. George's father formerly had some dealings with the Bourne Woolen Mills in the north. This gentleman known to Miss Brontë and her sisters is the son, Jason Bourne. And the present mill owner."

Desmond offered Rachel her champagne and she sipped at it, only half listening to him discuss with Dinnes-Evans whether the cravat would ever return to favor in place of the new cravat-tie, and if a monocle was actually the last word in style.

Rachel saw that little Miss Brontë had attracted an admiring group in spite of her quiet reserve. It was intriguing to note how the authoress fired up and became almost attractive when discussing subjects like the Tory Party and the Duke of Wellington, both of which she seemed to favor.

Rachel's party did not meet the Smiths again until after the final curtain. Strolling out just ahead of them, Smith stopped abruptly to speak with a dark, tall gentleman near the theater's entrance doors.

Rachel's heart beat faster. She saw George's friend only in profile but was positive he was the stranger on the Scotland Express. He looked even more stunning in full evening attire, all stark black and white. Friddy too recognized him and picked at the sleeve of Rachel's velvet cloak. "Is it he? Dare we join the group?"

But Smith's mother allowed for that. She turned back, caught Rachel's eye, and motioned her and Friddy forward. The gentleman seemed absorbed with Miss Brontë.

While Desmond and Dinnes-Evans hung about on the fringe of the group, George, in his mannerly way, presented the dark gentleman to the ladies present.

"Delightful coincidence, Bourne. Our second meeting in as many days." He explained to the other ladies, "Miss Brontë and Mr. Bourne are by way of being neighbors in Yorkshire."

How curious, and how revealing! Miss Brontë flushed when the man took her hand and bowed over it, yet they seemed to be the merest acquaintances. Perhaps *he* was the prototype of her novel's hero, and the hero of her sister's novel as well. He certainly could have sat for both portraits, though to Rachel he seemed more the callous and brutal Heathcliff than the warmly passionate Rochester.

Clare exchanged an excited glance with Rachel. It had been unlikely that the man's attractions would escape her. He saw Rachel but didn't look as though he would acknowledge their acquaintance. Indifference was the only expression she could read on his face.

"Miss Rachel Etheredge . . . Jason Bourne," the publisher said.

Desmond, ever resentful of any slight to his boyhood idol, added brightly, "I say—it is Miss Rachel *Hinton* Etheredge, to be precise. Father's name seems to have gotten lost in there somewhere. Everett Hinton."

Clare nudged him and hissed at his rudeness.

Jason Bourne bowed over Rachel's hand, but, as Desmond spoke, the man's fingers closed so tightly around Rachel's hand that she flinched. When he raised his head, his eyes had widened and his gaze swept over her from head to foot. She felt scorched. What plagued the man?

He went on to give Miss Fridd an unexpectedly warm smile, as if reminding her that he remembered their railway acquaintance.

Within minutes the parties separated, leaving Rachel with a challenging mystery.

During the first day or two after their meeting, Rachel wondered what events in Jason Bourne's life could have inspired the books of Miss Brontë and her sister. Or was it merely his appearance that they had borrowed?

On one occasion, when Miss Fridd unwisely mentioned "that gentleman from the railway carriage—such a nice smile!" Rachel cut her off sharply, "I've never seen his smile. Quite ill-bred, I thought him."

"Oh, Rachel, when I think of how he stared at you! Such intense interest!"

Rachel would like to have believed her, but she, too, remembered Jason Bourne's stare. Whatever his interest, it was hardly a pleasant one.

A week later, while Rachel and Clare rode in Hyde Park in hopes of a "chance encounter" with Clare's dashing Dinnes-Evans, Mr. Jason Bourne called at Berkeley Square and left his card. In the process he met Hesper Fridd, who reported the meeting to Rachel. "So gentlemanly, my dear. He almost seemed interested in my little efforts at conversation."

"Well, why not? You are a sensible woman. A deal more sensible than he is used to, I daresay."

Perhaps Miss Fridd read something in Rachel's disgruntled expression, for she added nervously, "He seemed most disappointed at not seeing you."

"Don't be silly. He despises me."

"Oh, no, Rachel. Not—despises."

"Did he frown or look angry when he didn't find me at home?"

"Well . . . no. He was very entertaining. Told me two modest jokes about"—she lowered her voice—"Prince Albert."

"Precisely. Probably thinks I am one of the idle rich, grinding the bones of the poor. Anyway, the dislike is mutual. I find him shockingly bad-mannered. I have never done a solitary thing to earn his hatred." She grew indignant thinking about the injustice of it. "And furthermore, I won't give him the opportunity to repeat his rudeness. The next time he leaves his card, tell Mrs. Brithwick to burn it."

48

"Rachel!"

She sensed around Mr. Jason Bourne an atmosphere of genuine hostility, of which she was the target. But she had never consciously hurt him, and she vigorously returned his contemptuous attitude.

Two afternoons later, coming down the stairs, she spied him in the hallway of her own home. Carefully dressed in black, with a narrow white cravat tied in the new fashion, he may have overwhelmed the little room but not small, pugnacious Mrs. Brithwick, the housekeeper, who ran the house and everyone in it.

"Indeed, sir, and what may your business be with my young lady?"

Rachel waited on the staircase, curious to hear his answer and to judge his manner toward her. Jason Bourne did not appear at all uncomfortable. He barely glanced around the entry and seemed, furthermore, to be smiling. A grim smile, perhaps, but anything was better than her exaggerated memories of his contempt.

"Our mutual acquaintance, Mr. George Smith, of Smith, Elder, knowing that my business took me to this area, has asked me to carry the several volumes of Miss Brontë's latest novel to Miss Hinton. The novel is called *Shirley*, I believe." Removing one glove, he held out the neat packet.

Mrs. Brithwick was not impressed. "Etheredge is my lady's name, sir. All legal-like. I'll trouble you for the packet, sir. Miss Etheredge will deliver her thanks to the gentleman herself, most like."

"And who is to thank me?" he asked, still amused. His strong, noticeably scarred hands maintained their grasp on Miss Brontë's volumes.

Mrs. Brithwick reached for the books, but he pulled them out of her reach, as if teasing an angry bulldog. Rachel decided she had better intervene before war was officially declared. She descended the stairs with leisurely dignity. It wasn't until she stood before Jason Bourne and asked him coolly, "How may I help you, sir?" that she realized he had known she was there all the time.

No doubt this explained his peculiar knowing smile. Not precisely disagreeable, but bemused. He offered her the wrapped set of books, for which she duly thanked him. But common politeness required her to hold him in conversation at least another ten minutes. He did not appear to be a tea-drinking man, still it was her only excuse for detaining him.

"I am about to take tea. Would you care to join me, Mr. Bourne?"

The gentleman was not to be outdone in politeness. "A pleasure, Miss Hin—Miss Etheredge."

She concealed her surprise, offering her arm to escort him into the long salon, but he deftly avoided her touch. She signaled to Mrs. Brithwick, who was standing at the back of the hall near the cellar stairs, to the kitchen area. Mrs. Brithwick's heavy frown deepened, but she understood and obeyed.

Rachel led the way to the far end of the green and gold salon, gesturing him toward the high-backed Hepplewhite chair. She settled herself and her sprigged dimity skirts over the sofa, suddenly aware that he was watching her every move with alarming intensity.

He seated himself on the edge of the chair as if he might get up any second and lunge at her. His position also brought him closer to her, though when she shifted her black morocco slippers uneasily, he made no effort to touch her. She felt like a specimen in a strange laboratory.

"You are staring, sir. I was given cow-pox serum when I was a child," she assured him with a lighthearted glint in her eyes. "I am not likely to transmit the disease to you."

She thought for a minute that she had finally reached whatever cold recesses made him dislike her. He laughed heartily and agreed. "The pox is one evil I never thought to take from you."

She ignored the possible double entendre. "I very much fear I cannot offer you my companion and dear friend, Miss Fridd. She is visiting her niece's family in Stratford."

"Indeed. Miss Fridd is a very worthy female. A trifle shy, I take it."

"Modest about her own excellent qualities," she added.

"Just so, Miss—Etheredge." For some reason he still had difficulty with her name.

Mrs. Brithwick appeared, followed by the parlormaid, Alice, who carried the tea tray furnished with Nicolette's delicate

French china, tea and lemon, small cakes, and a dusty bottle of what appeared to be heavy spirits. Rachel asked frostily, "What may that be, if you please?"

"Sir Thomas's rum, ma'am. For the"—just a hint of a pause— "the gentleman."

Rachel reddened with embarrassment and anger. Only hard laborers, seamen, and convicts were likely to drink rum at this hour. She opened her mouth to order it removed, fully intending to have a few severe words with Mrs. Brithwick in private, when Jason Bourne startled her by holding his hand out for the bottle and the pewter cup. "Thank you. You are very perceptive, ma'am. I will pour."

Mrs. Brithwick departed after a triumphant glance at Rachel.

Rachel poured her own hot, dark tea, not knowing what to say to this strange guest. The fragile china cup rattled in its saucer. Glancing at him beneath her lashes, she saw that his dark eyes followed her every move. They observed her discomfort, missing nothing.

She wondered if he was enjoying her unease and tried to make light conversation. Was he in London on business?

"Business and pleasure."

That told her nothing. "I understand you and Miss Brontë, the authoress, are old friends."

"I scarcely know the lady. My family attends services in the village of Haworth. Miss Brontë's father, the Reverend Patrick Brontë, is the curate at St. Michael's."

For the moment she set aside the Brontë matter. Of far more importance was her next casual question. "Your family?"

Again that peculiar gleam as he watched her. Had he read in her simple question more than she wanted him to know?

"My mother. And my sister, Maria."

He was unmarried. It was absurd that she should actually care. She drank more tea to compose herself and to compose her pleasant, noncommittal smile. "And they are visiting London with you?"

He winced perceptibly. "No." For some reason she had touched on a sore spot. At first, she thought perhaps his family did not get on well together. Then, with a rigid absence of the feeling one would expect in the remark, he said, "In the past two years I have several times visited London hoping to locate two

51

old . . . friends. A week ago I learned that both had died some years gone by."

"What a pity!"

"As you say. A pity. Fortunately, one of them left his family well provided for. Knowing the gentleman, I might have expected that. Still, I intend to do what I can to repay my friend. Through his family."

"That is very good of you."

"Not at all. I have had twelve years to think about my friend and what I owe him. And to make my plans, as it were." He had drunk the rum and set the goblet down with a click. He was charming again. "Now, Miss Etheredge, I have learned nothing about you. When am I to have the pleasure of escorting you to—" He broke off, shrugged, and added with a grin, "The theater? The opera? The races? In short, when will I see you again without being forced to fawn over Smith, Elder's ridiculous novels?"

She laughed at that, although she was puzzled that he held so low an opinion of her favorite pastime. Surely, even he must realize that he was, at least in outward appearances, the hero of those novels. She started to object to his opinion of the books, but he dismissed her with insulting ease. "Not my sort. Wild adventures, preposterous characters. Mad wives in attics. Evil gypsies. The entire parcel of tricks."

He was watching her with flattering interest, though he added indifferently, "But I can see those tricks appeal to you."

He rose unexpectedly. She walked with him to the front door. Mrs. Brithwick was there, hovering over them like a prison warden as she handed Mr. Bourne his top hat. But her presence had no effect on Jason, who seemed to have warmed considerably to Rachel after their little conversation. As though he had assured her of his honorable intentions and could now behave more naturally.

He took the hand she offered. Instead of releasing it, he bowed over her fingers and raised them to his lips. His lips barely grazed her knuckles, but the excitement of their touch spread hotly throughout her body. She contained herself and watched him leave without word of a future meeting. She felt excitingly sure that she had not seen the last of him.

FOUR

Ever willing to champion the cause of romance, perhaps with a hope that her friend's adventure might be contagious, Clare Lorimer suggested that Rachel give a ball and open up the Hinton-Etheredge ballroom to the first official entertainment since the deaths of Nicolette and Sir Thomas.

Rachel's eyes sparkled. "Do I dare? An unmarried young female with no male to play host?" But already she was making plans.

"I'll lend you Papa to make you respectable," Clare offered magnanimously.

"The next problem is how to include Mr. Bourne."

Both girls put their heads together and came up with a plan. Rachel would work upon Mrs. Smith's sympathies. The good-natured lady reserved her strict sense of propriety only for the girl she chose as her son's wife. It had been long understood between both women that Rachel was far too volatile to be the wife of a publisher, and with that danger averted, Mrs. Smith volunteered to find out for Rachel when Mr. Bourne would be returning to London. Invitations to a masked ball would then go out to include George's eager sisters and, of course, his handsome friend. It was to be understood that declining such an invitation would be considered an offense to Rachel's delicate sensibilities.

"He probably doesn't think I have any," Rachel admitted with a wry smile.

"Never you mind, my dear." Mrs. Smith patted her hand, obviously in a matchmaking mood. "It's my belief Mr. Bourne needs someone with your good nature. You will soften him, smooth away those rough edges. As it is, I'm afraid you may find him a very dour cloud hovering over your ball."

But Rachel was confident. "All he needs are a few smiles, some teasing, perhaps a little brightness." She looked out at the Smiths' Bayswater garden, where huge pale roses seemed to glow in the sunlight.

What had happened in Jason Bourne's life to explain his unsocial behavior? Rachel seized this opportunity to put together a few pieces of the mosaic. "Mrs. Smith, you mentioned once that Mr. Bourne had encountered some misfortune in his past. Are you permitted to give me the details?"

Mrs. Smith waved away this misapprehension. "No, no, my dear. To be precise, I have it at third hand. Miss Brontë, the authoress, made a similar remark to my son. But I doubt if even George knows the full story."

"At all events, a 'misfortune' suggests that Mr. Bourne was in some way a victim."

Mrs. Smith nodded. "Precisely my thought. Otherwise, I should certainly have dissuaded my son from his further acquaintance." She added with a small, reminiscent smile, "However, when he sets himself to it, Mr. Bourne can be quite charming, as I have discovered. And as my daughters will tell you." She had a sudden, anxious thought. "Perhaps a masked ball is too sophisticated for young ladies their age."

Rachel reminded her, "But if I engage to occupy Mr. Bourne's attention?"

"Well, perhaps—if their brother and your Sir Bayard Lorimer are to play chaperon."

"And you, ma'am, will you not reconsider and accept an invitation?"

Mrs. Smith jeered good naturedly. "What? Me? I'm afraid I

haven't the figure for it. I shudder to think of what costumes might fall to my lot. I prefer to picture my daughters. As shepherdesses, I think. Though I have no doubt they would prefer to go as Madame Pompadour or another of that ilk. And you, my dear?"

"The Empress Josephine, ma'am. Hoping to dazzle my own Napoleon. I mean to wear a gown my grandmama wore at the imperial court. My mother took great pains to preserve Grand-mama's ball gowns. I believe it was the only sentimental thing she ever did."

With Mrs. Smith's blessing and her promise to secure the elusive Yorkshireman for the masked ball, Rachel went about her household plans.

These included the renovation of the long, lovely upper-floor ballroom, whose ceiling and pediments, like the double doors, were all carved in the Palladian style, the cream walls accented by gold, with the long windows draped in soft green. The circular carved work in the ceiling, like the sun's rays ever widening from the sources, complemented three crystal chandeliers. Their hundreds of prisms were immediately dipped into special bowls of water and washed with great care.

They brought out the furniture buried in Holland cloth in the basement area and the attics, along with the elaborate draperies and silver, gold, and Oriental decorative pieces from other unused rooms.

By the time the warm June night of the ball arrived, Miss Fridd and even Mrs. Brithwick were almost too exhausted to care, but Rachel was still torn between hope and despair. She had received a message from George assuring her that "his party" would arrive as planned and found herself pacing through the house, touching objects here and there, nodding approval to the anxious housekeeper.

At dusk, as Brigitte ordered the old-fashioned hip bath up from the kitchen regions into Rachel's bedchamber, a second note arrived. Mr. George Smith was sorry to report that one of the members of his party, Mr. Jason Bourne, was delayed by personal business and sent his regrets.

"Oh, damn!" Rachel cried, shocking Miss Fridd and the very proper Brigitte.

The disappointment was sickening after all her plans. The

entire ball was being staged as an excuse to include the elusive Yorkshireman.

Angrily, Rachel bathed and perfumed her body and let herself be draped in the shimmering Empire gown, whose chalk-whiteness was softened in a startling way by Nicolette's ruby parure, complete with a small but spectacular tiara that glowed like coals of fire in her thick, light-chestnut hair.

Sir Bayard Lorimer and his party arrived punctually as Rachel started along the upper hall to check the ballroom once more. Her nervous apprehensions were only partially allayed by the excited praise of her friend Clare and the wide-eyed, "By heaven, what a beauty!" uttered by Desmond, who pretended to fall backward down the curving white and gold staircase.

Having enthusiastically complimented Clare, whose long golden tresses crowned a surprisingly sensuous Maid Marian, Rachel whispered, "He isn't coming."

Clare appreciated the earthshaking importance of this new development. "Rachel, how ghastly! After all your plans and preparations."

Desmond and Sir Bayard wanted to know what had brought about this curious mood on ball night, but Rachel pulled herself together, reminded herself that her pride was at stake, and tossed her head with a bright smile. She fastened the tiny white satin eye mask in her hair and fluttered her mirrored fan.

She felt intensely relieved when the first of the guests appeared in the entry hall below. As her footman announced each guest, Rachel stood beside Sir Bayard, smiling until the spread of her warm lips threatened to set them permanently in that forced greeting. She had been surprised by the number of acceptances the invitations had received. She reflected now that these delightful guests thought enough of her to enjoy her hospitality, and by implication, proved of far more worth than that wretched Mr. Bourne.

George Smith and his sisters were among the latecomers, Smith having waited until the last minute, as he told Rachel, in the vain hope that his friend could accompany the family. Rachel assured him that it did not in the least matter.

Presently, she and Sir Bayard left their posts at the head of the stairs, the older man anxious to adjourn to the card room, where his friends were settling down to a serious game of whist. A pair of dowagers who had been friends of her mother and stepfather had seated themselves across the ballroom to gossip about the young people, especially the shocking décolleté of one guest who came as Cleopatra and another as the sultana of Turkey.

When the dancing began, Rachel was led off by the faithful Desmond, looking especially handsome, like his friend Dinnes-Evans, in tight regimentals of a Wellington brigade at Waterloo. Rachel enjoyed Desmond's company because she could tantalize him to her heart's content without a second thought. She was a trifle more circumspect with Dinnes-Evans, her next partner, because she had no intention of upsetting her friendship with Clare, but, as she confessed to Clare halfway through the evening, "At least I can say I've been too busy to think twice about a certain someone."

It wasn't entirely true, but Clare nodded reassuringly. And it was Clare who, raising her winged mask, suddenly stopped with one hand in the air and stared through the doorway to the double doors of the upper hall.

"Well—well—well," she breathed.

Baffled by her behavior, Rachel swung around in time to see, standing in the doorway, a tall, trim gentleman with a distinguishing shock of blue-black hair. He was not costumed, but he looked strangely singular in his stark black and white evening clothes as he carelessly surveyed the throng through a narrow black eye mask.

There had been a break in the music, and since the evening was warm, the air was filled with rapidly waving ivory and feathered fans. The gentleman in the doorway smiled slowly. Rachel thought his scornful expression hardly flattering to her guests, and to her. Jason Bourne had indeed arrived.

She nudged her way gently, persistently through the dancers, arriving at the double doors just as the orchestra started up a rousing Vienna waltz. The dancers whirled away, around and around the room, her own partner, Desmond Lorimer, trying to follow her across the floor while avoiding the sweep of skirts as well as the rapid stomp of elegant boots and shoes.

Jason looked down at her. His heavy-lidded eyes, catching the light from the crystal prisms of the chandeliers, seemed to glitter as he asked her in his deep and suddenly familiar voice, "Our dance, I believe?"

She knew poor Desmond was standing there with his gloved hands held out, but she allowed herself to be swept out into the whirling throng, with one hand in her partner's, while Jason's other hand held her waist in a strong grip.

"Amazing that you should so easily recognize me," she told him boldly and a little breathlessly.

"Why is that?" But in spite of his teasing voice, he was looking over her head at invisible points near the ceiling. He swept her the length of the room in the dance but she persisted.

"I mean—considering how long it is since we last met."

"I have an excellent memory."

He whirled her past the wide-eyed Clare and her partner, and in those seconds Rachel found encouragement in his remark. At least, he went to the trouble of remembering her.

"What an excellent dancer you are!"

"Yorkshire is growing more civilized every day."

She forced herself to smile at his sardonic comment.

The waltz ended all too soon. Skillfully he brought her to a whirling stop in front of the young Lorimers and Dinnes-Evans. Rachel was just about to make conversation that would bring Clare and Mr. Bourne together when the maddening Yorkshireman bowed handsomely, then turned and strolled out of the ballroom. Rachel and Clare were left with open mouths.

"What an impossible creature!" Clare remarked, fanning herself indignantly.

Rachel refused to let them know she cared. Her smile was a shade more smug than she felt. "Yes. Isn't he?"

Clare broke down and whispered, "I hoped to tell him all the nice things I could think of—about you."

"And that was your only motive? How noble of you!"

Clare raised her eyebrows. "There may have been other motives. All wasted now."

"But he is attractive, you will allow."

"Devastating. But not, I think, easily broken to harness."

Rachel confessed, "I should very much like to try."

Half an hour later the dancers adjourned to the small dining room, where midnight supper was laid out in tempting array. But Rachel had lost her appetite. Desmond eagerly dispatched himself to attend to her plate, and she stood silently, observing the chattering crowd. She became aware after several seconds that a man had moved through the throng behind her and unexpectedly reached over her shoulder to present her with a glass of champagne.

She turned to make an excuse, pointing out that her partner was fetching her dinner, when she looked up once more into Jason Bourne's unmasked eyes. As unmasked, at least, as they ever were.

"Thirsty?"

She despised herself for her quick, pleased reaction. "Thank you. It has been a thirsty evening."

She put the glass to her lips, then murmured slyly, "Had I known you would eventually arrive, I would have ordered rum."

Looking directly into her eyes, he raised his own glass. "True. But one makes do with what is available. I have been known to drink bilge water, but I don't advise it as a steady diet."

She couldn't imagine where he had drunk bilge water. As a prisoner? Or a sailor in the hulk of a rotting ship? But it was not something one could discuss at a ball.

In spite of herself, she couldn't think of any small talk that would interest him. But he didn't seem troubled by her silence. He finished his champagne. She finished hers. He took the glass out of her hand. She noted his large hand, his long scarred fingers, and felt, too, the ecstasy of his touch.

They were standing near the wide-open green velvet portieres, which permitted a gentle breeze to sift in from the mews behind the house. Occasionally, the whiff of hay, old wood, and the fainter musky aroma of the stables reached the room. Out the window she took in the night's starry sky and a great crescent moon above the city.

Her face must have told him that this view stirred something in her, because she felt him close again, and his deep voice was unexpectedly warm. "So, even London can be beautiful! I hadn't thought to find it so."

She looked at him, faintly smiling. "In the eye of the beholder. I imagine you find your Yorkshire skies far more impressive."

"That would depend. Not in the cities, but certainly on the moors, where I live."

As always, she shuddered, thinking of the long-ago day she

was lost in the cow pasture. She felt one of his hands close upon her throat above her bare shoulder. She started. His voice asked with unexpected gentleness, "Are you afraid of me?" There was something else in his voice, a tension that puzzled and disconcerted her.

She turned to face him. "Not at all."

He looked at her for a long moment, during which time she held her breath. He reached behind her head, cupped his hand around the back of her skull, and held her there, staring at him, wide-eyed with suspense, while he warned her, "Perhaps you should be."

"Only . . . only of fields and open spaces."

She expected him to break into a smile but he did not. His eyelids flickered. He repeated, "Afraid of moors and open spaces? Interesting." He had said something like that before. Why was it of such interest to him, unless he wished to protect her from such places? He removed his hand with a deliberation that left her hopeful. Her scalp still tingled with the excitement of his touch.

The Smith girl's shrill young voice cut between them: "Mr. Bourne! They are asking my brother such questions about your friend Miss Brontë. I think you must answer them."

He looked bored as he turned away from Rachel to face her. "I am afraid I cannot help you. Miss Brontë is a much admired authoress and I am a poor sheep farmer. She earns her fame with her pen and I with my . . . sheep."

He bowed to Miss Smith, then to Rachel, and walked away. She watched his black figure cross the room, neatly threading his way among the talkative guests with their precariously balanced plates and their glasses of punch or champagne.

FIVE

During many spring nights Rachel lay in her frilly, dimity-covered four-poster bed reliving moments with Jason Bourne and trying to understand his strange moods.

Perhaps he had disliked her when they met in the railway carriage, or at the Italian Opera House, but something had changed his view of her since. Instinct and her own body told her that he was in some way attracted to her. Looking back on the day he took the rum from her tea tray, she thought his genuine interest in her began some time during that visit, and his conduct at the ball, while abrupt, was certainly romantic.

For several weeks after the masked ball he remained in Yorkshire attending to his sheep or his precious woolen mills, while Rachel wondered whether his mother or his sister would persuade him that he could not possibly be interested in a tiresome, rich young female with no experience whatever of rural life. She had always heard that people in the north lived, behaved, and were actually more primitive than Londoners.

From their meeting in the Berkeley Square house, and especially at the ball, Rachel knew that Jason Bourne aroused in her heart emotions she had never known in the company of any other suitor. She had been amused by some, like Desmond Lorimer, and disgusted by the obvious fortune hunters. But she had never been conscious of such a deep and passionate need to be possessed and gloriously ravished by such a man.

He returned from Yorkshire and invited Rachel for a fashionable afternoon drive in the park. He took her to a rowdy music hall, worse than any Desmond would have ventured in, and laughed as he watched her flush with the shock of it.

Clare tried to flatter her that his sporadic interest was real. His several invitations clearly showed that his intentions were genuine. Except that he also took George Smith's sisters and their mother for a similar drive in the park.

"But everyone is discussing his pursuit of you."

"Pursuit," Rachel repeated. "That is the problem. Sometimes I feel like a partridge pursued by the hunter's gun. If only I knew his true feelings."

"Whatever do you mean, Rachel? His pursuit—I mean, his attentions have been marked. How can you doubt?" She leaned closer, confidentially. "He's kissed you, of course? Or has he not yet attempted any . . . familiarities?"

Rachel was very much aware that good manners would prevent a gentleman from kissing her lips until he had spoken of marriage, but such delicacy hardly applied to a man of Jason Bourne's dominant nature. Yet he hadn't kissed her, except her fingers. And heaven knew, even that slight gesture managed to fire up all her passions. He had a trick of running one finger under her knuckles in a most sensuous way that aroused her as no kiss bestowed surreptitiously upon her lips by other hopeful suitors had ever done.

Was it a game he played? He must know his effect upon her. Or was he merely keeping a tight rein on his own passions?

Rachel didn't want to confess to her eager friend that this romantic figure had remained embarrassingly a gentleman.

She admitted finally, "No. But when we are very close, our bodies touching as we ride to the theater or through the park, I feel something in him. A heat. An emotion of some kind."

Then, for the first time, she saw him with someone else. Rachel spied her one evening about sunset, when she and Jason

Bourne were returning from an extremely pleasant drive, which had followed a walk above the green banks of the Thames. It had been half-stroll, half-drive, an idea of Rachel's that suited her companion. Her ancient coachman took them out in her equally ancient carriage. Rachel and Mr. Bourne got out at the river and walked up together, pointing out where it wound along below them, a long way off, appearing silver in certain light, now green, now brown. They argued over what its color actually was.

Out of politeness and a desire to keep his goodwill she surrendered. "Well then, it is brown. Now, we are truly friends. We have quarreled over the river."

He was looking less somber. His smile, on that sensuous mouth, made him appear unguarded, younger, especially since he wore no hat. His unruly black hair framed his head like a boy's cap. She felt encouraged after a few more such outings that he might even become human.

He asked, "Must we quarrel in order to be friends?"

She was disappointed that he could not see her point. Only true friends were close enough to quarrel. Strangers would remain coolly polite. But it was no use pointing this out. He would not understand. She said merely, "I trust we can be friends in spite of disagreements."

While they walked down the hill toward town, he drew her to him with his arm around her waist. She made no objection. She was excited by his closeness and she warmed to his next words.

"Let us not quarrel. We will have enough to quarrel about later."

She didn't question what he meant by this. She wanted to learn more about his habits and pursued the opportunity. "Do you like to walk?"

"I had better. I find it far easier to walk than to ride over the moors around the Hall."

"Your home?"

He was too casual. "Don't be impressed. It was once no bigger than a sheepcote. A barn and outbuildings. In fact, it was a sheepcote. The Bournes began on those moors." He looked at her. "It's just as well you enjoy walking."

Inside, she shuddered. The idea of being engulfed by the

moors of Yorkshire's West Riding struck her as horrible—a green monster like the meadow that engulfed her when she was four years old, leaving her to the mercies of a huge milk cow.

She managed a flickering smile. "Indeed, yes. They must be beautiful. The moors, I mean."

He studied her in such an odd, intense way that she felt sure he was about to propose. And though he did not, he did the next best thing. Moving with a deliberation that made her body excitedly aware of what he intended, he drew her to him, lowered his head, and touched her lips with his. His kiss was warm and tender; then, as she tried to break away to breathe, he held her breathless, crushing and bruising her lips, probing her mouth. When he let her go she almost lost her balance.

She laughed a little wildly. "What was that for?"

He shrugged. "An impulse. I wanted to enjoy the taste of you."

"Simple as that?"

"Of course."

She was too breathless to think straight. He signaled Claude, the old Etheredge coachman, and a minute later was giving Rachel a hand up into the open carriage.

They rode into the city making small talk, while she licked her lips, remembering the taste of him. There were no more hints about life in Yorkshire. They discussed the past opera season and politics. She asked whether the prince-president, Louis Napoleon, nephew of the great emperor, would yet become the ruler of France for life, as everyone was predicting.

"He will be emperor, mark me," the Yorkshireman said. "He is a shrewd man, and competent."

Rachel laughed at a memory. "And unmarried. To think I might have become the Princess Louis Napoleon, or even the empress of the French. My stepfather presented me to him here when he was a mere fugitive gentleman from France. They say he has a way with women. I found him charming."

"I can imagine he found you equally charming." Then he added, "Your own father. Do you remember him at all?"

"Quite well. But Mama preferred not to have me discuss Father." She flashed her lively smile. "He was a gallant. Forever in trouble over the ladies. I suppose you've heard how he died. It's common gossip. He was shot by a wronged husband. A sailor. Poor Father. He never could run fast enough."

She saw that her frivolous remarks about her father upset or annoyed him. He probably found her attitude toward her father disrespectful. She added hurriedly, "But I loved him very much. And I'm sure he loved me. He told me sometimes that in all the world I was the only thing he really loved. Of course, I never told Mama."

"He told you that, did he? Interesting."

It was a curious remark and she could make no sense of it. But something else had caught his attention. He sat up stiffly, looking out to his right as they crossed beyond Piccadilly Square. It was a district to which Rachel was often driven when she wished to visit a favorite bookshop or a perfumer's, but even in these advanced days of 1850, she would not walk unescorted along the street or the square as late as sunset.

The only women alone were females of the disreputable sort, obviously looking for a bed partner. Overdressed, in garments too heavy for the mild weather, they made overtures to every passing male, even those accompanied by ladies.

Among the strollers was a tall young woman dressed with provincial elegance in a velvet and brown plaid taffeta gown with a stiffened skirt and a velvet jacket that buttoned tightly over her thin bosom. She favored her left arm, which remained stiffly bent at the elbow. Her left shoulder hung slightly lower than the right.

The woman seemed to be drunk. Her brown bonnet with its silk rosettes had fallen off her head and hung from her neck by its gray ribbons. Her fine sand-colored hair flew in the breeze, giving her a hoydenish appearance that contrasted with her seemingly ladylike figure and dress. Surely this unfortunate woman couldn't be the object of Jason Bourne's interest. She tottered against a lamppost looking terribly alone among scores of passersby.

Jason was still staring at her when they crossed Piccadilly and headed toward Berkeley Square. He appeared thoughtful during the next minute or two. When Rachel attempted light conversation, she saw that he was clearly distracted. She was disappointed but not surprised when a minute later, he took her hand suddenly, kissed it in a most impersonal way, and tapped old Claude on the shoulder. "Stop here. I'm afraid I have neglected some important business. Forgive me. I'll call upon you soon."

She watched him, frowning, as he swung down from the carriage. She would have started away at a fast clip, but he read something in her face that warned him. He added, "One day, I will explain. Forgive me."

She smiled not wanting him to see she was hurt. But the lovely day had been ruined. He went striding back toward Piccadilly. She made her decision on the spur of the moment. "Claude, turn here and wait for me just beyond the corner."

"Miss Rachel, I'll not let you out here alone!"

She didn't trouble to argue but descended, carelessly pulling her full skirts away from the steps, and hurried after Jason, grateful that the crowded streets provided a little shelter for her in case he turned to look back.

By the time she reached Piccadilly, she saw him crossing the street with his arm around the drunken woman in the plaid dress. He was leading her, offering his strength to prevent her from faltering.

There seemed to be both love and tenderness in Jason's manner. He summoned a horse-drawn cab and got in with the woman.

Two men pushed against Rachel. One of them rubbed against her back in a suggestive way. Terrified, she swung around so fast her skirts brushed their legs. She glared at them, and they scuttled away, laughing. She returned to Claude and the Etheredge carriage, deeply troubled.

While riding back to Berkeley Square she made up her mind that the next time Mr. Bourne called upon her she would not be at home.

He failed to call, however, for three weeks. In the third week she gave up all pretense of pique. Even if that drunken misshapen harpy was a part of his past, he loved Rachel. She had his kiss to prove it.

One morning late in July, he was finally announced by Alice.

It took all Rachel's resolution to keep from running downstairs to meet him. She descended calmly, but her voice betrayed her as she called to him from the stairs: "Mr. Bourne! Where the devil have you been?"

That made him laugh. She thought it a lovely sound, a kind of pleasant, low chuckle.

"I found my sister in the city. She was . . . ill. There was nothing I could do but take her home as soon as possible. But all is right and in order now."

Rachel could not have asked for a better explanation. Only sooner. She hurried down the stairs. He took her hands, bringing her close to his chest. She knew her mouth quivered in nervous expectation, but this time he did not tease her.

Her lips found his, those voluptuous, wide lips of his, warm with passion. He took possession of her mouth, with the same violence, probing, rousing her body to press stiffly against his male hardness. His touch had the effect of bringing into her mind the most shocking desires. She wished his hands might move over her body in that sensuous way, this very minute, on the salon sofa. Or the floor. And she would surprise him by her own nimble, sensitive fingers.

Alice stood by, tongue-tied, delighted by the scandalous embrace.

Rachel finally became aware of her. "It's . . . quite all right, Alice. We are going to . . . be married."

"Are we?" Jason asked as they walked into the green and gold salon arm in arm.

"Certainly." She gave him a conspiring glance. "You might say, we were born for each other."

He pretended to consider. "Yes. I think fate intended us to meet. Perhaps it was all planned." Again, there was that curious pause, and the pensive mood that she noticed in him at odd times. "Planned by others who did not know it, long ago."

She wished his mouth did not suddenly have that grim look. If he could unburden himself to her, tell her what his past troubles had been, she would know how to sympathize. She backed away from her presumptuous joke.

"The others who intended us to meet may not have intended

67

us to marry. Very possibly, you are married already. Or I am." She wondered if her laugh sounded as forced to him as it did to her. She had not forgotten Miss Brontë's novel in which a man like Jason Bourne kept a crazy wife in his attic. She added, "Actually, I meant that proposal in jest. I merely wanted to excuse your conduct before Alice. You are not to take it seriously. I am far too happy in my present situation."

He seemed to ignore this. She had no idea what he was thinking.

Mrs. Brithwick marched in before Alice, who carried the tea tray. A bottle of rum, this time with the cobwebs and dust carefully wiped off, seemed awkward amidst the delicate Limoges china. On other occasions he had poured rum as a matter of course and more or less in defiance of Rachel with her pretty china cups. But today in a contrary mood, he waved aside the rum. "In honor of the occasion I think something stronger is in order. Mrs. Brithwick's hot tea."

Rachel laughed at that, but again when she poured, her fingers betrayed her uneasiness as the teacup she handed him rattled in its saucer. It was then that Jason put her doubts to rest.

He took the saucer, set it down, raised the cup in the hollow of his two palms, and brought it to his lips. His eyes studied her over the rim of the cup. She could imagine many emotions in those heavy-lidded eyes that sometimes appeared to burn as he looked at her. Even now she couldn't be quite sure that what she read in them was indeed a lover's passion.

Not even when he said quietly, "We can't make you a liar before Alice, now, can we?" She watched him, feeling more tense than ever. He said then, "Will you marry me?"

"Yes." Pride made her add in humor, "For Alice's sake."

Without getting up he set the cup down, pushed the tray out of his way, and reached for her. She was impressed, not for the first time, by his strength. He lifted her off the sofa and onto her knees before him. She raised her head for his kiss and felt his lips with their burning touch upon her throat, then upon the hollow between her breasts. She clung to him, so aroused she felt engulfed by tongues of fire.

She dismissed all reservations about his troubled sister, and his frequent disappearances, the tragedy of his life that had made him, perhaps, the prototype of two fictional characters written by two old maids. . . .

All those matters she could afford to put aside for the moment. She would assume her father's carefree attitude. Passion would come first.

SIX

Having seen her dream of romance suddenly come true, Rachel was too ecstatically happy to interfere with Jason's post-wedding plans. She agreed at once on a honeymoon in Paris, recently torn by its third revolution in less than a century. It was her mother's birthplace. She wondered if that was why Jason chose it.

She was careful not to pursue the problem of their future home. She assumed they would divide their time between her London house and his own mansion in Yorkshire.

She even thought it a brilliant notion that Jason should bring his sister, Maria, to stay with Rachel through the wedding preparations. Was Maria the woman she had seen him with on the street? She didn't like to ask, but she did want to know the woman before the ceremony.

Rachel was determined not to disturb any of Jason's plans. She was perfectly aware that her future husband was difficult and decisive and that she herself had been rather too accustomed to having her own way. She would work on that weakness. The fact that he loved her even a little was miraculous in itself. He was so exactly like the hero she had always dreamed of, a character out of a romantic novel.

Naïvely, she had supposed that her London friends would delight in her happiness. Their mild suspicion, triggered by the announcement, came as a dampening blow.

Both Clare and Desmond Lorimer had met Jason Bourne under unimpeachable social auspices. George Smith and Miss Brontë had vouched for the identity of Mr. Bourne. Tory Party members of York and Bradford answered Sir Bayard Lorimer's inquiry with the carefully worded assurance that Jason Bourne's credentials were solid: a respectable and moneyed party member, owner of lands in the West Riding of Yorkshire, as well as of the Bourne Woolen Mills, which he had recently reactivated after a long shutdown.

The question of why the woolen mills had been deactivated in previous years did not arise. This put to rest Sir Bayard's first fear, couched in delicate but unmistakable terms, that the Yorkshireman was marrying the heiress for her fortune.

Rachel was offended by the implication, and though she smiled when Sir Bayard came to her with apologies, she still secretly resented this insult to the man she loved. Fortunately, Clare Lorimer held no grudge over her brother's failure to win the race for the heiress.

"My dear, your Mr. Bourne is divine," she assured Rachel. "I have just reread *Jane Eyre*. I always skip the first part, you know, and begin reading where Mr. Rochester enters. And I must say, your Jason is far more handsome. How I envy you!"

Rachel found her own excitement hard to control. She insisted, "Oh, but he is much, much better than a mere storybook character." She did not add that even at this date, he still seemed to her in many ways as mysterious as the characters she read about.

"Well, I can only entreat you, if you meet any more Mr. Rochesters in Yorkshire, you must promise to send them down to London. I shall certainly make myself available."

Rachel hugged her and promised to send her all such paragons.

Ironically, it was Mrs. Smith who pointed out that Rachel's

beloved Mr. Rochester might turn out to be more of a malign and sinister Heathcliff.

"My dear, the wretched man actually spent ten years in prison."

Rachel knew that occasionally the toughest prisoners, the most violent men, had been forced to exist in the rotting interiors of aged, beached ships. From these hellholes they were dragged forth each day, heavily manacled and chained, to work on the docks or at other seaside fortifications. Whenever she saw such poor wretches, Rachel looked away, aware that they must have committed terrible crimes to be so mistreated.

With a pretense of calm she managed to ask Mrs. Smith, "What was his crime?"

"It is said that he attacked someone—a Lord Branscomb—in an argument over the rights of workers in the Yorkshire woolen mills. It was at a time when the hand looms and skilled home laborers had been replaced by machines. Years of great turmoil in the north."

"Was he for these workers or against them?"

"Oh, very much for them."

"Well, then," Rachel summed up triumphantly, "he was a hero and I'm prouder of him than ever. He did what my own father would have done in his place."

"My child!" Mrs. Smith stared, fanning herself vigorously. But she softened as was her good nature, and admitted, "George said much the same thing." She hesitated, then plunged onward with delicacy. "Still and all, marriage is a very intimate matter. And however romantic your Mr. Rochester may seem at a distance, a man who has lived like an animal in the hulks—well, you must take great care that he does not turn into a Heathcliff, hot for revenge against the people that sent him to that ghastly doom."

"I didn't send him to a ghastly doom."

"But—excuse me—the law gives all your property to your husband. You will always wonder if he married you for . . . Need I say more?"

Rachel snapped, "I devoutly hope no one else will." She realized the woman had her best interests at heart and added, "But thank you for your intentions. Mama was very shrewd. At least half her fortune was invested in France, and Papa could never get at it without her consent."

"The laws are even more strict in France."

But Rachel knew the ins and outs of her French funds. Some of these funds remained in the names of trustworthy Paris brokers. Rachel's husband would be dependent upon Rachel's own generosity with her French inheritance, and there was always the new French president, Prince Louis Napoleon, whose help she might count ,on, since her mother's money had helped to bring him to his present eminence. Besides, Jason Bourne had his own estate. He hardly needed hers.

She found the problem of Jason's family more troublesome. Jason brought his sister, Maria, to stay with Rachel during the weeks before the wedding. The sharp-tongued Miss Bourne relayed her mother's regrets. It seemed that Amy Bourne suffered from a migraine when she traveled and would not be able to attend the wedding.

Rachel saw through that at once. The woman didn't approve of her son's bride. That was obvious, although Jason phrased it differently.

Rachel's first formal meeting with Jason's sister, unfortunately, came hard on the heels of a moment's accidental eavesdropping. Alice had ushered Jason and Maria into the formal salon, where Rachel heard them as she crossed the Regency hall to meet them. Miss Bourne remarked sourly, "Your beloved does well for herself. I didn't know he was quite such a Croesus."

He? Rachel told herself she must have misunderstood. The pronoun was obviously "she."

Jason seemed torn between amusement and impatience. "Maria, my girl, if you are going to take this attitude, you would do better to stay in Yorkshire."

"I'll be good. It'll be no small effort, but I'll do well by you. As long as—" Glancing over at the open double doors, Maria broke off abruptly. Following her stare, Jason turned and saw Rachel in the doorway. Rachel noticed he showed none of the discomfiture that she might have expected in the circumstances. He crossed the room, bowed over Rachel's hand, and then, while she waited for the well-remembered touch of his lips on

73

her fingers, he raised both his hands, held her head between his palms, ruffling up her carefully coiffed hair, and covered her lips with his. Whatever pique she might have felt over their conversation was erased by his kiss. It raised in her a breathless passion that left her flesh tingling with desire.

Maria Bourne's laugh broke her reverie. "That brother of mine, he has no decorum," Maria remarked with a smile. "You will get used to it."

"I intend to." With lifted spirits she clasped the hand Maria offered to her. Warmed by Jason's impetuosity, Rachel welcomed her prospective sister-in-law with an embrace. She was sure the older woman would respond. Maria, however, suffered the embrace with a fixed smile.

The woman looked the way she sounded, crabbed and ill-natured. Her wide mouth seemed to have been pursed tightly for so long that wrinkles had begun to form, though she did not appear to be over thirty. She still carried her left arm in that curious way, bent at the elbow.

Heavens! Maybe it really was a deformity of some kind. Rachel felt guilty at her own secret criticism of the woman. Maria's hazel eyes proclaimed intelligence, but like her mouth, her flesh was already showing lines around the eyes and above the thin, sharp nose. Perhaps this was due to her drinking.

Rachel told herself that Maria had her own sorrows. It might even be that she was simply possessive about her brother. She seemed interested in the wedding preparations, so Rachel discussed the gowns for the bridesmaids, and the wedding's locale, which was to be the Berkeley Square house instead of St. Margaret's Church, the usual scene of fashionable weddings in London. But Rachel was not an aristocrat and often recalled her stepfather's reminder that she should be true to her bourgeois origins. "You will find them strong when you need them," he had said, and she saw no reason to doubt that wisdom.

"This house was the setting for my father and mother when they were married," she explained. "I would like to carry on their tradition." This mention of her parents caused Maria to look quickly at Jason. Her features twisted into a humorless smile. But Jason ignored the look, along with whatever message it contained. He put one arm around Rachel's waist, under her breasts, where she was especially sensitive to his touch.

74

"Why don't we show Maria to her room and get her settled? You must have quite a few plans for the rest of the day."

"I do. Maria and Miss Fridd, and my friend Miss Clare Lorimer, must choose their bridesmaid's gowns. Then there is the music to consider. The wedding luncheon. Dozens of things. What color do you favor, Maria, as bridesmaid?"

Maria shrugged. At the moment she was wearing various shades of deep brown, red, and rust plaid, not the most flattering shades considering her dull hair. "Blue, I suppose. Something light. Not that it matters."

But Clare would be sure to choose blue to complement her bright golden hair. A pity Maria had no taste for green. It would do wonders for her plain face, and flatter her hair.

The four women spent an enjoyable afternoon in London's best yard-goods emporium, choosing lengths of material that would then be created from their chosen patterns by Rachel's favorite designer.

Since it was to be a small wedding, the three bridesmaids, including Miss Fridd, would be especially noticeable. In order to reach a bolt of pallid baby-blue satin, Maria picked up a length of moss-green silk that happened to be in the way, and threw it over her shoulder.

Hesper Fridd exclaimed, "Dear Miss Maria, what an inspiration! It puts you in splendid looks."

She was right. The green seemed to bring a vividness to Maria's face, but in a way that also gave her hazel eyes a special glint of excitement. Maria hesitated. She swung around, eyeing the splendidly formal male clerk, who nodded in a thoughtful way, head tilted to one side, while he considered her. "Stunning. Most attractive." He ignored the problem of her left shoulder, and it seemed to Rachel that when Maria, too, ignored it, the awkward slope seemed to disappear. Maria was capable of a certain dignity, even elegance, when she regained her self-confidence.

Jason had said very little about the shoulder and arm problem. He had dismissed it abruptly as a street accident when she was sixteen.

While Maria was being measured for her gown, Clare Lorimer muttered to Rachel with a dry smile, "That suggestion about the color was a mistake. She will eclipse us all."

Rachel only laughed. It was all so marvelous. Jason Bourne was going to marry her. After all these weeks she still couldn't believe it. He had remarked once that she looked "enchanting" in a lace gown. For that reason she was having a Valenciennes lace wedding gown made in the newest style, with enormously wide, stiffened skirts to emphasize her small waist, and a wide boat neck of lace over the properly high cream-colored neckline of fine silk gauze.

Her chestnut hair peeked out in soft tendrils beneath a pearl-studded lace coif. Her delicate veil reached only to the hem of her skirts and added an exquisite flowing grace to the ensemble. Rachel chose to carry a bouquet of her favorite wood violets, carefully sewn together for the occasion so that they appeared to be spilling lightly down the front of her gown.

The three bridesmaids would appear in assorted pastels, blue for Clare, green for Maria Bourne, and lilac for Miss Fridd. All the silk gowns imitated the wedding dress in style. With them, each woman wore a silk bonnet of the latest fashion. It had all worked out so well.

One day Clare offered an unsettling comment to her childhood friend. "May I offer a warning?"

Rachel gave her a teasing, apprehensive smile. "If you must."

"Don't let Maria gain an advantage over you just to please Jason. She looks like a woman disappointed in life. She is bound to resent you."

"Then I shall ignore her resentment. But"—Rachel grinned—"I'll be charming about it."

Rachel suspected Clare might be right. Maria could conceivably spoil any happy gathering with her sullen moods. On the other hand, there were moments when Rachel believed the woman actually appreciated her friendship. Maria had a habit of watching her, looking her up and down and then just staring sadly into space. At such times Rachel tried to show her in every way that they would be friends as well as sisters after her marriage. She was still grateful that Maria had not embarrassed herself once since her arrival in London. Perhaps her brother had lectured her on the subject.

When they talked of household matters, Rachel often deferred to Maria's judgment—until she saw that this merely encouraged

Maria's unpleasant moods. Maria became abusive and superior, although from her conversation, it was their mother, Amy Bourne, who managed the estate in Yorkshire.

But Rachel was gradually learning more about Maria's peculiar troubles. Once when they were discussing Rachel's previous suitors, a matter that seemed to fascinate Maria, the woman asked, "This young viscount you were betrothed to. How did you feel when you realized he didn't love you—that he just wanted your inheritance? Weren't you horribly ashamed?"

Rachel was surprised by Maria's knowledge, but even more, by her vehemence. "Heavens, no! I merely canceled my wedding plans."

She hesitated, seeing the familiar resentful look creep over Maria's face like a mask. A minute before she had been interested, almost sympathetic. Rachel recalled her own pain and humiliation of the discovery that Viscount Ashwood had boasted at a hunt ball, in the presence of Bayard Lorimer and Desmond, and a dozen others. "Think I'd sacrifice my freedom for anything less than the Etheredge fortune?" he had bragged. "Why, the girl's French grandfather was a lowly peasant. We Ashwoods led armies in the Third Crusade."

"I suppose you never had the truth fed to you, as I have, and others," Maria baited her.

"Yes. I heard the truth. But I banished it. I wouldn't let myself feel rejected."

"But you were."

"Yes, I was."

"It hurt."

"I know."

They were both silent for a few seconds. Then Maria looked meaningfully at Rachel. "For me, it still hurts. I think of it every time I look in a mirror. Every time I go to bed at night. Alone."

Rachel reached across for Maria's hand. For a fleeting second the girl's scowling face softened into a kind of hopeful beauty. "Anyway, the illusion of being loved was wonderful, while it lasted."

Rachel nodded, more affected by Maria's remembered grief than by her own humiliation. She herself had recovered from the viscount's disdain very quickly. But it seemed clear now that

Maria's unhappiness had its source in an unhappy love affair of much more serious proportions.

Rachel tried to discuss the matter of his sister's past romance with Jason, but he only looked at her in that way he had, the large dark eyes luminous with what she supposed was love. His sensuous appeal washed away her questions. But sometimes she wondered if there wasn't humor in that look, as if he were amused by her. It was disconcerting. It mesmerized her when she most wanted to keep her senses about her. At such moments she felt he could make her believe anything. His influence was too strong. It disturbed her in ways far beyond sexual desire.

And in spite of everything, he pretended not to know what ailed his sister. She didn't believe him.

Nevertheless, Maria's mood occasionally softened under Rachel's casual but persistent curiosity. The woman was still abrupt; she still had a sharp, cutting tongue. But Rachel didn't mind that. In some ways, Maria Bourne was rather like Rachel's mother, Nicolette. The two women were outspoken and curt. Rachel mentioned this aloud one day.

Maria had turned on her furiously. "How dare you! As if I were remotely like that . . . that—"

Rachel was indignant. "You don't even know my mother. I meant it as a compliment. My mother happened to have been a remarkable woman."

Maria collected herself. She retreated rapidly, flicking her tongue over her dry lips. "I . . . I didn't mean that as it sounded. I'm sorry, Rachel. It's only the matter of age. Your mother had the benefit of maturity. I am still so young."

"Mother was a very popular and attractive woman. I only meant that her temperament was like yours."

"And a great compliment it is, too," Jason announced, coming into the room. He crossed the room, imprisoned both Rachel's hands, and bent his head to kiss her.

Rachel was relieved when this little storm blew over, but she remembered the curious moment of silence between brother and sister before Maria apologized. The two had looked at each other as if exchanging a signal, an ability to reach each other's thoughts. Then everyone was friendly again and she pushed the matter to the back of her mind. She could not help thinking, however, that there were moments when Jason seemed almost theatrical in his words and gestures, as if playing a role that happened to suit him well. It was an unsettling thought.

On her wedding morning Rachel awoke to the beat of rain-drops against the vines that framed her narrow windows. She sighed. Was that not bad luck, rain on one's wedding day? No matter. She was lucky to have Jason at all.

She stretched voluptuously, then reached out of bed to ring the bellpull. She drew the coverlet up again while she lay among her pillows, dreaming of the coming night, her first genuine night of lovemaking with Jason. She had certainly dreamed of that often enough. She remembered her discussion with Clare about all the aspects of the sexual act. But even in her girlhood she had never imagined her lover would be so romantic as this man.

How could she be disappointed? What could possibly go wrong in their marriage? Even Maria could prove to be a bless-ing. There were times when she forgot her prickly nature and behaved toward Rachel very much like a sister. As for Jason, Rachel had few illusions. She knew he would be difficult. But it was these dubious qualities—so reminiscent of her beloved Brontë heroes—that drew her to him. She could not complain.

There was a knock at the door, and then Maria entered hesi-tantly. "Do you mind?"

Rachel was quick to hide her surprise. "No. Please come in."

Maria settled herself on the side of Rachel's bed, watching her like a cat at a mousehole. "You're looking very pretty. You really care about my brother, don't you?"

"I love him more than anyone in the world."

Maria raised her eyes to some point on the wall behind Rachel. "That's nice. . . . Who's the gentleman?"

Rachel looked up at the oval portrait on the wall above her bed. Her father's blond good looks had always been noticed by women.

"My father."

"Very handsome. Of a type."

"Very handsome. Of any type."

"Jason says he died violently. All your family seems to have died violently. Is it a tradition or something?"

Rachel tried not to sound as resentful as she felt. "Father was shot, it is true. But mother and my stepfather were drowned in a ship collision. They were crossing the English Channel. It was hardly their fault."

"No. Of course not. I just thought—aren't you ever worried?"

"Worried about myself?" She looked intently at the woman, feeling undercurrents of a sort of hatred. Rachel had the ability to evoke a certain look in her gray eyes that threatened to freeze the recipient. It was there now. "Am I the victim of the fates, or something of that ilk?"

Maria blinked and swallowed. Her laugh revealed a hint of panic. "Did I sound like that? I'm sorry. But I'm delaying you. We mustn't do that to the bride. Will you be dressing soon?"

"Soon, yes."

Maria backed away, still awkwardly apologizing. "Don't tell Jason. You won't, will you? He made me swear."

"Swear?"

"That I wouldn't be . . . nasty. You know. It's just my way. I don't mean anything by it."

"I understand."

With a sudden eagerness Maria added, "I want us to be friends, I swear I do. You know that, don't you?"

"Friends," Rachel agreed. Maria departed, leaving the door ajar. Rachel called, "Would you mind closing the door?"

It slammed shut.

It took her an hour to recover her equanimity. Even when she was being dressed in all her wedding finery, surrounded by Hesper Fridd and the modiste, Madame de Laurier, she seethed inwardly at what she conceived to be a threat of some kind. It would be a happy moment when she got her husband away from the influence of that baleful sister of his.

The truth was, Maria Bourne needed a husband. She was much too old to be running about in her brother's shadow, and it seemed clear that her present erratic conduct was due to jealousy or perhaps envy. Rachel was convinced that Maria, having lost a worthless suitor, very naturally clung to the genuine devotion of her brother. Rachel decided that when she was safely married to Jason and he listened to her as a dutiful husband was bound to do, they must find a husband for Maria.

"That's better, dear. Don't frown," Miss Fridd advised Rachel as Madame de Laurier and her two flustered young aides moved around the hem of Rachel's gown on their knees. "Frowns are so unbecoming." Miss Fridd's eyes were bright with excitement. She had never looked better. Her lilac silk bridesmaid's gown did wonders for her thin, faded little face.

Rachel's laugh had a nervous edge. "Especially for a bride."

If only one could marry an orphan, with no family whatever, she thought. Marrying Jason apparently meant marrying two women who very likely began by disliking her for no better reason than their jealous need for Jason.

Mrs. Brithwick bustled in looking slightly stuffed in her new gray shot-silk gown. The rapidly opened door had brought a sharp breeze in with her, and Rachel shivered. In spite of her long lace sleeves, she felt cold. Then Mrs. Brithwick extended the bridal bouquet of violets, and the memory of that chill was tucked away, forgotten for the moment.

SEVEN

For her wedding, Rachel had chosen the little orchestra that played for the summer ball when she first danced with Jason. From her bedroom Rachel could hear the sixteenth-century tune played behind the bower in the Regency hall. She thought of Jason standing beside the improvised altar at the far end of the crowded green and gold salon. At this minute he probably wasn't the least bit nervous. She had no doubt he was exchanging pleasantries with his best man, George Smith.

Sir Bayard Lorimer knocked at the door, and then called, "Are we ready, Rachel?"

She wanted to say yes. This wedding was the culmination of her life, but for one instant, like a last, brief nightmare, she asked herself, *Is it too good to be true?*

"Rachel?"

She stiffened her backbone. "Yes, Sir Bayard, I'm ready."

His presence and the arm he gallantly offered were reassuring. They moved out into the hall, following the bridesmaids down the elegant white and gold staircase. Maria looked surprisingly beautiful leading the procession, followed by golden Clare and a radiant Hesper Fridd, who appeared to be at least ten years younger.

Rachel spied herself in the long pier glass and was hardly reassured, even by Sir Bayard's gruff, "Lovely, my dear. Completely lovely." She thought she looked stiff and unreal.

There was an audible gasp as those guests, craning their necks toward the open double doors of the long salon, first caught sight of the bride moving slowly down the stairs. But they must have been equally impressed by Rachel's charming bridesmaids, who were already entering the room.

The little orchestra finished on an off-note as Rachel was escorted to the side of the tall bridegroom. The autumn rain seemed to soften as Jason looked at her with obvious admiration. His eyes twinkled. She could not mistake his pleasure at the sight of her. Though she had resigned herself to the knowledge that her love for him was greater than his for her, she knew in this moment that he desired her. His smile warmed and reassured her.

She turned her attention to the Reverend Edward Culhane, Sir Bayard's godson, an attractive young man newly ordained and hoping to be accepted as curate at one of the parishes in the north, where his mother had been born. Thrilled, yet apprehensive, Rachel responded mechanically, aware at the same time of all the crosscurrents around her. Maria Bourne's attention was now captured by the reverend. Not surprisingly. The young man had a way of fixing his clear blue eyes upon each of the wedding party in turn, as if impressing upon them the special importance of that particular wedding vow. His excellent features and genteel manner seemed to impress George Smith's sisters as well. Obviously, with this approach the Reverend Culhane would go far.

He stopped speaking. Rachel started nervously when her husband tilted his dark head and brushed her lips with his. It was a disappointingly light kiss as befitted the solemnity of the occasion, and she was relieved when the guests began to mill around, Desmond claiming first embrace from the bride, while Clare, not to be outdone, kissed the groom. Watching this over Desmond's shoulder, Rachel thought that kiss took rather too much time, especially as Jason seemed amused by it. She didn't like to think he was so happy in Clare's embrace.

Among those thronging around Rachel, touching, whispering, and hugging her, she found her hand being kissed by the gallant Reverend Culhane. "I trust I may be added to the roll of your many friends who wish you a long and happy life, Mrs. Bourne."

She thanked him, giving him her most radiant smile, and expected him to move on, but he retained her hand while he added, "Perhaps, with any luck, I shall be selected for one of the parishes in the north, where you are to live. It would be an honor to think I might, in some small way, become your spiritual counselor."

Somewhat taken aback at this innocently pompous speech, she murmured, "I'm sure that would be very pleasant." She grasped the chance to turn his pointed interest in another direction. "But here is my new sister, Miss Bourne. Maria, have you met the Reverend Culhane?"

"Not officially." Maria was eager but trying hard not to show it. She offered her hand. He saw it an instant too late but saluted it with the faint touch of his lips. "Miss Bourne. You . . . er . . . reside with the bride and groom?"

Maria's decisive chin raised. "No. The bride will reside with my brother and me."

The young man colored at the correction. "Of course, very proper. Ah! Miss Lorimer, you are in excellent looks today."

And he excused himself, leaving Maria and Rachel to look at each other. Rachel understood Maria's feelings perfectly. No unmarried woman liked to be thought of as some kind of appendage. At the same time, she wondered if the Bournes expected her to give up her lovely home forever and go to live in darkest Yorkshire.

The matter would have to be settled. But not, she thought, on her wedding day!

Something tickled Rachel's ear. She was embarrassed but far from displeased to find it was her husband's lips as he whispered, "Must I carry you away from the religious community as well as from London's prize fops?"

She laughed and turned just as he kissed her, this time with all the attention and enthusiasm she had hoped for. She resigned herself to his arms. Someone started to applaud. Presently, the crowd joined in. No matter what might come after, she was supremely happy now.

"Come along, Madame Bourne," Clare called out gaily, "your guests are starving."

The party adjourned to the festive buffets in the dining room. George Smith raised his champagne glass to toast the bride and groom, and after toasts had been made and answered, the gentlemen bustled about filling Rachel's delicate Limoges plates for the ladies present.

Jason, who had a robust appetite, was piling pâtés and salads on Rachel's plate despite her protests. Suddenly, he noticed what she herself had been aware of for some time. The Reverend Culhane was still watching her.

"The Church of England must be desperate. They seem to be choosing their shepherds from the cradle."

Rachel laughed. "Such a nice young man. He'd be so right for Maria. Let's play matchmakers." Jason's sister stood alone at the far end of the buffet.

"Excellent. Anything to avoid losing my wife to such a heavenly rival."

She caught the Reverend Culhane's eye and then glanced at Maria. Culhane understood. He gave her his gentle smile and went off to assist Maria Bourne. Rachel thought the woman had never looked more appealing.

The clatter of silver and china was almost eclipsed by the voices that raised in volume as the champagne and punch diminished. Rachel had entered into the fun and excitement of the luncheon. Jason was close to her. He had removed her veil and kissed her frequently, little joking pecks, on the neck or top of her head, and all the guests seemed to be enjoying themselves, even Maria. She and the Reverend Culhane had their heads together, in an intense discussion.

"Look. They get on swimmingly," she told Jason. He glanced at his sister and the equally serious young reverend.

"Very likely discussing the worth of religion, or lack of it. Maria will take the negative." He raised her chin, examined her face, and grinned crookedly. "Don't look so shocked. Your husband shares her beliefs. Or should I say, her lack of beliefs, and with good cause." Before she could plead with him to deny his boast, he stopped her protests with a quick kiss and then another. "Hush! No arguments. Shall we go and change now?"

I must put an end to his giving me orders all the time, she promised herself. She looked at him, felt herself propelled along, out into the hall, and added mentally, *But not today.*

He did not release her until they reached the door of her own virginal bedchamber. She stopped. "I'm home."

"True. For the moment." He pinched her nose, then watched her go into the room.

Brigitte was waiting to help her change. Rachel was thankful for her brisk attentions. Her own fingers were so nervous she could only fumble with the tiny pearl buttons that ran from the back of her neck to the end of the basque.

When the wedding gown, its underdress, and stiffened petticoats were laid away, presumably to be worn at a distant date by her daughter, Brigitte brought out the carriage jacket of deep-blue velvet over a reversible taffeta dress with wide skirts that she would wear on the railway trip to Dover. They would then embark on the Calais packet at midnight to spend their wedding night on the choppy English Channel.

Rachel was a good seaman, having crossed the Irish Sea with her stepfather and her mother to visit his relations several times, but the English Channel had been the scene of her mother's death, and the idea that it would also witness her wedding night gave her twinges of fear. When Jason had made these plans, she had been too cowardly to object, reminding herself that nothing could happen to them while Jason protected her. It was unlike Rachel to defer to a man so readily, but she didn't want to begin her married life by making petty objections every time Jason offered a plan he spoke of as "delightful."

He stood waiting in a darkened recess of the hall when she came out. She was busy tucking the plume of her little velvet hat out of her eyes and for an instant did not realize that she was under his close observation. Startled, she tried to laugh away her uneasiness. "Good heavens! I didn't see you there."

To her surprise he didn't smile with all the warm excitement his presence usually brought. He had been staring at her, his expression darkly intense. Or sad. Yes, she decided. He was not happy. She called gently, "Did I delay you? I'm sorry, darling. Do we sneak out or give them that pleasure they are looking forward to?"

He took her arm, looked into her upturned face, and kissed her on the lips. His mouth lingered on hers and once again she gave way to passion at his touch. She clung to him gladly. However lighthearted he might have seemed earlier during the wedding festivities, he meant this. He loved her. She could have sworn to the depth of his feelings.

"I do love you so!" she breathed, taking his fingers and kissing them. Subtly, but unmistakably, he drew his hand away. She felt rebuffed.

"Turn around. We'll take the back stairs."

Puzzled, she found herself headed away from the Regency hall—they apparently were to sneak out by the servants' stairs. She whispered, "They will be disappointed."

"They've had their show. Now it's our turn. We want to get on with ours. . . . Don't we, darling?"

She didn't like this at all. Furthermore, as they crossed the lower floor, hearing the pleasant hum of the party in the long formal dining room, she caught a glimpse of Maria Bourne with one hand hooked around the newel post of the front staircase. Her champagne glass was tilted, and Rachel had an awful feeling that the contents had emptied out upon her mother's beautiful Persian rug.

Damnation! The woman wasn't . . . she couldn't be drunk! Rachel tried to call Jason's attention to the slumped figure, but he was hurrying her out into the mews behind the building. For her own peace of mind she told herself that Maria had behaved almost impeccably during her stay at Rachel's house and there was no reason to assume she had suddenly reverted to the folly of drunken behavior today.

Rachel was astonished to find her travel boxes and cases tied on the roof of the Etheredge carriage, the team fidgeting, and her old coachman huddled in his greatcoat, his face protected from the threatening sky by his wide-brimmed hat.

"But we didn't say good-bye to Maria," she ventured as Jason helped her up the carriage steps.

"I made the farewells for both of us. Better hurry, sweetheart. Looks as though there may be a downpour at any minute."

She settled herself without comfort. Rachel very much disliked being hustled about like this from her own house and in her own carriage. Furthermore, her new husband's face looked remote and preoccupied, as if deep thoughts occupied him, far from his new wife. Very little was said during the journey across the city. He didn't seem aware that his wife's silence was most uncharacteristic of her nature.

It was not until they were settled in the carriage of the Dover train, which pulled out past the depressing industrial slums of London, that Jason resumed his role as gallant bridegroom. He made some effort to see that she was comfortable, that she had a good view of the passing landscape—so much faster by train than by the old, familiar coach. He then settled back himself and made matters worse by watching her.

He had drawn the attention of two elderly ladies sharing the railway carriage, and they buzzed about him in whispers. They were obviously thrilled by his looks, and their bonnets nodded as they exchanged comments. Rachel caught the word "newly-weds" and frowned. For some reason it upset her to be thought a new bride. She caught Jason's reflection in the window glass and realized he was smiling at her.

Jason leaned over to ask her unexpectedly, "What does this put you in mind of?"

She caught her breath. The memory of that first sight of him rushed through her mind. She couldn't resist his smile that made his warm lips, his entire face, so very thrilling to her. She laughed, relieved to be free of the curious malaise that had troubled her since the wedding ceremony. "The Yorkshire train. I noticed you the moment you opened the track-side door. Did you see me at all?"

He nodded, his heavy-lidded eyes closing as he, too, remembered. "I thought you were too pretty. Empty-headed. Probably mistreating that poor little Miss Fridd."

"Oh?"

"And I wanted to kiss you."

"Ah."

"That annoyed me most of all. I remember how angry I was with myself."

He reached out and she let him draw her to him. The elderly ladies exchanged arch looks. Rachel cleared her throat, considering the right way to broach several important questions, but at her first words—"Seriously, darling"—he kissed her forehead and murmured, "Let's not be serious until we must."

EIGHT

"Darling, must we go aboard? Can't we wait until daylight and take another ship?"

He was warmly humorous but masterful in that way that always excited her. "What? And spend our wedding night in one of those drafty inns behind us there?"

He led her across the gangplank into the waist of the little three-masted bark, which appeared to carry only a half-dozen passengers, all males, each of whom looked tough enough to be a cutthroat, or at the very least, a smuggler.

It was already past midnight and this was no place to stand and argue. Rachel waited until they had passed the other passengers, who appeared to be making up their beds on the open deck. She avoided their eyes and let Jason lead her down the steep, narrow ship's ladder to one of the two cabins under the afterdeck. She hadn't expected much during the Channel crossing. Most vessels were far from luxurious. But there was something distinctly odd about this one. Several of the crew, the second mate and at least one of the sailors, had recognized Jason with a flip, informal salute as he passed.

Rachel looked around the little cabin, and guessed that Jason was putting her to some sort of test. She decided to play along with him. It was ironic that he should imagine she was more afraid of a spartan cabin than of the churning black waters she had seen a few minutes ago. She smiled pertly. "Perfect. A wedding night should be cozy."

He laughed. His hands reached for her throat. She made no move to resist. His hands fastened around the velvet bow that anchored the blue velvet hat. She then raised her own hands to stop him, but they were of little use against the steely strength of those lean, scarred fingers. He tousled her carefully groomed hair, shaking out the curly chestnut strands that glistened in the lamplight, before he kissed the side of her throat, where he had unfastened the ribbons of her hat.

"I do believe you love me, after all," she teased, aware at the same time that she was half-serious.

His fingers ceased their exciting exploration of her hair. The remark had caught him by surprise. He moved away from her to look into her face. His eyes searched her features, puzzled by her undisturbed reception of his conduct from the time she expressed her dislike of the choppy seas around the little bark.

She was determined not to give him again the satisfaction of seeing her cowardice.

He said finally, "Were you actually afraid of the sea? You are being very brave now."

"Of course." She glanced over his shoulder at the stern window of the cabin and showed her teeth in a mirthless smile. "Because I can't see the Channel from this spot. It was out there that my mother and my stepfather died." She raised her forefinger, ran it down from his forehead over the bridge of his nose. "And we don't want to follow them, do we?"

She saw that her sensuous touch disturbed him. Whatever the tension that caused him to behave so oddly, as if he loved and hated her at the same time, she had now completely confused him. If he expected to control her, and he had shown every sign of that intention in recent days, this mastery on her part might give her some leverage. She pursued her advantage. "Darling? This jacket of mine is a trifle warm for a wedding night."

His eyes glittered with an emotion she couldn't define. He

played to her mood gravely, and would have removed her jacket with excessive politeness if they hadn't both been startled by a heavy thumping on the cabin door. Rachel had suspected from the first landing on the deck that some of the crew were known to Jason from his prison years.

"That must be one of your old friends," she suggested as she unfastened the braid frogs down the front of her jacket.

He gave her a quick look with eyebrows raised, then opened the door, took in the cases and boxes belonging to them, and stepped out in the passage to exchange a few words with the crewman. When he returned, he found Rachel seated on the edge of the hard bunk with her jacket and shoes off, and her ankles displayed by the many folds of her disheveled skirt.

He caught his breath at the sight of her, from her tousled hair to those ankles, which she knew were excellent. Satisfied that she had disturbed him, she did not bring up the matter of his ruffian friends, or why he exposed her to this wretched crossing instead of more normal passages on the regular Channel boats. She was beginning to realize that her job was to persuade him she could make him happy. Perhaps he really had married her for her inheritance. No matter. She was a woman of considerable self-confidence. She felt that in the end he would love her for what she could offer in quite a different sphere.

Jason hefted the six pieces of their luggage, most of them hers, over to the corner beneath the stern window. She called out pleasantly, "One of my bedgowns is in that large case to your left, darling." He took the key she offered and unlocked the long leather case. He found her bedgown as she had packed it, on top of several garments suited to daytime and afternoon strolls. The gown was of sheer white silk with lace insets. He ran one hand through the translucent folds, studied his hand, and then laughed as he tossed the gown to her. "You might as well be naked."

"Would you prefer me so?"

She was sure he reddened a little, but he made a pretense of sophistication about it. "I like it. Wear it."

"Of course."

While she undressed he appeared to be shoving portmanteaus and cases out of the way. Suddenly, he loomed over her. The

92

walls creaked and the deck under her feet shifted, swayed, and she knew the bark was under way. In spite of all her resolutions to be brave, she gave a moan and covered her mouth with her hand. The lamplight flickered and was then blotted out as her husband's figure cast her in shadow.

She held her arms out to him as she had wanted to do during all the weeks of their courtship. She became aware of a smothering sensation, unable to see more than the top of his head. The black hair gleamed where the swaying lantern glanced off the coarse, vital strands. She would like to have run her hands over his brown flesh, and that masculine hardness of him. But his body crushed hers. Her own hands, trembling with the excitement he aroused in her, dug into his strong hips, moving to his loins as he entered her body abruptly. It was a rough taking of the virginity she offered so readily, but after the first painful entry, she felt with secret pride that perhaps her charms had made him so violent. She was not surprised by her own passionate acceptance of him. Her fingernails left bloody scratches on his flesh as her excitement mounted to a climax with him. She raised her hands to his head, caressing his hair.

Perhaps it was this touch that roused him to the present, to what she was—and why they were here. He raised his head; her hands fell away from him. He left her as she watched him. He grinned at her obvious admiration, but she felt, in spite of his bold pretense, that he was a little disconcerted by her quick adaptation to his lovemaking. Had his passion been meant to frighten her? He took up the black robe he had thrown over the one stool the cabin afforded, and he put his arms into the sleeves while moving to the stern window. He looked out, then held one hand toward her invitingly.

"Come. Say farewell to the White Cliffs of Dover. If it were clear, you could see the Pas de Calais off to your right. That's how close the two countries are."

She didn't want to give him the satisfaction of seeing her uneasiness, but still she hesitated, making a joke. "I'm not dressed to be seen by all those fish in the Channel."

"You look enchanting." She could not resist his further compliment. "If I had any talent, I would paint you as you are. Venus Rising from the Sea."

"Or the Nuptial Couch." She dropped one bare pale leg over the bunk's edge and then the other. She fumbled among the pile of petticoats and taffeta outer garments to cover herself. He insisted, "No, as you are."

But she dragged a petticoat after her. She swayed with the pitching and tossing of the ship until she reached him. He twisted the petticoat out of her fingers, opened his robe, and enfolded her in it, her flesh to his flesh, as if she were a part of him. Both of them became aware of a rising passion between them again. But instead, he drew her attention to the foggy view beyond the window. "You see, sweetheart? We are far from alone out in the darkness."

"Please don't remind me. It was a collision that killed my mother, not the water itself."

He hugged her to him with her head against his cheek. "I'm sorry. But I want you to realize you are safe."

She began to shiver in spite of all her efforts. She expected a note of superiority or sarcasm, and was surprised and touched when he kissed her hair, murmuring, "I don't intend to let anything happen to my enchanting Venus. Promise to believe that of me, whatever happens."

She nodded. He took that for assent.

"Then—no more fears?"

"Just don't leave me in a field with live cows lumbering around munching grass."

He chuckled. "Not even milk cows?"

"Especially milk cows." She could not forget those wide-open spaces in which Desmond had left her so long ago. Lost . . . in a vast nothingness.

She raised her head, peered out under his arm, seeing nothing but the vague outline of a lugger bound toward the English coast, and farther off, something huge, probably a four-masted bark with all sails set. She looked down quickly, seeing the foamy wake of their own little ship.

She could not resist confronting what had been on her mind before his lovemaking distracted her thoughts. "Those crewmen who know you, did you meet them while you were in prison?"

The arm that held her so warmly now felt hard, sinewed. He paused before the calm admission. "I knew Mrs. Smith had told you something about my—lurid past." He looked at her with those strange, somber eyes, whose black pupils always had their effect on her. "Why did you marry me? How much do you know?"

She soothed him first by brushing her lips along his bare forearm. "Darling, I loved you all the more." Before he could speak, she added, "You were condemned for defending those rebels in the north. People who lost everything when the machines replaced them in the mills. I was proud to love you."

He was silent for a long minute or two. Then, when she had begun to stiffen with apprehension, wondering if he resented her honesty, he lowered his head and kissed her mouth, silencing her nervous fears. Afterward, he looked deep into her wide, hopeful eyes, startling her with a plea that pierced her to the heart. "Love me, sweet. Not that stranger you gave your vows to. Love *me*."

She needed no second invitation.

She drew him back across the cabin toward the bunk, trying to show by her eyes and her gentle handling, how deep her love ran. A minute later, they lay in the narrow bunk together, her head in the hollow of his arm, her lips against his breast. When the swaying of the ship brought back her fears, he moved to return her earlier reassurance with his body. Taut and hardening again at contact with her flesh, he entered her waiting body again, this time gently, persistently, until she was once more aroused by his invasion. She locked her long slim legs around his hips, urging him, "Hurry! Hurry!"

She knew even then that her body would be sore and aching later, but her desire matched his. She would not have resisted, even if she were physically capable of doing so. From the moment she felt him within her, they were as one flesh, and all her doubts, her anxieties and fears, were briefly swept away.

Later, she slept in his arms, and only her dreams disturbed her. The figure of Rachel Hinton Etheredge Bourne was shrouded in darkness. That woman who was herself—for she stood off at a distance watching the figure—seemed to be weeping at a graveside. She couldn't understand at first why she wept, until she awakened in the first rays of dawn, hearing her voice whisper a name: "Father!"

Looking up, she found herself staring into the eyes of her

husband. Dark, with the pupils dilated, they seemed to burn into her. She tried to dismiss the matter by the casual remark, "I had a nightmare."

"What did you dream? Tell me." His deep voice, with its normally sensuous quality, was unexpectedly hoarse.

She tried to think back, wondering herself at the dream juxtaposition of her father and her husband. She had certainly never adored Everett Hinton as she adored her husband, and it was many years since she had cried at his funeral.

Perhaps the mental tie came because she first saw Jason Bourne on the day she had visited her father's grave. Maybe her conscience was chiding her for having so easily banished memories of him. She must persuade Jason to visit that grave with her someday. But meanwhile, her husband was her first concern.

She raised her hand to his face, touched his mouth with one finger, and smiled. "It was a silly dream. I seemed to be a child again. Darling, are we in the harbor? I hear them on deck."

He had recovered his normal manner as she spoke. She saw now that he had already gotten up and dressed while she slept. He smiled, slapped her bare hip lightly, and urged her, "Better wash and dress, unless you want to tempt those French dockworkers out there." He added with a return of good humor, "And they will never see a greater temptation."

Thank you, God, she thought. *We are returning to normal.*

The true, happy honeymoon could begin. All secrets between them had now been brought out into the open and disposed of.

NINE

During the next few days of their honeymoon Rachel Bourne saw no reason to doubt the rightness of her marriage. She did feel that some, perhaps all, of Jason's bitterness and his many moods would vanish once he confided in her about his years of suffering.

He would not. He was so secretive about his past, she didn't press the matter. Her job, as she saw it, was to show him that his imprisonment had only made her admire him more. The truth was, in her bedazzled state, he seemed especially heroic for his stand in a just cause. She knew very little about the cause itself, but such ignorance had not influenced her strongly expressed opinions in twenty-three years. It was unlikely to do so now.

They spent their first night in France at a quaint inn on the road to Paris. They wandered through the beautiful autumn countryside, venturing onto winding paths that led to small, neat châteaus tucked away from the highroad. The food at the inn was the best they had ever eaten, or so they thought at this moment in their happiness. They marveled at the French ability to slice a steak so thin that they could see their hands through it, or so Jason claimed.

"I'll wager this steak is as thin as your nightgowns."

Rachel was much amused. "I hope they don't understand your English here."

It was unlikely. His English still carried a hint of his Yorkshire accent, and he spoke little French—his knowledge of the language was based on an acquaintance with a Jersey smuggler in prison. Rachel's French was expert, if tinged with her own well-bred London accent. She suggested now that he should order a second steak, seared in butter, with those remarkable potato slivers that tasted salty and yet had a hint of their natural sweetness.

By the time he had eaten two steaks, he pronounced French cooking "Not bad. Not like our Yorkshire food, but perfectly adequate."

He couldn't understand why she laughed.

She considered their love life a huge success. She soon discovered that all her sexual discussions with her friend Clare Lorimer did not nearly cover the subject. She would like very much to have experimented in different ways of bringing her husband new sensual pleasures, but it was evident that he preferred to be her teacher. In fact, he wished to initiate any such pleasure, so she simply enjoyed herself in his arms and was convinced she loved him as no other man had ever been loved.

By the time they reached Paris a week later, they had heard opinions predominantly in favor of Nicolette Etheredge's friend, the newly elected president of France. Rachel was delighted to learn that the prince-president had returned to his offices in the Elysée Palace from political trips to Lyons in the south and then northeastern France. She was still debating how best to inform Louis Napoleon that Nicolette's daughter was visiting Paris on her honeymoon, when the matter was taken out of her hands.

They had rented the top floor of a former town house on the Faubourg St. Honoré, which Jason thought far too large an apartment and much too elegantly furnished. The settees, boulle cabinets, spinet, lacquer tea tables, sideboards, and bedchamber furniture collected by the owner, an ardent Bonapartist, were formerly the property of *ancien régime* families, many of whom had died during the Terror sixty years earlier.

Immediately upon settling in for their fortnight's stay in Paris,

Rachel received a note from Hesper Fridd, which hinted at future troubles: "I am the last to carry gossip, my dear Rachel, but I fear Miss Maria Bourne had just a sip too much of your excellent champagne on the wedding day. She became a trifle abusive when the guests were gone. But I took care not to provoke her. She slept late the next day and was quite herself afterward. However, when dear Clare Lorimer visited this morning, she happened to remark that the Reverend Culhane had left London for a Grand Tour of the Continent. When he returns, it is believed that he will be assigned to a parish out of London.

"This cannot concern Miss Bourne, but for some obscure reason she has been as cross as two sticks ever since. I hesitate to trouble you at this time, but would it not be better if Miss Bourne returned to her home?"

Rachel hinted at the matter to Jason, suggesting that perhaps Maria would be "bored" in London, but Jason took this badly. He seemed to think she was insulting Maria in some way. "Like all your family." This baffled her, but she decided his reaction stemmed from Jason's annoyance over her family's interest in the politics with which he disagreed.

Nor did Jason approve of the politics of their landlady, now traveling on a mission of goodwill to Austria for the prince-president of France. Jason was dubious about any meeting Rachel might attempt to make with Louis Napoleon. But the honeymoon had softened him, at least politically, and he was making an effort to match Rachel's good humor.

It was impossible for him to match her ebullience, her quick, fiery bursts of opinion, her passionate enthusiasms, which changed with every hour and every new or wondrous sight, but, at least, he tapered off his strange moods.

They had walked along the colonnaded Rue de Rivoli, where, according to Jason, Rachel spent enough money in the shops to feed a hungry army. She teased him out of his disapproval. They took a fiacre up the hill where the Arc de Triomphe loomed in splendor against a piercing blue sky, and they stood in awe in the nave of Notre Dame, looking upward into the dusty darkness, reverent of the fact that lovers had stood in the same spot six hundred years earlier and had seen the same marvels.

"And the same cobwebs," Jason teased.

It was hard to quarrel with him when he took her firmly in his arms and kissed her until she surrendered.

On one of these days of glorious good humor, days of eating, drinking, and loving, they returned to their rooms in the Rue Faubourg St. Honoré, still arguing pleasurably over Rachel's insistence that she should leave a message with the handsome guards stationed outside the Elysée Palace.

Jason said, "He is probably moving into the Tuileries by this time, being a Bonaparte."

"Don't be disrespectful," she pointed out. "We Etheredges have money invested in that man."

"You'll never hear from him. You never hear from borrowers. Don't you know that?"

She gave her hat and shawl to the stout little Alsatian maid who had been loaned to them by Madame Bertrand, their hostess. Rachel herself removed her husband's hat and the parcels they had purchased. Then she patted the back of the satin settee and invited him to sit down. "My poor hero! You must be bored and tired after all that shopping with me. Sit here and I'll be your slave. I'll remove your shoes."

His mouth tightened. "Don't. Slavery still exists. Men like me know what slavery is. It's no laughing matter."

She felt foolish over his reaction. It had been meant as a gesture of tenderness, and her feelings were hurt; so she shrugged and left him to the bustling ministrations of little Gretchen.

The concierge hammered on the door beyond the cool Empire foyer. It was not like the stout, ill-natured woman to climb four flights of stairs to the third floor. Rachel couldn't imagine what had happened—a fire? Unlikely. The solid stone house had withstood the street fighting of three revolutions.

"Monsieur, Madame, you are visited!" the concierge cried in her rapid street French.

Seconds later another knock came, authoritative and military. Jason opened the door. Rachel caught a glimpse of a tall, severe-looking man in a tight, buttoned three-quarter-length coat. The man stepped aside. He inclined his head slightly to his companion but made no effort to enter. Whatever Jason's private thoughts, he did not look surprised when their caller stepped into the little foyer.

At first sight of the short man with the mustache and small, neat beard, Rachel was so astonished she didn't know whether to bow her head respectfully to the president of France or curtsy to the prince, Louis Napoleon Bonaparte.

Breaking into a smile, the prince leaned forward and halted her wobbling curtsy. "Please, Madame Bourne. Spare the formality. My friend Madame Nicolette's child is my friend always." He spoke in his excellent, if accented, English, and glanced at Jason, still gracious but without the warm personal quality he reserved for women. His fine eyes looked deceptively soft, but Rachel noticed how carefully he observed her tall husband. Perhaps, in spite of Jason's respectful nod, Louis Napoleon guessed that dear Nicolette's son-in-law was not one of his admirers.

The prince's companions remained outside the apartment. Jason closed the door, assuming, as did Rachel, that they must be guards or police of some kind. The prince gave his approval by moving toward the chair Rachel hastily pushed forward. Instead of taking the chair, however, he seated himself on the settee, indicating that Rachel should join him.

Gretchen cowered in a corner, quite overcome, and Jason took her by the hand, leading her out of the little salon. When he returned, the prince indicated that he, too, might be seated in the chair the prince himself had refused. "Please, I like to think I am again among my English friends."

"Indeed, you are, sir," Rachel assured him.

"I have always found your land a refuge, at times when my own country was less hospitable."

Rachel fell into this trap. "And may it always be your refuge." She caught the faint quirk of humor at the corner of Jason's mouth and realized her implication that the president of the French might once again have to flee his country. She stammered, "Not that such a thing—I mean, we were so pleased when we read that in the plebiscite three-fourths of the voters chose Your Highness. What a triumph!"

"I am very aware of what I owe to my constituents," he said

gravely. "I am afraid I must still win the royal houses to our democratic processes. But at least, I may say I have the people of France with me."

"Your Highness must find the one-term law a handicap to your plans," remarked Jason.

Rachel twisted uneasily, wondering if there was a hint of sarcasm in this remark, but the prince appeared to take it at face value. "Very true. I understand the two chambers are considering a bill now to make a reelection possible. As you remarked very astutely, the improvement in labor conditions, the abolishment of so many injustices, cannot be accomplished in one term."

"That shouldn't be too difficult," Jason remarked, too casually for Rachel's comfort. "This morning in one of the quarters when the guards rode by we distinctly heard voices in the crowd cry, 'Love live the emperor.'"

"*Vive l'empereur*," the prince repeated softly, or was he correcting Jason? He took a deep breath and turned to Rachel, still holding her hand. "But what do we think of, discussing politics in the presence of a beautiful young lady? In truth, I *sneaked* out of my offices, as you British say, in order to invite you to a reception at the Elysée within the next week. We are neighbors, you know. Only five minutes away. It amused me to see if I might pay a call today upon a lovely young lady without arousing the gossipmongers who have linked my name with every eligible beauty in Europe."

"Your Highness need have no fear," Jason reminded the bachelor-prince. "Your name will never be linked with my wife."

Rachel cleared her throat hurriedly, but whatever the prince's thoughts, he was far too clever to reveal them, even to a beautiful woman.

"An admirable sentiment in a bridegroom." He stood up. Rachel and Jason arose immediately, and Rachel was given a better chance to study Louis Napoleon. He was not a tall man but he had a long torso. Everyone claimed he looked magnificent on horseback. She didn't doubt it. There was about him a presence, a quality of strength. Perhaps he was born with—but more probably acquired—the stance on the rocky climb to the Elysée

Palace. It was an admirable quality for a prince. Or a man. She believed Jason possessed it. But this was no moment for him to try and compete with the president of France.

She looked anxiously at Jason. He was behaving with brusque efficiency. He had already started for the door, as if to suggest that the prince had overstayed his welcome.

The prince took his time. "Your invitations to the reception are in the post. We shall be most pleased to see you. I hope you will express my warmest regards to the lady whose house this is. Madame Bertrand has been a good and loyal friend." He smiled pleasantly at Jason over Rachel's head. "Well then, I expect to see you both."

Jason showed him out, into the protection of several men in tightly buttoned black coats. All the way down the stairs Rachel could hear the concierge's hoarse voice repeating her lifelong devotion to the Bonapartist cause.

When he had bolted the foyer door, Jason crossed his arms, leaned against the door, and watched Rachel. He was smiling, but his smile made her uneasy. She bustled around straightening cushions and observing with an attempt at her own humor, "I suppose you are going to remind me that he didn't mention the debt. Darling, princes never acknowledge debts that involve money."

"Still, I imagine he got what he came for. The admiration of another beautiful woman."

Absurd! He was actually jealous. She dismissed this with the amusement it deserved. "He can't very well make me the president's wife. I'm already married to the prince of hearts. The finest title in the world."

"Ah! But how would you like to be empress of the French?"

The comment made her pause. Not that she had any ambition to be another of Louis Napoleon's mistresses, but she realized suddenly that she and Jason had been entertaining a man who might very well be an emperor in embryo. His uncle, the great Napoleon, had made it from a lower rung on the ladder.

"Jason! Do you think he has ambitions so high?"

"I'll wager he is emperor within ten years. Five, if he holds his present popularity with the masses." He repeated, "Empress of the French. How does it sound?"

"But he's not nearly tall enough," she teased. She had won, and pursued her advantage. "He's not the least bit like you. You were so dominating, and it's uncomfortable being around him. Having to stand and sit and do this and that. All the tiresome etiquette. Jason, let's leave Paris. Send a message to the Elysée saying there is illness at home."

For an instant she thought he was still angry, but then he reached for her, caught her around the waist, and lifted her off the floor. She screamed, but she loved it and wound her arms around his neck, drawing him to her.

"Emperor of Yorkshire, I love you!" she promised him.

His kiss silenced her witticisms. Perhaps he would take her to the Elysée reception, after all. She told herself, with some satisfaction, that she was beginning to understand how to handle him.

TEN

But they did not leave Paris, in spite of Rachel's generous suggestion. She would like to think Jason had agreed to stay because he knew how much she wanted to attend the reception at the Elysée Palace. Yet the motive came from quite a different direction.

The afternoon of Louis Napoleon's visit Jason received letters from both Maria and his mother. He said little about the message from Yorkshire, but his sister's story of unhappiness in London, where she remained in Rachel's house, was quite another thing. He was moody throughout the rest of the day.

And the next day, Rachel received her own troublesome mail, a note from the Reverend Edward Culhane. She read it aloud: "I depart Folkestone upon Friday, arriving in Paris in a fortnight. Dare I trespass upon your good nature long enough to ask if you will do me the honor of dining with me one night in Paris? The city is unknown to me. I should be delighted to have your company."

"'Arriving in Paris in a fortnight,'" Jason mocked. "Sounds

like the pompous fool. It occurs to me that we have engagements 'in a fortnight.'"

His absurd and pointless dislike of the man annoyed her. "He is a perfectly harmless man of the cloth. Everyone at the wedding liked him. Why, your own sister—" She broke off, entranced with a new idea.

Jason swung around, demanding harshly, "Why bring Maria into this? I know you dislike her, but what has she to do with this fool in sacred robes?"

"Wait!"

He saw the light of excitement in her lively, gray eyes. "What the devil are you thinking?"

"Maria liked Edward Culhane, and he is a perfectly respectable young man. Maria would enjoy Paris."

"Yes, but—"

"Can't we send for Maria? Have her leave for Paris by the Folkestone crossing on Friday and ask Reverend Culhane's escort when they accidentally meet?"

His scowl relaxed slowly into a grin. "Are all females such conniving wenches?"

"Of course. I won you, didn't I?"

He seemed happy again, or as carefree as his dark nature would permit. He was even amused days later when they were strolling near the Arc de Triomphe and encountered a troop of superbly uniformed horsemen heavy with gold braid. At their head, to the delight of the strolling citizens, rode the prince-president himself, in the handsome uniform of the National Guard. Even Jason was impressed. "I will say, he does it well. A pity he can't rule France from the back of a horse."

"Don't be nasty." But she didn't mind. Louis Napoleon passed by to shouts of *"Vive l'empereur!"* from the crowd. Rachel was surprised and impressed to note how many women curtsied, and how many men bowed. She, too, sank in a deep curtsy, her russet-striped silk skirts spreading in all directions, while Jason remained stubbornly unbending beside her, his tall figure and dark good looks making him stand out embarrassingly from the French around them. Perhaps it was this stance that attracted the prince's eye. Louis Napoleon turned slightly and, to Rachel's delight, recognized her with a bow and a smile.

After the procession had moved on, Jason muttered to Rachel, "You will be an empress yet." But he softened the jibe by taking up her gloved hand and kissing it. "I heard booing, too, incidentally," he reminded her.

"Did you? I heard nothing of the sort. Darling, could you be having trouble with your ears?"

"Not a bit of it. Shall we stop at one of those cafés for a drink?"

"Oh, let's! But not absinthe or those horrid things. One of the sweet drinks."

He raised his gaze to the heavens, or at least to the roof of the awning over the sidewalk. "It baffles me how this nation could have conquered a continent once on those damned sweet drinks."

"Very well. Have your stupid beer."

In excellent spirits, they sat down at the dusty little sidewalk table.

The next day Jason received a hurried scrawl from Maria. He showed it to Rachel, congratulating her upon the success of her scheming. "Maria has met the Noble Culhane. He graciously offered to escort her to Paris. When are we to celebrate the wedding?"

She refused to be teased out of her scheme. Propinquity had often done wonders. If only Maria wouldn't spoil it by her drinking, or some other calamitous mistake!

The two travelers arrived in Paris by a twice-weekly coach. The vehicle's bumping and rattling was an unfortunate contrast to the train Rachel and Jason rode from London to Folkestone. While Edward Culhane remained as polite as possible in the circumstances, Maria was still complaining when they all reached the Bourne lodgings. She favored her crooked left arm and shoulder more than usual, which made her look deformed, hunched over. From his furtive glances at his companion, Culhane must have noticed her discomfort.

Maria greeted her brother, suffered Rachel's embrace, asked where her own private bedchamber was, and retired. Within minutes, Rachel and Jason found themselves alone with Edward Culhane. It was painful to see the young man's obvious relief at Maria's departure. Rachel asked if she shouldn't go in and keep

Maria company, but Jason was adamant. "No. When Maria is tired she prefers to be alone. Like my mother, she suffers from a migraine." He then kissed Rachel's knuckles, making something of a performance of it for Culhane's benefit.

The young reverend, now relaxed, became much freer, more conversational ("gossipy as a woman" Jason later remarked). Culhane wanted to know about the president of France. Was he going to conquer the world like his uncle, or only the ladies' hearts? "As I have been hearing," he explained. "They do say he is—to borrow the vulgar phrase—'hanging out for a wife.'" He settled back comfortably for a long visit, unaware of Jason's dislike. "I would give a good deal to meet His Highness."

Fully aware of Jason's sentiments, and anxious to get Edward off to his own lodgings, Rachel answered overenthusiastically, "He wants peace. He is very intelligent. I can assure you of that. His Highness paid us a call recently. He knew my mother well." She caught the satirical look in Jason's eyes and added, "She dealt with him on a matter of business."

"And to think, less than five years ago, he was a penniless refugee in England. A remarkable race, these Bonapartes. So you have actually met him. How fortunate!"

"Your second theory was nearer the mark," Jason said. "The prince has great luck with the ladies. . . . But we are detaining you. You must be anxious to get settled. Suppose I have the concierge whistle up a carriage for you." He rose.

"Er—yes. Quite so. I really must—get settled, that is."

Jason went off to signal the concierge, leaving Rachel to express their deep gratitude to the young man. "It was so very kind of you to care for dear Maria. She had intended to make the journey with her maid, but at the last minute the girl took ill. We were so hoping to see Maria that she hurried off quite alone and unattended. I know you are thinking it was improper. But it was actually my idea," she added with perfect honesty.

Unluckily, he took this as a compliment to her own good heart, an idea that annoyed her almost as much as it clearly annoyed Jason when he came back to find Culhane bowing deeply over her hand, which he seemed reluctant to let go.

"Your devotion to your sister-in-law does you credit, Mrs. Bourne."

She stood on the balcony and watched Jason send their guest to his lodgings in a hotel off the Rue de Rivoli. Jason waved to Culhane as if to say "good riddance" when the old black fiacre with its patient mare clip-clopped down the street. Then he looked up at Rachel and started into the house.

She met him on the top-stair landing. "Thank heaven, the poor man is gone. What a bore!"

She put her arms around Jason, but he stiffened. "Save your relief. We haven't seen the last of him."

"I really think we should talk to Maria. Maybe we can give her a hint about pleasing Mr. Culhane. Father always said there were ways of pleasing, even if you didn't mean it. That is to say, if you wanted to be popular."

His reaction was cool. "You are certainly the woman to do that. But I don't advise it with Maria. And above all, don't quote your family."

She was astonished. "Why ever not?"

"Because . . ." He looked as if he would say something cutting. Then he went on, "Maria has no use for London fops. If you will excuse me, I am going out for a *Yorkshire Post*. There must be at least one in this benighted town."

She was almost relieved. Perhaps he would be in a better mood when he returned. Meanwhile, she would see what could be done with Maria.

She found her sister-in-law standing at the back window of her bedchamber, staring down into a tiny stone courtyard where a neighboring concierge was drawing water from the ancient well. Before Rachel could think of something to mollify the touchy woman, Maria surprised her by exclaiming, "I like Paris. It is real. Not like your pretentious London. Look down there at that old woman with the jar. And a minute ago I saw a child squat over in the corner by the ivy. That was natural."

Rachel decided not to point out that London, too, had its districts where the sanitation was not of the best. She was only relieved to find her sister-in-law a trifle less sour. She agreed: "Yes. I have always liked the French. I believe a great many British do not, but of course, my mother was French."

Maria's thin fingers drummed on the window. Her thoughts seemed far away. "And your father?"

Rachel remembered Jason's warning about discussing her "foppish" family and slipped over the subject. "He came from the north."

"Did your mother know about his—women?"

Rachel faltered, astonished at so forward a question. Hesper Fridd or Clare Lorimer must have been gossiping about Rachel's father. "Why should she? They didn't mean anything to Father. Just unprincipled women who deliberately threw themselves in his way. They knew he was married. They were no better than they should be."

Maria Bourne turned her head slightly, pressing the side of her face, her cheek and temple, against the cool glass. She said nothing for a minute. Rachel saw that her eyes were closed and her fists clenched. Obviously, she was suffering from a migraine.

Touched by the woman's genuine anguish, Rachel looked around for her sal volatile, found it in a drawer of the little inlaid dressing table, and offered it gently to Maria. "I'm so very sorry. Those jolting coaches always give me a headache, too."

Maria's eyelids snapped up. Her deep-set eyes blazed. "What a fool you are! You blind little idiot!"

Rachel gasped. Then she sighed, left the delicate tasseled bottle of smelling salts on the bed, and walked out.

Things improved by the time Edward Culhane came to take them to dinner. Jason spent a few minutes with Maria beforehand, and though Rachel hadn't mentioned her behavior, he must have guessed at it because Maria mumbled to Rachel, "Please accept my apology. I always say stupid things when I've a headache." She hesitated. "This is a poor time to mention it, but I've gone through everything in my cases and I've nothing fit to wear. My entire wardrobe is wrinkled. Do you have anything I could wear tonight?"

So that explained her apology! No matter. It was a heaven-sent opportunity. Rachel took her by the arm. "We haven't much time. But I've a perfect gown that would look lovely on you. Deep-rose barred silk. I'll get Gretchen to help us fit it on you." The idea of making her over was suddenly very appealing. They would conquer Edward Culhane if it took everyone in the house to do so. There was nothing really so wrong with Maria. She was simply a virgin who needed a man to sweeten her sour disposition. Having met the man of her dreams, Rachel was a great believer that love conquered all.

Maria had a natural coltish grace, a long-legged, determined walk that was neither fragile nor delicate in the popular style. But properly gowned, with her stiff left arm disguised by a shawl, for instance, she could be quite impressive. Her hair needed help. It was too fine and a dull sand color, all loose ends. Rachel studied it, then looked into the mirror at her own camellias, worn at the nape of her neck, one of them nestling on the side of her throat.

"I do believe they make my neck look short. But you wouldn't have that problem. Hold yourself still. Gretchen, bring some pins for her hair." Meanwhile, she unfastened the camellias and placed them rather daringly along the side of Maria's head and under her left ear. "Pin the rest of her hair firmly. Now, the flowers. . . . Oh, I love it! Now turn around to the mirror."

Maria's reaction was disappointing. "How patronizing you are! What pride it gives you to play fairy godmother! You love this, don't you!"

Rachel was wounded by the accusation, but even more so by the truth in Maria's words. She pretended not to take offense. "Well, look at yourself. What difference do my motives make when the result is so spectacular?"

Maria studied her image, her mouth twisted to one side. When she had rearranged Rachel's lace shawl, draping it over the crooked arm, even she was impressed. "Not too bad, really."

"Thank you." The woman did look remarkably attractive. Perhaps one shouldn't always expect gratitude.

Rachel's true reward was the look on Jason's face when he saw his sister. He was pleased, but it was Rachel he came to and Rachel he thanked, briefly, with one word, a quick kiss, and a long look into her eyes. It was enough. The only puzzling thing was his curious expression. If she hadn't known the idea was nonsense, she might have called it a sad look. Not regret, surely.

There was no explaining him sometimes.

He was clearly pleased when he saw Edward Culhane's reaction to this new Maria. The reverend's eyes opened wide. He started to say something, changed his mind, and greeted Rachel and Jason, but he lingered over Maria's right hand. He very

111

nearly raised it to his lips, then realized that such a salute would only be correct with a married woman. All the same, when the four set out for a well-known Norman restaurant farther along the street, where the select Faubourg became the more plebeian and historic Rue St. Honoré, Culhane took Maria's arm and made light conversation about their unpleasant but now amusing three-day journey from Boulogne to Paris.

Rachel wished her sister-in-law would not look at a man so directly when she disagreed. She was very opinionated; that same intense look might be seen over a pistol at twenty paces.

They ate upstairs at the restaurant, which was nearly deserted at this early hour, and Rachel had just begun to pick the delicious flesh of her trout away from a bone or two when a group of four gentlemen were shown to one of the empty tables across the room. Amid the white table linen and dazzling gleam of the many crystal wine glasses at each place setting, the men put their heads together to talk politics. One man, however, stocky, graying, with a wispy beard, looked around and saw the Bourne table. He broke into a smile, half-rose, and bowed.

To Rachel's surprise Jason nodded in answer, without much concern, but pleasantly enough. She broke in on an animated discussion between Maria and Culhane to ask her husband, "You know that man?"

"Certainly. We've conducted some business."

"But I'm sure he's a Frenchman."

Jason's black eyebrows were just a shade satirical. "Quite true. I am democratic. I am quite willing to discuss business with a Frenchman."

Unsatisfied, but not wanting to pursue the matter until they were alone, Rachel returned to her trout.

Before the Bourne party had finished its elaborate desserts, the man who had bowed to Jason got up from his table and came over to, as he put it, "Pay my respects to Mrs. Bourne and congratulate you upon your husband's financial acumen. You were wise to rely upon his expert knowledge."

The man must be talking about her mother's French estate. This was news, indeed. Edward Culhane raised his head and became interested, but it was Maria's reaction that alarmed Rachel. Maria shot a quick glance at her brother, then confined her attention to the *baba au rhum* as though deaf to what went on around her.

Jason remained nonplussed. "Darling, may I present Monsieur Raoul Meissen of the brokers Meissen Frères, who represent your French estate? My sister, Miss Maria Bourne, the Reverend Culhane . . . Monsieur Meissen."

Heads nodded all around, with the single exception of Maria, who kept her gaze concentrated on her plate. Rachel thought she saw the woman actually smile. No, it was a smirk. Maybe she suspected Monsieur Meissen's revelation would make trouble between her brother and his bride. For some reason, and in spite of Rachel's efforts to bridge that dislike, the woman was determined to keep the war going.

If only Edward Culhane could be persuaded to marry her! But it was almost too much to hope for.

While Monsieur Meissen lingered over Rachel's hand, another gentleman came over to be introduced as the aide to Monsieur Bacciochi, who was the prince-president's social secretary. He spoke in French, with a heavy Italian accent. "Monsieur Bacciochi asks me to inform you that the young lady and her escort will be issued an invitation to the Elysée reception, Madame Bourne. How shall the invitation be inscribed?"

Rachel introduced her startled sister-in-law. The handsome Italianate gentleman bowed. "His Highness always says—that is, it is his whimsical notion—that a reception should be blessed with as much beauty as possible, to leaven the amount of dull business transacted behind official smiles." He smiled suavely and departed.

Monsieur Meissen murmured, "A trifle grandiose, but he has a point. Incidentally, tickets to the reception are in great demand. Even the fossil Bourbons of the Faubourg St. Germain are beginning to clamor for them." The Bournes were suitably honored. Edward Culhane looked delighted to see Maria in this new light.

Rachel ached to ask the banker questions about her French bonds and properties, but she didn't want Maria and Culhane to know of Jason's unsolicited involvement in her matters.

Looking over at her husband, she saw that he had not touched his mocha pastry. He drank the last of his Bordeaux with an attentive eye to his sister. . . . He probably noticed how much Maria was drinking. Was that frown due to his concern for Maria? Or about the matter of Rachel's property? She was relieved to find him troubled, but she was not entirely reassured.

Had Jason married her for her inheritance?

When they left the restaurant that night, Edward Culhane was exuberant. He didn't seem to notice Maria's loud voice or her faintly alcoholic slur. Culhane talked on about the Elysée reception and the prospect of meeting Prince Louis Napoleon throughout the walk back to his lodgings. It was just as well. Although Maria gave him some attention, she had kept her eye on her brother and his wife, occasionally stifling a giggle.

Jason returned to the Faubourg St. Honoré with an excited Maria and a depressed, thoughtful Rachel. How much of her French estate was gone? She hoped at least he had gambled it on good solid stocks and properties. Monsieur Meissen seemed to think so. But nevertheless, she was deeply hurt by her husband's secrecy.

Undressing later for bed, Rachel automatically slipped on one of her trousseau gowns, wondering what she would do when Jason joined her in bed. If he did join her, of course. She wasn't even sure of that.

ELEVEN

It was well after midnight when she heard him come in from his small dressing area that had once been a powdering. He had thrown a robe over his broad shoulders, the gaslight from the hall behind him gleaming on his flesh. As always, and in spite of her cold determination to resist his power over her, she felt the now-familiar heat in her loins, her desire for him once again overwhelming her own strength.

She had long since overcome her shyness around his magnificent naked body. She stared at his thighs now, longing to welcome him into her own heated body. She found herself for the first time wanting him with more desire than emotion. . . .

She held her arms out to him. His robe dropped off. His past hardships had left his body firm and lean, yet she knew its suppleness, his tenderness that had surprised and delighted her. His skillful lovemaking further controlled her, and she was well aware of his power tonight as she surrendered to her feelings rather than her conflicting emotions.

How well he knew her, even in the short weeks of their marriage! He took her body at once, pulling her to him. His touch, as well as his strength, weakened any resistance she might have had. She groaned and urged him as always in whispers that were alive with her desire.

"Come to me, darling. . . ."

Her body throbbed with his pressure. His firm, passionate flesh within her brought her to ecstasy, her fingers biting savagely into his shoulders.

But a part of her remained detached, and watching: *Enjoy him. This joy will not last. You must not let yourself be conquered by a physical craving. You cannot trust him.*

Perhaps, in some dreadful way, she was not the Catherine Earnshaw to her beloved Heathcliff. She had so much wanted that role when she first knew him. Perhaps she was only another Isabella Linton, the besotted girl Heathcliff had used and despised.

Despised? That couldn't be true, she would sense that. Surely he loved her a little.

He seemed to prove that tonight. Or was it only sexual satisfaction that he sought when his lips brushed so sensuously over her breasts to her abdomen and between her thighs. . . . She wanted to scream with the ecstasy of his touch, but she did not scream. She remembered his sister, separated from them only by the hallway and the bedroom door, slightly ajar.

She caressed his hair and then her hands moved over his body, his thighs and loins. Her tantalizing hands lingered over his erection, his need for her. Maybe in this way she could bring him to love her as she so desperately loved him.

Hours later, when she was lying there staring at the high ceiling, Jason sleeping beside her, she felt his hand move suddenly. She remained motionless, pretending also to sleep. His hand found her thigh and rested on it. The heat of his flesh seemed to burn through her gown.

Did he think he could soothe away her suspicions and resentment over his secret handling of her fortune?

She slept at last. Her dreams were confused. She recalled afterward being haunted by images of a stranger who looked like Jason; yet, when she looked into his burning eyes, she knew he was her enemy. Why? What had her dream-self done to make him look like that?

* * *

That morning Maria wanted to visit the temporary tomb of Emperor Napoleon in the Invalides. The visit would give Rachel the opportunity she needed. She suggested that Jason take Maria while she herself visited a Paris salon to be fitted for a new chic Parisian wardrobe. Maria hesitated, as if the new styles might intrigue her. Then she dismissed such shallow matters. "Why don't we send a message to the Reverend Culhane and see if he wishes to view the catafalque?" she suggested.

"A capital idea," said Rachel. "He is so enthusiastic about the Bonapartes."

Before Maria and Jason started out for Culhane's hotel, Jason suggested that he would first escort his wife to the dress salon. Rachel tried to make her refusal sound casual. "Don't trouble, darling. I'll take my time. I love to window-shop. But I needn't tell you that."

He chuckled. "No. Whenever I think of Napoleon's beloved Rue de Rivoli, all I'll remember is starting and stopping. And gloves." He remarked an aside to Maria, "You'd think she had a dozen hands instead of just two. And very pretty they are." He reached for both Rachel's hands. She avoided the warmth in his eyes, smiling instead at his scarred fingers covering hers. For an instant she was afraid she might cry.

She felt him watching her closely. It was a searching look that made her more than ever conscious of her deception toward him. Suppose he *had* acted solely in her interest, as all husbands were presumed to do. Her actions today might destroy her marriage, destroy his love for her.

If he loved her.

He leaned toward her over their hands, as she herself had often done, and kissed her lips. A light teasing kiss; nevertheless, it shook all her careful resolutions. She asked herself if it wouldn't be better to ignore Jason's chicanery, his slyness, and let their lives go on harmoniously until . . .

Until he meddled with her estate again?

Until he took control of her fortune and lost interest in her?

"Darling," she murmured, looking into his eyes, "have a wonderful time, you and Maria. And miss me."

Those great dark eyes always had their effect upon her, searching her face now as if they were memorizing her features. "I always miss you when we are apart."

He kissed her again and his mouth lingered on hers. It was impossible not to respond. Her body yielded, and she couldn't help herself. She locked her arms around his neck. Their mouths were still exploring, finding new sensations together until they broke apart, laughing and breathless.

Aware that Maria was watching them, Rachel looked away, embarrassed. The woman's expression bothered her. It was sad, depressed, not what she would expect. No sarcasm, no contempt. Perhaps Maria was thinking of her own lonely life, the life that had never known such love. Rachel's heart went out to her. She turned to Maria and hugged her. "Have a *very* good time." The woman's body remained stiff under Rachel's good-natured embrace, but there was something in her posture that shifted, that seemed to suppress emotion. *Someday*, Rachel thought as she watched Maria leave with her brother, *we will be friends, you and I.* It might take a long time, but Maria had feelings. She could be won over, somehow.

Her thoughts returned to her troubled doubts. She dressed with quiet elegance, hoping to impress Monsieur Meissen that she was fully capable of handling her own monetary affairs.

The office of Meissen Frères was a narrow building like the others in the area, coldly beautiful, gray, secretive, and exclusive. The first thing Rachel saw as she stepped down to the cobblestones was the Vendome monument topped by the new statue of the Emperor Napoleon. She couldn't help wondering if one day her mother's friend Louis Napoleon would have his own statue. If Jason's suspicions proved correct, she might one day be able to boast that she herself had been an emperor's friend.

She was received by a serious young man with frosty eyes and the deportment of an usher. When she gave him her name, he thawed noticeably. "Monsieur Meissen will be delighted by your visit, Mademoiselle Etheredge—pardon, Madame Bourne. But at this moment he is closeted with"—he lowered his voice conspiratorially—"one of the Bonapartes. He should be with you in a very, very short time."

She allowed herself to be seated in the most comfortable chair the young man's office afforded, and she tried hard not to peer out the open door and around the pillars of the hall that led to the Meissen sanctum. Could the Bonaparte visitor be Prince Louis

Napoleon's cousin Princess Mathilde? Or was she still in the wilds of Russia with her royal husband (a dreadful beast, if the gossip were true)? Small wonder those same gossips also said the lady had taken a more pleasant male as her lover. It seemed a daring act, in view of her name and station, and Rachel admired her for it.

But the visitor proved to be a male, big and heavyset but otherwise bearing a distinct resemblance to his uncle, the great Napoleon. He must be Louis Napoleon's other cousin, the Princess Mathilde's brother. It was all quite exciting to Rachel, who felt more and more like an awestruck tourist.

He must be borrowing money, she decided, trying to keep her mind off her own problem. But all too soon little Monsieur Meissen came bustling out of his office to meet her. "Most delightful, madame. I could almost fancy I see your lovely mother before me. Not that you resemble Madame Hinton—pardon—Etheredge. But the same charm, the same—"

"You are too kind, monsieur. Actually, I have decided my mother was right in devoting so much time to her financial affairs, so I came to the wisest person I know for help."

Part of her attention was distracted by the Napoleonic money borrower who had gone out through the mysterious back regions of the offices, not the Vendome entrance. Obviously, he didn't want Parisians to know that he was hard-pressed.

Little Monsieur Meissen twittered. "*Vraiment*, madame? You flatter me. But come, why do we stand here when we may be comfortable?"

They walked together into the oppressively heavy office, with its oak-paneled walls and dark leather furniture. It was an airless tomb. The two long windows were closed, sealed against the cool autumn day by tightly drawn heavy velvet drapes, which looked as if their green folds had not been shaken since Waterloo.

But Rachel was here on business, not to criticize the ambiance. She leaned forward, conscious of her charm—and her neckline—as if to tell a secret. "My dear friend, you are a married man. You are aware that on occasion one keeps small monetary secrets from one's partner."

Monsieur Meissen cleared his throat. "I believe I comprehend you. As you are on your honeymoon, I imagine you wish to make a gift of some sort to your husband. A very knowledgeable gentleman."

Good Lord! Reward Jason for meddling with her inheritance?

She smiled. "Later, perhaps. But now I wish to test this great knowledge of his. What is your opinion of his various actions? I know you will be explicit. I am only a woman, without your brilliant mind." He swallowed that. She went on, "Can you tell me precisely what he has done?"

"Ah, but of course." He tinkled a little bell and another clerk arrived, an aged, dry-looking man with a scowl. He bowed to Monsieur Meissen. "You wished the file of Madame Hinton-Etheredge, currently in the name of Madame Bourne?"

The old man laid down the overstuffed portfolio, which he must have readied the instant Rachel swept into the pillared chamber of the sacred precincts. Meissen laid his hands on the portfolio, not even bothering to review the papers. "Monsieur Bourne," he began, "does not approve of steam."

"Steam!"

"Neither for the railway engines or ships. He has reinvested several of your mother's railway purchases. I confess I was reluctant. I personally believe steam is the energy of the future, but your husband . . . He is a country man, no?" She nodded. "Well, he prefers the horse."

She didn't believe that. Not for a minute. "But, why would he travel by train?"

"For practical reasons. So much more practical than the *diligence*, or, as you say, the accommodation coach."

"Yet you congratulated him on his business acumen."

"He sold your Spanish government bonds just before they plunged. Always prudent, in our opinion, and he has invested in Prussian government bonds."

"Why, for heaven's sake?"

Meissen shrugged with typically French eloquence. "He has heard talk of close ties between Queen Victoria and the Kingdom of Prussia. British money is being invested in Prussia. One knows also that Her Majesty is strongly influenced by her German husband."

"Isn't there a threat to France in all this German influence?"

120

He put his pudgy fingertips together and pursed his lips. "Our great continental enemy will always be Austria, madame."

Such matters meant very little to her at this moment. "Has he bought anything profitable?"

"Splendid country property near Fontainebleau. In a village called Barbizon. And one farming property on the Indre River, in the Loire region."

He'd been meddling everywhere.

She pulled herself together, forced her sweetest, most conspiratorial smile, and leaned closer toward him. "I must confess, monsieur, that I prefer the voice of authority to handle my French properties. Tell me now, isn't it possible to keep no one except yourself in control of them?" His friendly eyes told her he understood.

"Of course, purchases are often made in the name of the broker. My brother, or myself. These matters are handled in secrecy to prevent a rise in price."

"Excellent. I will sign whatever is necessary and I assume your company will keep the real owner's name secret."

He hesitated. "Within the law, your properties may be legally controlled by Monsieur Bourne. However"—she had been waiting for that word—"there are ways. Corporations unknown to monsieur. It is occasionally done."

"Excellent. I want all of my properties removed from my name except those he has already purchased. I know I can trust you. My mother always said you were the most brilliant man she ever knew."

"Did she? Nicolette was a *remarkable* female."

"Please send all communications to me at the home of Sir Bayard Lorimer in London."

"Not to your London brokers?"

The fewer people who knew of this, the better. She knew of only one person she could trust. "Here is Sir Bayard's address." She dipped his pen in the ink bottle and scribbled the address on the stationery he provided. Then she got up to leave.

She did not have to look back to guess that he was puzzled, or that she had aroused in him deep suspicions of her bridegroom. No matter. She was her mother's daughter. Nicolette had kept her fortune out of the hands of Rachel's father. Perhaps Mama, too, had had reasons.

Beneath all her resentment toward Jason's meddling in her estate was the fear nagging at her that he didn't really love her. In spite of the many times she assured herself of his sexual desire for her, she knew this was not love. But was there no more in his feeling for her than their happiness in bed?

Her fears and hurt pride only fueled this resentment; she would punish him with her only weapon.

TWELVE

In an effort to ease her guilt about lying to Jason, she stopped at a dress salon just off the Place Vendome, where she was received with open arms and a promise that both she and Miss Maria Bourne would be outfitted in the most fashionable creations of that noble house.

She returned to the apartment in the Faubourg St. Honoré before Jason and Maria. It gave her more time to regret what she had done. The necessity of her actions hardly soothed her conscience.

She spent the next half hour writing checks for the purchases she herself had made and added a second rent check for their landlady's account with Meissen Frères. When Rachel first told Jason she had sent a check to her mother's friend to obtain the Paris rooms, he had been angry, remarking indignantly that he could still pay for his own honeymoon. But when Rachel reminded him that the deed was done, he backed down. "Very well," he said, somewhat to her surprise. "It is your money." And now, with the second payment due, he had made no effort to pay it. Had he forgotten?

A uniformed aide arrived from the prince-president's offices with two more of the "tickets" for the reception at the Elysée just as the sightseeing group returned home. Maria came running up the stairs so happy that she hugged Rachel. "You've got the tickets! I saw that officer. Thank you, luv."

It was the first time Maria had ever used the working-class endearment with her. Rachel felt suddenly warm toward her sister-in-law. She banished her doubts for the moment and concentrated on the progress of Maria's romance. "You must tell the Reverend Culhane of his invitation," she reminded Maria. "Did you have a good time today?"

Jason's laugh revealed his excellent humor. "You should have seen them, sweetheart. You would have thought they were on their honeymoon." He slipped an arm around Rachel's waist, drew her close, and kissed the top of her head.

Rachel was especially pleased at his reaction. "I'm glad. Jason, I was talking to the *vendeuse* at Recamier's Salon today."

"Ah, yes, the shopping spree." He sounded casual, and yet, he seemed to be mocking her in some way. Did he suspect? Or was it only her guilty conscience that made her suspicious of everything he did? After all, it was his own conscience that should be troubled, not hers.

"Maria and I are expected at the salon tomorrow to be fitted for our Elysée gowns."

Maria looked almost girlish in her eagerness. "Oh, Jason, may I?"

"Of course, you may!" Rachel insisted.

Jason shrugged. "Why not? I would like His Highness to know I am escorting two beauties. He may be impressed." Maria flushed with pleasure. "One of the French tourists at the Invalides gave us some gossip that may be of interest to hopeful females."

"Really, Jason," his sister began, more flushed than ever.

Jason grinned. "They say Louis Napoleon has a penchant for light-haired beauties. The good Culhane was upset. He, too, seems to be attracted to fair women." Though he pinched his sister's chin, he was smiling at Rachel.

Maria's spirits were high that afternoon, and through the evening. The next morning she and Rachel discussed various styles for her gown.

"If only you weren't still a virgin," Rachel murmured, half out of sympathy. Maria's quick start told Rachel that she had been indelicate. "I beg pardon. I should have said 'maiden.' If you weren't a maiden, you could wear a green ball gown. But don't worry. You will look heavenly in white with a shawl. Perhaps layers of ruffles, and a —"

Maria wrinkled her nose. "Loops, festoons, anything. But not ruffles. I'm not the ruffles sort."

"You're absolutely right. Something more sophisticated, of course. You have a sophisticated air, and your features require a more subtle elegance. His Highness will be impressed."

Maria confessed, "I would rather impress the Church of England."

Rachel smiled with true warmth. "Maria, you will impress everyone there."

At the salon the two women found themselves in the capable hands of the glamorous shopkeeper. For Rachel, she chose a violet silk and tulle ball gown off the shoulder, with a wide overskirt tied by tiny violets of purple satin. To offset the gown, she would wear her mother's diamonds and amethysts.

On the night of the Elysée reception Jason announced with satisfaction, "There cannot be two women tonight who look handsomer than the Bourne ladies."

Edward nodded silently in agreement. His eyes wandered to the camellia nestled in the hollow of Maria's throat, which, like her face, blushed under his gaze.

Both Jason and Culhane had taken great trouble to match the women's elegance, dark Jason in his rigidly formal black and white, and golden-haired Culhane, perhaps equally handsome in his gentler way.

"In fact, you resemble a portrait in my home, a splendid-looking young man," Rachel told Culhane.

He looked pleased. "An ancestor?"

"My father." Although she spoke the truth, she had meant it as a teasing remark, but nobody seemed to appreciate her humor. She added hurriedly, "Which is a compliment. Father was handsome. In fact, he was very popular with the ladies."

A little red-faced, Culhane thanked her again, but neither Jason nor Maria smiled. Rachel looked distractedly out of the carriage window, embarrassed by her faux pas. They had just passed through the *porte cochére* of the Elysée Palace, to join the circle of other arriving carriages and teams, each of which stopped briefly at the formal steps to let out the guests before moving on around the inner court, where they would await the end of a long, festive evening.

Rachel walked ahead of their party, as if to impress her importance upon the others. Jason, however, would not follow her. With his long stride and a hard hand under her elbow, he guided her up the steps. By the time the women had been divested of their evening cloaks and swept out into the huge salon to meet their escorts, Rachel had forgotten the tension in the carriage. This huge gallery proved to be the most dazzling room Rachel had ever seen. She was awed by its splendor, as well as by the spectacular patchwork of uniforms worn by the numerous foreign visitors. For a man considered bourgeois by the ancient ruling houses of Europe, Louis Napoleon had managed to attract representatives of every royal family. Most of them looked far less civilized than the small genteel Bonaparte himself. Nor were they as well mannered, thought Rachel.

The Bourne guests made their way as best they could through the endless gossiping groups, while Maria silently counted the chandeliers under which they passed in the long gallery, whose large windows were draped with crimson and gold portieres. The columns of the gallery were aglow with lamplight. Rachel remarked to Jason behind her fan, "My presentation to Queen Victoria was nothing compared to this."

He regarded the breathtaking spectacle with a seemingly sardonic eye. "Merely the difference between reality and opera. You see here the first act of the Second Bonaparte Opera."

"In that case, I prefer the theater to the reality."

"Naturally, with your antecedents."

It was a spurious and unpleasant remark. Her lineage was all bourgeois, and he knew it. After all that had befallen him in his life, one would think he would be more resentful of royalty.

Families like the Bonapartes, the Hintons, and the Etheredges could not match them for ostentation.

"And the Bournes are superior?"

"The Bournes have always been and still are farmers. Here comes your opera hero." He turned to Maria. "Be ready to sink low. Our host has seen us."

Maria was looking flustered and awkward, her camellias wilting on her shoulder. She did not appear as happy as Rachel would have liked. Rachel glanced at Culhane and, to her annoyance, saw him staring back at her, his eyes warm. She frowned and gave her attention to the prince-president, who had left a group of generals, heavily encrusted with gold braid, and made his way toward the Bourne party, smiling and nodding to little caches of interested guests as he moved.

Both Rachel and Maria lowered themselves into deep curtsies, Maria covering the low bodice of her gown with her fan. She had evidently been practicing and performed the civility with grace. To Rachel's admiring eyes, Maria looked genuinely stunning. She was neither curved nor sweetly coltish, but she carried herself with pride and it suited her well. The drooping camellias had been thrust back behind her ear. The delicate lace shawl concealed the stiff set of her left arm.

His Highness greeted Rachel first, taking her hand and congratulating her on wearing "the color of the Bonaparte cause. A delicate compliment, madame."

Rachel had chosen violet because it was her favorite and one of her most flattering shades, but she diplomatically accepted the compliment. The prince turned to Maria, obviously impressed by what he saw. She had managed to rise above her own nervousness, perhaps put at ease by the man's gracious manner. The prince stood before Jason and Culhane. Edward Culhane's gentle smile and deep bow made it easy for Louis Napoleon to overlook Jason's barely perceptible nod.

There was a moment of awkward silence, but the prince, obviously practiced in proper deportment, directed his informal attention to the women present. He remarked to Maria, "It is an especial pleasure to meet the young ladies of that country I consider my second home. From my own observation tonight I am persuaded that all English females must be radiant beauties."

To Rachel's amusement Culhane flushed at the ease with which the compliment from the celebrated womanizer was bestowed. He once again seemed to reconsider his perception of Maria's beauty.

Louis Napoleon moved on to a Russian princess and her escort, and a stiff-necked, heavily decorated grand duke, and Culhane inserted himself, fairly gushing with pleasure. "His Highness was right, you know, Miss Bourne. You are looking—if I may say so—quite radiant."

"Merely a modest blush," Jason put in. But he, too, was pleased for his sister. He ran his finger over Rachel's cheek and remarked, coolly, "My wife, however, is used to such compliments. Not a blush in those alabaster cheeks."

Rachel tried to swallow her wounded shock. What had she done to make him abuse her in this cutting way? He had been cynical and dour since their arrival. Perhaps he hadn't approved of her flippant remark about her father's flirtatious tendencies. The remark could quite possibly be construed as disrespectful; country-bred people like the Bournes very likely disapproved of so casual a tongue. She wondered if he realized that when he lived with her in London, he would be shocked about much of the free speaking he heard in that cosmopolitan center.

Maria and Culhane appeared to be on more intimate terms once again. Their heads tilted close together, he was telling her of his wish for a curacy with the church in the north. Somewhat coyly, he mentioned Yorkshire's West Riding. Maria responded with an enthusiasm that must have told him he would have at least one eager parishioner.

Meanwhile, a stir rippled in the milling crowd. Several people shifted their positions and Rachel got a clear view of the latest group moving down the long gallery toward the prince-president.

Every candelabrum and wall lamp glittered upon the young woman escorted by a middle-aged man and woman. Rachel recognized the author Prosper Merimée and the chattering coquettish Countess de Montijo. But all eyes were on the younger woman. Tall and graceful, her golden-red hair sparkling under the light, her slanting blue eyes modestly downcast, Eugénie de

Montijo curtsied to the prince. The delicate white flounces of her ball gown dropped slowly about her, and Rachel found herself jealous of that marvelous self-possession.

At the same time, Rachel became aware of Jason's lips close to her ear. He murmured, "I'm afraid Maria, blond hair and all, has lost her chance to become an empress. Your friend Louis Napoleon is truly bewitched by that beauty."

So he was.

Rachel could only conclude that the prince had good taste. "It's just as well," she answered Jason's comment. "Maria would soon be homesick for England."

Jason laughed.

But since Louis Napoleon was the star performer of this delightful "opera" and he had evidently found a leading lady, Rachel couldn't take her eyes off the pair. It might have been this fact, she decided afterward, that made Jason choose such a moment for his unsettling disclosure. "By the way, sweetheart, I admire an independent attitude toward money as well as the next man, but nine thousand francs—that does seem excessive independence."

She stared at him, wondering if he had already found out about her order to Meissen Frères. "Nine thousand francs?" It was certainly an odd sum.

"Yes. Your note to Meissen Frères authorizing the second payment to Madame Bertrand for the rooms here."

"Not nine. *One* thousand francs. I remember."

He said quietly, "But your statement read ten thousand."

"Impossible! I don't make mistakes with money."

"You did this time. Nine thousand of them. Shall I show you the statement? Meissen's clerk sent it over while you were at your last fitting. I gave them a corrected check of my own."

His eyes glittered, like the eyes in her haunting dream not many nights ago. But there was something else in his face, a tense, troubled look, as he studied her for her reaction. What ailed him?

She managed to shrug off this absurd mistake of hers, which had obviously come about because she was upset over her Meissen visit.

"Thank you. I'm afraid I've been rather distracted; I've had so many things on my mind. Oh, do smile, darling. The prince and that pretty young Spanish beauty are looking this way."

All the concern in his face seemed to drain out, leaving him cool and sardonic. "Delighted to oblige. Shall I show my upper teeth, or my lower? Or both?"

She ignored him. Her own smile was stiff and unreal, her mind dwelling on that nine thousand francs. How had she made such a mistake? She wasn't just boasting to Jason, she truly was always careful about money.

THIRTEEN

Rachel was certain she would have grown to despise Jason had he excused his actions with her money, or tried to take advantage of her own careless handling of it. After all, his speculation had proved profitable for her, and in the case of her ten-thousand-franc mistake he had paid the rent out of his own money, just as he had wished to do weeks earlier.

What was her twisted, suspicious mind thinking of now? None of these little nagging doubts had occurred to her while he was courting her in London. Magical Paris was having a very unsettling effect on her—and its effect was not over, as she discovered on the last night of their stay.

"Jason, let's go home," she said brightly one morning while she watched his fact in his shaving mirror.

His eyebrows went up. He stopped shaving and passed the long blade slowly under her nose. "You are bored. You've won the heart of Napoleon Bonaparte's nephew and now you want to steal the worthy Albert from Queen Victoria."

She laughed at the picture he brought to mind of her making love to the staid and proper Prince Albert, but she persisted. "There is so much we have to do in beginning our married lives."

"I thought we had already begun in that direction."

His warm-eyed grin made her wonder how she could ever have lived all those years without him.

"It's true. We have begun, darling." She hugged him and he almost cut his throat, but he didn't seem to mind. He smeared her mouth with lather and laughed when she gagged.

Minutes later, while he finished dressing, he said casually, "Then you've given up your plans for Maria to become a curate's wife."

That took her by surprise and revealed to her once more her own self-concern. Ashamed, she protested, "No. Not at all. Couldn't something be done to bring them together? Edward wants a curacy in the north. Couldn't you influence the Reverend Brontë in your own district, perhaps?"

Immediately the all-too-familiar shadow darkened his face. He jerked at the newly fashionable narrow black cravat that took the place of the heavy, carefully folded cravats so long familiar to her. "I have no influence over Patrick Brontë. I scarcely know the man. I attend St. Michael's in Haworth as seldom as my mother considers seemly."

"Well, you do know Miss Brontë, and—"

"The woman pries. She and her whole family. They . . . document things. Or rather, they write fairy tales that have nothing to do with the world."

How little you know! she thought, watching him with all the excitement she had felt from the first moment she saw him on the Scotland Express; how he seemed to personify the fictional heroes she fantasized about. She reached up and caressed his hand. With a pang of passionate sympathy she felt the white scars on his fingers.

He looked at her. "Would you be happy if they married?"

The question was abrupt and angry, as if he suspected her of something. She tried to ignore its tone to answer him honestly, but when she tried to picture the soft, genteel clergyman as a lover, she had to stifle a smile. "Of course, I'd be happy. Maria is evidently enamored with the angelic creature. But that is her affair, and not mine, thank heaven!"

To her great relief, the dark, angry look softened, and he leaned over to kiss her forehead. "Actually, the matter is in the hands of the vestry committee, Haworth being a part of the parish at Bradford. So you think the Noble Culhane is dull."

She grinned. "What do you suppose Maria finds so attractive about him?"

"God knows. It must be the type. Look at the first man she ever . . . Damn! Nearly choked myself." He turned to her and she tied the cravat, her fingers lingering at the nape of his neck. How simple it was to settle problems with her romantic husband!

She pictured their return to the Berkeley Square house, where they would relive the ardent moments of their courtship. Now there would be none of the terrible uncertainty. She pictured him as master of the Berkeley Square household—but only in theory. Behind the scenes she would put things to right should he prove as ignorant as he pretended to be about London's fashionable life.

And, one day, they would visit Yorkshire and his ancestral estate. Perhaps in the late spring, when the weather improved. But in order to avoid any of the trouble that had briefly darkened her trust in him, she would secure her English estate—it would be beyond Jason's reach—except in case of her death. And this was an unlikely contingency, as he was over fifteen years her senior.

On their last night in Paris, Edward Culhane planned a dinner for the two couples at a restaurant only a few blocks from the Palais Royal.

"Not elegant," he admitted, "but truly French. In a cellar, matter of fact."

Jason was less than enthusiastic. "Good Lord! We came to Paris to eat in cellars?"

Culhane seated himself beside Rachel on the tufted satin love seat in the parlor. He was waiting while Maria freshened herself after a walk through the woods of the Champs Elysées. He explained, "I was sure Mrs. Bourne would appreciate its authenticity." She smiled and nodded. "And, appreciating the delicacy of Miss Maria's feelings, I wanted to explain to you my intentions toward her. But perhaps I am premature."

Heavens! Rachel thought. *What a pompous speech! But evidently quite sincere.*

"I know how Mrs. Bourne dislikes pretentious places," he went on.

"And pretentious people," Jason put in.

Rachel hurried into the breach. "It sounds nice. I'd like to leave Paris on a note of reality after all that splendor at the Elysée Palace." She liked the curate's naïve enthusiasm. "Who recommended it?"

"My concierge. She said Cardinal Richelieu's guards used to eat there, about two hundred years ago."

Rachel laughed. "After reading Monsieur Dumas's novels, I wonder if we wouldn't be invading enemy territory."

"Mrs. Bourne, only you could feel so strongly about the three musketeers," oozed Edward. "You have a delightful wit." He took her hand, just as Maria entered the room. She arched visibly at the sight of Culhane's grip on Rachel's hand. She gave her brother a quick, smouldering look. Rachel withdrew her hand.

"Maria, Reverend Culhane would like to invite you to dinner."

The girl smiled weakly.

"We decided to go along tonight," Jason added with forced enthusiasm. "But meanwhile, the worthy reverend is here for your promenade, Maria. Suppose we meet you at the café this evening. We have only a couple of hours to dress, and you know my wife."

And it was arranged. Culhane, blushing in embarrassment, defended his previous conduct as best he could while greeting Maria with a warm handclasp. "My dear Maria, I have been discussing my deep admiration for you, but I am precipitate. Are we ready?"

Still disgruntled, she took the arm he offered, and they left, Maria wearing an unbecoming scowl, Edward chatting amiably and a bit nervously about the cellar restaurant. It was Jason who voiced Rachel's silent thought. "What the devil *are* his feelings about Maria?"

She shrugged off his concern. "It may be his religious teachings. He seems to enjoy her company but he doesn't want to behave improperly." She gave him her most winning smile. "And he's afraid of you, darling. Who wouldn't be?"

His face remained dark. His fingers traced the scars on his other hand.

"Only a joke. A joke, dear." She had a feeling she hadn't reached him.

She dressed for dinner with caution—a subdued watered-silk gown, high-necked and modest.

"Oh, damn them!" exploded Jason from the parlor.

Rachel hurried in, still fastening one pearl earring.

"They've sent over two tickets instead of three for the Channel packet."

"Good heavens! You mean one of us must swim across?"

He forced a smile. "Unless we steal Culhane's own ticket."

"I'm afraid Maria wouldn't like that."

He studied his pocket watch. "We should be leaving for the restaurant now. But I might just make the Channel Shipping Company before they close." He glanced around, looking for the frock coat he would wear to the restaurant. "I'm afraid I'll be late to meet Maria and her curate, sweetheart. You take a carriage and I'll meet you all there."

"Oh, no! Let's go together."

"We can't very well. They'll be expecting us. If we don't arrive, they may come back for us. A great mix-up over nothing."

"But, monsieur," Gretchen protested, "it is so dark. Madame would—"

Rachel said, "Can't this be done tomorrow before we leave?"

Jason was already getting into his coat. "We can't put it off until tomorrow if we are leaving at eight in the morning, now, can we? I'm sorry, sweetheart. Give Maria and the Noble Curate my apologies. I'll join you shortly." He kissed her and was already opening the door when she called out, "Where, for heaven's sake?"

"La Fleur, of course. Between the Palais Royale and the Marais somewhere. The coachman will know."

Rachel felt abandoned, being left in this awkward position, and yet, there seemed to be no other way of handling the situation. If Jason sent a messenger to the Channel Shipping offices, it would take just as long, and quite possibly a messenger would make a mistake, or be fobbed off with the wrong tickets. Jason should have examined the tickets when the messenger brought them, Rachel reasoned, somewhat satisfied at finding this small point of blame.

She lingered as long as possible, rather hoping to find Jason and the others all waiting for her. Finally she went downstairs, had the concierge whistle up a horse and cab, and stepped inside the dingy, foul-smelling buggy.

"La Fleur, please."

The old man turned to look at her. He was heavily wrapped in a muffler that revealed little but his bored half-closed eyes. "Madame said . . . La Fleur?"

"*Oui*. La Fleur."

He shrugged, climbed upon his box, and they trotted off.

She was perfectly capable of traveling alone, she thought with some pride. She had done so on occasion, when Miss Fridd was ill or engaged with her family. Her maid, Brigitte, was much too officious to take on any pleasure trip. But after weeks in her husband's company, she missed him tonight. She had no idea of where she was going, the streets dark and eerie in this jumbled, ancient section of the city. The crowds had thinned out, all the respectable Frenchmen having departed to their mistresses before going home to dinner.

Rachel bundled up in her cloak and thought about the return to London with Jason. Thoughts of their passionate nights, of their romantic compatibility, warmed her more than the furred collar of her dark winter cloak. Other women had problem marriages. They married men who despised them or were singularly unattractive, men who ignored them. How lucky, and how clever she was to have waited until she was twenty-three to marry! She knew she had been judged somewhat odd by her friends, who suspected she was either sexually cold or far too demanding in her choice of a husband. They must be envying her now.

The carriage wheels jolted over loose cobblestones. She stirred, shifting her position. How dark it was among these ancient, crumbling stone mansions that had seen the torturous doings of Catherine de Medici with her twisted brood! Rachel looked out at the alleys crushed between great seamed walls, and wondered what creatures watched her from that blue darkness.

What a strange location for a convivial dinner party. Her opinion of Edward Culhane's good sense was considerably reduced.

The coachman pulled up unexpectedly. Rachel looked out and around. Squeezed between two of these grim walls was a café whose *terrasse* tables and chairs had been stacked for the night, the chairs balanced precariously on the tables. The sounds emanating from the door of the café suggested quite a gathering within. She paid off the coachman and raised the latch on the door under the swinging wooden sign that read LA FLEUR.

Her first glimpse of the interior told her that this was no place for a future curate of the Church of England. The fumes of wine, of gin, absinthe, and other unsavory liquors, overwhelmed her like a slap in the face. Nor was this a restaurant of any kind. A café, perhaps. There was a long communal table covered with paper, where half a dozen raucous males and females drank what would probably be their dinner. The room with its dusty rafters and the haze of the newly fashionable cigarette smoke looked and felt sinister—perhaps it was the way the café's patrons glared at Rachel, sneering and laughing to one another about her—the women especially. Tattered harridans, not too young either. She could easily believe their mothers had sat knitting beneath the guillotine during the Terror.

She wondered if this could properly be called a cellar. Obviously, there was no Culhane party here. The barman, who was most likely the patron of the café, came out from behind the zinc bar wiping his hands on his heavy, soiled apron.

"Madame?"

She wanted to back away, but found her pride. "I'm afraid I have mistaken the address. I was to meet my husband and friends at La Fleur."

His big toothy grin expelled whiffs of strong spirits as he reached out to stall her departure. "Just so, madame. Will you wait at the table? It is a pleasure to make the introductions."

Evidently, he believed she was here for another purpose, referring to her "husband" as a pretense. She said coldly, "Thank you, no. I see I have mistaken the address." She turned and reached for the door latch. The landlord's big hand closed over hers, unnervingly strong. She forced herself to conceal her fear. "Monsieur! Your manners hardly make it worth my while to come here again." The repulsive man was too stunned to be amused by Rachel's insistent propriety. His hand slipped off hers.

A second later the door was pushed open and Jason stood there, at center stage of the action and, thankfully, quite the hero she always thought him to be. Somewhere he had lost his hat. His black hair was windblown. His eyes glittered, but whether from anger or humor it was hard to tell. He knew at once that the barman-patron was annoying Rachel, and forceful and indignant, he shifted her neatly out of the way. "My wife desires to leave. Do you mean to stop her?"

The patron considered Jason's well-dressed figure with self-righteous disdain. Then his gaze lowered to Jason's bare hand, flattened against his own breast, threatening him. Something about the scarred fingers. He blinked and shrugged. "Madame said she was waiting for you, monsieur."

"And I am here."

"Perfectly true. May I . . . er . . . seat you?"

Jason smiled grimly. "Not tonight." He ushered Rachel out into the street, which was deserted except for a horse and cab, apparently Jason's. The coachman, a lean, spry little man, leaped down to help Rachel into his cab. She asked no questions until she and Jason were on their way.

"A change of address?" she remarked sarcastically.

"To the Café de Flor, of course. Sweetheart, you gave us quite a scare."

"Jason, I was sent to La Fleur and I went to La Fleur."

He put his arm around her. "No, sweetheart, I told you to meet us at the Café de Flor. It is in the Rue Montpensier, near the Palais Royal. Remember? Ned Culhane told us. Matter of fact, it was only five minutes from the Channel Shipping bureau. I got there, found you hadn't arrived, took a cab back to the rooms—I didn't know what to think. Thank God for that gargoyle of a concierge. She heard you tell the cabbie 'La Fleur.'"

Once more, she appeared the fool. She persisted. "You did *not* tell me it was De Flor. I heard you say very plainly—*La Fleur*."

But she was beginning to wonder. It was an easy mistake to have made.

He shrugged. "If I had said La Fleur, Rachel, the cabbie would have driven me there from the shipping bureau; so I couldn't possibly have said it, since I arrived at De Flor."

She sensed something amiss in his argument but she was too tired and relieved to pursue the matter. And he did make sense. She settled back, allowing herself to be cradled against his shoulder.

"Anyway," she insisted, getting in the last word, "I can't wait to get back to England. We can't very well have these misunderstandings there. I know London too well."

He smiled.

PART TWO

ONE

Yorkshire

It was only to be for a brief visit: "Just long enough to meet my mother." Jason had promised that.

Rachel's plan to go directly to London had been overruled by Maria and even by Edward Culhane. He believed that his presence before the Bradford Parish Committee would improve his chances of being appointed curate to one of the vicars of the West Riding.

"And you, too, can meet mother," Maria reminded him. "I am persuaded she will speak for you. The vestry listens to Mama."

Jason was behaving so beautifully, affectionate and teasing in his "Rochester" mood, that Rachel couldn't disappoint him. She agreed to remain on the barkentine while it dropped passengers off at Dover before sailing up to several northern ports. The Bournes and Edward Culhane disembarked in a windy mist at the Yorkshire harbor of Scarborough.

The resort town had been described to Rachel as a lively, beautiful place, with splendid cliffs above the blue waters of the harbor and magnificent sunsets. Rachel found it bitterly cold, depressing, and, not surprisingly, deserted. The quay was shrouded in fog, and the cliffside hotel, a red brick affair, compared unfavorably with Rachel's recent memories of elegant Paris, or of London.

But they were there only one night, and her growing pique at having been dragged to the town without as much as a stopover at home in London provoked her husband's contempt.

She remained in a huff while the party arranged for three bedchambers in the empty hotel plus a sitting room. Except for the clergyman's room, Jason paid the reckoning as usual, and Rachel made no effort to use her money.

But her volatile nature wouldn't permit her to remain angry— and especially not silent—for very long. An hour later the little group gathered for a stroll down the cliff road to the long stretch of sand below. None of Rachel's previous sulks seemed to have any effect on Jason. There were moments when she suspected he was amused by her attitude, perhaps even pleased, though she couldn't imagine why. Maybe he felt that he could tame her by these methods, make a dutiful, shadowy wife out of her. And if that was so, Jason didn't know her at all.

All the same, it was lovely to be on good terms again, strolling along the sand holding hands, kicking the sand up like children, laughing at the vigorous salt wind whipping across their faces, lashing their hair.

She cried, "I've never looked worse. But I like it."

He shifted one arm to her waist and squeezed. "So do I."

Maria and Culhane walked ahead of them, a more sedate couple. When it came to romance, Maria did not share Edward's reserved nature. Several times she raised her hand to touch Culhane in some way, his hand, his shoulder, and one time, daringly, his hat, which threatened to blow off.

Rachel saw Culhane shift his position to avoid the blast of wind, putting space between himself and Maria. It did not appear to be deliberate. He gave her one of his gentle smiles. But the gesture seemed too dismissive for Rachel's discerning eye, and she suspected his passions were inadequate for Maria's needs as well.

She whispered to Jason, "Is he human? He practically admitted to us that he loves her."

Jason had also seen the same gesture, and he gave Culhane's back what Rachel thought of as a dark, rather frightening "Heathcliff" look. She wondered how far his hatred of anyone would take him. It wasn't a pleasant thought.

Rachel tried to be generous about Culhane. After all, he was a clergyman. Perhaps he felt that touching Maria in a proprietary or sensuous way would be a sin before their marriage. She couldn't deny the man's gentle good looks, and his manner. Elegant but gracious, he had the charm she remembered in her own father, but none of Jason's vitality. Well, he was Maria's choice, not hers.

The windswept sand near the stone jetty was dotted with a few people, some of whom seemed to be tourists. Rachel stared at them disinterestedly, her gaze straying to the vast blanket of sea.

"I thought you were the young lady who cowered before open empty spaces. You seem to be enjoying yourself now, on the beach, near the ocean."

"I'm with you. That's why." It was true. The beach didn't seem quite so threatening. There was the town itself, still alive with people behind those shutters, and now, coming toward them near the jetty, were people, normal human beings. Besides, she was far too occupied with the pleasant contact between the two of them after their quarrel.

Maria stopped suddenly and turned to Jason. She was tense and white-faced, her teeth biting hard into her lower lip. "Jason, look!" she called.

He had already seen the stylish little blond woman moving toward them on the arm of an elderly gentleman, possibly her father. She wore a black mourning bonnet with white ruching to frame a pretty but petulant face. Mourning or not, she took care to reveal the yellow ringlets of her hair that greatly softened the severity of her close-fitting black bodice, the pelisse and wide skirts of which flew out like one of those French balloons ascending.

Clearly, she was an acquaintance of the Bournes, someone

whom Maria either feared or disliked. But it was Jason's reaction that intrigued Rachel. He seemed to be restraining himself from any show of emotion, but she knew him well enough to guess that certain fires burned behind that dark, almost malign mask. What motivation from the past fueled those fires? Passion not yet spent? Clearly this was more than a casual acquaintance.

At the sight of Maria, and especially Jason, the pretty widow released the stout gentleman's arm. She ran toward them on her small dainty feet. "It can't be! But it is." She looked over her shoulder, gesturing to the old gentleman. "Papa, do hurry. Here is Jason. Our Jason." The woman had used Jason's Christian name. Obviously an intimate friend. Rachel hoped she was merely a relative.

Jason strolled toward the widow, his arm still tightly around Rachel's waist. He managed to edge his sister out of the way, almost behind him. More oddly still, Maria seemed to want to be hidden there, obscured by the others, as if she were afraid of the young widow.

Jason inclined his head politely to the woman, then to Rachel's pleasure, he added, "Sweetheart, may I present Miss Cecily—"

Mrs. Debenham, Jason. You've forgotten. My poor Andrew has been gone these past sixteen months," the lady scolded prettily. "Papa, here are Jason and . . . My dear, you haven't presented the young lady."

Jason said tightly, "Rachel is Mrs. Bourne. My wife. And here are my sister, Maria, and our friend the Reverend Edward Culhane. Mrs. Debenham, Mr. Humphrey Wentworth."

Gentlemanly old Mr. Wentworth shook hands cordially with everyone. He seemed to approve of Edward especially. Rachel quickly sensed that he was avoiding Maria. Another mysterious romantic entanglement? Perhaps the old gentleman had been interested in Maria and she refused him.

Jason urged Rachel while apologizing brusquely to the Wentworths, "We won't keep you. If you will forgive us now? Coming, Maria? Culhane?"

He had caught Edward in the middle of Mrs. Debenham's gushing compliment. "My dear Reverend Culhane, we are delighted by your presence in Yorkshire. You may believe me, we have a great need for a curate in Wycliffe Mount, across the moors from Haworth, but a part of the same parish. My beloved husband—my late husband, I should say—had considerable properties in the West Riding."

Culhane beamed. "Nothing would be more satisfactory, ma'am."

Maria had already left him in order to join her brother and Rachel. Rachel reached for her hand, touched it. Maria did not respond. Rachel said brightly, "I'm afraid we really must hurry, darling, if we are to keep our dinner appointment."

The gratitude in Maria's vague, uneasy smile was unmistakable. Both women offered Mrs. Debenham a half-curtsy in parting. To Rachel's annoyance Cecily Debenham returned the gesture with a deep, graceful curtsy directed at Jason and Culhane.

"We must meet again," she called to the two women. "What a delightful chat we will have! So much has happened since those dear days. Unforgotten, I assure you."

"And good fortune to you, Reverend Culhane," Mr. Wentworth called, having bowed to the ladies.

Culhane bustled after the Bournes, naturally pleased as he reached them. "Such a friendly pair! I was unknown to the lady and her excellent father, yet they treated me as a friend like yourselves. If all of Yorkshire is like this, I shall be a very contented man."

It may have been Rachel's imagination but she thought the Wentworth-Debenham woman's voice sounded a bit brittle when she spoke those last words, "Unforgotten, I assure you."

But Rachel was chiefly interested in Jason's attitude. He had behaved like a spurned suitor or worse, a spurned lover. It was unlikely that such a pretty woman could injure him in any other way. Why else should be behave so abominably to the woman?

They had walked back past the harbor and were headed up the hill toward the hotel before anyone but Culhane said a word. Even he finally surrendered to the generally somber mood. Rachel was wild with curiosity, but she was determined to say nothing until she and Jason were alone.

It was not until they reached the inn and settled themselves that Jason offered an explanation to Edward's tentative questions. "The woman was betrothed to me some twelve or thirteen years ago."

Of course. From the sight and feel of his anger now, Rachel was sure some residue of that love remained after all these years. Otherwise, he would hardly care so much. This didn't explain Maria's peculiar reaction, but the Bournes had a strong family loyalty. Perhaps Maria was afraid Culhane would learn of her brother's prison record, if indeed he hadn't already. Culhane was a protégé of Sir Bayard Lorimer. It seemed odd that Sir Bayard hadn't told him something of Jason's past, with the idea of preparing the clergyman in case he heard the story from a less amicable source.

As difficult and secretive as Jason was, Rachel knew that sooner or later all secrets between husband and wife should be divulged. She couldn't remain ignorant.

Suppose he refused to explain himself and his past to her. To live without Jason . . . even the thought weakened her.

Culhane seemed aware of the awkwardness of the meeting with Cecily Debenham and her father, but he rushed on hopefully. "They seem to have influence in the area." He gave the pale and silent Maria an arch look. "I'm convinced they will help me obtain a curacy. That should make our—my plans more definite."

Maria ignored this and turned to Jason. "I didn't know they had settled in the region. If so, what were they doing here in Scarborough?"

He shrugged. "I heard something of Debenham's holdings in Keighley and Wycliffe, but they lived in Leeds during Debenham's last years. In the Wentworth house. As for Scarborough, it must be some sort of vacation."

"One can only hope they keep their promise to speak for me," Culhane persisted. "They seem very good-natured."

"Wentworth is a good sort but not very astute. We used to work together for the Tory interests. He was forever trying to persuade me that the mill workers were not my concern. I should like to know whose concern they were, since his kind threw them and their families out in the cold."

Later, when she and Jason were alone, she asked with more calm than she felt, "Darling, did she break off the engagement because you were sent to prison?"

He looked at her, frowning. "Why do you ask that?"

148

"Well, you did say the engagement ended twelve or thirteen years ago." Her laugh made him stare. "Darling, what a fool she was!" She reached out, touched his cheek. "But for my sake, I'm glad she was a fool . . . so very glad." She kissed his cheek. To her surprise he did not respond at once. He took her wrist, brought it down from his face, and let it go, looking down at her in that dreadful, somber way. As if he were sorry for her.

She couldn't quite believe her own reading of that expression, but there it was. She withdrew from him, tired of this nonsense, this silly game he played, as if everyone in the world was responsible for his private torture. Someday he would have to face the truth.

As much as she loved Jason, she knew that he had a volatile temper and that perhaps his indignation on behalf of the mill workers had brought him to prison. Why should he act as if his wife, who loved him, not to mention everyone else who crossed his path, was somehow to blame? And what was he afraid of from Mrs. Debenham? His emotions, and Maria's, seemed unfairly violent in the context of the widow's "crime." What harm could *she* have done to him or his family?

Rachel's anger over this incident was stronger and more threatening to their marriage than her silly pique earlier in the day over their abrupt change in travel plans. Nor did her mood improve when he behaved as he had this morning, treating her attitude as a temper tantrum.

One evening she asked him who was responsible for his mills in Leeds and elsewhere.

"Nahum Cload, naturally. I would have no other. The man grew up in the mills. He knows the problems."

"Are there still so many problems? Have you solved the matter of the machines that displaced the handlooms?"

He looked up impatiently from a short business note that seemed to occupy his attention. "Sweetheart, you are not equipped to handle mill problems. I'm certain you wouldn't know a millhand from a machine worker."

She was annoyed and a little hurt, but her anger grew when she thought seriously about the thoroughness with which he conducted his business. Obviously, from the beginning of their honeymoon, he had known they would return directly to Yorkshire, avoiding all contact with her home and everything she regarded as necessary to her life. And he had never mentioned this to her.

He went on talking to her later about casual, impersonal matters, made his usual derogatory remarks about Edward Culhane. She responded to his chatter. But her manner and voice were superficial and light. She might have been once more the London belle, flirting, smiling, without a sincere bone in her body.

He noticed her frivolousness and scorned it. No matter. He must learn that his own theatrical performance could grow tiresome. She wondered if he knew how overly dramatic he seemed.

She was also more than curious to see what would happen when next he met his onetime beloved. Could he actually despise the woman? Was he angry with Cecily Debenham because he had once loved her so much? Perhaps she had been his first love. Such tormenting doubts did little to improve Rachel's nervous anticipation of the evening ahead.

TWO

Edward Culhane entered the sitting room, looking, as usual, handsome and friendly. The warmly lit room accented his shining hair and bright smile. At moments like this Rachel almost preferred the young clergyman's harmless good manners to the cutting sarcasm of her more impressive husband. But every time she looked at Jason's tall figure, cut so starkly in black and white, her heart betrayed her, her pulse racing with longing for him.

While they waited for Maria, she flirted with Culhane, who was at once drawn as a moth to flame into her orbit. "What a pleasure it has been!" he said with enthusiasm. "From the moment our leisurely journey began, there in Paris, weeks ago."

Jason, pacing nervously with frequent glances at Maria's door, corrected him. "Your journey began *before* you crossed the Channel, or have I misunderstood?"

The comment aroused Rachel to her own disgraceful manners. Playing with Culhane was dishonorable to Maria, and her shame did not improve her disposition.

Culhane archly fed Jason's disdain. "Precisely. The moment I met Miss Bourne as we crossed the Channel. I confess I should never have enjoyed France so much without the Bourne family. And then, how could I forget the appearance Miss Maria made at the prince-president's reception? What a stunning creature! And after all our adventures, now we meet the Debenhams who—"

"Wentworth and Debenham."

"True. I had forgotten. Mrs. Debenham strikes me as a tragically young widow, but I daresay her husband was somewhat elderly."

"I believe so."

"Yes. The sort with a great income, which naturally would prove attractive to a young, naïve woman. But perhaps that was not the case. I should imagine that—"

"What the devil is keeping Maria?" Jason cut in.

Rachel snapped her fan shut and hurried into the breach. "I'll find out."

"No!" He knocked heavily on Maria's door. A voice within said something indistinct. "It's Jason," he called. "I want to talk to you."

Rachel listened. The Reverend Culhane had never seen Maria intoxicated; it seemed as though Maria had somehow gotten hold of a bottle. She mumbled something to her brother through the door. A minute later the bolt slipped back and Jason went into her room.

Rachel, talking rapidly, tried to divert Culhane's attention. "I'm afraid Maria has these occasional migraines. She is quite an intense young woman. Sensitive and delicate. A fine person in every way."

"Yes, indeed." He lowered his voice, confessed with shy pride, "It is my intention to ask her mother for her hand when the proper moment arrives."

Good heavens! Hadn't there been enough "proper moments" in these past few weeks? But, of course, the Reverend Culhane always acted with infuriating propriety.

She didn't know what to expect when Jason came out of his sister's room, but apparently he had satisfied himself that she would be all right. He looked tired and as aloof as he had appeared earlier. Rachel felt the rift between them more strongly than ever. They couldn't go on like this.

Jason said calmly, "My sister is suffering from a headache. All that sea air, no doubt. She is in bed now. She asked that we dine without her."

Rachel started across the room to Maria's door, but he put his hand out to stop her. "She will do better for the rest and quiet. She hopes you will both forgive her."

Culhane, too, had been concerned. "Perhaps I might see her for a moment, if it is proper. To wish her well, let her know we are thinking of her."

"I think not." He was in one of his sarcastic moods. "She is not quite so far gone as to have prayers said over her."

Culhane reddened, speechless. This was going too far. Rachel cut in, "Really, Jason. Edward didn't mean anything of the sort."

"Well then, my apologies, *Edward*. Come along, or we will miss our supper, as well as dinner."

Rachel restrained her anger to remind him, "We should have a tray sent up to Maria. If nothing else, at least tea and cakes, or something of the sort."

"Later."

None of them were in good spirits when they entered the old-fashioned northern dining saloon of the hotel, with its large fireplace, wall of crockery, and a number of vacant tables carefully laid with mended white cloths, meager glass settings, and heavy silver. Two tables were already occupied, one by a rather boisterous family, and the other, by Cecily Debenham and her father. In contrast to the more lively group, Cecily and her father, though seated close to each other and obviously on good terms, dawdled with their food, looking bored.

They were both delighted to see Rachel and her escorts. Mr. Wentworth got up at once and trotted over to them, forestalling the forty-year-old waitress, who came forward at a sedate pace, looking in her competent unpretentious way very like a local millhand's wife.

Mr. Wentworth's chubby face beamed upon Rachel. "How very kind of you to relieve our solitude, Mrs. Bourne . . . Jason . . . Reverend Culhane. Do permit us to play host. This wretched place is death so late in the season. . . ." He addressed Jason, who was looking around for another table. "Where is Miss Maria?"

"She's not feeling well," Rachel explained. She felt compelled to compensate for Jason's rather impolite reticence. "We have been traveling for four days, and I'm afraid we are all exhausted."

Jason pretended to be distracted, but remarked, "We spent our honeymoon in Paris. An excellent setting for romance, as my sister and the Reverend Culhane discovered." And with this he stared directly into the gentlemen's eyes.

Culhane stammered, "Yes, in-indeed. I haven't spoken to M-Miss Maria's mother yet, but—būt I have hopes."

Rachel puzzled over Wentworth's reception of this news. His pink lips pursed in consideration of the fact. He very nearly frowned before remembering his good manners. "Well then, that is romantic. My dear Cecily is quite a romantic herself."

Jason looked anything but flattered, with a contemptuous smile that he didn't trouble to hide. Wentworth shook Culhane's hand. "We must hear the details. Come, come. Mrs. Bourne, may I offer my arm?"

Rachel caught Jason's quick, disapproving glare but let herself be piloted along, partly because Wentworth moved as inexorably as the tide, partly because she was still disturbed and angered over Jason's conduct that night.

The gloomy world outside had been closed off by pale draperies that appeared to be alive with cabbage roses. A miserly fire of peat and wood flickered now and then in the huge fireplace. Rachel was wearing a plum silk gown, modest enough in Paris, but revealing somewhat more of her throat and bosom than seemed to be suitable here. She had observed at once that Cecily Debenham was primly clad in an expensive high-necked black taffeta, with ruffles and a wide skirt. She also wore a great deal of jet beads, which made her gown noticeable across the room. Her flaxen hair was arranged with cool elegance, and did little to warm her brittle personality.

She waved to Rachel—ignoring her ex-betrothed—her fingers extending an invitation. Puzzled by Cecily's interest in her, Rachel allowed Mr. Wentworth to present her at the big table. Mrs. Debenham was gracious. In spite of her beauty and her age, somewhere in her early thirties, her manner reminded Rachel of Queen Victoria receiving her subjects.

"Dear Mrs. Bourne, how fortunate that we were thrown together in this slapdash fashion! I have so looked forward to hearing the story of your romantic marriage. The Wentworths and the Bournes will always be political allies, you know, however far afield our destinies may take us."

"Indeed?" Rachel replied with equal poise. Mr. Wentworth pulled out a chair for her. Cecily beckoned Culhane to her other side.

Wentworth was all goodwill and showed a tendency toward subtle yet annoying physical contact. He eased her into the chair, pushed his own plate, glass, and silver utensils over to the next chair, and then patted her forearm and squeezed her hand reassuringly. "My lass here, she enjoys a little chat now and then with another lady. You must tell her all about your betrothal. She sets great store by such matters. Don't you, luv?"

While Mrs. Debenham agreed and chattered on with a gleam of sharp interest in her pale eyes, Rachel glanced at Jason. He had seated himself across the table between Wentworth and Culhane, neither of whom would be likely to improve his disposition.

The supper menu was brief: hot tea, cold meat, slices of beef, and the superb York ham, currant scones left over from high tea, and cheese and apples.

Rachel found herself nodding, smiling, and agreeing absentmindedly with whatever Cecily said. The woman rambled on, "I am delighted you adored Paris. . . . Where did you meet Jason? . . . Did you know dear Maria at the time? . . . I gather this is your first visit to Yorkshire. . . ." There were other personal but charmingly expressed questions.

During the meal Rachel looked across the table several times but never caught Jason's eye. Suddenly, she found herself remarking casually, "But I understand you were once betrothed to Jason when you were both . . . some years ago."

Cecily laughed with that brittle tone, which was becoming rather irritating. "Indeed, yes. I was scarcely more than a child, but Jason was so impetuous. Well, you know Jason."

"How very true!" Rachel thought ironically of how long she had pursued Jason before he decided to marry her.

"I daresay you are wondering why I broke off our betrothal,"

Cecily was loose-tongued now, willing to confess. "In those days I sensed a violence in him, a strange, almost dangerous quality. His passion for me was too great. Quite unsuitable. And then, of course, I was proved correct." She whispered, "That Branscomb incident, you know. But I expect he's told you."

"Indeed, yes." Rachel didn't dare reveal how little she knew of the political quarrel that sent Jason to prison.

Mrs. Debenham turned to Culhane, full of enthusiasm. "I am certain you will exactly suit our parish." He warmed to the flattery and she went on, "But you, sir, do you think our northern ways will suit you?"

He blushed. "I will treasure your own graciousness, whether I am accepted or not. If I may say so, one seldom encounters a young lady of such delicacy." Both Jason and Rachel looked at him. He swallowed and added quickly, "In these matters."

"You are too kind. We northern folk tend to be rather less refined than our city friends."

Rachel shifted in her chair and smoothed the several yards of silk in her skirt, as a none too subtle hint that Wentworth was making a nuisance of himself. She caught Jason's eye, indicating that she was about to make their excuses and leave. He nodded. He shared her disgust with the scene between Cecily and Culhane, if not between Wentworth and herself. She thought it better not to call his attention to that.

Culhane was explaining all the innovative plans he had for the northern church, but broke off to stare at Rachel. His lower jaw dropped. His eyes widened and he stammered, "What . . . Is she . . . ill?"

Jason stood up, knocking over his chair with a terrible crash. He, too, was staring. But not at Rachel. Something in the room behind her.

Maria Bourne wandered into the big, spare dining saloon, barefoot in a floor-length nightgown that was curiously graceful in spite of its many cotton folds. The long, full sleeves were drawn in at the wrists with green ribbons, and around the waist and sleeves; yet she looked and moved in a sensual way that was entirely unconscious. She looked like a lovely specter, her pale hair tumbling down her back.

She mumbled, "You forgot me. I'm . . . I'm . . ."

Was she sleepwalking? She glided onward, moving slowly, the gown billowing out around her. Mrs. Debenham gasped. The Reverend Culhane started up as if to help Maria. Rachel moved toward her, but Jason got there first, scooping his sister up in his arms and starting for the staircase in the dingy hall.

Rachel rose to follow them, then stopped, knowing the crucial thing in Maria's life at this minute was to convince these staring witnesses that it was the headache or sleepwalking, not drunkenness, that caused this melodramatic appearance.

"Those dreadful physicians!" Rachel complained, quickly inventing a story. "They insist that a dose of laudanum will cure the pain. But I'm afraid the drug only puts a sufferer into a deep sleep. And now, this mesmerized state . . . all the fault of that medicine."

"Shocking! The poor girl!" Cecily murmured with tight lips. "I'm very much afraid of laudanum myself. It was recommended for Mama, I remember. But I place no reliance on it."

Culhane nodded.

"Well I'm sure that by morning she will be again herself." Rachel prayed this was true. From her experience with Clare Lorimer's drunken brother, Desmond, Maria would be intolerably cross tomorrow morning, and complaining of worse than a headache.

What was this sinister mood evoked by Cecily Debenham and her father that their mere appearance should drive Jason to such surliness and Maria to drink?

THREE

Edward Culhane behaved considerably well, wandering disconsolately around the Bourne sitting room during the evening, punctuating his progress by frequent pleas, forgetting his previour rebuff. "Perhaps if I offered a few prayers by her bedside . . ."

Jason was curt. "Certainly not. She will be herself presently."

Rachel tried to ease over his abruptness, afraid it might breed suspicion. "Thank you, Edward, but I rather think she must rest now."

She remembered that encouraged sleep was the worst treatment for victims of laudanum overdose, and added quickly, "Jason walked her up and down so much, she must be very tired."

"This is so unfortunate."

Both Jason and Rachel glared at him.

"I mean," he explained, "migraine in one so young. I had a great-aunt who suffered tortures from the headache."

Aware of the deadly effects of gossip on a woman's reputation, Rachel remarked, "I do hope Mrs. Debenham and her father understood."

"Oh, most kindly, I assure you. Mr. Wentworth even suggested that my presence on the journey from Scarborough to Keighley might be, as one puts it, not appropriate, considering Miss Maria's illness. They thought if I traveled with them, I might have the immediate benefit of the Wentworth influence in the parish, but of course, I refused. My place is with my dearest Maria. If I may call her that."

Rachel knew Jason wanted to be rid of him. He was an awkward encumbrance. Any moment he might discover the truth about Maria's real condition. But Rachel smelled danger in Cecily Debenham and Reverend Culhane's shared company. Culhane was susceptible to the widow's flattery, and perhaps to her cold good looks as well.

Rachel was beginning to have serious doubts about his union with Maria. Despite Maria's faults, her occasional lapses from sobriety, and her frequent bursts of sulkiness or temper, she was too good for a man who could be so easily seduced away from her. He might be sincere, but he was superficial. Nor did she think more highly of herself at that moment, when she reflected that she had also betrayed Maria by her flirtation with Culhane. She was so used to regarding the tricks of fan and smile as mere games in London, it seemed second nature, until she realized what that sort of game might mean to a woman like Maria, so very much in love with the Reverend Culhane.

Eventually, Culhane gave up the vigil and retired to his room. It was shortly afterward, nearing midnight, when Jason, having briefly looked in on Maria, came out to get Rachel. "She wants to talk to you. Alone."

Rachel hurried in. She had hoped to reassure her sister-in-law and perhaps raise her spirits. She suspected that depression over something, perhaps a fear of the widow's rivalry, had driven Maria to drink nearly half a bottle of gin, which the lower orders still referred to, with reason, as blue ruin.

Maria sat up in the feather bed, leaning forward, holding her tousled head between her palms. She peered up under a shower of hair. "Close the door." Rachel did so.

"He doesn't want to see me again, does he?"

Rachel rightly guessed how much she felt, but she believed it indicated even more optimism if she gave a teasing answer. "Of

159

course not. That's why he waited out there in the cold sitting room so long, begging Jason to let him come in and comfort you."

Her pallid features brightened. "Did he? Oh, but he mustn't see me. Do you think he guessed the truth?"

"He knows you have a headache. A migraine. It was unfortunate you took that laudanum. Maria, you were walking in your sleep."

"Laudanum. Mother uses it. I never take it. But I did go downstairs, didn't I? You were at supper and I was late, so I went down." She covered her face and groaned. "It's vague from there on. I seem to recall I found myself half-naked."

"Yes, you were wearing your nightdress."

Maria groaned again. "Like Lady Macbeth."

"More like Ophelia."

Maria brushed hair out of her eyes. Hope softened her tortured face. Maria patted the bed beside her long, lean body. "Come and sit on the bed. Here. You must be tired. I can see that." Her self-control broke and she pleaded, "Forgive me, luv. You've been kind and tried to help. But you see, you of all people could never understand."

"Perhaps I could if you explained."

Maria spat out a humorless laugh. "That I could never do. But some day you'll understand without my explaining." She felt Rachel turning away from her and reached out. "Don't go yet. I want to ask you about Edward Culhane. I sometimes wonder what you really think of him."

Rachel chose her words carefully. "He is not like Jason."

"No. But I have enough strength for both Edward and me. I love his gentleness." Emotion crept into her voice. "He can be so tender and warm."

"So can your brother. Yet, he is very . . . different."

Maria stared at her. "Edward likes you. He sets great store by your opinion. But you're not fond of him are you?"

"I certainly will respect him if . . . when he marries you."

"But you see, I've spent my life in the turmoil of Jason's passions. It's like standing on the shore at the edge of a raging torrent. You know, sooner or later, it will wash you away."

Rachel had never heard her sister-in-law refer to her brother in this way. The family loyalty was too strong.

Maria's face was blank, dreamlike. "I loved someone when I was very young. Not good or kind or gentle like Edward, but I thought he was all those things. . . . But now, I've found someone who is truly everything I loved long ago. Edward's affection for me, his goodness and gentleness, will wipe away the memory of . . . that other. It will give me back my pride in myself. Everything I lost long ago." She caught Rachel's hand. "I couldn't stand it if I lost this one, too. I would hate the world."

For the first time Rachel sensed that she and Maria shared an emotion. She herself loved Jason with the same passion Maria felt for her fragile little curate.

Maria sighed, and lowered her head. "I won't keep you any longer. I know how tired you must be."

"But we are truly sisters now." Rachel leaned over and hugged her, then apologized when Maria moaned with pain. "I'm sorry, dear. Just remember. Tomorrow . . . not too early . . . you will feel much better. And your gentle curate will be waiting."

Rachel returned to the sitting room. Jason stood at the window across the room with his back to her. He seemed entranced by silent, sleeping Scarborough. She said nothing but went into their bedchamber, where she undressed, yawning again, trying to summon up some encouraging thoughts about Maria and the Reverend Culhane.

She had stripped to her petticoat, when she felt her shoulders clenched by two powerful hands. She winced, but the force of his grip was not as disconcerting as her quickening blood, the rising desire within her body. Tonight, especially, she resented his power over her.

For the first time in their experience together she willed her body to resist him, knowing he would resent the refusal. He would undoubtedly be hurt and retreat into one of his moods.

He did neither. For an instant his fingers were still, then they moved over her shoulders to her forearms. She was intensely aware of those hands, warm and strong upon her flesh. He drew her back against his body. She stiffened in opposition, but her resistance had little effect.

She became aware of his lips upon the crown of her head and then his deep voice. "You know me very little, sweetheart, if you think this performance will discourage me."

"It isn't a performance."

"You want me. You know you do. I can feel it in your pulse. Here." His heavy, sensuous lips lingered on the pulse point at the side of her neck. She shivered with anticipation but tried to turn away. He must not be allowed to treat her as he had today and then control her by his lovemaking whenever he chose the moment.

He bent his head farther. She made out the blue-black gleam of his hair as his lips found the hollow between her breasts.

"No." Again she tried to avoid him, but her body was pressed back against his and she could not release herself.

He raised his head and suddenly swung her up into his arms with her bare feet dangling like a rag doll over his arm. Her struggles seemed to amuse him. She heard the low, chuckling sound of his laughter as he strode across the room to the big feather bed. In spite of a small, nagging fear of him when he behaved like this, she felt, instinctively, that he must love her or he wouldn't behave in such a sensual fashion.

Or had he behaved like this with Cecily Debenham long ago? The violent, passionate man Cecily had shuddered at.

She forced herself not to make any helpful effort when he tore her frilled petticoat away from her pale, golden flanks. She pushed vainly, trying to turn her body from him, but his knee imprisoned her and seconds later he was upon her. All his driving force took possession of her until they were joined and her body shuddered under waves of ecstasy.

Whatever his intention, and she didn't fool herself that love drove him tonight, at least he shared her passionate climax. The throb of physical desire still held them together. She yielded at last to her own bodily demand. While her mind despised this weakness, she freed her arms, locked them around his neck, whispered the warm words, the sensual demands, she would never have uttered aloud. The hard flesh of his neck and shoulders yielded under the kneading and tickling of her fingers, while his lips aroused her abdomen and her limbs once more.

Even tonight, in their mutual anger and resentment, they repeated those first moments of true union as if setting aside the problems of their daily lives for the morning. Jason murmured the endearments she wanted to hear, and she reassured his apparent doubts for the thousandth time, "Of course, I love you . . . ." And breathlessly, "whatever you are, whatever you do . . . I adore you . . ."

She still found it puzzling that he so desperately needed to hear her confirm these feelings.

And yet, afterward, when she had almost resigned herself to becoming the devoted and docile wife he seemed to prefer, he did not sleep with her. None of the warm, close companionship followed their lovemaking. He left the bed, went back into the sitting room, and she spent the rest of the night in the cold, solitary splendor of the bedchamber, alone.

Curiously enough, in spite of Maria's often sulky and unfriendly manner, it was she who brightened the late-morning breakfast and the departure by various train connections for Leeds, Keighley, and their final destination, Bourne Hall at Haworth.

Having witnessed the sufferings of a few people, even her father, on the morning after a drinking bout, Rachel marveled that Maria could be so cheerful. She knew, however, that Edward Culhane's presence and his solicitude had a great deal to do with her good humor, for his interest in her welfare soon turned to her interest in his and brought out all her latent qualities. Certainly, neither Jason nor Rachel enlivened the day or the journey. Rachel had awakened angry with herself for yielding to him the previous night, more especially since he hadn't the decency to share her bed afterward. She felt that he had treated her like a common trollop, using her body but too fastidious to share her bed.

Jason, on the other hand, appeared to resent her cool morning greeting—or did he regard it as indifference?—and he became as cold and aloof as he had been on the Scotland Express the first day she saw him.

In this state Rachel sat glumly, pretending to be absorbed with the passing scenery while listening with envy to Maria and Culhane's convivial chatter. Maria, animated and warm, hung on his every word, flattering him with her complete attention. Rachel understood better circumstances that might have caused the tragedy of Maria's first romance. Maria was constantly touching him, using any excuse to fuss over him. Her attentions threatened to smother him, her own worth greatly sacrificed. It was as if she were telling him, "I am yours, completely. I am worthless without you. I am nothing in myself."

She should take care lest Edward come to believe her. But this was advice that Rachel could not possibly give her.

Because of their late start, they spent the night at Leeds, much against Maria's wishes. She detested the crowded, smoky mill city. But as they were to remain there for no more than a meal and a night's sleep, Jason managed to persuade her.

As they arrived at the dingy station hostelry, a cinder flew into Maria's eye. Edward offered his handkerchief to remove it, but the linen was creased and heavy. A softer material was needed. Rachel opened the drawstrings of her cluttered handbag, but she had forgotten to put in one of her own soft lawn handkerchiefs. Maria's own handkerchief was soiled after she had eaten, feeding Culhane pieces of an apple on the train, so they were forced to use Jason's heavy handkerchief.

Later, when they were preparing for the afternoon dinner, Jason knocked over Rachel's bag, which she had laid on the little round table under the single window. He picked up the bag to tie the drawstrings, which were loose. He stopped suddenly. "What the devil? Why did you refuse to give Maria your handkerchief? Are they that precious to you?"

There they were, two handkerchiefs, still neatly folded, one lace-trimmed, but both were soft and would have served Maria very well.

"It can't be! I could have sworn . . ." Had she thoroughly rummaged through the bottom of the bag? Obviously not. "I'm sorry. I guess they just slipped down and I didn't find them."

His voice cut deeply. "Or was it because you saw Maria enjoying herself with Culhane and you were jealous?"

She reddened with anger and shock. "Jealous! I don't even like the man. And I certainly wouldn't do anything to hurt Maria." His accusation was so unfair and so very wrong she wanted to cry, but in his present mood it would only amuse him. She added haughtily, "Think whatever you like. But Maria will know better."

He became tolerant, kind. "Well, we'll forget it. I don't know why you require such a huge bag."

You may forget it, she thought, *but I won't!*

FOUR

Instinctively, Rachel sensed that there would be more such surprises upon her arrival at Bourne Hall.

The Bournes dropped off Edward Culhane in the city of Keighley, where he was to meet members of the Bradford committee and their vicar to discuss appointments throughout the moorland area of the West Riding. He was buoyant and optimistic about the possibilities.

"I feel it must happen," he boasted to Maria, whose hand he daringly kissed. "The appointment will be mine." Then he added, "When the Wentworths arrive, they have promised to speak for me, as you know." Sensing Maria's disapproval, he hurried on, "But that shan't matter to us, unless they occupy too much of my time. And I promise you, I shall not let them prevent my visits to Bourne Hall."

To Jason he promised, "As I have confided to your dear wife, sir, I shall soon pay my—er—respects to the senior Mrs. Bourne."

Jason's eyebrows and his sardonic expression should have told the innocent Reverend Culhane that this news was hardly a surprise; the satisfied Culhane left in excellent spirits.

By the time the three Bournes set out for the three miles to Haworth, Jason seemed to share Culhane's spirits. He and Maria had an entire volume of anecdotes they planned to tell their mother, Amy.

Though a prey to nerves, Rachel felt better at first as they rode through the rolling autumn landscape. She had been warned by many Londoners that the moors were "frightful" after the heather blackened and winter approached, but she could see the mauve beauty as soon as they passed the bounds of Keighley itself. The enormity of the moors—like great trackless, rolling fields with ferocious cows—only occurred to her in later minutes, as she realized their distance from the cities. Even the towns, if they did indeed exist out here in the vastness of nature, managed to make themselves invisible.

She drew nearer to Jason, in need of the warmth and comfort of his body. Maria grew more and more restless with anticipation. "It seems months since I was home. How I wish I might run on the moors to the far beck at this minute!"

"Soon," Jason promised her. With loose reins he had given the young mare her lead. He looked at Rachel. Surely, she was not mistaken. She read concern and an anxious note in his question, "How do you like it? Do you think you could ever feel something for this country?"

He reached out as he spoke and pulled her close. She hadn't the heart to disillusion him, and her love swelled at the feel of his arm around her. She tried to laugh. "It's so grand. Almost infinite. If only I can get over my ridiculous fear of cows."

Maria burst into her natural moorland dialect, "Ye'll be seeing no' but a sheep on the heath."

"No cows?" Rachel joked, more lightly than she felt.

Maria's expression was gentle as she gazed upward toward the high green sea of grass and dying heath. "I had a lamb, once. Moogin his name was. Now I have his daughter. Her name, naturally enough, is Parkin."

"Parkin!" Rachel had heard her father mention the word once or twice. "That's a form of gingerbread, isn't it?"

Jason was pleased that she knew. "So is moogin. It's one of the local names. Maria's Moogin lived a long, healthy life, and I may add, died a natural death. He was buried like any respectable member of the family."

Maria touched her hand in a friendly way. "Aye, we'll do well, you and me." The hint of the Yorkshire country in her voice seemed to Rachel like a welcome.

She studied the low gray York stone walls that occasionally split that rolling green eternity. Jason pointed to them. "When you are walking, as we all do hereabouts, never cross over one of those walls without the owner's permission. They wouldn't hesitate to shoot at you."

"More likely set their dogs on you," Maria put in.

"How jolly!"

Jason hugged her. "You'll do well. All you need remember is that we Yorkshiremen are proud. We may not be lace-edged, but we are as good as any Londoner."

She was amused at his vehement pride, but she was pleased by it, too, and determined to honor it. She had been snatched away from her civilized world, but because she loved Jason, she was willing to give this primitive world a chance.

Despising her own cowardice, she looked out again from the warmth of Jason's arm to that enormous green monster everywhere encroaching on the muddy road. "It's like a great dragon, lying there in wait. Look. It seems to be breathing."

"That is the wind blowing over the juniper and heather. It's too late in the season for the heather to be seen in its real glory. But you can still see the hint of color in it." She heard in his voice again the abiding love he bore this forbidding landscape. "You may walk for hours and never see a sign of habitation if you don't know where to look. Maria was forever wandering over the moors looking for young Moogin. She usually found the rascal munching grass by our own front gate."

Maria said, "Edward likes pets. He said he understood very well why I spent an entire night looking for lost animals."

"And so do I." Rachel began to reminisce. "I never got on with Mama's gorgeous yellow cat, but once, Papa gave me a puppy for my tenth birthday, and when it got out I had to chase . . ." She heard her own voice trail off, feeling their attention dissolve. It was always that way when she talked of her own past, especially her parents. They didn't seem to be listening to her. They were looking out at a downward sweep of the road and then across to what appeared from that angle to be a riverbed. Rachel saw the beginnings of the steep hill George Smith's mother had described, which led steeply upward to the town of Haworth.

Rachel wondered if the horse and cart could manage the climb. The hazy orange sunset gave the landscape a pleasant glow, lighting the austere gray stone buildings of the village perched at what she assumed was the top of the hill. That area must be Haworth. Unbelievably, there appeared to be rolling moors still higher, beyond the last roofs of the village.

At the foot of the hill, to Rachel's surprise, Maria jumped down from the cart and went around to her brother's side. Jason gave over the reins to her and also climbed down. He explained to Rachel, "We spare the nag on the hill."

Rachel wouldn't yield to anyone in her love of animals. She got down while Jason assured her, "It isn't necessary, sweetheart. Maria will take the reins, I'll carry some of the baggage."

"So will I." She reached for one of her own portmanteaus and the ribbons of her hatbox and plodded up the hill over the rough stones, trying to keep up with Jason. But his long legs ate up the distance, though he loaded himself down with half the Bourne baggage.

He turned at the top and waited for her to join him. She was no faster than the old mare and cart. He laughed at her stunned expression as she finally reached him. She turned, breathing hard, and saw the second steep hill almost at right angles to the first. Much of Haworth village bordered this second cobbled street. It was a long way from the unpretentious elegance of Berkeley Square. It was, indeed, a long way to anything remotely resembling Bourne Hall.

Jason had no free hand to help her up the second hill, but he modified his stride to hers and laughingly encouraged her, "Only a few more steps. That's my girl. One foot . . . one foot . . . Up there at the head of the street, on your left, is the Black Bull Inn. A noble edifice where the locals hide from their wives."

"Shall I look to find you there?"

He leaned over, encumbered with their boxes and cases, and

to the interest of passersby, he kissed her cheek, only just missing her bonnet.

"Not yet, sweetheart. We are still only newly wed."

She had been conscious of a peculiar sound echoing up the street as they climbed. Now, aware of what appeared to be hostile eyes, she looked around. Without stopping, she tried to study the people who were to be her future neighbors. She heard a few voices. These people did not share the voluble, gossipy manner of the inhabitants of London's streets. So what was that curious hollow sound that echoed through the steep canyonlike street? Looking down at the feet of the hurrying villagers, she found the source of the noise—the clogs that many of them wore to protect their feet from the damp and the moor paths. Some of the women wore old-fashioned iron pattens, such as Londoners wore a century earlier, as protection from mud, slops, and the cold.

The faces she saw struck her as being hardened from the elements, slightly darker than the complexions in southern England. No one looked friendly; yet when some recognized Jason, they nodded and smiled and their countenances lit up like low-burning coals under a current of air. One man with half his front teeth missing hailed him in a dialect totally incomprehensible to Rachel. It amused her to hear Jason return his greeting in an equally foreign string of sounds.

Most of the villagers eyed Rachel curiously, but no one seemed surprised to see that she was trudging up the hill carrying a portmanteau and a beribboned hatbox.

Maria and the horse and cart came along, slowly, with a kind of mechanical determination. Rachel wondered how anyone could possibly survive the winters. She felt suddenly that they would have to go down to London soon or they might be sealed up here away from the world, like being buried alive. It was curious that the residents looked so determined, so strong and normal. Perhaps this purgatory was good for them.

Many of the buildings were stone-roofed, which surprised her, but she told herself it was all of a pattern with the forbidding aspect of Jason's world. The wide windows leaning out on the street reminded Rachel of the story Mrs. Smith had told her about those competent hand weavers of Yorkshire. "They all worked handlooms. They were individuals, those people. You will not credit it but many of them were females. They wove and carded their wool—or did they card and then weave? They sat in those big windows to do their work. But they're all gone now. Only machines, and in the cities. The great cities of the north."

Rachel could almost see those weavers working in the long window fronts of the houses, but it was an illusion. There was precious little private weaving now. Still, these people did not look poor. They looked reserved and private and highly independent, and they seemed to respect Jason Bourne.

Maria called out, "Come aboard, Rachel. We can all ride now." She held her reins in one hand and beckoned.

It was all so primitive. Certainly no one in the cities lived like this. Rachel kept her feelings of superiority to herself and climbed up into the cart with the help of Maria's extended hand. Jason threw the cases into the cart and mounted on the other side to take over the reins. As they passed through the village under the watchful eyes of villagers hurrying home in the dusk, Rachel looked around for the great family house, Bourne Hall. But there was nothing resembling such a structure anywhere in sight. The largest building was Reverend Brontë's church—a historic stone edifice whose square tower cut into the sky. It was made of the same gray stone she saw everywhere. Depressing, thought Rachel. And more depressing because nothing else in the village could possibly be Bourne Hall.

She kept up a spirited conversation, not wanting Jason and his sister to suspect the depths of her displeasure. As they passed through the village, Maria was greeted by several locals hurrying home, huddled over against the gusting westerly wind. Many of the people wore black, which only added to the gloomy atmosphere.

"Is there a high mortality rate here?" she asked in reference to the black. She was perfectly sincere. Maria looked indignant; Jason answered with a short bark of laughter. "Last spring Otho Bradford died of a belly ailment. He was near on eighty and it was commonly said that he died prematurely. I could point out half a dozen ninety-year-olds among those vigorous country folk we just passed."

"But we've children aplenty as well," Maria informed her with understandable pride.

Rachel sighed. She had a mental image of herself tossing out her entire lovely wardrobe and bundling herself in dull, practical black stuff gowns. On her carefully shod, narrow feet, would she, too, be soon wearing iron pattens? This was not at all what had been in her mind and her dreams when she married Jason Bourne, and he knew it. Had he deliberately forced her into all this?

As they rode through Haworth, they were again surrounded by the high rolling moors. The long northern twilight was fading.

"Have we passed the Hall? Or missed the turn? There doesn't seem to be anything out here. It's like a vast green sea."

"The Hall isn't in Haworth," Jason told her. "Remember? I said there would be many occasions to walk. But three miles can hardly be called a walk. A little stroll, perhaps."

"How lovely."

There was nothing in sight but the land, an infrequent stone wall, the carters' track, and on the near horizon, slow-moving creatures that must be sheep. They were hardly impressive enough to terrify her. What an absurd fear it was! Cows! On the spur of the moment she determined to conquer that problem at least, before she left this strange, somber country.

The road began to descend a little hollow, the muddy wheel ruts deep where runoff from the higher banks collected. A clump of trees hid the rise on the far side. She thought the first odd shapes must be gaunt thorn trees, with bushes clinging around them, and small berries of some kind. The horse and cart rattled down into the hollow and started up past a huge chestnut tree that Jason said had been blasted long ago by lightning. It still stood, spreading its bare branches wider than many a healthy tree.

Beyond and behind the tree the road wound up another slope past a giant sycamore, which stood as sentinel before a low stone building of two stories. The forbidding Jacobean facade was softened by several fruit trees in the small enclosed front garden.

Around the house the moors spread to the far horizon. Seeing it at dusk after a day of tedious traveling, Rachel shuddered to herself inside her cloak. She made a valiant effort to smile as Jason announced proudly, "Bourne Hall. This is your new home, sweetheart."

Impossible, she thought. *I must be having a nightmare.*

He jumped down, went quickly around the cart, and held his hands up to lift her down. She slipped into his arms, felt the stones under her feet, and stood there in the muddy road, wondering if she would disgrace herself by crying.

A yellow-haired young man came around from the south end of the house and pushed open the low, ancient iron gates. He had the appearance of quiet, muscular competence. He gave Jason a nod, greeted Maria. "Good having you home, mum," and skimmed over Rachel with a simple, "Mum?"

Jason slapped his broad back. "This is Nahum Cload, sweetheart. Nahum runs the mill, the farm, the sheep, and the Bournes. All well with Mother?"

Nahum swung the cases easily down from the cart. "Well enough, allowing for all those good works that keep her from sleep and food. Aye, she was in Oakleigh nigh on sixteen hours this day. There's sickness in the Row, down by the river. I went and fetched her home."

"Good lad," Jason said.

Maria called, "Mother? Are you home?" and hurried along the stone path to the heavy oak-reinforced front door.

Feeling lost, Rachel picked up her hatbox and one of the valises Jason was unloading. Nahum carried some of the heaviest baggage, including a long box containing three of Rachel's most expensive evening gowns. Guiltily, she avoided looking at the box. She couldn't see any possible use for a trousseau here in this godforsaken country.

The two small mullioned windows flanking the front door gave little promise of cheerful rooms within. A date carved over the lintel of the door read "1592." She wondered if the interior was as dark as that weathered date, but a warm surprise greeted her entrance.

The long sitting room–parlor spread the length of the house to the right of the little entry hall. It glowed with light from several lamps, but especially with a blazing fire in the huge fireplace at the far end of the room. Long casement windows obviously let light into the room by day, but the drapes were closed now against the misty night. Two settees, carefully carved— probably by local craftsmen, for they were far from perfect—

172

helped divide the room, reducing the spaciousness into cozy, more intimate sections.

Behind Rachel, Jason murmured in her ear, with a tone of quiet pride, "The small woman by the fire is Mother." He set down several cases, went to the slender, worn-looking woman standing with Maria, and embraced her. He kissed her faded blond hair and, with one arm around her, turned to Rachel, who stood awkwardly surrounded by luggage, wondering if she should make the first advances. Or would the woman think she was being forward?

"Mother, I have brought Rachel home as I promised you."

Amy Bourne was much paler than most of the Yorkshire villagers Rachel had seen thus far. A rather fragile woman, she was not nearly as awesome as Rachel expected. Her mouth was pursed, and wrinkles had begun to distort it, but her faded looks lifted with her gentle smile. Only her eyes, very pale and tending to water a bit, seemed less than friendly. They were searching eyes, with a penetrating power that Rachel felt at once.

The awkwardness of her situation made Rachel more nervous. She held out her hand, trying to make her own smile less forced. "I'm pleased to meet you, ma'am. Jason and Maria have talked so much about you."

"My dear." Amy Bourne took her shoulders in small-boned fingers, somewhat as her son did occasionally, and barely kissed Rachel's cheek. "Welcome home."

Home? Rachel, desperately anxious to conceal her inner panic, returned the embrace with feverish enthusiasm. She could not let this frail, gentle woman know how horrified she was. Whatever they believed, she *would not* be left here to perish!

FIVE

Rachel was sure she'd have violent nightmares, perhaps tossing and turning for hours, incarcerated as she was in this old house far from civilization. The first evening, Jason left with Nahum Cload to sort out some problems with the mills and the estate, but the hours before their early bedtime passed quickly for Rachel as Mrs. Bourne acquainted her with the house. True, she made it obvious that Rachel's position in the household was equal to Maria's, dutiful and subservient; yet, Rachel was much more optimistic than she had ever thought possible when she went to bed that night.

She was awakened by a faint sound nearby in the dark, unfamiliar room. She opened her eyes and, looking over Jason's head, could make out only the outline of huge, heavy furniture. The drapes had been tightly closed by the parlormaid. Groggy, she dropped back on her pillow. The faint sound of a human groan jerked her awake once more. Jason stirred restlessly, obviously deep in a troubled sleep. A lamp in the hall gave off a knife-edge glow beneath the door, and she caressed his hair hoping to comfort without awakening him. He groaned again and thrashed, raising his head. To her dismay he stared at her in the dark and drew away from her in unmistakable repulsion. He reached for his robe and got out of bed.

It had no doubt been a dreadful dream. She forgave the way he repulsed her, realizing it must have been a product of his nightmare. Perhaps he had confused her with a figure from his past.

Very quietly, she murmured as he wrapped the robe around his lean, powerful frame, "Is there anything I can get?"

"No." He waved away any effort on her part. "Be silent. Don't remind me of"—he changed the direction of that curious sentence—"of what happened."

"Why should I? I have no part in your past."

He had started toward the casement windows. He swung around so swiftly she shrank back as if there were danger in him. "Oh, my dear, you are very wrong about that."

It made no sense at all. Hurt, angry, and afraid, she wanted only to turn her back and try to sleep again, but she told herself she was no longer the coddled young girl. She was an adult, and his wife. One of her vows had been to understand and help him if she could. She got out of bed, took up her own robe, and swung it around her shoulders. The room felt encased in ice. She started toward the door.

Three strides brought him to her. "Where are you going? You are not going to run away from my bed. Do you hear me?"

The night was cold and her robe had not yet warmed to her body. She told herself angrily that it was not fear but the frigid air that made her limbs tremble. "I am merely going to light the bed lamp from the hall light. Then you can tell me whatever you wish about your dream. It may help." She shrugged, and his angry hand fell away from her. "Or, it may not."

She returned with the lighted bed candle in its old, well-polished glass chimney. He seemed to have softened. His spirits were somber. Old memories of sufferings, no doubt. Remembering what he must have gone through, she felt that she could forgive him almost anything at this moment.

He parted the drapes angrily and stood staring out at the moor. It was not a view she had yet come to cherish. She had not once looked at it since her arrival in this house, knowing it would terrify her more than anything, but there were some things that had to be faced. Especially if she was going to help this domineering, impossible, and, yes, beloved man.

She crossed the room, came up behind him, and put her arms around him, hugging his chilled, stiff body. "I'm still here, love, if you need me."

For one terrible instant he shrugged off her embrace. Then he swung around, pulling her close. "No, my love. Not you. It's . . . something else. Long ago. Come, love, look out at your kingdom."

She saw only endless rolling green seas that seemed to ripple in the foggy moonlight. "Where is the village?" she asked, hoping to fasten on some landmark, some sign of life in that dead stillness.

"You can see the Haworth road from the front windows. This is the back of the house; it faces east. Many a time I've walked to the far beck in that hollow where the trees grow. In the north—you can't see it from here unless you look far out—you might catch a glimpse of the Withins."

"Withins?"

"An old farmhouse. It was deserted some time while I was in the—was gone. I've heard gossip that Miss Brontë's sister Emily set her novel in Withins Rise. You get a magnificent view of the surrounding countryside from there."

Rachel asked excitedly, "You mean, that is Wuthering Heights?"

He kissed the top of her head. "No, sweetheart. Only the location. The manor house in the book would have been much larger, I should think. But if you stand on that hilltop some day when the wind freshens suddenly, you'll agree it's wuthering, as we locals say."

"Then you did read the books. Did you know the authors were actually the Reverend Brontë's daughters? I mean, when you read them?"

"I cared very little, one way or the other. They were too farfetched. Absurd. No one exists like those storybook creatures."

She smiled to herself, then rubbed her cheek against his scarred hand. "Do you think you will ever be able to tell anyone about this? And the other things that were done to you?"

He withdrew his hand. "This wasn't done to me. At various times I did it to myself, in a manner of speaking. Handling cement and ship's tackle. And fighting an Irish rogue who stole a bit of sacking I slept on in the hulks. We used broken knife blades, bits of stone, anything sharp."

"Oh, how dreadful!"

He laughed off her horror. "Lord love you, no! Niall and I became comrades before he was moved to dockwork near Portsmouth."

"Why did they give you such a terrible sentence for merely attacking an earl in a quarrel about politics?"

He rested his chin on her head and stared out at the moors. "There were two of them. They wanted any excuse to silence me. I'd caused them enough trouble in the meetings. In some respect she had nothing to do with it."

"She?"

Rachel sensed that he hadn't intended to say so much. He retrieved his former ground easily. "I mean—a woman saw us. She was of no account. At all events, the earl testified, and since he had more influence than I, well . . ."

"Oh, my darling, *darling*!" She turned in his arms and hugged him as hard as she could. "I'll make it up to you. I'll make you forget all those terrible years."

There were no more disclosures of the dark years that night, but Rachel vowed to herself that one day she would bring those ghastly memories of his out in the light, and when that happened, the ghosts would be exorcised forever.

In the morning, Jason left to investigate the Bourne Woolen Mills and the workers whose own tribulations were so closely bound to the Bourne family. Rachel had become used to late risings on her honeymoon and was a little put out to find herself alone in bed when Dilys, the parlormaid, brought her morning tea. She would have been quite willing to rise with Jason. Dilys treated her like a privileged guest instead of as the mistress of the house.

She wondered how she ever would occupy her time until Jason returned. The morning tea was hot and strong but she drank it hurriedly. She washed and then dressed in the simplest, warmest clothing she could find. She went down to breakfast, pretending a calm she was far from feeling.

As she feared, the rest of the family had finished their morning meal, although it was barely an hour after sunrise. She felt all the humiliation of a person who lolled about in luxury, demanding to be attended to while the rest of her family was hard at work. As she ate thick, chewy Scottish porridge in the cold dining parlor, she was informed by Finbar the dried-up, frigid butler that "Mistress, she is off to Hardcastle Bridge to care for the townsfolk. There's typhoid."

"Did Miss Maria go with her?"

"Nay. She's off to the Far Ponden Beck. There's the sheepman with his back giving him pain."

Rachel was more annoyed than abashed. "What problems are left for me, may I ask?" It was purely a rhetorical question.

"Well now, Miss—Missus, as I should say—there'll be the folk off Hepton Clough. Miss Maria, she'll be going there this evening, afore sunset. Plain hunger it is with them. What with the last of the Heptons laid off the Debenham Mills nigh onto Keighley."

"I see. And where may I find this Hepton Clough? And what would Mrs. Bourne take to these Debenhams?"

"The Debenhams, mum, is them as made the hunger, you might say."

It appeared that the family of Jason's late betrothed was not in great favor among the moors. She wasn't sorry to see that. "Very well, Finbar. You will tell me what I must take and how I am to reach the good folk."

"Aye, mum. There'll be baskets, napkin-covered and that. With soup and all."

The eternal preoccupation with soup as a remedy for the poor always baffled Rachel. Surely, there must be more practical gifts, such as money and jobs. It seemed strange, and even more rude than strange, that the entire Bourne family should vanish from the house even before their newest member had been awakened. She almost felt a conspiracy existed to make her feel unwanted. But she refused to believe she was shunned so. As Finbar slipped out of the dining parlor, mouselike in his silence, she called to him, "Did anyone leave word about seeing me later in the morning? To introduce me around the estate so that I may be acquainted with it?"

Finbar's sharp nose twitched. "Nay, mum. The rich young lady will not be troubled is what I heard. We've the word to treat ye fair, since ye'll be a guest, in a manner of speaking."

"I am not a guest, Finbar. I am Mrs. Jason Bourne."

He looked back at her with a smirk, his lizard eyes still glittering. "Aye, mum. That's as may be," and he was gone.

Odious little man! Dislike was one thing, but he showed every sign of despising her, and that was another matter entirely. She could never remember having been despised by anyone, except the proud golden cat owned by her mother, who had clawed and spat at her for thirteen long years.

Returning to breakfast, her fork toying with the slice of cold mutton that arrived with her eggs, she listed mentally all the things she might do in order to fit into this highly reserved ménage and become accepted as one of them.

First of all, she would bring soup—or whatever one took in Yorkshire—to the unfortunate folk of Hepton Clough. She didn't like to complain to Jason and his family, or to earn the servants' respect through such shabby means. But if all else failed, she would suggest sending for her own people, a polite form of blackmail. But that would have to wait until she became certain of the desperation of her predicament. The mere thought of her own Mrs. Brithwick in a row with that nasty little Finbar made her laugh softly, shocking doe-eyed, pretty Dilys, who came to clear away the table. Rachel got up, determined to start building her reputation with these people at once.

"Dilys, is it very far to the Hepburn Clough? I understand they've fallen on bad times. Perhaps I can take Miss Maria's place and save her the trouble."

"Well now, ma'am, that'll be a kindness. Miss Maria sometimes overdoes. The cold creeps into her shoulder-like. But it's Hepton. Hepton Clough."

Every time she opened her mouth it seemed she made a fool of herself. She retreated, smiling. "*Hepton* Clough. Is it difficult to reach? I've no intention of getting lost in this desolate wasteland."

"Just a skip-stone away, ma'am. Right yon, past the Blewe Farm. You cross the Withins Trail yon. Past the little beck by the falls. They're a sheep farm like my own folk." She stopped in the doorway to add with a touch of pride, "I'm the first in that valley sent to school all the way to. Keighley," then she rushed away, rattling crockery.

Rachel sighed, leaned against a casement window, and looked out at this ground-floor view of an appalling moorland ocean that spread before her.

How far was "a skip-stone away"? Would she be welcome or resented? Above all, when would Jason be returning?

If only I could count on at least one friend here! So far, there were none.

SIX

The morning was gray, with bright patches of blue in the enormous sky overhead. The cook, a tall, stout good-natured Northumberland woman with a vaguely Scots' burr, promised Rachel, "There'll be them that's glad to see your sunny face, Miss Rachel, ma'am. We're a sober lot and we could use a bit of sweetness-like."

Rachel had never thought of herself as sweet. She had always been much too volatile and given to moods. She made up her mind to remain on her best behavior with Mrs. Hannah Peebles. True, the cook's breath exuded a scent that suggested she was no teetotaler, but perhaps she needed a little liquid cheer in this climate, populated as it was with such self-righteous citizens.

It was Hannah Peebles who took time from her baking long enough to trot around the front of the house with Rachel and point out the path to Hepton Clough. "Take care now, Miss Rachel. There's a hundred crossings made by the sheep, but you must not take them. Straightaway will do it. You fetch up at the Blewe Farm and down in the hollow, then across to the Heptons'."

181

A wind was blowing up. *Wuthering*, Rachel thought, oddly excited.

Mrs. Peebles smoothed back a thick strand of graying hair that brushed her eyes. "Big Hepton has a taste for the good Scots' brew."

"Good Scots'?"

"There's none better whiskey in the land. Och—it's a dark delight, is true scotch. Big Hepton is a man of his fists, with a wife that—" She shrugged. "Well then, she's one of them females as likes to be beaten. Thinks she's somehow less than Old Hepton. It's my notion he pleasures her by his cruelty."

"Heavens, what a family!"

Mrs. Peebles was pragmatic about it. "There's many marriages like that. The wretched female overloves a brute, more than his worth. Mark me, it's a bad business, too much loving and no return. I'm not that kind. No. Not Hannah Peebles. Even-up it was with me and Peebles." The cook's grin was mischievous. "Though I daresay he thought he loved me more than I loved him. I let him think so. Good for the dear lad's soul." She lowered her booming voice to confide, "There's some in this house would do well to heed what I was saying. There's passion in that poor lady that puts a man's back up. Too much passion. Makes them afeared they'll be gobbled-up-like."

Rachel guessed at once that she was referring to Maria. Was it so evident then? She knew how disastrous it would be if such gossip spread. "Forgive me, Mrs. Peebles, but that can't be true. I came to know her quite well on my honeymoon, and I assure you, she was much admired. His Highness, Prince Louis Napoleon, took an enormous fancy to her, and the Reverend Edward Culhane has every intention of asking for her hand. So you see, they respond to her feelings."

Mrs. Peebles looked pleased. "It's surely a good thing to hear. Miss Maria has her crotchets, like all of us, but she's a fine, feeling woman. If only she holds back some of those feelings."

"I'm sure she will. Are you certain this food will be of good use to the Heptons?"

"Most like. It'll feed the boy and that's the thing. Young Tam Hepton is a fine little lad. You'll find my currant scones tucked away in the basket. They're for Tam."

"I'll remember. I keep to the path till I pass the Blue Farm, avoid the sheep trails. Beware of Big Hepton, see that Little Hepton gets his scones."

Mrs. Peebles clapped her floury hands, laughed, and gave her blessing.

The clouds had blown across the sky, leaving a palette-shaped splash of blue over her head. Though the ground underfoot was still soggy from a late-night shower, and the western horizon promised more of the same, Rachel preferred to put her faith in the omens overhead. Her wine-colored leather cloak enveloped most of her wide skirts. The hood would serve if the rain blew up. Only her shoes were not sturdy enough to be practical, but she vainly refused to wear the more sensible pattens.

She had scarcely stepped off the soggy Haworth road and onto a path paved with brown leaves, gravel, and what remained of the autumn heather when she saw a lamb gamboling along, rattling the bell around its neck. This must be Maria's pet, Parkin, the daughter of the celebrated Moogin. She was a jolly sight, another good omen, and Rachel walked on, smiling to herself.

Other sheep wandered over the upper range of moorland at a distance, but for the most part the area in three directions appeared to be uninhabited, even by sheep.

After some minutes she became aware of the many hummocks of ground that were responsible for the disappearance of all habitation in these moors. Many people lived here but they seemed to be chameleons. They absorbed the texture of their surroundings, and doubtless, while she saw nothing, their eyes, and the eyes of the creatures hidden in all this lonely green splendor, were watching her.

She shivered. It was necessary to remind herself that she was behaving bravely, conquering a fear that had pervaded her life.

The path climbed over a rise. At the top of the rise she stopped, shivering, awed by the deep valley below, and the endless heath beyond that seemed to climb to the open sky and go on forever. It was here that she saw, far away to the north and east, a huddled farmhouse only half-sheltered by a tree or two that looked black against the heavens. This gloomy habitation clung to the high slope of the moors and she assumed it must be the farm called Withins by Jason. But to Rachel, it would always be Wuthering Heights.

She shifted her basket and started down the slope past tangled bracken and heather that must have made a breathtakingly beautiful carpet a month ago when seen from the moor heights. The overflow of the last night's rain poured down over rough steps in the rocky bottoms here. She stood between two gaunt birch trees, trying to remember whether this setting had appeared in Miss Brontë's *Jane Eyre*.

Rachel considered resting on one of the flat white rocks in the stream, but it would mean venturing out from stone to stone, possibly plunging ankle-deep in that icy, foaming water. Instead, she crossed by an improvised bridge made of wide stones. A few bilberries still clung to the far bank of the stream, and she thought somewhat cheerfully of how beautiful this ravine would be in summertime.

A flurry of noise stopped her as she climbed the far side. A flock of birds rose from the bushes, frightened by something about the ravine. She looked up and gasped at the sight of a big, broad-faced cow. At that instant she saw a ferocious mastiff staring down at her, with canine teeth shining and mouth salivating. She heard its low-throated warning growl.

Abandoning all pretense of bravery, Rachel let out a screech. More birds rushed upward into the rapidly clouding sky. The huge dog raised one paw tentatively, as if debating between a descent upon her down the side of the ravine or a broad leap onto her shoulders. He loomed so close over the edge above her that she could almost smell his rancid breath.

Rachel bit her lip nervously. The mastiff pawed the edge of the ground again and then pawed the air just above her. Dirt, pebbles, and a bit of bracken showered Rachel's face. She blinked and coughed. Angry now, she forgot her immediate fear and yelled, "Down!"

Much to her relief, he accepted the tone rather than the command and retreated a few steps, still growling. She climbed out of the ravine, swinging her basket, whose napkin covering had blown off and now floated below her, down the stream. The dog sniffed at the smell of food. He stopped growling, slouched toward her, and suddenly sank down on his haunches. He raised his powerful head and stared at her.

If he could have spoken, he couldn't have been more eloquent about his desire for the contents of her basket. She looked around, saw nothing but rain-shrouded vistas of green moorland interspersed with shallow valleys, and no human owner for this dog, who was staring at her as if he might substitute her body for the food in that basket she now held high over her head.

"Oh, all right!" Her mercy journey had very likely failed anyway. This walk was taking forever and she hadn't seen a farmhouse that remotely looked "Blue." She removed one glove, reached into the basket, took out a greasy bone that felt as if it contained considerable meat. The thigh of a goose, or a large hen. It ought to satisfy this four-footed monster. She threw it at him.

He caught the meat in the air and had crunched down upon it, doubtless devouring bones and all before she was a dozen steps along one of the many sheep tracks that crossed at this point.

She looked back but did not stop. "No. Down!"

But he knew now where his next meal would come from, and his lean flanks suggested that he had not found food any too plentiful lately.

She waved the basket, striking his nose with the corner, but he thought she was teasing him and growled a warning.

"No, I said! That's enough. Now, behave yourself. Go home." She had never seen such a huge, red, wet tongue.

She looked around helplessly, all her old fears superseded by greater problems. For some reason, she felt an incongruous sympathy for the monster, obviously starving. She wanted to pet the great shaggy, unwashed head, but managed to refrain from any signs of friendship. She must maintain her advantage.

Seeing him shift his gaze to her hand, she ordered him "Down!" but the tightening of the muscles within the ragged, dirty coat also revealed his bone structure. Hungry as he must be, the poor creature had not yet attacked her. He was not wild. He must belong to some family in the neighborhood. She reached into the basket, found a chunk of Mrs. Peebles's fresh-baked bread, and before the hungry dog could leap at her, tossed it into the blackened heather that bordered the path.

The dog made a lunge for the bread, scrambling around in the prickly brush until he found it. He settled down to chew it in spite of the prickles and stabs of the brush around him, while Rachel hurried on.

The path took many odd turns and became increasingly hard to follow. Often it disappeared into the heath around it. She found herself retracing her direction and then crossing trails that should have been her original path. Meanwhile, the mastiff, having finished the bread, trotted along behind her. It occurred to her about this time that she must be on the trail to the dog's home farm.

A sheepcote attached to a low, whitewashed cottage was hidden away on the brow of the hill to her left. She decided to ask there about the Blue Farm. The Blue Farm, she devoutly hoped, would help her to the Hepton place. However, she had not counted on her monstrous companion, the mastiff. He stopped when she stopped, fastened those huge teeth on her cloak, and pulled so hard she heard the tear as he took a triangle out of her cloak.

"In heaven's name, you monster!" she yelled, but he merely wagged his rope tail and nosed her over to a track that ran in a northwesterly direction, away from the little farm so temptingly close.

No matter. It was evident from his condition that his own farm had just as much need of her. With great daring she patted the dog's bony back.

"We'll go to your home, you great monster. Be easy."

Surprisingly enough, he seemed to understand. It must have been the tone of her voice. She hoisted the basket, now somewhat lighter, and marched on, her confidence increased.

Overhead the clouds gathered in ominous black piles, and Rachel thought longingly of turning back, but she wasn't at all sure the dog would permit her to do so.

Over the next ridge, the wind snapping in her face, she did not see any signs of life. But the mastiff picked up speed, as if headed somewhere. A minute or two later she made out a flock of black-faced sheep wandering up the rise toward her. The mastiff barked fiercely, scattering them back down the slope, thus announcing to Rachel that she was now on his home ground.

She frowned into the gray murky air and made out the white-washed farm somewhere above the valley bottomland. With spirits renewed, she started down along one of the sheep tracks. She had just reached the valley bottom when she discovered that the ground was slipping away beneath her shoes. She raised one foot, felt an unpleasant sucking sensation as she drew up the other foot, and realized she had landed in boggy ground.

What more can happen? she wondered.

She saw the dog, trotting with far greater ease along another sheep track, headed up toward the farm tucked away in a fold of the upper moors. Rachel found that, stepping quickly, she would not sink. It was hard to guess where the bog holes were deepest. She dragged her feet through the mud, with its disgusting viscous quality, and ran after the dog.

A big sycamore tree sheltered the outbuildings of the dilapidated farm. Judging by the noises within these sheds and the enclosed yard—there was livestock about.

She reached the small house itself, which seemed to consist of two rooms, one for eating and general living, the other for sleeping. There were worn and mended drapes at the narrow windows but no curtains. At least, the shutters were still open to the gray autumn light.

She wiped her feet on the flat stone plate before the door and knocked. Getting no answer, she called out. The wind swept her words away, and the dog leaped upon the door to help her. A few seconds later there were sounds within. A querulous, whining female voice addressed the dog, "Away, Alfie. 'E know better nor this racketing."

The words sounded like a mixture of English and some foreign language that she couldn't be sure she had heard correctly. Except for the reference to Alfie, her canine friend. Rachel smiled. The name seemed highly unlikely. He looked as if he would answer to some great Norse name, wild and dangerous.

She called out again, "It's Mrs. Bourne from Bourne Hall. I've lost my way, ma'am. I'm looking for the Hepton farm."

The bolt was shot back on the door and a lean, youngish female with glazed eyes and a fixed, frightened grin peered out at her. The woman's lank mouse-colored hair was straight and stringy, swept back to a knot at the nape of her neck, though several strands had slipped down over her eyes. She seemed terrified of everything except, surprisingly enough, the ferocious Alfie. As she looked Rachel over, her fingers teased Alfie, who leaped up and licked them.

"You be the lady to the Hall? 'E've been a long time comin' to these parts. Miss Charlotte said 'e'd be here while the heather was still fresh. Miss Charlotte an't with 'e?"

"Miss Charlotte?"

"Reverend's daughter. She comes here, but she mustn't. Miss Charlotte is a good, kind lady, but my man, he cannot abide such like. He don't hold with them as spies on us like we was needful. We an't needful, not quite yet, so 'e says."

Rachel didn't want to get involved with "him" and his dislike of kind-hearted, caring women like Miss Brontë. "Can you tell me if I am on the right path to the Hepton farm?"

The young woman looked around behind Rachel in a furtive way. "'E didn't see him?"

"Me? No. I didn't see him." The woman's husband, no doubt.

"He's comin' any time now. He was over to Oakleigh for the work that's promised, but he's not well liked. He'll be that cross if there's nothing for him to do. He's a good worker, but God knows there's been nothing for that long ye'll not believe how long."

It all fit together. Rachel ventured to guess, "You are Mrs. Hepton?"

"Aye. What else?"

Rachel glanced at her basket, very much aware that the Heptons would not receive the Bourne gift with thanks. She devoutly hoped that Mr. Hepton would not arrive while she was here with her unwanted offering. Mrs. Hepton followed her glance. She seemed to panic, reaching out, exclaiming, "'Tis food? Cakes for the lad? If only . . . D'ye see him on the path? He's due. Overdue, indeed. I daresay he's stopped for a dram at the Black Bull."

Rachel looked over her shoulder but saw nothing remotely resembling a human being on the bleak horizon behind her. She thrust the basket at the woman. "I'm afraid your dog got at the fowl. I lost the bread as well, but he seemed to be starving."

Mrs. Hepton's flickering smile broadened. "Alfie? 'E mustn't think on it. Alfie's best fed of the lot of us. Not but what that's little enough. All the same . . . I'll take it. My Tam is a good lad. Mayhap there's a bit of Mrs. Peebles's scones."

"There are." Eagerly, Rachel pushed it into her thin hands.

"By the by, Mrs. Hepton, is there a shorter way back to Bourne Hall?"

Mrs. Hepton pushed Alfie down. He sulked away, tail between his legs. Rachel could see that she was not going to be invited inside to rest a few minutes in the dark farmhouse before her long journey back over the moors. The room itself was sparsely furnished with a settle, an ancient scarred pine table, two rickety chairs, and a huge Scottish wall of crockery. Rachel saw no signs of the boy Tam. It looked like a bleak life for a youngster.

Mrs. Hepton pointed to a confusion of sheep tracks far north of the path by which Rachel had arrived. "Make straightaway over yon knob. Carries to Pondon Beck. It's off right hand to Haworth. The Hall's on that road."

"Thank you. I hope Mr. Hepton won't object to the basket. It was well meant."

"Of course, ma'am."

Rachel stepped backward into the path. She was turning to leave when a small object grazed her cheek. She heard the crunch of a heavy boot on the stony ground and guessed at once that the Terrible Hepton returning from the outbuildings had either thrown a stone or shot at her.

SEVEN

"No, luv!" Mrs. Hepton cried. "She's from outside. She meant no harm."

Rachel felt a drop or two of moisture on her left cheek and touched it gingerly. The whirring thing must have been a sharp pebble. It has passed her close enough to raise blood, but the wound was not serious.

She was so angry she almost lost her fear of this wooly-headed man in the heavy, worn lamb's wool jacket and knee breeches. He made no effort to hide the handful of pebbles he carried, his scowl even more intimidating than Alfie's.

Rachel drew herself up. "How dare you, sir!" she cried melodramatically, and would have gone on in this theatrical vein were it not for the wild-eyed panic of Hepton's wife. "Oh, my God in heaven, 'e have raised blood! Now we are in trouble. She's from the Hall."

Hepton's scowl mellowed at her words. "You're old Jason's woman?"

"I am. And he means you well."

"Well, now." He scratched his head and let the pebbles drop

one by one from his fist. "Ye have brought charity, I'll be bound. Hepton takes no charity from any, not even Jason Bourne."

She thought she saw a way around this. "Actually, it wasn't Mr. Bourne who sent me. It was . . . another member of the household. I'm sorry to intrude. My husband wouldn't approve of our visiting you uninivited."

"Och, 'tis of no matter. I expect ye meant well." He approached her. Like his mastiff, he was a little overwhelming at first, but she stood her ground hoping for the best. She could forgive the prickle of the scratch on her cheek if she might win the friendship of creatures like Big Hepton and Alfie. His wife was perhaps more worthy, but the woman cringed in the doorway looking from one to the other as if she expected her husband to murder his visitor at any second.

"Thank you, Mr. Hepton. I am glad you understand." She plunged on while she had his goodwill. "Is it possible that my husband could help you?" His wild eyebrows rose, and she hastily added, "To find work? I know he has been away for some time. Our honeymoon, you know. But now that we've come back—at least, for a short time—I would be most happy to mention the matter."

"So as ye make plain to the man that we're not needing it." Rachel looked at him innocently. He added while his wife held her breath, "But I'll be pleased to speak to them as wishes to make hire of a man that knows the mills. None better, excusing the boast."

"All the truth of God, it is," his wife assured Rachel.

"I do not doubt it." She suddenly felt the effects of her long trek; she ached in every bone. Looking up at the sky, she saw dark rain clouds billowing. She must leave at once, or be caught here, exhausted.

She held out her hand to Hepton. "Good-day, sir."

Caught unawares, he hesitated. "Mayhap ye'll take a dram of some'ut to warm the walk home."

Out of the corner of her eye Rachel saw Mrs. Hepton's panicky shake of the head. She refused quickly, sensing Mrs. Hepton's relief. Big Hepton seemed almost reluctant to see her go. He offered his big paw and shook her hand vigorously, as if she were a man of great strength. He walked across the path with her and a few yards along the sheep track. "If Jason says there is a place for Hepton," he reminded her, "well then, aye, ye'll say, Hepton is his man."

She smiled, thankful for the first glimmerings of softness in his rugged face. Really! He was so very like his dog, Alfie, and like Alfie, he appealed to her. She wished she could have seen the face of the boy Tam when he discovered the scones, but no matter. She had had enough for one day.

She started over the knoll of late grass, trying to keep to one sheep track. The air grew colder, the wind swirling down from the northern heights. It was tipped with ice, and she hurried on, anxious to make her way down into more protected valleys. She felt herself in one of her nightmares, a huge expanse as desolate as the moon, with herself in its midst, running, running . . .

The first raindrops prickled her face. Within seconds they became a downpour.

She was tempted to run, but she must carefully watch her route. The track before her blurred into a dozen runnels, any one of which might be the correct path, the others leading her in circles just as sheep wandered for days, perhaps even weeks.

She hadn't counted on the extraordinary darkness that dropped over the moors with the storm although it was barely past noon. She stopped, the rain pelting her back, and studied what had been, a few minutes before, the moorland rolling toward the wide horizon. To reach Bourne Hall she must keep to the southeast, no matter where the sheep tracks ran. But which way was southeast?

She considered the distance she had come, and calculated roughly the direction she was seeking. She was astonished at her own practical handling of the matter. On the northeastern horizon a crooked tree bent from the wind beside a farmhouse that might be the Withins farm. She chose it as her guiding star. She must move southward, away from it, and a trifle westward, remembering the farm's position when Jason had pointed it out from their bedroom window.

Bless you for creating Wuthering Heights, Miss Brontë, she thought. *You may have saved me from wandering forever like those poor sheep.*

Rachel plunged away from her lodestar, aided in part by the

push of the windy rain behind her. She reasoned hopefully that it would be better in the valley. There she might escape the worst rushes of wind. Toward the bottom of the ravine she made out a great black clump of darkness, which she thought at first must be bracken or stunted trees. Eerie sounds came from this pitch-black mass, noises she took to be crosswinds swirling along the little trough in these eternal moors. They sounded like souls writhing in hell.

Conscious of her childhood fears, she tried to avoid this strange phenomenon, but at the bed of the ravine she found the soil muddy and viscous again, sucking at her shoes as she crossed the boggy ground. Losing her balance and teetering in the horrible mud, she cried out, dragging her left foot up only to have her right foot sucked down as she tried to get a footing.

She toppled over, face-down in the mud, and screamed as she clawed around her, finding grass and a rocky surface. Turning her head and flailing her arms to get on her feet, she saw giant creatures wading toward her, all in black except for the unwieldy gray bundle in the arms of the biggest. . . .

Not a creature. A man. She could not mistake that yellow hair blowing wild in the wind. Nahum Cload waded to her rescue. Huddled in his arms was a surprisingly docile lamb. Like Nahum, it was covered with mud. "Mrs. Bourne! Is it you? They're scouring South Moor for you. When we come upon the poor creature here, Tam and me, we thought it might be you, at first. Thank the good Lord it weren't! Tam, give the lady your hand."

No need to give the boy the order. Tam Hepton, a tousled, friendly lad of about twelve or so, pulled her up on the firm earth and tried in vain to brush off the mud that already crusted her cloak, her hood, and the right half of her face. She thanked the boy, shakily, torn by relief, fear, and fury. "Is it far to the Hall?"

"Lord love ye, no, ma'am," Nahum assured her. "Just a skip-step yon."

But Rachel knew all about "skip-steps" and wasn't the least surprised to discover that they still had over two miles to walk before they would even see the welcoming lamplights of the old house.

Nahum soon dropped the rescued lamb and sent him on his

193

way after the confused and scattered flock. "Lean on me, just so, ma'am. 'E'd ought to be to home no time now, and they'll be that pleasured to see 'e. They're real worrit-like."

I hope they are worried, she thought. They deserved to be, sending her off into the wilds like that, without a decent road or a place to rest. Jason would be shocked to find out how his servants had treated her.

Yes. Let them all be as "worrit" as could be!

Stumbling along between Nahum and Ted Hepton, she refused indignantly when Nahum offered in a gingerly way, "Happen I could carry ye, ma'am, and make the going easier."

"Certainly not. I shall walk in just like any good Yorkshire-man."

Nahum Cloud laughed. "Excuse me for saying, Mrs. Bourne, but ye're far too bonny to be one of the locals."

Tam agreed eagerly. "Aye. Truly."

It was hard to be angry with them after that. Anyone who could see beauty in a mud-encrusted, bundled-up female like herself at this moment was a friend to be treasured.

They reached the Haworth road after interminable plodding over the moorland wastes. She was sure she would never be able to make those last steps to the Bourne house in the distance, but the thought of vinegar-faced Finbar with his original suggestion, the parlormaid and her hints, and worst of all, "friendly" Mrs. Peebles, gave Rachel the incentive she needed. It was most important that she should make an entrance worthy of the Italian Opera at Covent Garden: head high, and smiling, with just a touch of arrogance. Never let these strangers know how they had cowed her. She was not Big Hepton's wife.

She stumbled on the doorstep. Nahum reached for her arm, and she resisted angrily. "No. I wish to go in alone."

He seemed to understand. He stepped back with Tam, and before she was able to thank either of them, the boy hurried off toward the moors again and Nahum turned back to follow the South Moor path. Doubtless he wanted to tell the searchers that the lost outlander had been found.

Dilys came to the door. She threw her apron up in her delight at the ghastly sight before her. "Oh, ma'am! I'm that glad to see you! And me thinking you was down some pothole! Do come in."

Rachel breathed deeply, moistened her lips, which tasted of grit and grass. Her smile wavered, but it was there for Dilys and Mrs. Amy Bourne, who came up behind Dilys in her quiet way. She held out her thin hand, smiling. "My dear child. Come. We'll get you warm. What a dreadful ordeal! No. Say nothing." Rachel opened her mouth to accuse the servants who sent her on this terrifying ordeal, but Amy hushed her prettily with a finger over her lips. "Later, my dear," she admonished her mildly. "Dilys! Miss Rachel must have a hip bath prepared in Jason's room. Immediately."

Jason's room. It was the least of the annoying remarks made by this woman in her ladylike manner, but it added fuel to Rachel's resentment. She was rushed upstairs still too angry to speak.

It was difficult to broach the first complaint with Dilys pouring deliciously hot water over her shoulders. The kitchen maid arrived with hot tea to warm her interior as well while she sat and soaked in the old tub that was shaped rather like a boot. Rachel wondered what sort of conspiracy had sent her out on the moors in the threatening weather to a destination that, if not dangerous, was most certainly unpleasant.

She was still soaking in the hip bath when Jason returned home from his search. She heard his heavy boots racing up the stairs an instant before the door was flung open. It hit the wall with a crash. Rachel anticipated his outrage with satisfaction. His conduct would certainly demonstrate to this household the depth of his concern for his wife. She looked up with a ready smile, but her smile faded at his glowering face.

"Are you completely without common sense?"

She froze. The girls stared at him, terrified. Rachel was instead more indignant. After all she had been through! Foul-tempered Heathcliff, indeed.

"Ask your household, sir. And don't use that gutter tone with me. I am not one of your serfs. Dilys, the soap, please."

But Dilys only looked at Jason's towering, muddy figure, her pretty face goggle-eyed. He dismissed Dilys with one hand before removing his sodden glove. "Leave us."

My God! Rachel thought. *Queen Victoria herself couldn't be more imperious.* Aloud she said sweetly, "Dilys, please leave the soap."

The girl fumbled, dropped the soap into the tub, and scuttled out, followed by the even more timid kitchen girl.

Jason took a long deep breath, searching rather theatrically for patience. He finished removing his gloves and threw them upon the big armchair that was his favorite. He reached the hip bath in two steps. "Why did you do such a thing? Have you any idea how dangerous it was?"

"The water is growing cold. Would you mind handing those towels to me?"

He reached for the biggest towel, holding it open. Standing behind her he wrapped it around her shoulders. His hands hesitated on her body, then he stepped back and she stood up, her body dripping, her hair piled high on the crown of her head, and her pale flesh gleaming in the firelight. She began to dry herself. She prompted him over her shoulder, "You were saying?"

He took up the second towel and circled the bath until he faced her. His scowl remained but his lips moved in that familiar, sensual way. He wanted to kiss her. Good. He was softening, and he couldn't keep his eyes off her body.

Time to sheathe the sword.

"Darling, I wouldn't have dared venture out to the Hepton farm without advice from the household."

He stared, the scowl deepening. "Advice? They couldn't have told you such a thing. They were both away when you left the house."

"They?" Why was he so violent about his mother and sister? They had nothing to do with it. As he said, they were far from her when she was more or less shamed into making the walk. "Of course not. I said 'the household.'"

Looking into her eyes, he took the towels from her hands and began to dry her body, but his mind was clearly distracted by two opposing matters of concern, the physical and the mental. "By 'the household,' you mean the servants?"

"Especially Finbar. I may have misunderstood the motives of Dilys and Mrs. Peebles. In fact . . ." She considered the question. Busily scrubbing her body until it was pink, he ordered, "Stretch your arms out."

She did so. He used the towel to draw her to him. She gasped at this contact of her bare flesh with his wet and muddy black storm coat, but he held her close, lowering his head until his lips brushed hers. His mouth crushed hers with a hot and ruthless force that drained her of protests and managed to excite her in spite of his violence.

She suspected that some of his pent-up anger and worry over her adventure added impetus to his force, as if he wanted to punish her and to yield to his own pleasure at the same time. She was very glad she had stood up to him earlier. She felt that it was the only quality a man of Jason Bourne's history would respect.

But there was, of course, a last word to be said, and in the end, she realized that the truth had somehow been twisted so that she appeared stupid, an inexperienced and addlepated amateur.

Later that evening, Jason called for Finbar. He bowed stiffly to Jason and Amy, then stated in his dry, scratchy voice, "Aye. Miss—that's to say, Missus—said to me where was the mistress and Miss Maria. I said they was off to help them folk as is in a bad way. Miss said what would Miss Maria do when she come home. I said, visit the Hepton farm, most like." He bowed again, looking to Amy Bourne for approval.

Amy nodded. "I think I understand. Rachel merely wanted to play at becoming one of the household. But, my dear, you need never again do anything so foolish. We accept you as you are." She smiled, reached over, and patted Rachel's curling fingers. "And such a pretty member! We must keep you safe from harm."

As if I were a china plate, Rachel thought resentfully. But Maria added her friendly suggestion, "We'll go together next time you want to roam the moors. Take up a lunch and do it properly. Anyway, it was a kindly thought of yours. And, Jason, it showed her courage as well."

Finbar backed away from the table. Just before he left the room he glanced at Rachel, his thin upper lip twisted slightly into an ugly leer. She was convinced that his malignity was deliberate. But why?

Jason seemed determined to continue his investigation. "Shall we have in Dilys and Mrs. Peebles? You said they all conspired in this business."

"Oh, dear," Amy Bourne complained with an anxious look

toward the dark hall leading to the kitchen, "she will be so cross. She must have sat down to her own supper by now. Things were in such turmoil at dinnertime when you hadn't returned," she explained to Rachel, "that I'm afraid Mrs. Peebles has had nothing to eat since breakfast."

She is not the only one, Rachel told herself, but she shrugged and said aloud, "I'm sure we all misunderstood one another. Let's say no more."

"That's my good lass," Jason encouraged her with a smile.

Amy Bourne smiled, too, and resumed her supper, but Maria sat staring at her full plate, looking thoughtful.

EIGHT

Everyone was excessively kind to Rachel for the next week. The attention was harder to bear than the snide trick that sent her to the Hepton farm on her first day at Bourne Hall. Mrs. Peebles remained friendly, apologizing in her own way: "I'd no notion, ma'am, that you'd never walked these moors afore. I was that surprised when I heard." Rachel was glad enough to keep her good opinion and not make trouble for her. It was with considerable relief that Rachel urged Jason to join the family at the church services in Haworth. Perhaps Miss Brontë would be there, a sympathetic friend. Having made several visits to London, sought out as she was by distinguished writers, politicians, simple celebrity seekers, the woman would be fascinating to talk to. A refreshing companion once that outward shyness was conquered.

Jason was not enthusiastic, but the gentle coaxing of the three women he loved was too much for him and he ended by ordering Nahum to harness the pony and cart for his mother and Rachel.

"Maria and I will walk."

Resenting the implication, Rachel spoke up. "I'll walk as well.

I'd rather." This wasn't altogether true, but she certainly didn't want to ride to the village like someone's aging mother while the others walked. Jason agreed at once. He started to help his sister into the cart, but Maria hesitated. "If I am to ride, I had best change these ugly boots. I want to wear my Paris shoes."

Rachel looked down at her own pretty leather shoes, made especially for her by her favorite London cobbler. She had already ruined one pair of shoes on her ill-fated Hepton visit. Too late to retreat now. The family would despise her. She stepped aside, ignoring Amy Bourne's soft-voiced objection, "Are you certain, Rachel? It is all of three miles."

She hadn't thought it was so far, but no matter. She craved contact with civilization. After her first blunder on the long moorland walk, she had been confined to the house and the companionship of servants, the occasional company of Amy Bourne doing needlework, or Maria dreaming aloud and making plans for her life after she married Edward Culhane.

The reverend had sent her a note in care of her mother, announcing his planned arrival in Haworth very soon. Maria took this to mean the Bournes' first excursion into the village and she half-expected to see her beloved on this brisk Sunday.

The weather was brilliant, the skies never more blue, the air bracing, and the pleasant scents of late autumn made Rachel almost exhilarated for the moment. Maria came back to the cart and settled herself beside her mother, and the older woman took the reins in her small, thin, unexpectedly strong hands. Jason reached for Rachel, put an arm around her waist, and told Amy, "We are ready. We'll give you a race for it."

Amy nodded but reminded Rachel sympathetically, "You must not let this naughty boy overdo. If you tire, please tell us at once."

Feeling Jason's arm, holding her solidly against his body, she grinned up into his face. "Highly unlikely. I have never felt better."

"Nor looked better," Jason told her, squeezing her ribs.

Maria watched them and remarked to her mother, "What gallantry! I must teach Edward to follow our Jason's habits, Mother."

Amy Bourne flicked the reins. "Dear, he is the Reverend

Culhane. I don't like to hear you speak so disrespectfully of him."

Maria rolled her eyes and then winked at Rachel. "Mother may be in the fashion, but she isn't very romantic."

It felt good to be on such free terms with Maria. Her dull blond hair was brightened by the sunlight as it stole out in wisps around her blue silk Sunday bonnet. Rachel hoped Maria's beloved Edward Culhane would see her today looking just as invigorated as she was now.

But it did occur to her often that losing the companionship of Maria during the long boring days ahead would throw her more and more into the company of Mrs. Bourne. Jason's mother was always polite, but it seemed impossible to get close to her, unlike Maria, who revealed her feelings violently and could be counted on not to play the turncoat.

Perhaps Mrs. Bourne was simply slow to display her affections. She had never shown anything but good manners and kindness to Rachel. It wasn't her fault that Finbar persisted in menacing her, or that Dilys spoke so often of the public good accomplished by Maria and Amy Bourne. Nor was it anyone's fault, Rachel knew, that she herself had led a purposeless life since arriving in busy Yorkshire.

The distance to Haworth by road was three miles. Jason explained that it was a little less by the moorland path. Either way, it was no place for Rachel's delicate kid slippers. Jason proved to be patient about it, but he had to stop incessantly while she made her way around puddles and patches of mud. Once he picked her up bodily and boosted her over a rut in the middle of the road, but in general, she insisted on making her own way.

When they came in sight of the Reverend Patrick Brontë's gloomy square-towered church, looking so like a medieval relic, no one was more relieved than Rachel. Her shoes were somewhat muddied but not quite ruined, and no one seemed to notice them. She and Jason were among the last to arrive at the stark ancient village church. Looking down the steep Haworth hill, she saw, even on the sabbath, a mass of black-clad citizens.

Among the younger women there were some daring girls in bright cheerful bonnets, but there was no mistaking their interest in and disapproval of young Mrs. Jason Bourne in her frivolous full-skirted gown of golden-brown taffeta, with a bright bonnet and a cloak to match.

Mrs. Bourne presented Rachel to various village acquaintances, but the one she most wanted to meet, Miss Charlotte Brontë herself, had already entered the church. Rachel was distracted trying to catch a glimpse of the tiny, quiet woman near the window, and missed Reverend Brontë's ascendancy of the pulpit.

The reverend had a booming voice, forceful and intelligent, and it was clear to Rachel that he placed a great deal of importance in his daughter's opinion of his words, for he seemed to continually turn his head toward Miss Charlotte. Maria whispered to Rachel that the Reverend Brontë had been nearly blind from cataracts until recently, and this recovery from blindness, plus the appalling loss of three of his children within a year, had made his remaining daughter doubly dear to him. He seemed like a sensible man, severe but just, who evidently had an excellent relationship with this lonely spinster, the last of his six children.

As the worshipers left the church in the bright sunlight, Amy Bourne presented Rachel to Miss Brontë. The little spinster smiled faintly. "Mrs. Jason Bourne and I have met before. At the Italian Opera."

Rachel was pleased to be remembered, although very much aware that she was being closely scrutinized by those curious nearsighted eyes that evoked a sensation of cold fire.

Rachel said, "I am delighted that you remember me. You met so many of your eager admirers that night. I certainly add myself to their number."

Miss Brontë continued to look at her, squinting slightly. Rachel felt that those eyes saw through her—all her pretenses, her foolishness, her uselessness. The woman seemed not so much to be judging as studying her.

Her compliment had disconcerted Miss Brontë. That lady's lips tightened, and she looked more angry than pleased. It occurred to Rachel, much too late, that Miss Brontë was very firm about separating Currer Bell from Charlotte Brontë.

"I beg your pardon—you must be mistaken." The writer turned half-away from Rachel, groping nearsightedly for the hand of Mrs. Bourne.

Realizing that she should never have alluded to Miss Brontë's identity as Currer Bell, Rachel stepped back, ashamed. Out of Miss Brontë's hearing, she murmured, "I can see it now. In Miss Brontë's next novel I shall probably appear as the repulsive villainess."

Jason grinned. "Come away. I'm afraid you don't quite fit into the village just yet." She started to argue, but he covered her mouth with his hand. "Sweetheart, the Heptons think you are the wonder of the world. Nahum claims you were a real soldier on that return across the moors." He added the final accolade, "And your husband thinks . . ." He squeezed her chin between two fingers and kissed her pursed mouth.

She responded with delight but was well aware of the disapproval among the churchgoers around her. As they started out into the cobbled street, the townspeople made way for them.

"They act as though we had the plague," she whispered.

"Don't worry. They will eventually agree we are eccentric. They are fond of eccentrics."

Engrossed in themselves, they were startled when a voice, familiar though breathless, called up to them from the street in front of the Black Bull Tavern. "Mrs. Bourne. A miracle. And Mr. Bourne—Jason. How good of you to meet me! I cannot imagine how you knew the exact time of my arrival."

"Good God!" Jason muttered for Rachel's benefit. "Our hero has arrived. . . . Good-day to you, Ned. Let me take your valise. You look a trifle winded. Did you walk up both hills?"

Edward Culhane shook hands with Jason and bowed gallantly over Rachel's hand. He was still out of breath, but Rachel was pleased when he looked around, over her hand, searching for Maria. "And where is my . . . Miss Maria, if I may ask?"

"Still at St. Michael's with my mother," Jason said. "They'll be glad to see you."

"Your mother, too? Ah, excellent. I mean to see her as soon as possible."

They walked up past the church together. Edward Culhane's blond and delicate good looks attracted considerable attention from the villagers. He had a way of looking at strangers with gentle, friendly reserve, as if he were approachable but not forward. Rachel recognized the quality as useful for a man of the church.

Maria was deep in conversation with her mother and Miss Brontë, when she looked up and saw Edward. Nervously fidgeting with the ribbons of her bonnet, she let them go now and started toward him over the cobblestones. Her bonnet fell back and dangled from her shoulders by its blue ribbons as she broke into an excited run. Edward, conscious of the proprieties, walked toward her with moderate speed. When they met, he kept her from throwing her arms around his neck by seizing one of her hands in a tight grip and bringing it to his lips.

Mrs. Bourne joined the group a moment later, with her pleasant smile and guarded eyes.

Although Jason was not particularly fond of Culhane for a number of reasons, he joined Rachel in his amused sympathy for his sister over her overt display of affection.

"You've been missed, old lad. Anyone can see that," he said to Culhane, who was looking tenderly into Maria's eyes.

"How dear of you!" Culhane murmured to Maria. "Of you all," he amended, and still holding Maria's fingers by their tips, he turned to Amy Bourne, bowing respectfully.

"Mother," Jason prompted Maria, who was still tongue-tied with passion, "our good friend and traveling companion, the Reverend Edward Culhane. Of what parish, Ned? Did you get the appointment?"

Culhane blurted out his success, hardly able to contain himself. "Thanks, indeed, to that good churchwoman Mrs. Debenham and her father, Mr. Wentworth, I am very nearly assured of the curacy at St. Anthony's in Wycliffe Mount, which serves the spiritual needs of the surrounding villages."

"A good churchwoman, indeed," Jason repeated with a bitter laugh that Rachel found most unpleasant. She watched for a similar reaction from the Bourne women. They all seemed to detest this Cecily Debenham. Jason must have loved his onetime betrothed very much. But surely, after all these years, they could forgive her.

Amy suggested that they all return to Bourne Hall for Sunday dinner. "It will be a cold meal, of course," she reminded Culhane. "The staff does no cooking on the sabbath." Rachel felt her usual disappointment at the family's strict adherence to religious observations, but at least Maria was happy and Jason seemed relieved at his sister's prospects for romance.

It was decided that the Reverend Culhane should guide Maria home in the pony cart while Mrs. Bourne walked the moorland path with Jason and Rachel. Amy insisted on it, and no one argued with her beyond the polite amenities. It was not a popular decision with Rachel, who thought one three-mile walk was enough for one day, but she couldn't bring herself to object and appear frail before these sturdy people.

As the path crossed the Haworth road, Culhane leaned down from the cart to tell Jason, "I have several pieces of mail for you, Bourne. They arrived at Scarborough after you left. Mrs. Debenham held them for me. That is to say, for me to deliver to you."

Jason shrugged. "No matter. Probably French debts."

"Oh, no." Culhane had missed the humor. "From London. Stock and bond brokers, I should think."

"Ah! Let us hope Bourne Mills haven't tumbled. I've just hired three new hands." Just then he caught sight of Mrs. Hepton and her son, Tam, crossing the path on their way to the Hepton farm, accompanied by Alfie, who leaped around ahead of them having a splendid time. Rachel felt secretly pleased to have played such a role in Big Hepton's employment. She had done at least one creditable thing since her arrival.

Seeing the Bourne group, Tam nudged his mother. The poor woman looked perennially browbeaten, if she wasn't beaten in any other way. She walked rather stooped, as if under a tremendous burden. Rachel wondered if Big Hepton was responsible. She was sorry to think so. Like Alfie, he had seemed to possess some rather endearing qualities.

Prodded by her son, Mrs. Hepton came over to Jason with a furtive side glance at Rachel. She expressed her thanks for putting her husband to work, speaking so rapidly in a combination of dialects that she was unintelligible to Rachel. Jason received her gratitude with gracious casualness, but it was Mrs. Bourne who took the woman by the arm, walking her away from the others to discuss her problems.

Tam smiled shyly at Rachel. Seconds later, Alfie, too, saw her and came galloping across the dying heather to leap upon her. Both Tam and Jason were shouting, both trying to place themselves between Rachel and the great mastiff.

"Down, Alfie!" shouted Jason, alarmed.

"Alfie likes 'e! Alfie's a friend," Tam reassured her.

She was proud of Jason's surprise when she pushed him away and seized Alfie's fur behind the ears as the dog leaped. "Good old Alfie. No food, but here . . . you'll like this." She buried her fingers in his fur, massaging his ears. If he had been a cat, he would have purred. His great tongue tried in vain to lick her.

Jason and the boy Tam watched with open-mouthed admiration. But along with Jason's admiration there was amusement. "Now I see why you got on so well with Big Hepton," Jason teased.

Her friendship with Alfie did not produce quite the same reaction from Amy and Mrs. Hepton. Amy swung around and rushed to save Rachel. "Jason, what can you be thinking of? Save the child."

"What? And spoil poor Alfie's good time? My delicate London wife has him mesmerized."

"Oh, Master Bourne," the Hepton woman sputtered, "I'm so sorry. Poor Alfie don't get the food as he had ought. But your lady, she fed 'im." She shivered and looked over her shoulder anxiously. "All well and good, but Hepton mustn't know. Violent is that man. My poor Hepton is a killin' man when the mood is on 'im."

Tam looked away, ashamed, but Jason shot back, "Rubbish! I know Hepton. He's not such a bad fellow. And he's always been a good worker. Debenham Mills make a habit of letting their best men go. All I need do is rehire them."

Mrs. Hepton looked at Amy Bourne with her woeful red-rimmed eyes. "'E been that good, mum, there'll be no thankin' 'e. Sending the basket by yon lady."

"Nonsense. You belong to Bourne Mills now, my dear, and we have the care of you. But do come along to the Hall. Cook will have something for you, I daresay."

"And scones for Master Tam," Rachel called out as she and Alfie hurried along, flanked by Jason and the boy.

Tam's green eyes were lively. "Och, aye. Happen she will."

They reached the Hall somewhat after the horse and cart, and while Nahum led the animal away, Edward Culhane sorted out the mail he had been given by Mr. Wentworth. There were notes for Rachel from Hesper Fridd and Clare Lorimer. She grew homesick at the sight of their familiar handwritings, but wondered why no other mail had come.

That afternoon Rachel overheard Amy Bourne exchanging cross words with Jason about one of the letters. It seemed that Mrs. Debenham had written to him, and Amy disapproved of the correspondence. "Then leave the matter to me." This was Mrs. Bourne. "I have not forgotten what was done to us, if you have." It could only refer to Cecily Wentworth's breaking of the betrothal long ago. But Jason's angry reply sounded as if he had forgiven Cecily and was in fact defending her.

"No. I forbid it. . . . Let all that wait for the moment." She murmured something in a low voice, and he went on brusquely, "Well then, I have changed my mind."

"Shameful! Shall I tell you what weakness it is that moves you?"

"Be silent!" he roared imperiously.

Rachel would have smiled at the familiar tone, but the hurt was too great. Until now she had not dreamed he still cared so much for the Wentworth woman. She rustled into the drawing room unable to contain her emotions. "Good heavens, Jason! They can hear you clear to Haworth. Is your mail that bad?"

He appeared very agitated, his face thunderous and his hands working nervously, one fist grinding inside the other palm. He ignored her comment and moved to the front casement windows, where he could see Maria pointing out to Edward Culhane what remained of the summer garden.

Unflustered, Amy Bourne touched Rachel's hand. "My dear, what are you thinking? You must not judge a conversation by the bits and pieces overheard."

"I was not eavesdropping, if that is what you mean to imply."

It was rude, but Rachel was not in the mood to be polite. She had no reason to worry about her manners. Mrs. Bourne remained annoyingly compassionate. "Believe me, my daughter—and I feel that you are my daughter, in a sense—we have no secrets from you. That is why we shout so loudly about . . . about . . ." For a second she hesitated, shot a glance at Jason, who jeered without turning around, "Aye. Tell her, Mother."

Rachel appreciated the delicacy of the moment and tried to save them all from embarrassment. She felt proud to have handled the situation so sensibly. "Please. I know Mrs. Debenham is involved. You see, Jason told me about the broken betrothal. Naturally, these feelings can't be entirely obliterated. . . . Is that the case, Jason?"

He looked sharply at Amy. "Do you want to answer that, Mother?"

The woman appeared pleased by this blunt truth and took Rachel's hand. "It is nothing, dear, except simple remembrance, the old affection that Jason once had long ago for Cecily." Jason grimaced, but his mother said firmly, "It has nothing whatever to do with his feelings for you."

"God, no! Rachel, come here."

She wanted to balk at the order, but something in his face, the way his mouth tightened as if he were in pain, drew her to him. She would like to have kissed away his pain, but she had her own hurt. She had silenced her pride for months, sensing that her love was far greater than his. Now she had what seemed to be proof.

She hesitated, but he reached out for her, drawing her close, apparently unaware of her resistance. Behind them, Mrs. Bourne obliquely took credit for making peace between them, a peace that Rachel was far from feeling. "There, you see, my dears, how easy it is to forget that wretched Wentworth woman?"

She had managed to remind Rachel all over again that there was a rival. Curiously enough, the reference upset Jason even more. He looked after his mother's slender, departing figure in its sweep of gleaming gray silk and muttered, "I wish to God we could bury the past."

No one wished it more than Rachel.

NINE

Amy Bourne confronted Reverend Culhane's request with commendable moderation. She stipulated that her daughter must be adequately cared for by a man with an ambition to excel in his profession. But even the most concerned mother would be reassured that Edward Culhane possessed such ambition.

Jason, too, was anxious to see his sister happily settled, and it was only to Rachel that he confided his own private concern over the approaching marriage. "Maria is like all of us Bournes. She has a great deal of love to offer. I sometimes wonder if Culhane can appreciate that. He seems such a milksop."

Rachel had to admit there was some reason for his fear, but she didn't appreciate the possible correlation of her own character with that of Culhane. Something of her thoughts showed in her manner and the way she stiffened. He smiled. "No, sweetheart. You aren't a milksop. But there are relationships in which one party gives and one receives . . . affection."

"Passion."

"Passion, yes." He wound a loose curl of her hair around his forefinger. "Do you believe that Culhane is capable of passion?"

"At times, I think."

His forefinger bent over the curl and he pulled hard. She cried out indignantly.

He reminded her, with a grim edge to his humor, "Please, no jokes of that sort."

Annoyed, she pulled away from his hand. "I answered your question. The man has a very strong passion, I have no doubt, a passion to be archbishop of Canterbury."

He pulled her hair again but managed to elude a playful slap as she pawed his cheek.

"Yes, he is ambitious. No question about that."

No more was said about the bridegroom's qualifications, and in days to come, Rachel wondered if she had discouraged Jason from confiding in her. Her regret grew as preparations began to be made for the wedding celebration. Instinctively, she felt that something was wrong in the relationship between bride and groom.

Edward Culhane's new post called him back to Keighley, but he made frequent trips to Haworth. He had become acquainted with the Reverend Patrick Brontë, and one day, while admiring a miniature of Maria that she herself had presented to him, he confided to his betrothed and Rachel, "I hope I may say this without sounding like a coxcomb."

Maria said quickly, "You could never be that."

The miniature had caught Maria's strange, almost desperate tension. Edward showed it proudly to Rachel while remarking, "I may say, ladies, that the Reverend Brontë has indicated that he might have preferred me to his present curate, the Reverend Arthur Bell Nicholls."

Rachel was not surprised. Culhane had a way of making himself liked, whereas young Nicholls was of a more serious nature, a man whose personality was not so outgoing. Somewhat to Rachel's surprise, for she hadn't noticed the matter, Maria said wisely, "Small wonder. I've a notion Mr. Nicholls is interested in Miss Brontë. Her Papa has had so many tragic losses, he certainly wouldn't welcome the loss of his last child."

"By marriage?" Rachel asked, intrigued at such romantic notions of the staid young Reverend Nicholls.

"By marriage or any other way. I don't believe Miss Brontë

suspects anything. She would certainly discourage the poor man." Maria looked out the window at the dying autumn landscape, which held a curious sharp-edged beauty in the cold sunlight. "I must say, if it is true, I pity Arthur Nicholls with all my heart."

Rachel and Culhane looked at her in surprise. Culhane took her hand. "Your kind heart does you justice, Miss Maria, but such people must endure their own fate."

Maria turned on him and Rachel. "You don't know what torture it is to love, to give yourself to, someone who despises you."

Rachel remembered another conversation like this before her marriage. It still had a painful significance for her.

But Culhane was uncomfortable. He chided Maria with gentle humor. "Dear one, you need not fear such a disaster from me. I will never despise you."

Maria raised her head, reached for him, and hugged him. "Oh, Edward, promise me. Please."

Rachel looked away, embarrassed at her intrusion. Such words should be exchanged in privacy. Rachel could sense Culhane stiffen when Maria displayed such out-and-out vehemence.

The next day Amy approached Rachel with her plans for Maria's wedding. "The ceremony will be at St. Michael's of course, but our personal guests must be brought back to the Hall. I shall expect you and my son to act as hosts with me. The bride and groom will leave shortly after for the Reverend Culhane's new residence at Wycliffe, near Keighley. He is making purchase of an old but well-kept house, very seldom used by the previous owner, I understand."

"I'll be glad to help in any way."

"Good, my dear. And one more favor. Mr. Culhane tells me he would like help in furnishing a house for him and Maria. He suggested Mrs. Debenham, but I am persuaded she is the last person Maria would suggest." She added with just a tinge of malice, "It was Mrs. Debenham's idea that we send Jason. She felt that between them, she and Jason could satisfy Maria's tastes."

Rachel was pleased at the prospect of escape from the confinement of the Hall, even if it would throw her into the company of Cecily Debenham. Perhaps, by her superior conduct, she could show Jason that he had done well to marry her rather than Cecily.

Jason noticed her pleasure at riding with him to Keighley in the little pony trap. "You look quite spirited, sweetheart. Is it the idea of escape that cheers you up?"

"Escape?" But, of course, it was.

"From the house. You needn't stay inside the Hall every day if you find it tedious. I've no objection if you want to visit the sheep farms with a proper escort. The boy Tam Hepton might be an excellent guide. Or Nahum, when he has the time. Always providing these proud farmers will receive you."

"And how will I know which family will welcome me?"

"Next Sunday I'll introduce you to other members of the parish. Or try the stationer Greenwood's shop."

They were silent while the pony took its careful way down the double Haworth hills. When they were on the Keighley road, with its rolling heights and depths, Jason glanced at Rachel, frowning. "Has something happened? Has Mother offended you in some way? Don't be afraid to tell me. I can't do anything if I don't know about it."

"Nothing like that." She felt it was not the time to mention her displeasure with Finbar. The old family retainer always managed to treat her with exaggerated politeness, as if she were merely a guest. But it was hard to find fault with a man who behaved with perfect propriety. His leer and that knowing look in his little eyes were not matters that she could report without feeling like a fool.

"Well, I hope it isn't Maria. You and she have been getting on quite well lately. I know she is quick-tongued, but she has been much more pleasant since the betrothal."

"No, no. It's just that I keep hoping my friends at home will write more often."

"Sweetheart, we hoped you'd feel that this is your home."

She sat up angrily. "I don't know where you got that notion. You promised me this would only be a short visit. Long enough to become acquainted with Amy."

He didn't deny it. "Yes, but I hoped you would come to love it as we do." He hesitated. She sensed his growing tension. "What

212

do they say, these London friends of yours? I thought—I was under the impression that they said very little to you."

She laughed without amusement. "Your impression is correct. Clare says almost nothing, and my dear Friddy says less than nothing, except that they miss me." She grumbled, "And I have an awful feeling that they *don't* miss me. London is very exciting now, with everyone visiting Prince Albert's fabulous Crystal Palace, and the opera opening. The parties and balls. Strolls in the park. Or drives. And we do our part for the less fortunate as well, though you may not believe it. We visit the poor and bring more practical help than soup, I may tell you. These are the things I've done all my life."

He concentrated on the road, guiding the pony and the wheels so that they just missed the depth of the wagon ruts. "Do you really find Haworth so unbearable?"

"Not exactly." Honesty compelled her to admit, "Sometimes I like it. Today, for instance. That cold blue sky, and the moors. They have an eternal look to them, as if they are endless. Not like confined, crowded London. Still, I would like to think I had a choice in the matter."

Unexpectedly, he asked, "How would you like to visit London? Perhaps for the winter."

Visit? Once she got him there, she would make it so delightful he would want to stay. However, she was willing to be fair about it. Summers in Yorkshire, then the rest of the year in London, or traveling.

"Oh, darling, I'd adore it!"

His grim features relaxed. "Then, so we shall."

Her own spirits uplifted by his magnamity, she began to make plans aloud. "We will buy something nice for Maria's first home as Mrs. Edward Culhane. And some new bed sheets for the Hall. And I must shake up Sir Bayard. He is holding my dividend payments. He must think we are still on our honeymoon. It's rather careless of him. Those dividends might be making money. They should be put to use."

"You have a singularly mercenary nature, for a female."

"Not at all. Mama was the same. Monsieur Meissen agreed with me."

He made no reference to the Frenchman but he must know by

now that she had put most of her French investments beyond his reach. He did not look at her. He was maneuvering the cartwheels to avoid a countryman striding along in the road, swinging a gnarled stick.

"That may be. But you would do well not to scold your friend Sir Bayard. He has done his part. Naturally, I have already reinvested the dividends, as you suggest."

Words almost failed her. "You mean—you received my money and didn't tell me? And then you reinvested it—without telling me?"

"*Your money?*"

She refused to let herself be stared down by those deep black eyes. "Common courtesy, if nothing else, should have made you tell me."

"My dear dutiful wife, I am telling you now. Have you forgotten your wedding vows so soon?"

She had sworn to obey him. She had sworn that what was hers she gave to him. And the law *would* give it to him, whether she wanted it that way or not.

TEN

What really angered her was once again her own carelessness. She had known in Paris that he had made his own investments with her money. They may have been investments for their mutual profit, but she had wanted control over their financial transactions, at least those involving her money. Why hadn't she gone through with her plan of securing her funds beyond his reach? This would never have happened to Nicolette Hinton Etheredge; Mama kept too close an eye on her estate. This was all her own fault.

But it wasn't too late. Let him play with these dividends. She would notify Sir Bayard that the rest of her funds and investments should be hidden, held by Sir Bayard for her under another corporate title. She tucked her hand in his palm. "How did you invest it? I hope you were clever about it."

He seemed relieved that the matter had been so easily settled and even offered to relinquish some of his power, much to Rachel's surprise. "If you especially want to make these arrangements, I've no objection. But if I may say so, I made one or two good moves."

"I'll trust your judgement," she acquiesced, still a trifle miffed. But she, too, was relieved that the sharp edges of their quarrel had been blunted for the time being.

Apparently he had given more thought to their discussion than she had suspected, for when they had passed around the outskirts of Keighley headed toward the rural market town of Wycliffe Mount, he announced suddenly, "I believe I will stop by my bankers in Keighley while you are choosing furniture for the house."

"Why, in heaven's name?"

"I want to show you what has been done with your dividends. If you wish to sell, I've no objection."

"Do you mean you will leave me alone with Edward Culhane?"

"With Cecily Debenham to play chaperon."

"Ugh."

Jason grinned.

She saw very little of busy Keighley, a town whose somber air reminded her of other faceless towns she had passed when returning from those quick trips to her father's grave near the Northumberland border.

Gothic and forbidding, the low uneven skyline was contrasted by more cheerful activities and signs of life that passed her watchful eyes. The town was totally unlike her effete, elegant father, and even now she found it hard to believe he had once been born in this strong, vital north country. "Papa was born in a town like this. I was surprised at how small it was, father being so sophisticated and . . . well . . . gentle."

"Gentle?" he repeated. "Your little papa was gentle?"

"Certainly. I hope you don't judge him by the way he died. Father was easy prey for aggressive females."

Jason did not respond, but checked the pony. "The Wycliffe Inn is somewhere hereabouts. Keep a weather eye out for it. An old half-timbered pile. I wonder if we will find the worthy widow already on the premises, wooing our Ned."

"Heavens, I hope she isn't trying those tactics." Seeing his look, she added, "For Maria's sake, although perhaps she sees something in him that we do not."

"She was always a fool when it came to men."

They reached the coach yard to find Cecily Debenham already arrived, and laughing merrily at something Edward Culhane had said. He seemed inordinately pleased, which was not surprising. Rachel could not recall one clever thing he had ever said in her presence. Cecily was no doubt capable of bringing out all his latent wit. She tossed her head back, golden curls bouncing, and laughed again.

Rachel suspected she had seen Jason and was performing for his benefit. Jason, for his part, seemed preoccupied. He helped Rachel down, turned her over to Culhane, and asked for directions to Culhane's prospective house. "I will meet you there. I have business in Keighley, but it shouldn't take long. Good-day, Cecily. So you are now an authority on the furnishing of religious households."

Undaunted, Mrs. Debenham offered him her hand, obviously expecting him to put his lips to the delicate fingers. Rachel stifled her amusement as Jason shook the fingertips instead, then kissed Rachel quickly on the lips, and returned to the two-wheeled pony trap.

Both women watched the pony and cart leave, then Cecily murmured to no one in particular, "Poor dear."

Edward Culhane proudly escorted the two women along the road, turned at a cross street, and shortly thereafter arrived at a secluded brick house on the outskirts of the town, set back from the road behind huge sycamores.

"Behold!" Culhane announced with a wide sweep of his arm.

The house was not large—two stories, with an attic floor—but after so much gray York stone, Rachel liked the dusty red brick and felt that Maria would be pleased with it. It was a truly magnificent wedding present, though Rachel suspected, perhaps unfairly, that Culhane's motive was twofold—to please his bride and, equally, to impress the vicar of Bradford.

"Lovely, sir, as I said a fortnight ago when we discovered it, and I must say in all modesty, it grows lovelier every day."

So Mrs. Debenham had been involved in the finding of the house! The knowledge would not be likely to please Maria. But the woman had been right. The house, with its untended grounds and low stone wall, was a splendid purchase. The wrought-iron gate swung from one hinge and the stepping stones of the walk were obscured by overgrown grass, but the building's charm was in no way marred.

Mrs. Debenham went ahead, the hostess of the event, with Rachel trailing after her, intent on Culhane's enthusiastic reportage. "How good she has been, Mrs. Bourne! Taking endless hours to find exactly the right house for us. A true Christian spirit. She is so fond of the family, you know. The original . . . misunderstanding . . . was unfortunate."

"Misunderstanding?"

"An incident Mrs. Debenham explained to me recently." He lowered his voice. "After Jason's, er, imprisonment, naturally Mrs. Debenham—Miss Wentworth, as she was then—was shocked. You may imagine. No gentleman of her acquaintance behaved in such a violent fashion. And apparently, my Maria defended Jason to Mrs. Debenham."

"Good. I am proud of Maria."

"Yes—yes. And I, too. But she provoked Mrs. Debenham . . . or at all events, that is what I gather. And poor Mrs. Debenham said something to Maria that Jason overheard."

There must have been more to it than that, but Cecily evidently had no intention of showing herself in a bad light.

"And that is why the betrothal was broken? Surely, Mrs. Debenham broke it when she first heard of Jason's quarrel with the Tory peer."

He shrugged. "Quite understandable, though. A lady of Cecily Wentworth's antecedents."

"Do I hear my name bandied here, sir?" Mrs. Debenham asked coyly. "Have you the key, Reverend Culhane?"

But the door was unlocked, and opened into a dark entry. A tall red-haired woman of forty-five to fifty greeted them. She was dressed primly, perhaps a bit oddly. Her voice and her diction did not quite match the appearance she gave of high respectability. She was an interesting study in contrasts and looked rather good-natured.

"Good-day to you, sir. Ladies. You said you would plan the furnishing of the house today. I thought as how you might be wanting a few of my pieces, which I'm willing to let go at what you might term a good price."

Cecily Debenham was less than gracious. "Perhaps. But unlikely, I should imagine."

Her cool manner aroused Rachel's curiosity about the red-haired woman, whom Culhane introduced as Mrs. Gantry, the former owner. "Mrs. Gantry owns extensive properties in Leeds." He gave the woman his most pleasant smile. "I see no reason why we should not at least look at her pieces, since she is so obliging."

Rachel was eager to argue with Edward, if only to contradict Cecily. "I should think some of the original furniture just might do. We have only to recollect what Maria prefers at the Hall. Edward, perhaps Mrs. Gantry has a love seat like the oaken set Maria always preferred in the small parlor."

Mrs. Gantry brought them through an impressive long drawing room cluttered with dark Jacobean furniture. The room, overwhelmed by the large pieces, lacked Amy Bourne's tasteful arrangement. Culhane hesitated over an elaborately carved sideboard that dominated the north end of the room, and Rachel tried to attract him toward the less heavy pieces, such as a gaming table, small and charming, that she thought Maria would like.

Cecily Debenham seemed quite taken with the other rooms in the house. She moved on, chattering away to Mrs. Gantry as if they had been lifelong acquaintances. Meanwhile, Edward listened to Rachel's opinions about the various possible purchases.

They reached the small parlor behind the drawing room. An oval portrait of Mrs. Gantry had not yet been removed from above the fireplace. Rachel and Edward studied it while Cecily again slipped out of the room toward the front entry.

Rachel heard the clip-clop of a horse's hooves. She turned to look out across the untended lawn to see if it was Jason, but Mrs. Gantry intercepted her, pointing to her portrait. It was handsomely done and showed the woman at her best, a few years younger, with the attractive face of a tolerant, worldly creature, her red hair worn in the fashion of the late 1830s, with many side curls; yet, for some reason, it did not look ridiculous.

"I looked like that when I had my first lodging house in Leeds. Did very well, I must say. I took in only gentlemen of the highest sort. Tory was my party. More genteel-like."

"Yes, indeed." Culhane seemed taken by the area above the mantel.

Mrs. Gantry asked brightly, "Happen you've got a portrait of the charming bride that would just do where mine hangs?"

"Matter of fact, I do." He produced the miniature Maria had

given him and held it before him. Mrs. Gantry looked at it with interest, then frowned.

Culhane explained, "I should like to have this copied by a reputable portrait painter and hang it there. Just so. It catches those speaking eyes of hers."

Mrs. Gantry surprised them by the strength of her agreement. "Those eyes. Yes. I have known only one woman with those tragic, expressive eyes. A young female who visited one of my gentlemen back in the late thirties. She was desperately in love with him. And the real tragedy is, he didn't give a groat for her. Tried to drive her away, but . . . Well, they're always pitiful. The ones that love even when the gentlemen have no use for them—always excepting the usual uses."

"Madame," Culhane said repressively, "such insinuations are not for decent ears."

Rachel laughed off Culhane's concern. "Nonsense, Edward. It doesn't concern me. She only says Maria resembled this unfortunate woman."

"Nevertheless, the insinuation . . ."

"Even if it had been so, the girl was not at fault. I mean, Mrs. Gantry's 'gentleman' was no gentleman, so far as I can see. Actually, I'm sorry for the girl, poor soul."

Culhane seemed more excited than the subject deserved. "But the story might spread. And Maria has mentioned that she was in Leeds to visit her brother during those years. What if someone should misunderstand?"

Rachel took the miniature from his hand and put it in Mrs. Gantry's palm. "How utterly absurd. Can you see any real resemblance, beyond a slight expression around the eyes?"

Mrs. Gantry puzzled over it, but her answer was firm. "It is the very face. But I'm likely wrong. It was back in '37, I think. However, the beads . . . I'd dare swear I saw them beads flashing on her neck. Kind of like garnets, they were. I saw 'em the night she tried last to see him, poor creature. How she clung to him! He had to throw her off."

Rachel was exasperated. "Have you ever seen Maria wear garnets, Edward? I can't even tell what color this necklace is. I should think it might be . . . anything else." She looked at Culhane's face, thoroughly disgusted at such craven behavior.

"Can you imagine Maria clinging to a man and being thrown off?"

"Certainly not." He pulled himself together. "But I don't wish this story spread about. It would be disastrous to my calling. To both of us."

"You have only to consider the awful injustice you do Maria in wasting a moment on it. Maria is too attractive a woman to be that desperate over a man who despised her.

But she had said the wrong thing. The shock she read in Culhane's eyes told her the words she had used had served an opposite purpose. She felt the ghastly silence in the room and swung around. Behind her, Cecily Debenham stood in the archway, an audience to this little dispute, and with her was Jason, looking as if he had turned to stone.

ELEVEN

A memory came rushing back. Rachel heard again that heard-wrenching cry, "You don't know what torture it is to love, to give yourelf to, someone who despises you."

Only a person who had suffered much anguish could have uttered such heartfelt truth. The girl Mrs. Gantry described was very possibly Maria. And Rachel had pointed this resemblance out with devastating accuracy. Culhane himself had been privy to Maria's vehement demand for love and commitment. She saw now the growing horror of suspicion in his face, realizing that she had planted the seed.

Rachel could understand Jason's strong reaction. As for Maria, whether or not the poor woman was indeed she, then Maria would certainly hate the woman who dragged this sordid story into the light and caused Edward Culhane to make comparisons.

Rachel attempted to shrug off the ghastly business, hoping someone else would come to her rescue. "All this has nothing to do with our affairs here. Edward, are you going to take the little gaming table? There is also a mirror in the entry hall. I think it would exactly suit Maria. Don't you agree, Jason?"

"Aye, indeed," put in Mrs. Gantry, sensing that the sale of her furniture might be in jeopardy. "We are talking of the bride's house, not the doing of strangers, years gone by."

Cecily Debenham gave Jason a quick, furtive glance, and then a wistful smile that accompanied a shake of her black bonnet with its pale rosebuds.

Jason remained silent. His eyes seemed to burn as they stared at Rachel. She looked away. He was only worsening the situation.

Edward Culhane moistened his lips, cleared his throat, and said hoarsely, "I like to take my time . . . consider before I make purchases of . . ." He reached into his waistcoat, drew out his handsome gold timepiece while everyone stood still with an elaborate pretense that nothing had happened. "Have we really spent so much time here? And I have an appointment with the vestry committee within the hour."

Mrs. Gantry still seemed confused by the cooling of the atmosphere. She bustled around nervously. "Maybe tomorrow, sir. That'll fit me right well."

Culhane glanced at his watch again as if he had forgotten what he read a minute ago. "Eminently satisfactory. If there are no objections, I believe I shall return to my lodgings. I must retrieve some papers and . . . er . . . copies of sermons that I am turning over to the committee for their perusal."

"Naturally, sir." Cecily Debenham's voice held just a hint of sadness, as if only discretion and good manners prevented her from pouring out her sympathy to the suffering curate. "I suggest we all leave matters in abeyance for the moment. We can always take this up another day."

Holding on to her pretense like a bulldog, Rachel insisted, "I think that is quite unnecessary. Jason is here now, and he and I know exactly what Maria likes. We may lose that pretty little table if Mrs. Gantry gets another offer." But Jason had begun the determined retreat to the front door.

Cecily lingered only to pat Edward Culhane's hand and whisper something to him. Rachel strained to hear the words. "I know the facts," Cecily whispered. "I will explain. Later."

What a vile creature! And for all her pretty ways, how singularly devoid of common humanity!

Culhane's face showed the terrible dejection he must have felt, his thoughts torn by doubts, for he knew his career would be destroyed if ever his wife's purity was questioned. Rachel despised him for his lack of faith in Maria, his narrow, un-Christian view of her, but from a practical perspective, she knew he was correct in his fears.

She stopped long enough to ask the puzzled Mrs. Gantry, "How did the Reverend Culhane come to make your acquaintance, in regard to this house?"

"Well now, that's the puzzler, ma'am. It was Mrs. Debenham, that widow there that's cutting out so fast right now. It was her that also said to me only minutes gone by, 'Get the gent to show you the little painting he has of his betrothed.' But I didn't have to. He saw my portrait there—a very good likeness even if I do say so myself—and then he brings out that little portrait. Did the gentleman think his betrothed was the lady I talked of? Most unlikely, I'd say. Not a female betrothed to a churchman.".

Rachel denied everything with confidence she didn't possess. "His betrothed was a child when the female you spoke of was in Leeds. It is a pity he did not recall that. But he will. You could hardly have seen a girl of ten, could you?"

"Surely not, ma'am. Well on in years, I'd say. Nearer eighteen. Tell me, ma'am, in confidence, d'you think he'll be coming back to buy my pieces here?"

"Of course, he will," Rachel lied, "but as you see, he is a busy man. He may have to postpone the matter a few days. Of course, if my sister-in-law hears how she was so shockingly mistaken for a woman nearly twice her years, she is liable to break the betrothal herself. Imagine! A child of ten being mistaken for . . . Well, I'll take my leave now. Thank you for your kindness."

"You will speak to the young lady, ma'am? Tell her it was all a silly bit of nonsense, and not to take any note of it?"

"I only hope my sister-in-law will see it in that light, but I can't promise anything. She is a very strict churchwoman."

Mrs. Gantry followed her to the door insisting that she understood and would wait in good faith. "Ten years old, well, I just guess not. Bless me, what nonsense it was, and all!"

Rachel left her, praying she had been convincing. She dreaded confronting Jason, but she wanted to have the matter settled.

She marched out along the stepping stones toward the road. Jason stood there rubbing the pony's withers, his back turned to the Reverend Culhane and Cecily Debenham.

Cecily made no effort to approach Jason. Culhane's stammers met no reply; he waited a second or two, then walked down the road with Cecily.

Jason was alone. Clearly, he preferred it that way. Rachel's feelings of fear and guilt were slowly being overpowered by a growing impatience. His conduct only gave credence to the story about Maria. "Darling," she called out to him, "I'm ready."

He reached for her hand and helped her up into the pony trap. His eyes had that stony look again, like coals after a blazing fire has burned itself out. Neither of them said anything until they were on the moorland road to Haworth. Rachel's anxiousness grew. She remembered, wary of the way he had hurt her before. The business of the French securities, lying about his intentions when they came to Yorkshire—and she had forgiven him.

Her nature was quick to anger, quick to forgive. But his was far more turbulent than she had ever imagined. And this sullen mood was pure childishness.

"Darling, nothing will come of this. Mrs. Gantry knows that Maria was only ten or so at that time."

"Mrs. Gantry. Hardly an achievement! We need not concern ourselves over the former mistress of a brothel."

"Jason, good heavens!" Where had he learned that bit of ancient history? "Just give Edward a few hours and he will be galloping over to Haworth to name the wedding day."

He was silent, studying the reins. At last he said, "We will not see Ned Culhane again."

"I'll wager you ten guineas that he paid no attention to that mere coincidence. If you'd like, I'll see to it myself that he is made aware of the truth."

He looked at her, "I think you've said quite enough. I suggest you say as little as possible before you destroy us all again with your—"

"My what?" she demanded, enraged.

After a lengthy pause pregnant with the anger between them, he added, "Your babbling today has threatened Maria's happiness."

"My 'babbling,' as you call it, has accomplished far more than the cowardly activities of Edward and your precious Cecily and you, all combined."

His voice remained quiet and calm, but deepened rather frighteningly in its force. "You have destroyed my sister's life by everything you said. Do you understand that? Or is that insensitive Hinton soul of yours too dense to understand what you've done?"

"My insensitive Hinton soul tells me you are being deliberately obtuse."

"Don't fling your fancy London words at me. I'm only a poor oaf of a northman who speaks the language straight out. Every word you spoke today was a further warning to Culhane against my sister. He may be a stupid clothhead, but he certainly understood what you were saying. The question is, Did you do it deliberately, out of malice? I know you never liked her. Or was it pure stupidity?"

She was too shocked to answer and simply said tiredly, "It must be stupidity because I still don't understand what I did that was so terrible. It isn't as if there were any truth to it. You and Maria could prove it was just a horrible coincidence, couldn't you?" She looked at him. "Couldn't you?"

He kept his eyes on the distant horizon, where the sun had begun to set behind the high rolling moors.

She understood at last that her worst suspicions were confirmed. Sensing his hostility, she shifted in her seat so that she was no longer touching him, and settled down in proud, lonely misery for the rest of the trip home to the Haworth hills.

At the foot of the first hill she got out without being told, though she saw that he had intended to hand over the reins to her. He guided the pony up the lower and then the higher hill while she plodded along beside.

That night she was aware of all the old evils, the village smells, the open drains that spread typhoid, the privies and urinals behind the narrow, secretive stone buildings. All the ugliness that had seemed mere mystery and romance when she read about them.

Was it this way with her dark, glowering Brontë man as well?

TWELVE

The next three days were the longest of Rachel's life. She found Maria's enthusiasm and her constant talk of the coming marriage fearful and unbearable. "Christmas is nearly upon us," Maria would say. "We'll have to consider how we will fit both a wedding and a honeymoon into the time left before New Year's. We want to return for the present giving at New Year's."

With a sinking heart Rachel realized there was no way Maria could avoid the damage Cecily Debenham could do if she really did know something. As for Rachel's own holiday plans to leave the north with Jason, well they would have to wait at least another month or more before departing from this alien country.

Meanwhile Maria chattered happily. "Bourne Hall is always open to the people of the neighborhood for Christmas Revels. They come from Haworth and all the sheep farms and as far as Keighley and the surrounding moors. I only hope they will be as happy as I am."

Rachel heartily agreed with her. "With all my heart, I hope 1851 will be the happiest year of your life, dear Maria."

But the fear haunted her.

Bold as Jason might be in his daily life, he had obviously lacked the courage to tell his sister what had happened that day in Wycliffe Mount. And it was hard to guess whether Amy Bourne knew. The woman remained polite and well mannered, never demonstrative but always showing a pleasant willingness to accept Rachel as the necessary appendage she was.

Finbar either knew or suspected something was amiss. Although Rachel rose at five in the morning with the rest of the family, there never seemed to be anything for her to do. Finbar's malevolent glances reminded her that he was conscious of every tension in that big house.

Curiously enough, there were times when Rachel thought quiet, self-effacing Nahum Cload was the only person who really understood her position. He didn't seem to know what had happened at Wycliffe Mount, but he acted as if he wanted to make up in some way for Jason's coldness. Furthermore, she realized from the way he watched Maria that he had loved her for a very long time. Maria seemed scarcely aware of him, except as her brother's friend and a useful manager of the Bourne enterprises. One evening, after the young man had gone off to his meal in Mrs. Peebles's kitchen, Maria remarked, "Nahum is as much a part of the Hall as those casement windows are. A good man, but no woman is going to have him because, to tell you the truth, Rachel, he has no personal charm. Nothing. One might as well be attracted to a pillar or a . . . a pewter cup."

A pity. And probably true, Rachel thought, but she liked the man, all the same.

She did not mention to anyone the fact that Jason had never turned over her dividends and newly invested bonds to her. Nor did she care to ask Jason for them. It would be too much of an accusation at a moment in their relationship when the slightest harsh word might pry them apart forever.

On the night of the day they had visited Wycliffe they shared nothing but the big master bed. Once, in the middle of the night, he left the bed and went to the windows in his robe as he had on that first night. She saw him raise one foot and prop it on the footstool while he massaged his anklebone. She guessed that the deep scars of the ankle irons must ache, and she ached for him, longing to comfort him. But the moonlight illuminated his face as he looked toward the bed, and she could almost imagine she saw hatred in that glance.

Her imagination, no doubt. He had no reason to associate her foolish "babbling" that day with the early crime against him. Feeling quite alone in the dark, Rachel said and did nothing, and he came back to bed.

For two nights they spent the long hours like this, as far apart in the bed as if she were in London and he alone in Yorkshire. On the third night he reached for her and she came to him willingly.

The day had been no different from the last two, with Jason off attending to the mill concerns, which he had promised to show her one day but never did, and Rachel in the kitchen with Mrs. Peebles, learning to make the parkin and baked apples the family were so fond of.

Rachel hoped the feud was over and that Jason had decided to forgive her. Their lovemaking began tentatively—and then accelerated into the passionate union they had always shared. Although she and Jason did not sleep in each other's arms that night, they slept more securely, and Rachel looked forward to an improvement in their daily life.

But the next morning they continued the frigid politeness that existed between them, and only Amy Bourne's calm, unexcited friendliness made the hours bearable. Certainly, Maria's feverish joy did not help matters.

"He is coming this afternoon," she announced, looking into the kitchen, where Rachel, Mrs. Peebles, and the kitchen maid were working on the two o'clock dinner.

Mrs. Peebles's big face beamed. "That's the good gentleman. The reverend always has a fine word to say for my beef and 'taties. We best add a mite to them apples, too. The reverend likes 'em sweet, don't he, Miss Maria?"

"He has a sweet tooth right enough." She turned to Rachel. "Tell me again about the house. I know I shall love it. I do wish he hadn't wanted to surprise me with the furnishings, but his taste is excellent, don't you agree?"

"He has superb taste." And then, trying to hide the doubt in her voice, she asked, "Did he say anything else in his message? I suppose he sent his love."

"Of course, he did. I mean to say, the same as that. The message was short. He hadn't time to send more. I have no doubt the lad stood at his sleeve waiting to take up the letter. But it says, 'May I come today, my dearest Maria, on a matter we must discuss?' That'll be the wedding. What else could it be?"

"What else, indeed?" Rachel could only hope.

Perhaps it was Rachel's imagination but Mrs. Bourne appeared to devote special attention to her daughter, looking at her with more tender regard than the undemonstrative woman usually showed.

Maria asked her mother nervously, "Shouldn't we send for Jason?"

"Why, my dear?"

"I thought it would be pleasant for the Reverend Culhane if the family were all here. To make plans."

Mrs. Bourne gave this and some private thoughts of her own cool consideration. "You may be right. I'll send Nahum when he returns from the Heptons. Mrs. Hepton has been taken ill. I've no doubt that ruffian husband of hers has beaten her again, poor creature. Yes, Maria, I think we shall call your brother back."

Maria clapped her hands. "Yes, indeed, poor man. He's been looking wretched lately. All those problems at the mill, I don't doubt. But this is the day to remember! I'm glad it's sunny. I want always to think of today as sunlit and bright. I am going to change now. Which would you wear, Rachel? My green silk or the rust plaid?"

"The green, by all means."

Rachel found herself wishing harder than ever for Maria's happiness. She knew there was a great deal of self-interest in her prayer, wondering how long she would remain unforgiven if things went badly for Maria.

During the hours before Edward's arrival, the household was frantic with preparation, as if the young curate had never visited before. The excessive anxiety worried Rachel. Surely, they didn't all suspect something was possibly amiss! Only Maria remained unwaveringly optimistic.

She called Rachel into her bedchamber, which was littered with discarded garments, and hugged her. "You cannot imagine what it feels like to wait for so long, hoping, praying, wondering if you will ever find love again, once you've lost it. Then it happens. Happiness once more."

"It is wonderful. I felt that way falling in love with Jason."

"Oh, well. Jason. But he is so self-contained, so big and strong. As you may have guessed, I prefer elegance and gentility, a kind of gentleness in a man."

Rachel thought back. "Jason can be gentle, too."

"I know that. No one knows better. But Jason doesn't need anyone. My Edward needs a woman of strong mind, a woman like me."

Rachel thought defiantly to herself that Jason *did* need her. However, this was Maria's day, providing all went well and Edward Culhane behaved like a man and a gentleman, so she did not argue the point with her.

Rachel was especially pleased when Maria took her arm and they descended the front stairs together. At the foot of the stairs they heard voices by the low stone wall beyond the tiny front garden. Maria rushed ahead, leaving Rachel by the newel post while she peered out through the narrow window beside the door.

"It's Edward!" She struggled with the heavy door.

Wary of Maria's excitement, Rachel reached for her. "No, Maria. Let him come to you. You mustn't be so terribly eager." But her smile was one of perfect understanding.

Maria stopped, frowned at her, then she, too smiled. "You are right. I must be calm, and let him approach me. I shall be Queen Victoria herself." She made a dreadfully serious face, all pompous and fat-cheeked.

Rachel laughed. "Not quite so prim. Just keep to the notion that you are the equal, if not the superior, of our precious Reverend Culhane. And any other person."

"I am his equal. I shall keep saying that. But, oh, Rachel, he is so very handsome, he takes my breath away!"

"And so are you. You look absolutely regal."

With the same nervous intensity that she showed in all her emotions, Maria hugged Rachel and stood beside her waiting for the front door to open. "Perhaps he wishes to move ahead our wedding date?" she whispered. "I shall be very calm and let him persuade me."

Jason opened the front door, stepping aside for Culhane.

Rachel tried to read something of her husband's mood in his face, but he maintained that grim Byronic expression that had always appealed to her. Only now she was infuriated by his stoicism, though she thought she detected a slight uncertainty in his eyes. She hoped he, too, was not anxious; there was enough of that in the house already.

Edward hesitated in the entry hall. He had seen Maria on the staircase. She looked her best, flushed and vivacious, but careful not to rush toward him. Rachel slipped away from her side and around the newel post into the shadowy rear hall. Jason joined her without speaking to her. His mother passed him, her gray silk skirts sweeping around his legs as she went to greet Culhane. There was something slightly eager in her manner, not like herself at all, but very like her daughter. Rachel hoped Culhane would not notice.

"Dear boy, how good to see you again! You are looking well. How is the house coming on?"

Culhane was not looking well. He appeared pale and reserved, but he smiled quickly before kissing Amy's hand. "You have always received me so generously, ma'am. Like your daughter, you are always gracious, no matter what the . . . ah . . . occasion may be. One may always count upon that."

"Dinner will be ready within the hour," Mrs. Bourne reminded him, then turned to her son. "Jason, you can remain here for dinner, I trust."

"Yes. Maria and I were going to bring Hepton's wife into town if her condition warrants. The boy defends his father, but that may be natural. I only hope Big Hepton isn't responsible. He is a good worker."

Despite all her warnings to Maria to remain reticent, Rachel asked eagerly, "May I go with you instead? I got on very well with the family that day."

She had to be satisfied with Jason's absentminded, "Perhaps. We'll see." He was watching his sister and Culhane as they walked to the door together, with Culhane's hand under Maria's silk-clad elbow, tenderly proprietary. They walked off together, Rachel, Jason, and Amy watching the departure.

"It's damnably cold out," Jason commented.

But Amy Bourne shook her head to silence him, unwilling to break the mood of the two lovers.

Without a further word, Jason excused himself to attend to some business matters with Nahum Cload, leaving Rachel alone with Amy.

"May I help you?" Rachel volunteered. "I suppose the reverend will be staying the night."

Mrs. Bourne looked out at the sky, where the clouds raced across that enormous expanse, pursued by the wind. "I shouldn't be surprised. The weather looks unpromising. But Dilys will have seen to his room. And I doubt if Mrs. Peebles would welcome any help in her precious kitchen." She smiled to soften the refusal. "My dear, I do appreciate your wanting to help. I know this house must be dull for you after your exciting life in London."

Rachel remarked, somewhat ironically, "I find it quite exciting enough here, I assure you."

Amy pretended not to notice Rachel's dry tone. "I shouldn't wonder, after that dreadful day with the Heptons."

"Not at all. Actually, I liked the Heptons, and to tell the truth, I do wonder if Mrs. Hepton doesn't go on a bit about her husband's cruelty. He seems far more lucid than she."

Clearly, this observation upset Amy. "I have never known Elfrida Hepton to tell an untruth."

"I'm sorry. I didn't mean to imply that. I was thinking that perhaps she isn't aware that she exaggerates."

"Well, we won't concern ourselves with such matters today. I'm sure her injuries must be real if she says they are. Nahum told me she refuses help, but I imagine she will speak more freely to a female."

Amy put an arm around Rachel and propelled her over to one of the two settles that faced each other comfortably in front of the peat-burning fireplace. "Why don't you sit here until our happy lovers return with their plans all laid."

Rachel gritted her teeth but obeyed. She didn't want to cause further upset within the household by refusing to be treated like a guest. The Bournes had enough to cope with.

To her intense relief Maria returned soon after, her arm entwined with Edward's. They both looked tense and rather pale, although Rachel hastily concluded that might be due to the brisk westerly wind. Maria was laughing, the sound rather loud and brittle; Rachel hoped it was her imagination. Edward's countenance remained somber as Amy came to greet them. "All the plans worked out, I trust."

"Certainly, Mother. We are very methodical."

Finbar stood just behind Mrs. Bourne in the background, all in black except for the homespun collar of his shirt. His narrow little eyes were fixed upon the lovers, but he glanced from them to Rachel as though he saw some connection and didn't like it.

Mrs. Bourne sent him to fetch in Jason. "We will all sit down to dinner, and the two of you must regale us with your news. Tell us what you have planned."

Culhane and Maria exchanged looks. Culhane cleared his throat. "You are really too kind, ma'am, to take in a poor way-farer, as it were."

Maria laughed.

Dinner was filled with tension. It seemed to Rachel that she talked too much and too fast, but when she forced herself to be silent, she noticed that the others were fully as bad. Even Jason seemed overtalkative, discussing mill affairs that couldn't possi-bly interest the new curate of Wycliffe Mount.

It was Amy, finally, who broke the tension. "My children, you are going to tell me, I trust, that you have set that important date."

Maria looked at Culhane, who smiled, dropped his eyes, and fumbled vaguely with his napkin. He looked suddenly miser-able.

Maria spoke up with somewhat forced vivaciousness. "Ed-ward has been very sweet, just as I knew he would be. I ex-plained about the Christmas Revels, and the Bourne tradition of celebrating so grandly. New Year's comes directly after Revels. It would ruin all the family plans if we made any of our own before everything else had been done just as usual."

Rachel held her breath.

"Then when is it to be?" Mrs. Bourne persisted.

Maria leaned forward, her eyes glittering. "The most heavenly time. In the spring. Or, just possibly, the very first day of sum-mer."

Culhane looked up. His smile wavered, but his voice was firm. "Maria felt that we should not hurry into a relationship that must endure all our lives. I suspect she is a trifle hesitant to move so far from all of you, her family." He turned, laughing nervously, to Maria. "Sometimes I suspect you care more for these great gloomy moors than you do for me."

"Oh, Edward, you are so silly!" Maria teased with a shrill voice. Rachel would have guessed she was tipsy, but there was no liquor at the table. "Yes, I am in love with this dreadful old dungeon of a house, and all those bleak moors," Maria said, "but perhaps I have just a smidgen of affection left for my Ned." As Maria realized the painful truth, her contempt for Culhane grew. The dinner broke up slowly, in a kind of nervous disarray.

The Reverend Culhane was not so hypocritical as to accept the Bournes' hospitality for the night. As early as he could politely escape, Edward Culhane made his excuses to Mrs. Bourne and said good-bye to Maria in the entry hall while a horse and buggy waited for him out in the Haworth road.

He made his farewells alone, to Maria. She did not go out on the road with him, retreating instead to the lowest stair, where she had earlier stood to await his arrival. Both Mrs. Bourne and Rachel waited, not wanting to intrude, until Maria turned to them. But Jason could not wait. He came around from the back hall, reached over the newel post, and touched her arm. For an instant she said nothing. Then she swung around to him. "Bad for his career, he said. You know. Marriage at this time."

She started to laugh bitterly, but he caught her hands. "Don't. The fool isn't worth it. What a shabby creature! He doesn't deserve you."

She shook her head. "Don't worry. I was Queen Victoria. I kept my pride. When he told me it was . . . over . . . I held my shoulders firm, I smiled. Like this." Rachel heard the anguish in her voice, and her own throat closed painfully. Minutes later, it also occurred to her that Maria's tragedy might well be her own.

THIRTEEN

Much to Rachel's relief, two visitors from the village arrived for tea early that evening. The old gentleman was a veteran of the Napoleonic Wars, and his daughter, Miss Oakley, had been a schoolmate of Amy's at the Young Ladies' Academy in Leeds.

Maria remained indisposed. Mrs. Bourne explained smoothly, "One of her migraines, poor soul. I very much fear she inherits that unhappy condition from me."

"Indeed? Poor Maria. What a trial that girl must be for you!" Miss Oakley was an abrupt, opinionated woman who did not mince words. Apparently, she had ruled her father's household for the past quarter-century. She was extremely hardy and had no patience with the weaknesses of others; she blithely dismissed Maria's condition. "Then we are fortunate in meeting young Mrs. Bourne here. Amy, you did not tell me she was so pretty. I'm sure this marriage must have put the local noses out of joint."

But this praise was wasted on Rachel, and she attempted to change the subject. But Amy Bourne's strange gaze disrupted her train of thought. Rachel expected anger, resentment, even hatred. Did she not blame her for Maria's unhappiness as well?

Yet what Rachel read in Amy Bourne's pale eyes was a rather speculative look, followed by the faint social smile she gave the servants and other inferior beings. Nothing seemed to ruffle Amy Bourne.

"Rachel is new to the shire. She hasn't been able to meet many of the people in the village. Not since that dreadful day when she was lost on the moor. She had the entire household in an uproar! But our Nahum Cload found her."

Rachel could not help interjecting, "Or I found him, in a manner of speaking. I was caught in a storm."

Old Colonel Oakley combed his side-whiskers with his fingers. "Aye, it can come over nasty when it's wuthering."

"As for myself," said Miss Oakley, somewhat testily, "I refuse to let myself be lost. I face the elements and I say, 'Storm as hard as you like. It's you or me.' And to this day I've never been lost, not even when I toddled across Ponden Beck when I was four."

Rachel set her teacup down, trying to conceal her shaky hands. "I had the opposite adventure at four," she confessed with a nervous laugh. "A boy, a playmate, left me in a great field and turned loose an enormous cow. I was ridiculously terrified. I'm afraid I've never quite gotten over it."

The Oakleys exchanged looks of astonishment. The colonel repeated, "A mere cow?"

Miss Oakley, true to form, assured her, "If I'd had you in my keeping, my girl, I'd have sent you out into a cow byre. Let you face a dozen cows. That would have cured you right enough."

Rachel smiled weakly. Suddenly she felt an unpleasant grip at the nape of her neck. It was Jason, who had walked unnoticed into the parlor. He scolded them sarcastically, "Oh, I beg to contradict you, ma'am. Rachel is a tender creature, so dainty and defenseless, she might have fainted dead away."

"Don't be ridiculous!" Rachel snapped, "I wasn't afraid of the Hepton's dog, was I?"

"Well now, there's something," said Miss Oakley, her smile an accolade. "I will admit I have a fancy to old Alfie myself, though I daresay, he'd bite off your head if he were hungry enough."

Jason settled himself on the arm of Rachel's chair, with his hand under her hair, his thumb and forefinger still a vise at her neck. What had seemed a loving gesture became increasingly ennervating.

She wondered if this was to be part of her punishment—the constant reminder that her head was on the block. She tried to shake off his grip, but to her embarrassment, he only exerted more pressure, his palm closing around the back of her neck.

She knew it was a game with him, but she was also terribly aware that with just the right motion he could break her neck at the spine. He must have learned the trick in prison; perhaps he had even killed men in this fashion.

The Oakleys and the Bournes were still discussing the Hepton family. "You may talk of Big Hepton's evil ways," Miss Oakley was saying, "and the good Lord knows it's been whispered about for ages, but I was ever a friend to the big lad."

Rachel clapped her hands, unexpectedly freeing herself from Jason's hand. "I feel the same. He is a well-spoken person. I'd swear to it."

She suspected she had done more than defend a rough man she scarcely knew, a man who had at one time tried to harm her. Jason's release told her she had spoken up for his own beliefs about Big Hepton, and he was pleased. His hand moved over her neck again, this time deliberate and sensuous. She took care to ignore the subtle communication that had just passed between them, for a far more serious matter still separated them. If they made their peace over the matter of Big Hepton, he would resent his own weakness and blame her.

That night Jason accompanied Rachel as she climbed the stairs to their bedroom. His companionship, and all its implications, both relieved and pleased her. Perhaps he had decided that she was not so much to blame for Maria's shattered dreams. It had taken him a long time to reach that conclusion, but didn't the circumstances make his uncertainty understandable? He had spent ten years unjustly imprisoned. And if what he had revealed about Maria's past was true, she had suffered an emotional blow equally as traumatic as his; now it seemed the trauma had been repeated.

The door of Maria's room was ajar. They walked past quietly. "I want so much to comfort her," Rachel said. "Point out how unimportant he is. She is worthy of so much better."

"Say nothing. She might guess your part in it."

"But I had no *conscious* part in it. I think your friend Mrs. Debenham told him everything."

He was skeptical. "Cecily has always known. She might have told him at any time these past few weeks."

"She was waiting for the perfect moment, when someone else might be held responsible for betraying Maria. And I blundered into her little plan."

"*You did a great deal more than that, luv!*" There was no mistaking Maria's shrill voice. Through the crack in the door they could see one of Maria's eyes and three fingers.

"Maria," Rachel spoke calmly to her, "you have no reason to think I betrayed you. I was merely careless, and repeated things you yourself told Edward and me."

Jason pushed open the door of Maria's room and went in. "Maria, we know Cecily is behind this."

"Not this time. I accused him of listening to her, but he said it was Rachel who made him see the truth. Cecily merely reaffirmed what happened that night in Leeds."

Jason said evenly, "He knows the entire story?"

"All except who . . ." Maria hesitated. "He asked me if it was true that I was . . . involved with a Tory worker at Mrs. Gantry's house. I said it was. Jason, I couldn't lie." She began to weep, sniffing back the tears. "Why did Rachel do it? I loved him so . . . He even let me make up that story about delaying the wedding. He saved my pride. He did that much."

"The devil with that fool! I wish we had never met him."

"But Jason it was all part of the plan. Your marriage to Rachel—"

"It's all been idiocy. We should never have involved ourselves in anything so medieval. Now, my girl, let me give you some stout advice." He slammed the door and Rachel heard no more.

It was enough. She leaned against the wall, trying to tell herself she hadn't heard his words. Marrying Rachel had been *medieval*? Maybe the family was simply against marriage. But hadn't they encouraged Maria?

Her head spinning, she made her way to Jason's bechamber and dropped into the big chair by the window. Like Maria, she, too, wondered if her life was over, her life with the man she loved.

When Jason came in a few minutes later, it was all Rachel could do to keep from blurting out that she had heard his miserable words. But he would probably give her some far-fetched excuse, that he had learned to love her, that he had simply meant something else, that she had not heard correctly, and of course, he would accuse her of eavesdropping. She had to find some way to prove, to herself, at least, that he did truly love her. That his feelings for her ran more deeply than the physical bonds they so ardently established. But was it worth trying to hold a man who did not love her, who thought of their marriage as a farce?

He undressed, methodically removing the dress coat and old-fashioned, snow-white cravet he wore at meals to please his mother. She watched him, loving each moment, thrilled as always by his proximity, even giving him a wan smile when he looked over at her.

Shaking inside, she huddled there, wondering what to do, whether her marriage was over. Wondering how she could possibly tell herself nothing had changed and just go on, thriving on his presence, accepting the small crumbs of affection he offered.

He removed his crisp white homespun shirt and, draping it carefully over a chair, studied her. "Sweetheart, I know you didn't mean to cause trouble with that infernal idiot. Maria will forget him. He isn't worthy of her. We all know that." He held his hands out to her. "You mustn't mind Maria. She doesn't mean half of what she says."

She stared at him. She could not bring herself to tell him it had not been his sister's dreadful words but his own that wrenched her heart. But she did not pursue what was really on her mind. "Then you no longer blame me?"

His expression told her that he forgave her once more, as if she were afraid to cross his surly moods, and that he must be, would be, kind. He reached for her, but she rose from the chair and avoided his embrace, turning, instead, to remove the mauve sash of her gown. She wanted him to understand that she was not begging his forgiveness or Maria's. She felt she had saved her pride, but the reward was hollow.

He was only deterred momentarily. He touched her waist, moving his hands along the tight bodice, then down her back. She inhaled deeply, as if trying to avoid his hands on her hips, but the warmth of his hand seemed to burn through her clothing to her flesh.

"Let me undress you," he murmured.

She longed to say, "I want you. Touch me. Love me." Only the last was impossible. She found herself struggling against his own strength.

He drew his hands through her hair and tugged at her gown. In another minute he would have her dress off. He was breathing heavily, her own pulse competing with his.

She stopped struggling with him and looked up into his eyes. "Do you really love me?"

His eyes widened. "Why do you doubt me now? Because Maria accused you? Naturally, she believed whatever Culhane told her. She was always a fool for men of that type. And they invariably fail her."

"Maria is no longer the issue."

"What do you mean?"

"Jason, I know why you married me."

His eyes seemed afraid, but she knew him better than that. His only fear would be for his welfare, perhaps some remnant of his past. Some other emotion, but not, surely, the fear of losing her!

Fear of losing her money?

He spoke calmly, "So you know why I married you. Tell me. I thought I knew at least that."

"Was it because of my money, the inheritance from my mother and my stepfather?"

He looked stunned. Then his face broke into a grin, laced with what was unmistakably relief. And then he laughed, and with such abandon she had to silence him.

"Maria will hear you!"

"Let her." He embraced her impulsively. "So you think I was motivated by your vast estate. My dearest love, tomorrow we are going to visit the Bourne Mills, you and I, and I'll prove to you that Jason Bourne need not marry for money."

Sweet relief let her be convinced for the moment. But her common sense told her that she had not mistaken his remark to his sister and, worse, Maria's comprehension of his words. With a gnawing certainty, she knew their marriage was over. It had never existed, not like other marriages; she had always known he didn't love her as she loved him.

FOURTEEN

She slept badly, haunted by dreams. She relived the scene over and over, Jason's words a cruel echo that jarred her awake.

Jason, too, was restless throughout the night. He would leave the bed, walking through the darkness to stand by the windows, staring out at the austere beauty of the moors. Frequently, he would turn and look across the room at the bed, or at Rachel. On moonlight nights she could not mistake the tenderness, even sadness, in his face.

On the cold December day when he took her to see the Bourne Mills on the outskirts of Leeds, he talked animatedly about the mills. But Rachel barely heard his words, reminding herself that she must soon leave him. She could not remain where she was not loved. She had not yet written to Sir Bayard Lorimer to find out to what extent her estate had been infiltrated by Jason. She didn't want to know until the last minute, until everything was over between them.

She took what pleasure she could from the following days. There had been snow in the night, and when they left Bourne Hall, the moors were peppered with white. She wondered how the sheep farmers and their families could ever find their way over those endless undulating hills. The prints of boots and accompanying paw marks of local sheep dogs crisscrossed the whiteness everywhere.

They stayed that night at the hotel in Leeds. The next day Jason proudly guided the mare and the buggy over to the Bourne Mills in a suburban area beyond the city limits. The Bourne Mills proved to be impressive even to a Londoner. She had pictured a large, forbidding edifice of provincial gray stone. What she saw was a series of whitewashed wooden buildings clustered around one taller building, which was topped by a gigantic smokestack spewing black fumes of smoke into the murky sky. The entire area was encircled by shrubs and trees that lined a muddy creek along one face of the properties.

"It isn't as terrifying as I expected," Rachel admitted when the mare drew them over a plank bridge and onto the grounds of the mills. Only a few workers wandered over the grounds. A stocky black-haired youth met them. He seemed to get on well with Jason, the way Tam Hepton did. The boy looked at him with a reverence that pleased Rachel. It suggested that Jason treated his workers well, that he would, in the future, be a good father. She felt a pang of sadness as he took her arm, reminding her to be wary of her skirts, which spread out ridiculously like sails in full wind.

Each floor of the central building contained a different block of noisy, rattling machinery. She expected to see spinning wheels, shuttles, and heaps of wool waiting to be spun mechanically and rapidly in some fascinating way. But such machinery was now obsolete and had given way to stocking frames operated mechanically by workers who hadn't any interest in the types of cloth or patterns or even threads that they produced.

Rachel noticed that the long rooms were not heated, though the day was cold, that in fact several of the women operating the machines wiped sweat off their brows. No one seemed to be suffering from lack of warmth. One middle-aged woman, strong-armed and competent, greeted Jason and "Mrs. Jason." Others looked up from their frames to smile shyly at their employer. The woman exclaimed loudly, "Aye, mum, Master Jason's stood friend to us since time out of mind, and t'other way, too. We all said when those dandy lords made him all that trouble, they was deserving of a cuff on the muzzle and we would've cheered him on. Why, one of them lords didn't even—"

Jason excused himself, smiled at the interested, curious faces, and ushered Rachel out of the long, noisy room before the woman finished her praise.

Rachel noticed several children scurrying about, carrying small bundles and helping the women comb wool at separate hand-weaving looms for personal piecework. Jason explained that several families, himself included, preferred their clothing handwoven.

Rachel was less interested in the hand-weaving than in the children. "Are they permitted to see their parents? Or are they indentured to Bourne Mills separately, as they are in London?"

"The children work *with* their parents. They aren't permitted to work the full period. Sometimes as many as ten hours, never more. And with time for bread and beer, or a fuller meal if it's wanted or needed. The mothers like it. It saves them money and time, and the children are better fed than they would be at home."

"Do they see their mothers, then?"

"The women they are working with are their mothers, for the most part. Or, in the case of Sally Mangum, she has her two nieces in hand. My mother has attempted a schooling system for them, but they pay little heed. Mother believes that they must at least know their letters."

Rachel's reluctant respect for this indefatigable woman grew. *If I were to live my life out here*, she thought, *I would dedicate myself to such a cause.* Aloud she said, "I've tried to work with the Lorimers to improve conditions in the London shops, but we've not succeeded as you and your mother have. Now I have a fresh incentive. I'll take Clare by the scruff of her neck and make her see what must be done."

Jason nodded absentmindedly, seeming not to notice the implication of Rachel's words. Her heart sank further when he announced that he wished to return home that same day, although they had planned an afternoon tea and a romantic late supper at the hotel. "Maria isn't quite herself these days," Jason explained, "and I don't like to throw her entirely in mother's care."

They picked up his valise and her portmanteau from the hotel and left the city. They traveled along a road they hadn't taken before, past the gray slag heaps that were another product of the industrial revolution that had so drastically changed the once rural area.

The carriage wound its way through the patches of snow that dotted the moors. Rachel found herself thinking of stately Bourne Hall as her home. She never dreamed she could develop an affection for this desolate spot, and now she would have to leave it. Well, she had been uprooted before, and she would bear it now. She was not quite as weak as the Bournes seemed to fancy her.

They didn't reach Bourne Hall until late that evening, but Mrs. Peebles had prepared high tea for them, which was every bit as delightful and warming as if Rachel were back in her house in London. There were meat pasties and the Banbury cakes Rachel had adored from infancy. She went to sleep nourished and content, and awoke the next morning with an optimism she hadn't enjoyed for weeks.

For several days Rachel determinedly kept to this belief, reinforced by the fact that at least nothing had changed for the worse. But it was a negative kind of happiness. She breakfasted with Jason before sunup in the mornings, hoping, though she did not say so, that he might invite her to accompany him to his mills and other enterprises.

One morning her impatience peaked. "Let me go with you," she pleaded. "I could help you. You saw the workers in Leeds, how they looked as though they wanted to know 'Mrs. Jason.' Please, it would mean so much to me."

"Definitely not, sweetheart." He kissed her with absent-minded tenderness. "You've no notion what that area is like. It would shock a lady like you."

"I've seen the Thames, Jason. I've seen bodies . . . well, a body removed. It was partially . . . eaten, and dreadful, but it didn't scare me. I'm really sturdier than I look."

From the hall Rachel heard footsteps on the wooden floorboards. She turned to see Maria standing in the doorway watching her. Her gaze was unnerving. This sneaking up on others seemed to be a game Maria played. Rachel tried to accept it as a friendly gesture on this morning. "Good heavens, you startled me! Have you eaten yet! Mrs. Peebles's scones are superb."

Maria remained silent. She looked frightful, her hair uncombed and snarled, her dress disheveled and missing one button. She also appeared to have been drinking. Rachel wondered where she had gotten the liquor. She wouldn't have been able to buy it at the Black Bull Tavern. No lady would ever visit such an institution, for it was common knowledge that the tavern doubled as a brothel.

Rachel tried again. "A pity it isn't a very good day for walking. Otherwise, I might go into the village and post some mail. Do you have any I might carry for you?"

Maria's lips moved before she spoke. "No need your going. Leave them in the pewter dish on the sideboard in the passage and Mother will have Nahum take them." She stopped leaning against the open door and moved to the table, lurching ever so slightly, her eyes still on Rachel. "Maybe I will have some of those scones. And a Banbury cake."

"I'm afraid the tea isn't hot."

"We'll settle that." She eased herself into the high-backed chair on Rachel's left, reaching for the maid's bell, which she rang wildly. When the kitchen maid stuck her head in, Maria snapped, "More tea. And heat the pot, in heaven's name!"

"Aye, ma'am." The girl bobbed a curtsy and obeyed.

Hoping to soften Maria's surly mood, Rachel said, "I wish I could find a place for myself where I might help out. I've asked Jason, but—"

Maria read sarcasm in the remark. "We are all aware that a fine London lady needn't ever raise a finger to help those less fortunate. Up here in the north we believe our people are worth a few hours' time. Aye, and money and care, if need be."

Bewildered, Rachel raised her voice. "I didn't for a minute imply that it wasn't a worthy act. What makes you think . . . Oh, dear. I can't seem to say anything right."

"You'd do better to keep silent; you may believe that."

Rachel realized Maria was incapable of thinking rationally.

There was nothing she could do but walk away. She pushed her chair back, excused herself, and left the room, dropping her letters in the pewter plate on the hall sideboard.

Half an hour later, too restless to remain in her room or wander about the house, Rachel dressed for a walk to Haworth. This time she did not hesitate to carry pattens to protect her feet from the dirty snow and the mud. Cheered at the prospect of mail from London, she stopped by the sideboard in the hall, but her letter had already been taken up, probably by Nahum. There was no sign of Maria.

Out on the little stone walk Rachel fastened on the pattens and set out along the curving road to the village. She knew she could save time by cutting across the rolling moor as she and Jason did when they went to St. Michael's in Haworth, but she was not going to take any chances in the moor path today. She was tired of being considered a burden to the Bourne family.

At a turn in the road she met Nahum coming back from the village. The sight of the quiet, somewhat dignified man gave her an idea. "Could you look in on Miss Bourne?" she asked him. "She wasn't in very good spirits at breakfast. She might need some friendly attention."

"Surely, ma'am, I'll do that, and gladly."

He had gone on before she turned to ask, "You left the post to be mailed?"

He looked surprised. "Aye, ma'am. To be sure."

"Good. I want my London friends to know what the Great World is like beyond Tower Bridge."

He hesitated, staring at her. His yellow hair, tossed by the chill wind off the moors, fanned out around his face. It was a curious expression, but so many of the looks these people gave her seemed odd. She had stopped worrying about them.

By the time she reached Haworth, a high, hazy sun slightly warmed the steep main street of the village. She remembered what Jason had suggested about acquainting herself with the stationer and his patrons. In this way she would discover which farmers welcomed visits or who needed help.

She was just entering the shop on the pretext of buying letter paper when she saw a tall, thin woman in a carelessly buttoned overcoat crossing the graveyard toward the rear of the Black Bull Tavern. Her yellow hair was unkempt and hung loosely down the back. It was Maria.

Rachel looked around. The gates to the churchyard were closed, and there seemed to be no quick way to get into the tavern except by the front door. The street was comparatively empty, but Rachel imagined she saw faces peering from the long front windows. Gossip would soon destroy whatever remained of Maria's reputation.

Rachel walked rapidly past the churchyard with its ominous flat stone slabs. The tavern was just beyond, its windows overlooking the gloomy site. Behind the churchyard, the neat rectangular gray parsonage also looked out upon the dead. Small wonder the Reverend Brontë's daughter behaved so oddly with strangers. Such a view was bound to have grimly colored her childhood.

Rachel hesitated in front of the tavern, looking carefully around her, wondering how many people were watching. A rugged-faced elderly man striding up the street had to step aside to avoid her, his black-clad figure appropriately sinister. He would not likely forget her face; they had met almost nose to nose.

Rachel sighed and opened the door, stepping into semidarkness. Several men sat around a table drinking ale. They looked properly indignant at the sight of her. She avoided them, turning her head and hoping her bonnet concealed her face. She drew a long breath and marched ahead with whatever pride she could muster. The rustle of her taffeta skirts sounded oddly out of place.

Trusting only her judgment, Rachel approached the man she assumed was the keeper of this menagerie. But before she could inquire about Maria, she saw her, sitting quietly alone in a dark corner. The tavern owner was watching Maria, whose pale face gazed bleakly ahead. Rachel squared her shoulders and walked up to the bar.

Seeing the landlord's shocked expression, Rachel explained, "I've come for this woman, who, as you can see, is rather ill. You may appreciate the delicacy of the matter. And allow our departure to proceed without difficulty."

The landlord agreed in haste. "Nay, mum. Ye've the right of it there. Privy door it is, askin' y'er pardon."

She went to the table and, against Maria's mumbled objections, helped her up from her chair. Maria lashed out, tearing the sleeve of her dress from its shoulder seam as she lunged toward the front door.

"This way, out the back," Rachel whispered anxiously.

"Don't touch me, you Hinton baggage!"

Maria threw off Rachel's hand and burst out onto the cobbles of Haworth's main street, and headed toward home. Before Rachel could reach her, she lurched to one side, lost her balance, and struck her bad shoulder against the stones.

Rachel knelt beside Maria, saying nothing, fully aware of her hatred, but feeling also the pain that Maria must have endured as she twisted her stiffened arm. From the movements around them Rachel had no doubt the whole village must have witnessed this appalling scene.

Struggling to help Maria to her feet without hurting her bad shoulder, Rachel was aware of the presence of a man and woman. They bent down to shield Maria from the gaze of passersby. Rachel found herself face to face with Miss Brontë and her father.

What impressed her most was the Reverend Brontë's efficient handling of the situation, as though he encountered such sights every day. She was almost afraid to look at his daughter, guessing how Miss Brontë despised "worthless Londoners" like herself, and now she would surely believe further disgrace had come to the Bourne family. The face of the little authoress was rigid, unfriendly as ever, but there was anguish in her eyes, and Rachel remembered her lost, dead brother, Branwell, who must have suffered like Maria in his wasted passions.

Rachel took Maria's uninjured arm and thanked the Brontës. Maria tried to pull away immediately, but at least she could walk and her head was up, her back straight, pride in every bone and muscle.

"I tripped," she explained to the world.

At a loss for words, Rachel tried to thank the Brontës, but the reverend forestalled her. His harsh, worn countenance softened. He nodded simply, and they walked away.

It was enough. Rachel remembered hearing Miss Oakley gossip about the family, telling with ghoulish pleasure how the Reverend Brontë had gone many nights to find his son and help him home across the churchyard from this tavern. No man knew better the tragedy that faced Maria Bourne and those who loved her.

Maria took a few steps, her torn sleeve fluttering in the wind like the unkempt hair that gave her a strange, Medusa look. Rachel glanced behind her at the Brontës' turned backs, bobbed an exaggerated little curtsy, and called to them clearly, "Good-day. Good-day. I'll see you at service on Sunday."

FIFTEEN

It would have been impossible to hide Maria's mishap completely. She had spilled some rum down the front of her dress; the scent of liquor was unmistakable. Luckily, she had the woolen cloak, which Rachel threw over the woman's shivering frame. She prayed that no one walking over the moor path would approach close enough to guess what had happened.

Not that the gossips wouldn't take care of that! Miss Oakley and her kind would soon spread the story.

Rachel tried desperately to think of some explanation for their behavior. Illness was the most obvious possibility. Everyone knew that brandy was a remedy for many maladies, including a delicate woman's fainting fit. The important thing was to have an excuse that would serve publicly. No matter whether it was privately believed. The Bourne defenders would have a barricade to stand behind.

Most of the way home Maria maintained a haughty reserve, struggling off Rachel's steadying hand. Rachel had little doubt that in the end it would be she who received the blame for this incident. She thought of Amy Bourne's cold smile. Why this curious vendetta against her?

As they tramped along through the thin, crusty coat of snow, she burst out suddenly, "Why do you hate me, Maria?"

Maria stopped. She was shivering again in spite of the cloak that concealed her thin arms and her bad shoulder. She appeared transfixed, staring at Rachel. "Why? Do you know—can you have any idea what Jason suffered all those years? And me? It is like dying—and now I'm dying all over again. And Mother. Do you think she didn't suffer?"

"Of course, I know. And I understand. But what have I to do with all this past suffering? It was not I who sentenced Jason. It was not I who made that man behave so abominably to you when you were barely out of childhood. Do you blame the entire world for your misfortunes, or is it just me?"

Maria clasped her hands as in prayer, shaking as if the effort to speak was unbearable.

Rachel nudged her forward. "I know you are not in your right mind, but that wretched little man wasn't worth all this suffering. Now, come along before you disgrace yourself again. Think how Edward would love that."

Maria, taken aback by this sudden arrogance, lost her voice and trudged silently along beside Rachel. She was red-faced, in a furious sulk. Rachel wondered if Maria had ever been disciplined by her mother. Even Jason seemed overly cautious with her. It occurred to her that Maria was oddly childlike, a creature who had never known a harsh word from those she loved. It explained a great deal about her. She was six years younger than Jason, and the child of her mother's middle years. Then, at the age of sixteen, she had given everything, all those passionate feelings, to a scoundrel, who heartlessly abandoned her. After that came the tragedy of her brother's imprisonment. She and Amy had comforted each other in their shared sorrow.

No one had even told Maria, "You cannot do this. You cannot have that. You cannot give all your trust to this man."

No one ever told me, Rachel thought, feeling again that pang of sympathy for Maria's loss. Both women knew what it was to love a man who might not return that love.

As Bourne Hall became visible on the near horizon, Maria spoke aloud to herself, "Little man? . . . He was rather little. I never thought of him that way." She looked ahead at the house on the rising slope beyond the Haworth road. Her voice hardened. "You don't love a man because he is big and brave, or little. He loved me, and you ruined that love by coloring his feelings for me."

"Maria, has it ever occurred to you that it is you, *your* weakness, that caused you such unhappiness?" Rachel snapped. She was sick of all this self-pity, even her own.

Maria remained silent until they reached the house, where Amy anxiously greeted them. She looked at Maria's slovenly figure, her glazed, sullen expression, and turned to Rachel. "What have you done?"

Rachel threw up her hands, shrugged, and stomped up to Jason's bedchamber, still wearing her pattens. Maria and her mother simply stared up at her, thunderstruck by her behavior.

Some time after five she rang for Dilys. Finbar came instead. Dear Finbar, undoubtedly sent by Amy Bourne as some kind of punishment. Rachel refused to be cowed by the man. "Please send Nahum Cload to me. I have some mail to be taken to the post tomorrow. And have my tea brought as soon as possible."

"Tea is being served in the small parlor, ma'am." He coughed, a dry sound that did not conceal his crooked little smirk. Perhaps he simply couldn't help himself. The smirk was part of the armor he wore against outsiders like herself. "The mistress told me to inform you that you are expected in the small parlor, ma'am."

I see we are at war, she told herself. Aloud, she said, "I understand. However, you may tell the cook that Mrs. Bourne requires tea and biscuits in the master bedchamber."

He backed away, and out the open doorway with his usual hauteur.

Less than half an hour later the kitchen girl arrived with Rachel's tea tray. Her pinafore apron was spotted and her hands were filthy. Rachel assumed this ensemble was for her benefit, but it only hardened her resolve.

So it was easy enough, after all, to overcome Maria, her mother, the servants, and even her own shyness. She just wished she could practice the same command over her own body. She was so nervous, her heart was beating so fast, that the tea turned her stomach, and the biscuits crumbled dryly in her mouth.

The kitchen girl returned shortly to take away her tray. Rachel's anger had not slackened. The girl shuffled into the big masculine room sneezing into her hand. She used the same hand to collect the uneaten sweet biscuits. When she kicked the door open with her knee, Rachel got up, furious and repulsed. Obviously, the girl's habits were due to lack of training, but she would not have been tolerated as a member of Rachel's kitchen staff in London.

Rachel followed the girl to the door and said quietly, "Sophy, throw away those biscuits when you reach the kitchen."

Sophy blinked. "Eh, mum? Mistress don't like us to be wasteful."

"Never sneeze into your hand, Sophy. Use a handkerchief. And never, above all, serve food to me in that condition."

"But mistress wants—"

"There are two mistresses in this household, do you understand? And I, for one, insist upon sanitary conditions."

Rachel saw fear in the girl's eyes. She felt guilty but took care not to let her weakness show. "You may go now."

Sophy shuffled away. Rachel was about to close the door when she heard the sound of Maria's laughter from the dark hallway. Rachel looked out the door and saw Maria leaning against the wall, massaging her temples. "There is no hell like an aching head! You're so clever with that wretched child. Can you cure real misery?"

"A hot drink often does the trick," Rachel responded cordially. "Is there any coffee around? Or even tea. Papa often relied upon fruits when we could get them."

Maria moved slowly toward her, still close to the wall, as if afraid she would fall down without its support. She groaned and closed her eyes. "Do be a friend and bring me something. Anything."

"I'll see what I can do." Rachel started toward the staircase. She was stopped once again by the sound of Maria's laughter. "It really is good to hear someone stand up to Mother. Bless her, but she is formidable. She is so busy helping others that she forgets sometimes how much Bourne Hall needs her."

"Thank you. I don't want to make trouble, honestly, but that girl and her dirty habits!"

"And a private tea tray in your room, and the rest of it." Maria rubbed her head again, groaned, and then flashed her surprisingly attractive grin. "You may as well prepare yourself, lass. Mother is probably informing Jason of today's chapter in your criminal career."

"Criminal!"

"You've interfered with Mother's running of the household. You've led me into temptation and disgraced me in front of the Reverend Brontë and his daughter. . . . Didn't I see them over there enjoying my little display?"

"As a matter of fact, they were very kind. They helped us. You were ill and asked for some spirits for medicinal purposes. Nothing out of the ordinary." Rachel went on, far more calmly than she felt, "I came along, surprising you, and made you stumble."

"You're a better liar than Cecily Wentworth."

"No! I hope I am not quite in a class with Mrs. Debenham."

Maria laughed. "Well, I'm certainly obliged to you. And if it's not a bother, I believe a cup of tea might soothe my aching head."

"At once."

Thankful for Maria's sudden good nature, Rachel was nevertheless wary of an equally sudden change of heart. On her way to the kitchen she passed the small parlor where Amy Bourne sat quietly working in her ledger on the mill accounts. Miss Oakley and her father, the colonel, chatted meanwhile over tea. It seemed odd that Amy entertain in such a fashion, but it was clear that her guests accepted her work as a part of her feverishly busy life.

Rachel went into the kitchen, startling Sophy, whom she found drying her hands on a threadbare towel by the fire.

"Washed 'em, mum. I did. I swear," the girl cried.

"I know, Sophy. Thank you. Is Mrs. Peebles around?"

"Out with Mr. Nahum, mum. It's to do with the mutton and all."

Rachel heated the old chipped teapot, brewed tea exceptionally strong even for the Bourne household, and carried it up to Maria along with several thick slices of Mrs. Peebles's gingerbread. Maria grabbed the tray out of her hands. "Many thanks," she said and turned away. Then she stopped. "A little man, you said?" she asked abruptly.

Rachel was confused, then remembered her warning to Maria about Edward Culhane on the way back from the village.

"Yes, Maria, little and shallow."

Maria looked thoughtful as if she were re-forming her image of Edward. "Aye. That'll be my Ned." Leaving the door open, she carried the tray to her bed and settled herself on the edge of the heavy comforter to drink the tea.

From downstairs came the echoes of Miss Oakley's farewells, her loud, horse-neighing laugh reverberating as she passed the foot of the stairs, and the colonel's sudden greeting, "Well, my boy, so you're home from the mills. Gad's life, you work harder than your people do!"

Jason had come home.

Rachel wondered how long it would take him to reach his room. If Amy Bourne did not delay him first, she felt she would have a much better chance to explain the morning's events. Her pleasant scene with Maria had somewhat mellowed her resolve to present him with an ultimatum, but a great deal depended on whether his mother was able to lay forth her delicate, veiled complaints before he saw Rachel.

She went to the door and heard Jason's booted footstep on the stairs. Encouraged, she hurried across the room to settle in her chair beside the writing table.

Several minutes went by and he failed to arrive. It grew more and more obvious that Mrs. Bourne had intercepted him. Rachel bit her lip and sank lower into the chair. No doubt she had lost this battle as well. Now there could be no turning back.

SIXTEEN

She heard his footsteps but did not look up.

"So here you are," was his greeting as he strode into the room. Removing his gloves, he looked very businesslike. His shoulders were damp, and black tendrils of his hair had blown across his forehead. The weather must have turned bad again.

She did not rise to meet him but instead looked up, offering her most winning smile. "Yes. Here I am."

He reached for her, asking whimsically, "What? Am I in such bad graces that I am no longer 'darling'?"

He stood over her and stroked her hair, but she turned her head to avoid his caress. She borrowed strength from the bedpost behind her. "You've talked to your mother."

"No," he answered casually. Then he smiled. "We don't talk to Mother. She talks to us. In her own quiet way. I take it that you went into Haworth, forced some gin down Maria's throat—"

"Rum."

"—rum. Then you were rude and cruel to poor helpless Maria. You called her—"

"I said she had taken leave of her senses over a very silly little

257

man who wasn't worthy of her and she shouldn't disgrace herself again. But you must know that. I'm sure Maria has told you all my sins."

"I haven't seen Maria."

"No need," his sister said from the doorway. She looked disheveled and suddenly older than her years.

"Are you feeling better?" Jason asked.

Maria shrugged. "To be quite honest, no." She looked at Rachel, "Though the tea helped. Thank you."

Jason looked at both women as if he couldn't believe any of this. Maria grinned. "Jason, she called my loving betrothed a dull little man." Her eyes flashed. "Do you suppose I would have found the other one little and dull if he hadn't gone home to his beloved bitch of a wife?"

Jason winced at Maria's choice of words. "May I suppose you two are friends at last?"

Maria shrugged. "You may suppose anything you wish. That is your affair." But her amused glance at Rachel was genuine.

Jason got up. "Well, this armistice is long overdue. May I suggest that as soon as I've washed off the snow and the night air and the problems of the damnable Bradford works, we might go down to a hot supper together, we three?"

It had all gone much better than Rachel had hoped, but her relief was short-lived, for nothing had actually been solved. As long as they shared the dinner table and the household with Amy Bourne she had no reason to believe anything had changed. Rachel realized she must confront Jason directly with her doubts and fears. She must be true to herself, for to assuage the pain with politeness would be the most disastrous farce of them all.

In a cowardly fashion, however, she put off the moment for another hour or two. Was it not possible that Amy, too, could undergo a change of heart and accept Rachel's efforts as they were intended?

She did want to settle one matter immediately. "Darling, if Maria didn't tell you all about our little adventure today, how did you hear of it?"

He and Maria exchanged looks. He said quietly, "I think you know."

To which Maria added, "I might have said something about it to Mother. I did a little babbling, as I vaguely recall."

"Maria and I can tell you exactly what happened," Rachel assured him. "Maria was in town and suddenly took ill. She had asked for a bit of brandy to revive her, but it didn't seem to help. I was passing by her on the street and we literally collided. It was all rather frightening business but not scandalous in the least."

Jason looked at her for a long minute. Then he raised her hand and kissed it. Maria watched them, sighed, and went off to her room, mechanically smoothing her hair and rumpled dress.

She looked much better when she joined them at supper some time later. Mrs. Bourne, however, appeared rather careworn, her eyes red and sore from concentrating so intently upon the many cramped figures in her ledger. She was her usual quiet and undemonstrative self. "All of you down to supper? Excellent. We missed you at tea, my dear."

Rachel said, "Thank you. I had it served in our room."

"Perhaps, dear, next time you might give me a hint of your intentions and I will explain to the servants. We are very proud, we Yorkshiremen, and we do not take readily to orders from outsiders."

Rachel exchanged a quick glance with Jason, who smiled as if gently urging her on. Rachel straightened her shoulders and replied, "How very true! But the girl, Sophy, must learn not to handle food with soiled and unclean hands. However, I have every confidence that in time she will be as efficient as the servants in my London house." She added a friendly *coup de grace*, "It requires only a little firmness, you know."

Amy Bourne's face flamed. Rachel realized she had probably never been so brought down in her own or any other house. Even Jason and Maria appeared stunned.

In silence the four sat down to the small but adequate supper. Rachel forced herself to lead whatever stilted conversation there was. She kept her voice light, her manner casual, but there was a gently firm tone in her voice that refused deference to anyone.

She knew Maria was puzzled. She could not even imagine Amy's secret reactions, but her greatest triumph was Jason's apparent admiration of her new behavior. He sat eating his soup, breaking off pieces of toast, and chewing each piece with his black eyes intent on Rachel. He did not smile, but she could have sworn those formidable eyes were amused.

Gradually, Amy Bourne recovered her usual calm. Between them, Rachel and Maria made it easy for her to rejoin the conversation. They discussed only general topics, which did not leave room for hurt feelings or arguments. Jason, too, played his part, and to Rachel's secret relief the evening ended on a superficially pleasant note.

Maria walked with Rachel and Jason to the stairs. "Well, good-night," she said, yawning. "I've still got that infernal headache. But I've something else, too."

"What's that?" Jason came up putting his arm around her.

She looked around at him. "My talisman. A wise person told it to me. 'He is a dull little man, unworthy of me.' I repeat it to myself and it seems to help." She hurried on up the stairs.

Jason turned in confusion to Rachel. "I feel as though I were in Paris again. I need a translator."

Rachel laughed and took his arm. "Come along. I very much hope Maria—my friend Maria—is on her way to recovery."

As they went on up to their bedchamber he remarked thoughtfully, "I only wish it might be as easy to win Mother over."

It seemed to Rachel that the proper moment had arrived. When Jason closed the bedchamber door, she took a few deep breaths. "Jason."

He reached for her, teasing. "Jason, darling."

"Well then, Jason, darling. You must listen."

Just a shadow of the old somber look came over his face. "We are to be serious, then?"

"Very. Our whole lives are involved."

He perched on one arm of the chair, his mouth hardening a little. "You want Mother to treat you like a married woman and not like a second daughter. I agree."

"Jason, darling, there cannot be two Mrs. Bournes in one house. Not any house that is meant to be my home."

He frowned, rubbed his hand over the back of his neck. "It is difficult. Mother came to the Hall as a bride. The house had been practically in ruins for about ten years after my grandmother died. Mother loves the Hall, very much the way she loves us."

She was shocked at his misunderstanding. "Never! I had no

notion of such a thing. Of course Bourne Hall should belong to her and to Maria."

He remained reasonable but confused. "You're not asking me to leave those two women here . . . two females alone. Sweetheart, what's come over you?"

"They got on for ten years without you."

She wished at once she hadn't said it. The old coldness crept over his face—what she had once fondly thought of as his Heathcliff look. Now she was frightened of the effect her boldness might have on him. "I didn't mean that. Please, forgive me."

But she knew she was right. His silence worried her. He rose and stood before the windows, as he had so many troubled nights before. Finally, he said, "I can still see the Withins up there on the moor, in spite of the snow. It looks strange. Sinister."

"Rather sad, I think. It's so lonely."

He did not answer. Then, in the still-awkward voice of a man talking to himself, he murmured, "How could we?" His fist came down hard on the chair back. The sound made her jump. "How were we capable of it?"

Sensitive to the precariousness of this moment, Rachel wondered if she had understood him. She pretended to laugh. "I hope you aren't asking . . . how you could have married me?"

The stoic frigidness seemed to melt from his face. He became, once more, the deeply caring man she loved. She was glad to see the brooding hero of her past disappear. Heathcliff did not promise much for their future. He warmed her with his smile, though it had in it something haunting and sad. "No, I wasn't thinking of our marriage. Not in the way you mean." He backed away from the window and moved toward her in the smoky light of the lamp. "Loving you, sweetheart, was the one thing I am not ashamed of in this—" He stopped. She sensed he had been about to say more. "In this world," he finished.

She asked barely above a whisper, "Then what are we to do? We must leave here. It is the only answer."

He drew her against him and she let him take her, but he must have known he had not won. She was excitingly, almost painfully aware of his heavy heartbeat, his lean torso, the hardness of him. He wanted her now. But this perfection in their married life had nothing whatever to do with their future. Without much hope, she waited for him to make a decision.

And he did. "Yes. You need to get away from this climate for a time. There is so much I have to say to you, but this isn't the place. Shall we go down to London for a visit?"

"Oh, Jason, I would love it. Beyond anything."

"But we must be home for Christmas Revels."

There it was. The snag. She raised her head. "Darling, this isn't our home. It belongs to Amy—to your mother and Maria, until Maria is married."

He still held her, but he asked quietly, "Do you really expect them to live alone? Have you ever known a proper household in which a woman like Mother lived alone?"

"Yes, I have," she reminded him. "My own household. I lived alone for three years, except for a hired companion."

He had never considered this before. He seemed encouraged. "Quite true. Of course, you were in a large city where every comfort was available."

"And your mother lives in a small area where she is known and respected by everyone. In practice, she should be safer than I was."

He gave a short laugh, not without humor. "At least, here on the moors she is unlikely to be snatched up and carried off by an ex-convict galley bird."

"And that is the most fearsome hazard of all." She kissed him, happy for the first time in so long. Her mind was already at work. London! And at Christmas time!

"I'll write Friddy," she said with a grin. "I'll tell her she must have the house ready. And Clare, for she must be prepared to entertain us royally."

He groaned. "Must she?"

"It's been a long time since the Elysée ball, darling," she reminded him. "I'll tell her—only a very little ball."

"If you must, you must." Jason grinned, giving in.

Rachel could hardly contain her joy. And as he removed his cravat, she stilled his hands, letting her own carry out the task. She knew their small triumph was not hers alone, but theirs together. And it was just the beginning.

SEVENTEEN

Amy Bourne ticked off a dozen reasons why her son and his wife should not visit London so close to the holidays, although Rachel had thought she would be glad to be rid of at least one of the pair.

"There is so much to be done before the Revels," Amy reminded them, and Rachel in particular. "My dear, you would find it most interesting and instructive. Naturally, there will be the usual adorning the Hall for the occasion. I think I may invite that poor Mrs. Hepton and some village girls to help out." She explained graciously to Rachel, "Your advice would be invaluable on the decorations. We festoon the house with twisted ribbons and paper. Then there are the crackling fires, the Yule log, a splendid roast of beef, and our good Yorkshire ham. And the guests arriving, ringing sleigh bells. And musicians for the dancing, you know."

"It sounds delightful," Rachel admitted.

Mrs. Bourne was determined to offer the olive branch. "Though I daresay you will have your own suggestions. I am told the celebrations in London are wonderful to behold."

"Yes, yes," Jason interrupted. "She knows the whole of it. Rachel will do her part. She always does."

For some reason, all his mother's efforts at friendliness seemed to annoy him. Rachel couldn't imagine why. She herself suspected the woman had guessed they would be moving elsewhere and wanted to prevent it. It was perfectly natural. Rachel was far from holding that against her.

Maria was less voluble one way or another. She shrugged as she said good-bye to her brother and Rachel. "I knew you were certain to go. I went to London myself before you were married. Did you know that, Rachel?"

Rachel started to say, "Yes, I knew." Then she remembered seeing Maria that day near Piccadilly Circus and went on quickly, "Jason told me you had been to London."

Much to her surprise, Maria offered Rachel a farewell kiss. "We may as well, being sisters and all." Rachel embraced her in agreement.

Amy Bourne reminded them once again, "We cannot have the Revels without you. Don't disappoint us, and the entire moorland hereabouts."

"Certainly, Mother. We aren't deaf. We would never be anywhere but home at Christmas. Stay well." Jason kissed his mother. "I don't suppose it would do any good to ask you not to work so hard with the mill families."

She shook her head, smiling. "I cannot help what I am. If I did nothing, I should be dead in a year. In a week!"

Rachel did not doubt it. Amy Bourne might be less than competent as a mother-in-law, but in her efforts to educate the millhands and their families, seeing to all their needs, she was more than admirable.

I wonder if I could ever be so useful, Rachel thought, and said her hesitant good-byes to Amy Bourne. She tried to appear friendly and warm, but her honesty would not let her be hypocritical. "Jason will be home for the Revels. . . . When I visited the mill near Leeds, he told me all the wonderful things you did for those people. Perhaps, someday, you will teach me how I, too, can contribute to your work."

Amy Bourne smiled. Only her tired eyes remained alien and

remote. "If you say so, my dear." Her fingers curled into her palms.

Though both appeared to be in a holiday mood, Rachel and Jason left the Hall with very different thoughts. In Rachel's mind lingered the image of Amy Bourne's stubborn aloofness. Jason seemed troubled as well. She asked him lightly, "Do you remember the first time we met in one of these cars? You looked so cross. But you were quite taken with Hesper Fridd. She told me you were a kind gentleman."

He took her hand. "I was never that."

"What did you think of me?"

"What a very self-centered question!"

"Be honest."

He ruffled up his hair with her own hand as he appeared to think. "You were beautiful—"

"Ah."

"—and shallow, and selfish."

"Not worth a second glance?" She remembered that journey and how, every time she had looked at him, he was absorbed in his *Yorkshire Post*. "And did you glance at me a second time, even though I wasn't worth it?"

He grinned. "A hundred times, as I recall, though I wasn't going to give you the satisfaction of knowing it."

She asked curiously, "Then why were you so cold when we were introduced at the Opera House?"

He changed the subject, looking out the train window. "Nottingham. We should be in London in a few hours." He didn't look happy about it.

The house in Berkeley Square stood very much as she had left it on her wedding day. It seemed so long ago. Rachel thought back to that day, the image she had of her romantic new husband. He seemed almost magical—an unreal creature out of a fantasy. But how different and how much more wonderful he proved to be!

They entered her mother's elegant foyer, ushered in by Mrs. Brithwick herself. The housekeeper was as bustling and efficient as ever. Her heavy face looked fairly pleased to see them but she reminded them at once, "Take care. Your boots may mar the floor, sir."

"For heaven's sake, Mrs. Brithwick!" Rachel began, just as she would in the past. But she silenced herself. She didn't want Mrs. Brithwick's wrath to fall upon Jason for having provoked the woman so innocently. Rachel wanted Jason to feel at home in her house.

Outwardly, he appeared to be just as impudent and charming as ever with her servants. He chucked Mrs. Brithwick under her chins, apologizing as he would have done when first visiting the house. "And a rare beauty it is, Mrs. Brithwick. Thanks to you, I don't doubt. But you were always perfection at your job, ma'am."

"Well now, Mr. Bourne, that's as may be. What'll you be saying to a wee tot of rum, like in the old days?"

"I'd say you are an enchantress, ma'am. The bottle must be shrouded with cobwebs."

Mrs. Brithwick made a prim face as he recalled her own disapproval, but she softened and even chuckled to herself, then went off to order the scullery boy around. Remembering those bottles brought to Jason so insultingly, Rachel felt a little guilty over the way she had taunted Amy Bourne for her servant's dirty habits.

The returning honeymooners were greeted with gentle excitement by Hesper Fridd, who was so glad to see them that even Jason claimed he felt finally welcome. Hearing their voices, she had rushed out of the sewing room to greet them. "How delightful to have you back, dear Rachel! And Mr. Jason, too, if I may be pardoned the familiarity."

After Rachel had hugged her, Jason embraced her hardily, embarrassing the older woman, but obviously thrilling her to the core. "Miss Hesper, you must now be my guardian as well. Nothing less will do," he told her, to her great pleasure. "After all, it was you I saw in the railway car, long before I fell under the spell of this trollop."

"Trollop. Oh, dear!" she twittered. "He is only teasing, Rachel."

"Trollop, indeed. I know when I have been insulted."

Jason reached past Miss Fridd and pinched Rachel's cheek.

"Rachel, dearest, you will want to pay a call on the Lorimers at your earliest convenience. Or shall I send a note to Miss Clare and Sir Bayard? That naughty boy, young Desmond, has been by any number of times to pay his respects."

Rachel explained to Jason, not without some secret pleasure, "Desmond was very keen to marry me, you know."

"No. I hadn't known. Can't wait to meet the chap. We will have so much in common."

She laughed. "Don't be grumpy. His great interest was my estate. If he could have married that and not me, I am sure he would have considered it a perfectly satisfactory match."

Shocked, Miss Fridd protested, "How can you be so unfair, Rachel! He dotes on you, and well you know it."

Rachel realized she would have to watch her words. There was still something of the brooding Jason that was sensitive to her flip attitude. He might also remember her similar accusation regarding his own interests. Mrs. Fridd excused herself, leaving Rachel and Jason alone in her bedchamber.

She realized almost at once that Jason seemed oddly out of place in the delicate, pale room. No muddy pattens or boots had ever entered here, and the view was only as inspiring as the chimneys of London. But if Jason felt any contempt for the atmosphere, he made no unkind comparisons aloud, nor did he comment when she went around touching all the individual pieces of furniture, few of them comfortable but all a sign of affluence. The decor was not her own taste, however, and she pointed this out when he asked, "Did you choose that chaise longue? That clothespress? The four-poster?" The bed was so delicate it shivered when he sat upon it.

"Oh, heavens, no! Everything you see—was Mother's. She had wonderful taste." She sat down to demonstrate the uses of the little white chair before the elegant and fragile dresser. She looked at it curiously, realizing something she had never known before. "It's not a very comfortable chair. But then, antiques never are." She remembered another odd matter and made the comparison that must have been in his thoughts. "Our furniture at the Hall is antique, too, isn't it?"

"I imagine so."

"But more comfortable. Well, Mother was a great believer in appearances."

"Mothers can be a trial," he sympathized, and she raised her chin, ready to take offense at his comparison of Nicolette Etheredge with Amy Bourne. A fair consideration made her smile instead. She was picturing Nicolette's arrogance, her possible prejudices against Jason had they lived under Nicolette's roof. Such criticism seemed to her a betrayal of her mother's memory. But the truth was, the elegant house struck her as cold, a museum. There had been no love in it.

Perhaps it will seem more like home after Jason and I have lived here a few days, she decided, remembering how warm and personal the big bedchamber at Bourne Hall had grown with the weeks. This house was indeed of such warmth and humanity.

She looked at Jason, studying his broad shoulders and the width of his hands laid flat on the bed. His personality seemed to fill the room and made her constantly aware of his discomfort. Though he probably hated to do so, Jason was trying very hard to fit into her world. He was, or tried to be, good-humored about it. He had been astonishingly patient, so far. But his very quietness troubled her.

That evening at supper, Jason asked wryly, "Why do I imagine I am in Paris again?"

Through the habits of a lifetime, Rachel's menus were invariably French in style and content. He considered the delicate white sauce over the sweetbreads, while she said on an anxious note, "You like it, don't you?"

"Very good. As a change."

But he wasn't enjoying it. Rachel felt that for a normal diet it was too rich, and yet it lacked substance. She wasn't sure why. She decided that when she returned home, she would adapt these French recipes to more substantial northern fare.

During their night in Nicolette's bed they clung together as if this were the last refuge they could share in a pattern of their lives that seemed to have its answer somewhere between her world and his.

The next morning, accustomed to rising early, Rachel reached for her mother's worn petit-point bellpull and upset the entire household. Mrs. Brithwick wasn't up yet from her basement quarters. The maids had barely risen, and only the illiterate scullery boy was on duty with his bellows, blowing fires into flames in the various fireplaces and the kitchen stove. He panicked at the summons but arrived shakily in Nicolette's white bedchamber tracking ashes on the exquisite Aubusson carpet.

Rachel sighed and, catching Jason's grin, swallowed the scolding she was about to administer. In a warmer voice she asked the boy to deliver a message when Alice arrived, Alice being the most responsible of Mrs. Brithwick's staff. "Just say we would like our tea as soon as possible." Can you remember?"

"Aye, mum." He scratched his tousled head. "I'll try, mum. Alice be mighty cross these hours."

"Nevertheless, you will try."

He beamed. "That I'll do." He sauntered off, leaving Rachel exasperated and Jason amused.

They were at breakfast two hours later with Hesper Fridd when a boy brought the answer to Miss Fridd's note informing the Lorimers of Rachel's arrival. Miss Fridd was delighted. "Dear Miss Lorimer will pay you a call within the hour, Rachel. And such news she has to tell you! I mustn't say a word. It is to be a great secret until the Lorimer Christmas ball, but I am persuaded Miss Lorimer will confide it to you and Master Jason today."

Jason winced at the title. "Miss Fridd, you may call me anything you like, and I hope you will use my Christian name, but 'master' is suitable only for five-year-olds. Remember, I am a West Riding farmer lucky enough to have been educated like a gentleman. But I am not a gentleman."

Clare Lorimer swept in shortly before noon. She paused, as if in awe, before she gave Jason her hand. She looked him up and down, then whispered to Rachel while embracing her, "You traitress! How could you keep this handsome creature all to yourself up in dreary Yorkshire? If it weren't for my adorable Roderick, I should be quite green with jealousy."

Rachel obediently asked the obvious question. "Then you are still escorted by Mr. Dinnes-Evans? With your popularity, Clare, I expected you would have a dozen more hopeful suitors by this time."

"Then Friddy has kept my secret!" As always, from the top of her bright blond head in its sassy blue taffeta bonnet to her dainty feet, Clare Lorimer glowed with friendliness and good humor. "Come. Do let us sit down. Miss Fridd, come along. And Mr. Bourne, you must hear me as well. Don't make excuses and run away."

Jason strolled behind them into the green and gold salon. Rachel wondered what he was really thinking. He had behaved gallantly, and yet, knowing him so well, she could detect that his thoughts were elsewhere. His manner remained distracted.

Clare was scarcely settled before she poured out further hints of her exciting news. "Papa is making the announcement at the Christmas ball, but I cannot possibly keep the secret so long. More than a week."

Rachel thought with a bit of disappointment of her promise to Amy. It would be too bad to miss the Lorimer Christmas ball. She had attended the affair every year since she was fourteen; as a child she had watched with awe, accompanied by Clare and Desmond, from the Lorimer gallery. Nicolette had danced at the ball during both her marriages, effortlessly securing her position as the center of attraction with her French wit and impeccable style.

But Rachel had given her word. Clare sensed the reluctance in Rachel's enthusiasm. "You will be there, surely?" she asked rather indignantly.

They were seated together on the gold and green-threaded sofa with Jason opposite them in a chair, but Rachel could feel her husband's tension, as if he were beside her. He was waiting for her to speak up. "Clare, I'm afraid it won't be possible. You see, Christmas Revels is the most important family holiday of the Yorkshires. It is a time the whole community waits for. Bourne Hall is the center of the festivities and we must be home for Christmas Eve."

"But you are home."

Jason raised his head. Rachel knew he was studying her. "Did I say 'home'? It was instinctive. But, yes, I suppose it is true. Jason and I will soon be setting up our own household." She smiled at Jason. "I don't think London will ever be my home again. Perhaps only during the court season."

"But this lovely house, what will become of it?"

Jason reached for Rachel's hand, "Why not save it for our firstborn."

Miss Fridd cried, "Dearest Rachel! Is it true?" and Clare echoed, "Are you really?"

"Not at the moment," Rachel said quickly, feeling somehow that she had disappointed them. "But one never knows. Now, do tell me what is to happen at the Christmas ball."

"My betrothal. I am to be *Mrs. Roderick Dinnes-Evans*."

Although her obvious hints had deprived the announcement of its due surprise, it was received with suitable cries of joy and good wishes. Jason joined the congratulatory group, adding, "From my own long experience, I can recommend the institution. May I wish you every happiness, Miss Lorimer?"

Clare was so excited she kissed everyone, including Jason. "I must go," she said. "I've spent a scandalous amount of time here. But if you are returning to the north so soon, we have a great deal to do. A visit to the opera to exhibit you two. You make such a handsome pair."

"We met at the Italian Opera," Rachel reminded him. She asked Jason, "Wouldn't it be appropriate? I would love to retrace those steps, relive our meeting."

"As I recall," said Jason, glancing at Miss Fridd, "there was one other enchanting woman present."

"Dear me," Miss Fridd said, shyly, "I thought you had quite forgotten."

"I can hardly forget the most crucial decision I ever made." He spoke so soberly they were all silenced. He was staring out the window of the parlor, as if searching for a more pleasant memory. He recovered at once, adding cheerfully, "The decision to marry the most intriguing woman I had ever seen." He looked at Rachel, and now, for a moment, the two other women seemed to fade from the room.

Clare broke the spell. "And now, I must go, truly. Des and Papa will want to know all your plans."

She stopped in the foyer. "Heavens! I nearly forgot. Papa is most awfully anxious to speak with you, Rachel. Something about that tiresome estate of your mama's."

Rachel was casual. "At any time. Jason and I will always be available to Sir Bayard."

Mrs. Brithwick opened the street door and was signaling to the Lorimer coachman down the square. Clare stopped in the doorway. "Yes, well, it's very tedious business and Papa is the old-fashioned sort. I think it might be better if you see him alone."

Jason relieved the sudden tension in the room. "Thank you, Clare. That's probably good advice. I've never understood the half that solicitors and bankers have to say. I'd just be in the way."

"Wonderful." Clare embraced both women and gave her hand to Jason. "I only hope Roddy and I will be as happy as you two, so long after the wedding."

EIGHTEEN

Jason offered to accompany Rachel to the huge old building off Grosvenor Square—the town house in which the Lorimers had lived for what seemed like forever. Sir Bayard's title was bestowed through the intervention of a grateful prince-regent for his efforts in stabilizing the British government funds during the Waterloo Panic. However, in the rise of the Welsh Tudors, the Lorimers had been on the winning side and managed to remain there ever since. Technically not of the aristocracy, they were received everywhere in a way that Rachel would never experience. This fact made her perversely proud of Jason's boast that he was no gentleman.

She would like to have shown Jason the Lorimer family treasures, which dated back to Henry the Second, but Sir Bayard paid her a call, eliminating her own visit, before Jason could order out the team and carriage. Rachel was relieved, for Jason could thus remain elsewhere in the house during the meeting and not seem deliberately shunted out of the way.

Sir Bayard made Jason's exclusion from the meeting more uncomfortable by bringing Desmond along, clearly to occupy

Jason while Rachel and Sir Bayard talked. When Jason saw the two men alighting from the heavy, old-fashioned coach, he groaned. "Am I to entertain that pretty prig?"

"Try to be patient with him," Rachel begged. "He is a very silly boy but he means well."

"God preserve me from well-meaning fools. I knew enough of them in prison."

They heard voices in the foyer, the enthusiastic greeting of guests. "Sir Bayard? Master Desmond. Mr. Bourne and the mistress are in the drawing room. This way, gentlemen."

Sir Bayard walked heavily into the room, hefting his walking stick, and marched forward to greet Rachel. He gave Jason a nod before bowing over Rachel's hand. Desmond, meanwhile, sauntered in behind his father. He kissed Rachel's hand wordlessly, then shook Jason's. There was a moment of awkward silence, during which it seemed there were too many people in the room. Then Jason, remembering his position as host, signaled to Desmond. "Come along, my boy," he spoke cordially. "What do you say to a nip of something while these two talk investments and government funds?"

"Well, sir, sounds like just the thing. Mighty good to see you, Rachel. Daresay your marriage broke my heart."

She laughed. "I don't doubt it was soon mended. You never looked handsomer."

He had to be satisfied with that. Somewhat smugly, he let himself be taken away by Jason. In Rachel's opinion Jason was a little too eager to get the matter settled. It seemed probable that he had nothing to fear and she was relieved about that, but she would much rather have postponed all business as long as she could, now that the moment was at hand.

Sir Bayard massaged his side-whiskers, cleared his throat, and, worst of all, gave a furtive little look over his shoulder. Rachel resented this on Jason's account. "I shouldn't be concerned if I were you, sir. My husband is not an eavesdropper."

"No. I understand. Naturally not. A gentleman, and all that."

Rachel smiled, remembering Jason's insistence that he was "no gentleman." But aloud, she agreed. "Exactly so."

Sir Bayard had brought with him a heavy, narrow leather case that looked like a flat valise. She had seen expensive cases like this in the legal offices of London and they frightened her. They suggested crime and criminals, solemn subjects. She said lightly, "I see you have the problems of the world well in hand."

Sir Bayard merely cleared his throat. His thin knotted fingers drummed on the chair arm. "May I?" He indicated the tea table near his elbow.

She shrugged while he took out one sheaf after another. Most of the papers were not bonds and coupons as she had expected but letters, written in a broad, scrawling hand. She was not close enough to examine the writing but a cold hand seemed to clutch her heart. The letters were so very like Jason's scrawl.

She reminded herself that it was only natural. Jason had acknowledged his correspondence concerning the recent dividends. He had used her dividends to purchase railway stocks and then resold them to please Rachel. Surely, these were the letters. She decided it was good strategy to wait until Sir Bayard made his accusations and then point out to him how Jason had canceled his original orders. Doubtless, Sir Bayard would mention the losses she had sustained in the purchase and rapid sale of the new stocks. But these, of course, were Rachel's fault.

"My dear child," Sir Bayard began, "there has been a great deal of activity in your investments lately. I feel I must warn you, as an old friend, that your dear mother, God rest her soul, would be shocked."

"Oh, nonsense. Mother was not a saint, Sir Bayard. And I am persuaded that only the loss of half the kingdom would shock her."

He raised his head. His wise, kindly eyes seemed to peer into her soul, reading all her insecurities. "And the half *your* kingdom?"

"I hardly think we need concern ourselves with matters so . . . improbable."

He riffled through the papers, then took up several bonds, inserting his gnarled fingers between certain sheets to mark the problems he wished to de-emphasize. "Rachel, within two months your entire government securities and many other bonds have been reduced by nearly one half."

275

That shook her. Instinctively, she searched for answers that would eliminate her deepest fear. Had Sir Bayard been dishonest all these years? Was he in serious trouble? How easy for him to "borrow" on the funds of other trusting friends and to replace them at his leisure. Or perhaps Desmond had done so, forged names, used the money to pay gaming debts or to purchase that splendid wardrobe of his. Better yet, someone in his employ.

But she was grasping at straws. She knew. She had always known. She had been silly to think Jason could ever return her love for him. But she was certain he loved her a little. And now he was doing his best to right the situation he had created. Wasn't he?

She pulled herself together, managing a disdainful smile. "Those letters from my husband must have told you that he was following my instructions."

"I see." His aging face looked more wrinkled than ever. He fiddled with the sheaf of papers. Somewhere a clock struck half-past-four.

"As my husband, Jason has access to every shilling I own. All my properties. This house. So I don't understand your concern."

He nodded gravely. "I appreciate these facts. Trust me to know the law, at all events. But this is quite a different matter. During the past two months your properties have been systematically decimated."

"Decimated? You mean—liquidated? Sold out? Certainly. We . . . we needed the cash in hand. We are about to build a huge, magnificent mansion in Wycliffe Mount." *Wycliffe, of all places*, but her thoughts were running in circles.

Silently, he reread letters at random, still fumbling to discuss some further unpleasantness. "Rachel, my child, I could understand that. Such conversion of property to cash is almost commonplace these days."

"And in this case, I encouraged him."

"You encouraged him to make these preposterous investments?"

So it wasn't a matter of out-and-out theft. She felt a gush of relief. "We are not all as brilliant as you, Sir Bayard. I freely admit that we made some mistakes, especially when we sold those railway bonds so quickly. Or were they stocks? My husband advised me to retain the railway bonds, and I insisted he sell them. You see?"

He thumbed through the letters, found one, pulled it out, and handed it to her. She was too nervous to read it. All the words blurred and ran together, but she pretended to examine it.

Assuming she understood, Sir Bayard gestured toward the letter. "If he advised you to retain the railway bonds—"

"Which he did. He said railways would soon take the place of other modes of transportation."

"The mail coaches, for example? And the old stages?"

"Precisely." She was triumphant.

"Then why does he exchange your bonds for shares in a coach line near Bristol? And a Yorkshire stage line? The new railway has taken over most of their business. And that tin mine in Cornwall—my dear child, that mine is on the verge of shutting down. There are three or four similar investments here."

Rachel felt herself perspiring. "It was all my notion, unfortunately. It annoyed me that Jason should so often be correct. I seem to have put holes in my own pockets, as you may notice. We actually had words over some of those letters I forced him to post to you."

Sir Bayard pursed his lips as if to keep himself from saying something cross. He was probably utterly disgusted with her. He had adored her mother, adored most particularly her financial acumen. And now Rachel had destroyed that. Apparently a considerable portion of her estate was gone, and Jason was responsible.

For what purpose? None of the investments mentioned by Sir Bayard had gone into Jason's pockets. He could hardly be the owner of failing tin mines, abandoned stagecoach lines, and the rest.

Sir Bayard saw her bemused air and went fumbling on. "I do not quite understand why you failed to reply when I warned you by letter."

A creeping dread made its way into her heart. She tried to appear nonchalant. "Oh, well, a letter. You know how we were traveling constantly. I'm afraid I didn't always read everything I received. You must remember, I was on my honeymoon."

"You did not even read one of my four letters? My dear Rachel!"

Four letters had been held from her, probably burned. To Sir Bayard, Rachel's apparent dismissal of these matters must have destroyed whatever respect he may have held for her. She sounded exceedingly unlike Nicolette's daughter, and very much like a stupid heiress with no sense of duty. She was ashamed, devastated by the shock of Jason's betrayal. She had always been proud of the way she handled her estate.

Rachel smiled, a false smile, stiff and too broad. It was disavowed by the glazed look of shock that he must have noted in her eyes.

"Poor Sir Bayard! Have I disappointed you?"

Put on the defensive, he admitted, "I was always very proud of your mother. I felt that she had a mind almost as sharp as a man's. I hoped that you, too, would show a similar interest in your financial investments."

"Shocking, I know." She heard himself playing the flippant, empty-headed fool, but if she said anything remotely near the truth, she would give away her secret and, worse, perhaps burst into weak tears.

Rachel's refusal to see the gravity of the situation seemed an open affront to Sir Bayard. He began to gather up papers, bonds, letters, and his own notations. He said stiffly, "I had better delay these discussions until you are in a more serious mood. I fear that, in a manner of speaking, you are still upon your honeymoon."

She arose with him. "Yes," she said absentmindedly. "I believe that must be the answer." She put her hand out, and asked too casually, "May I keep some of the letters for a time?" He gave her a sharp look and she knew he suspected the truth. She hurried on, "I want to reread them and see just what foolishness I forced poor Jason to write."

He hesitated, his fingers shaking a little as he debated the danger of letting them get out of his hands. Surely, he knew Jason could not be prosecuted. As Rachel's husband, the estate belonged to him. Perhaps he suspected that she would destroy the letters—an action she would undoubtedly regret.

Actually, Rachel had every intention of destroying the letters, but something of her mother's cautious nature made her reconsider such impulsive, and martyred, behavior. Her sense of betrayal was too deep. She surprised her own ears by the coldness of her voice as she assured him, "Don't be alarmed. I am not quite the fool you think I am. I only wish to keep certain letters. Not all of them."

"I see." Regret and genuine feeling for her came to take the place of his brief disappointment. "As you wish. Which letters are of interest to you?"

"The stagecoach line from Yorkshire to London. And the ones immediately after the letter that sold out the railway shares. That was within the past month."

"Indeed, yes. I was appalled. I wrote to you a little more than a fortnight ago the last time, begging you to reconsider in the matter of the coach lines, if you recall."

It all seemed to be Amy Bourne's doing. That was why Rachel had received so little mail. She must ask Nahum about it. He seemed to be an honest man, even though he was faithful to the Bournes.

"Very well." She gave him her hand. "I do appreciate all you have tried to do in my behalf. Even though, as I say, it was my stubborn insistence that made Jason buy those preposterous shares."

"And bonds."

"Bonds, all of it. Then we understand each other, Sir Bayard?"

"Perfectly, child." As they walked to the foyer, he added, "I am proud to discover you are your mother's daughter, after all. I feared for a little while . . . but there. We need not discuss it. . . . You will take great care." He looked up the stairs. Desmond was hurrying down, loose-limbed and carefree as ever. He had obviously drunk his share of Jason's rum. More demerits for her husband. Sir Bayard's taste ran more toward port and Madeira.

Rachel was still secretly troubled over Sir Bayard's warning to "take great care." Jason and Sir Bayard had inclined their heads to each other with a cool formality that did not escape Rachel's notice. At the doorway Sir Bayard looked back. "Don't forget, my child," he said to Rachel. "You may always call upon me, at need."

"Of course, Sir Bayard."

Jason stood behind Rachel as she waved good-bye to the Lorimers. He had his arms around her waist, his fists under her breastbone. He was in excellent spirits and murmured into her ear, "That fellow doesn't like me. Probably thinks of me as a blackguard or an ex-convict."

"He never mentioned your past."

It was curious, she thought, that Jason seemed to have no fear of what Sir Bayard had disclosed to her.

"The boy Desmond has a taste for liquor but not a head for it."

"He isn't used to rum. It's not exactly a gentleman's drink."

He squeezed her waist. "But I keep telling you, I'm not—"

"I know." She longed to let her head rest back against his cheek, and to relax in his sensuous and skilled hands. She would have given up all the money just to know he had not deceived her. But the evidence was there before her, in her hands.

With his lips close to her ear, he suggested, "Shall we go upstairs? Now, this minute."

She was so tempted to escape with him, as though all his sins would be erased in their passion. "At this hour? Darling, it's nearly suppertime."

"We may have supper when we choose. Pretend we are back in Paris. Tell Mrs. What's-Her-Name we will not dine for an hour."

She swallowed. "Jason?" she said.

He smiled into her eyes. "We are very serious when we use that tone." His gaze shifted from her face to the folded sheaf in her hand. She felt the warmth of his arms leave her body as he backed away slowly. "Ah, business, I see." He tried to retain the light, teasing manner, but she guessed it was an effort. "There are many women, sweetheart, who would find the bedroom more enthralling than a financial report."

Her smile was set and studied. "I'm not many women, darling. I'm the daughter of Nicolette and Everett Hinton. And it took a long time to accumulate those millions. I wouldn't like them to vanish in a matter of months."

"Has something happened to your estate? What is Lorimer about?"

"Lorimer isn't about anything. He merely reminded me that my English holdings have shrunk by almost one half."

"Good god! How could that have happened?" He smiled. "Sweetheart, you shouldn't have let me sell those railway shares."

She had rolled the letters into an even tighter cylinder. "Then you still believe the railways are worth more than tin mines?"

"Tin mines?" He sounded genuinely confused. "I imagine there are tin mines and tin mines. They are not in the range of my experience. I can tell you the worth of every woolen mill in Yorkshire. Will that do?"

She refused to be distracted. "Then you would never invest in tin mines? Even if I asked you to?"

"I think the purchase of stock in antique transportation would be disastrous. Now, may we find out what the Lorimers have done to your estate?"

She handed the roll of letters to him. "Sir Bayard was forced to make those purchases. He had instructions from me."

He took the roll, shaking his head. "Rachel, we discussed this some time ago."

He unrolled the letters, recognizing his own writing. He said at once, "This is the time you objected to the railway shares I'd purchased. You recall, I asked Lorimer to repurchase those bonds in the old mail-coach company."

She said nothing and he turned to the second letter.

The house seemed very still. From the kitchen Rachel could hear the clang of a dropped pan, the stabbing of broomstraws against the wall where Alice was sweeping the hall at the head of the stairs. Out in the street there were hoofbeats and the rattle of wheels. Then silence again.

Reading and rereading the letters, Jason turned and walked into the drawing room. His dark weathered face looked pale.

Her heart was beating so fast it threatened to suffocate her. It seemed an endless time before he looked up and handed the sheaf of letters to her. "It seems clear enough."

"Jason, tell me the truth. Is this your hand?"

He shrugged. "The evidence would seem to be overwhelming. I can hardly deny my own work."

Her legs failed her and she sat down suddenly on the hard love seat. Her heavy skirts whirled out around her, and he reached over as if to support her. She avoided his eyes. He took her chin and forced her to look at him. "Sweetheart, I can sell the Bradford Mill. It's not as large as the Leeds Mill, but it may fetch more at a quick sale. Mother had an offer this spring." His grip tightened. "Please, sweetheart, you aren't listening. I have properties in Keighley that will sell eventually, with patience. And we can certainly borrow against the Leeds Mill."

She wanted more than anything to believe in his sincerity. She wondered if she could ever trust him again. Her smiled wavered. He kissed her. All the same, there was no mistaking the anxiety in his own eyes.

"We'll leave tomorrow for home," he promised. "I should have the Bradford sale well in hand by New Year's."

The property had been in the Bourne family for centuries. And he would sell it at once, to help in paying her back. But why had he done such a thing in the first place if he must sacrifice so much now? Or was this, too, a lie? Was this a bluff? Perhaps he thought she would weaken. She felt herself come perilously close to—no—she would make him prove his intentions.

But he offered no explanation.

She looked up at him, at the troubled face, the eyes that seemed to love her so deeply. She asked the one obvious question, "Why did you purchase failing companies? I could understand if you tried to make a profit. But why deliberately try to destroy my—the estate?"

He recovered his confidence. She hardly knew whether he was joking or serious when he explained. "I didn't like being married to an heiress."

This was so absurd she burst into laughter. "So you tried to reduce my worth."

"Your monetary worth."

"And now you want to pay me back? Has it occurred to you that your own estate is at stake as well?"

He stood up and turned away. He seemed absorbed in the view of the square out the windows. "That was inevitable."

Did he mean that he regretted what he had done? Did his family suspect, or were they even more closely involved? She made up her mind to settle this mystery once and for all. She would give him the chance to repay her, by New Year's, as he promised. She did not believe he could do it. In any case, their marriage would soon be over.

It had always been too good to be true. There were no Brontë heroes in real life.

NINETEEN

Home to Bourne Hall. In spite of herself, Rachel remembered many rooms in the house with warmth and affection. Besides the master bedchamber, there was Mrs. Peebles's kitchen. She even looked forward to the small parlor and the ancient drawing room with its massive beams and various comfortable corners.

Her feelings for Jason remained precarious. She loved him as much as ever, perhaps more, now that she was convinced their married life was almost over. They had not made love since the day she discovered his lies. On their last night in London he had taken her hand, looking at her with that gaze that made her tremble. Yet she found herself withdrawing from his advances as she never had before.

He understood. His mouth tensed, but in his dark eyes she read his true feelings. As if they had been discussing her estate all evening, he said thoughtfully, "The Bradford matter should give us little trouble, and I've remembered some government bonds in the family. Together, they will give you something less than half the worth of the properties you lost. The rest can be made up from loans on our other properties."

She came so close to giving in, to saying, "Let that be all. I don't want any more. I forgive you." But she couldn't. The money was less important than the lie. He had let her believe he knew nothing about the other letters, the demands that Sir Bayard make those preposterous deals, and he had condoned his mother's confiscation of her letters to and from Sir Bayard.

He made no further overtures to her on that night, or the next night in Leeds. They were almost excessively polite to each other, but in her mind what had once been between them was slowly dying.

They arrived at Bourne Hall to find the old house a flurry of activity, busy with Amy Bourne's hardworking army of local people. She appeared glad to see both Jason and Rachel.

"My dear, how good to see you," she said, embracing Rachel. "We are in desperate straits. Will you please see to the women in the lower hall. The locals simply refuse to cooperate. They will not match the hall decorations to those across the beams in the drawing room." She went on in her low, confiding voice, "You might hint that it is done thus-and-so in London."

Jason was cross. All the way home to Leeds he had been rigidly proper with Rachel. She reflected bitterly that she and Jason had regressed to the way they had been when they first met—socially correct, their conversations filled with a twist of irony.

She was glad enough to go to work and let others carry up her things, arranging her clothing in the old clothespress, while she helped the women decorate one of the archways between the hall and the drawing room. Though still suspicious of every member of the family, she was pleased when Maria joined her. Among other things, she wanted to find out if Maria knew anything about Jason's plot against her estate. Maria seemed sober and curious about what they had done in London.

"You were there so short a time. Did you see the Crystal Palace? And the opera? Wasn't that where you met Jason?"

"We had intended to go, but somehow there was always some other affair to attend." Rachel nailed up a green ribbon streamer and then a red one. She watched Maria furtively. "Sir Bayard Lorimer came to see me about my estate and some heavy losses in my British bonds."

Maria wrinkled her nose. Her thin fingers remained steady as they twisted together red and green ribbons and raised them to her. "That will give it variety."

Rachel tried again. "Are you interested in bonds and securities and such matters?"

"Ha! If it were my doing, I'd let the gentlemen play at such stupid flummery. They are forever losing, anyway. Gamesters, all of them."

"Even Jason?"

"Oh, well, Jason has a good head for such things. Let Jason have the care of your precious bonds. He'll make you rich as Croesus, I daresay."

"Does he often buy into failing companies?"

"Jason? Why, he's as sharp as Mama when it comes to money. I'm the only stupid one in the family if it's a matter of investments to deal with. Show me a sure and certain bond and inside a fortnight I'd have it reduced to tuppence."

"I suppose you would sell out railways and buy in accommodation coaches."

Maria grinned. "Very likely. I'm fond of horses. I wouldn't trade you one horse for all those great puffing black monsters. . . . You missed that spot above the clock."

Just before teatime, Jason and Nahum returned from an inspection of the sheep on the moorland. They had been afraid that an epidemic might have started up among the flocks, but luckily the fears were groundless. The sheep in question had injured itself in the local bog that Rachel recalled so well from her walk to the Heptons.

Nahum explained to Amy Bourne and the other anxious wives, "'Tis no more than a skin mold from the bog. No cause to worry."

The working women all adjourned now to the crackling fire in the small parlor and were served tea and sweet biscuits. "Like we were gentle-born," Mrs. Hepton murmured, ever pointing out how obliging their hostess was.

The other women, most of them sheepmen's wives, pretended to ignore this fawning comment. They were a proud people. They found it quite natural that they should be treated like "ladies," since they knew themselves to be anyone's equal.

Rachel liked their spirit. She thought Londoners could learn from these north country people.

Rachel went upstairs to wash and change before joining the others. She met Jason in the bedchamber—he seemed to have been waiting for her. The idea made her nervous—he was looking very businesslike and determined.

"I want you to promise me, sweetheart, you won't do anything, make any decision until I return."

"Where are you going?"

"To Bradford. I want to see the purchaser I have in mind."

And then, presumably, the slate would be rubbed clean. He would repay her, one way or another, and they would resume their married life, full of deceit and further lies. Did he honestly think she could forget so easily?

"What will be gained by that?" she said quietly.

"I will explain. I promise you. But I must repay you first."

He understood her hesitation as a promise. "I hope to be back in time for the last of the Revels tomorrow night. As they say in those novels of yours, 'I'll ride like the wind.'"

After washing in the now-cold water, she changed and went down to join that hubbub in the small parlor. All the women seemed to be talking at once. She heard Amy Bourne's voice in the kitchen doorway, her usually quiet voice raised in anger. "How could you have done such a thing? It is theft, pure and simple."

Amy had a dish of scones in her hand. She slammed it down on the old pine table in the kitchen. Several scones jumped out, and while she picked them up, Jason walked away without saying another word, either in extenuation or explanation. He departed through the pantry to the back of the building to saddle his mare for the ride to Bradford.

Rachel started forward, calling to Mrs. Bourne, "Was that Jason? Did he tell you he was going to Bradford?"

"Yes. And on the eve of the Revels. Was there ever such a man!" She reached across the table to get fresh scones. "He tells me he sold some of your property without your consent."

"Very true."

Mrs. Bourne looked down at her hand as if she wanted to avoid looking at Rachel. "The law, I believe, permits this. I would like you to know that I do not hold with it. My husband, Jason's father, would never have dared. There was not a day when he could have done as well as I have done. And for over ten years without a man's help. He will repay you and he will never touch any property of yours again."

"I know that." Rachel did not doubt the woman's sincerity.

"I trust that you do. Apparently, he thinks this marriage was a mistake. However"—she closed her eyes, then opened them abruptly—"he has changed since you came along. You've been good for him. I hope you will not make trouble for him with the bankers." She put one hand out, thought better of it, and turned away, mumbling, "Not that you could, in the legal sense. He is your husband."

Rachel could promise her nothing. It was a game of honor that she played. She had not promised Jason. She would not promise his mother. She would not lie to either.

Having received no answer, Amy picked up the plate again and moved along the festively decorated hall, her skirts swaying in a dignified way. Rachel realized that she was not nearly as noble and useful a woman as Jason's mother, but she couldn't help feeling Amy Bourne's usefulness in the world was almost excessive.

A commotion out in the little patch of garden drew Rachel to the front door. She was rather relieved at the distraction, having been involved in a boring conversation with families unknown to her.

Maria had opened the door to help Finbar, who was out on the cobblestone walk, trying to lift a fallen man. Rachel joined them and found that the man on his knees was the sheep farmer Hepton, his grizzled beard sprinkled with mud and ice. He was drunk and had tripped over a broken cobblestone. The ground was still partially frozen. Snow dappled the dead vegetation and all of the rolling moors beyond.

Hepton's black storm cloak glittered with the snow that had been gently falling. They got him to his feet. He shook himself like a great hound, muttering angrily about something Rachel could not understand. By the time she got him into the entry hall, he had worked up to fresh indignation. "What've ye done to my woman? Where's my woman? I come home to a cold house and naught but the dog and my son to greet me. I've mouths to feed. Where is she?" He struck out wildly in her direction.

Rachel eluded his fist and he fell against the paneled wall, still bellowing his outrage. Rachel tried to prop him up, but he tried to push her away.

A whirlwind seemed to tear into the fracas, and Rachel found herself under attack by Mrs. Hepton. "Lay hands to my man, will 'e, miss? 'E've no call to treat him so shabby. There, there, man. I'm with 'e. It's me. Come along, do. Aye. The night air will put us to rights." She swung around on Rachel. "'E've no call treatin' us like we was dirt. I'll do 'e a mischief, I will. Learn 'e that Hepton's a proud man. Not to be mishandled. Always interferin', are 'e? Next time . . ."

Amy Bourne made her way among the three women crowding the arched doorway. "There, Mrs. Hepton. It is over and done with. Finbar, will you . . ." But Finbar, nursing a black eye and a bruised elbow, was being helped to his quarters by Maria. Mrs. Bourne turned to a startled Dilys, who stood on the staircase with her mouth open. "Will you help Mrs. Hepton? Ask Cook for some basilicum ointment. It should take care of those bruises."

She then returned to the small parlor, shooing the women in with her as though they were cackling hens. "It is a cross the poor woman bears. She is quite saintly about it, I do swear. But I daresay he means well when he is sober. It is a pity he has taken such a dislike to my daughter-in-law."

Resentfully, Rachel noted that he had behaved in the same way to Maria and Finbar. Hepton's heavy black muffler had fallen on the doorstep. She picked it up and threw it around her shoulders. She walked to the back of the house, where the moors and dells beyond spread out to the eastern horizon. Rachel was always conscious of the old, abandoned farm on the northern horizon and stared up that slope, trying to make out the huddle of buildings more clearly. Suddenly Nahum appeared behind her. His light hair was already sprinkled with a few snowflakes, and in the gray-white light of the snowy landscape he looked rather ghostly.

"Is that old farm inhabited?" Rachel asked him.

"Oh, aye. It's used for picnics, and that. I've walked to Wycliffe over that hill, and on to Keighley. Took a pony cart once, we did, Mrs. Amy and me, with Miss Maria betwixt us. Miss Maria's shoulder was giving her bad pain and Haworth road was closed by a crossing accident. Sheep wagon and Colonel Oakley's gig come to fists over who had the right of way."

Rachel looked up the exposed and weathered slope to the huddle of buildings the locals called the Withins. Nahum had not mentioned Jason.

"Was that while my husband was . . . away?"

"Aye. Whilst he was away to prison."

"I have the impression his neighbors hereabouts sympathized with him, that they thought none the worse of him for what happened."

"That'll be the truth on it, ma'am. Them two London swells as caused it was deserving of worse and they put him to prison false-like."

The mention of Jason's name brought her a pain burning like a physical blow. How long before that pain would ease? Perhaps he couldn't help himself when he committed those crimes, told those lies. Maybe there was a reason. If she could only believe there was a reason overriding all else, she could go on loving him. Suddenly weary, she said good-night to Nahum.

She went to bed depressed and alone that night, but the next day was Christmas Eve. The Revels would begin at five o'clock, and neither Rachel nor anyone else had time to be melancholy. Rachel had dreamed that Sir Bayard visited her, sad-faced and apologetic, confessing all the accusations against Jason were merely an untimely jest.

For some reason the dream soothed her. She found herself believing it was a sign. It meant, somehow, that Jason was innocent.

TWENTY

Everyone arrived at the Hall in good spirits. Heavy boots tramping over the village trail had marked a path across the moor. The Haworth road was likewise devoid of snow except for a few drifts of kicked-up mud and debris.

Looking toward the northern horizon, Rachel saw tracks carved over the melting snow on what she assumed was a footpath past the abandoned black silhouette of the Withins.

Remembering that Nahum had taken the pony cart over that trail, she almost envied him. Someday, perhaps she and Jason would walk there, carrying a lunch. Surely, if he recovered what he had destroyed, he could be welcomed back? Forgiven?

Hearing the fiddlers tuning up, she went down to await the first guests. She had chosen her dress carefully, dismissing the elaborate ball gown she would have worn in London or Paris. The deep-rose taffeta gown had long sleeves slit to show the white silk sleeve beneath and, with its triple-tiered skirts, was guaranteed to keep her from drafts on the chill winter night.

Her light chestnut hair shown richly in the light of candles, wall sconces, and oil lamps. Dilys had arranged her hair, permit-

ting the more unruly strands to creep out around her face, reliev-
ing the severity of the fashionable style. The effect was somewhat diminished by the early arrivals, friends of Amy Bourne's
from Keighley, each of whom arrived in full ball dress, complete
with bared arms, plus bare bosom and shoulders, a great deal of
floating gauze and festoons of lace.

Rachel told herself that she was being correct. The others had
dressed absurdly for this climate and for the time of year. All the
same, she felt a trifle underdressed. Her only consolation was
that Amy Bourne and Maria likewise wore long-sleeved winter
gowns. Maria came after Rachel, grumbling. "My basque is too
tight. I can scarcely breathe. Mrs. Hodges always scrimps on
materials. I should have gone to Bradford to have it done
properly."

Rachel thought Maria looked elegant. She was wearing
maidenly white, not her best color, but a set of topaz jewelry did
wonders to bring out the haunting beauty of her hazel eyes.

"You look splendid. If Prince Louis Napoleon could see you
now, you would be Princess Maria in the wink of an eye."

Maria gave a hoot of laughter. "My dream was to be Princess
Culhane. I wonder who that lucky bride will be."

Rachel thought at once of the obvious candidate. She had a
strong suspicion that Cecily Debenham had not brought about
the exposure of Maria's past out of pure altruism or high moral
standards.

But she hoped there were more pleasant matters to occupy
Maria. Nahum was organizing the musicians, discussing sheep
problems with one male guest, mill problems with another, and
generally making himself indispensable.

"Amy counts on Nahum a great deal," Rachel remarked carefully. "He seems to be a thorough gentleman."

But Maria was not interested. "Good heavens! He's not my
sort at all. I like a man whose edges are refined."

"I guess I didn't know. I hoped—"

"Well, don't! Nahum? He's a heavy-handed, coarse-talking
farmer. When I've been loved by gentlemen like Edward
Culhane and . . . Never mind!" She walked away.

Rachel hoped Nahum hadn't heard Maria's shrill voice, but as
he crossed the hall with an extra chair for crotchety Colonel

Oakley, he gave Rachel a wry little smile. She was sorry. It seemed unjust. He was a fine, handsome, decent man. Why couldn't Maria see that?

Why couldn't I love someone other than Jason? she asked herself. You couldn't force love. Perhaps you couldn't force yourself to forget love.

She drifted back into the kitchen, which was scented with the spicy aroma of apples. The whole house smelled of apples. And spiced cakes, scones, and heavy cider, along with grog and hot rum and Madeira or port for the elegant guests. Rachel was astonished at the amount of people who turned out for the event. She had no idea the Bournes had so many acquaintances. Once she came upon Amy Bourne in the kitchen leaning tiredly against the table.

"Are you ill? May I get something for you? Wine?"

Amy brushed aside the offer. "Thank you, no. Water will do. I'm afraid I am growing too old for this sort of thing. The noise, the voices, the confusion." She drank from a scarred pewter cup, remarking over its brim, "And I am worried. Jason told me of the losses incurred from his misuse of your property." She looked suddenly old and fragile. Her voice broke. With painful intensity she said, "The sacrifice he is undertaking to make good those losses is a grave one. Are you certain he is guilty?"

She poured the rest of the water into the pan beside her hand. "We will lose everything. Almost two centuries of work and struggle and hardship have gone into the Bourne properties. After Bradford, he intends to take loans on the Leeds Mill. There will be nothing left."

Feeling as if she herself had committed the crime, Rachel ventured, "Perhaps it won't be necessary to make the larger loan. He said he would sell the Bradford Mill. And some other things. . . ." Her voice trailed off. She couldn't bring herself to say, "Forget the entire debt. Let us go on as before. Let us trust each other. Let us keep lying to each other." She couldn't say it. Perhaps to Jason, but not to Amy Bourne. She couldn't help sensing that she was being manipulated, and it angered her.

She said, "I'm sorry," and left the kitchen.

Back in the parlor she found Miss Oakley was enthroned in a corner, where she could criticize the dancers, who were laughing, boasting, flirting, and enjoying themselves to the tune of fiddles, a drum, and Maria's flying fingers at the pianoforte. The woman motioned to Rachel. "Where might your husband be, Mrs. Jason?"

"In Bradford, ma'am. He's pursuing an offer for the sale of the smaller mill."

Miss Oakley frowned and pinched Rachel's hand, drawing her closer. "I don't like the sound of that, my girl. You'll not find a better family to look out for its people than the Bournes. If they must sell out, it will be a great calamity for the area."

"I'm sure you are right, ma'am."

"Well then, my girl, rumor says your father, this Etheredge man, left you very well breeched."

Was there a conspiracy abroad? Rachel would not have been surprised to learn that Amy had urged this conversation upon her good friend.

"Mr. Etheredge was very kind to me, but he was not my father."

"Indeed! I had no notion." She looked over Rachel's shoulder. "Amy, why doesn't our Jason apply his wife's riches to preserve the mills? He does us all a disservice by his whims. He should think of us."

Amy looked pale and tense. "These matters cannot concern my daughter-in-law. She is not a Bourne, nor is she a native of the land."

Miss Oakley sniffed. "Come and sit beside me, Amy. You look exhausted. Now, what is this about the girl's father not being Etheredge, that rich nabob? You'll not be telling me there was something havey-cavey in her parentage."

"Hardly, ma'am," Rachel put in, less offended than amused. "My mother was widowed when she married Mr. Etheredge. My father was actually a good Yorkshireman, born near the edge of the shire. He—"

"Jason is expected by morning," Amy put in unexpectedly. "He knows how disappointed the family would be if he were to delay his return past Christmas day."

"A cold Christmas will greet him, mark me. I felt the wind from the west when we arrived tonight. It was wuthering."

Nahum Cload came by and Miss Oakley signaled to him with

a long, knotted forefinger. "There's a waltz, my boy. I am persuaded this young lady will not take it amiss if you lead her into the dance."

Nahum's eyes questioned Rachel, who smiled in agreement. She had always pictured herself dancing in her husband's arms on the night of the Christmas Eve Revels. But the music was sweet and tempting, so she gave herself into his arms and they whirled out among the bright, full skirts and the black trousers of the other dancers. Since she had hoped to play matchmaker between her earnest partner and Maria, it was disappointing to see how little Maria cared to see them thus entwined. As Maria's fingers danced over the keys, her eyes dreamy, she was no doubt remembering those dances with Edward at the Elysée ball.

The Reverend Brontë's daughter arrived well into the evening, wearing the plain puce-colored gown she had worn to the Italian Opera in London. Rachel very much wanted a chance to talk with her, but she stayed only long enough for a courtesy call, inquired after Miss Oakley's rheumatism, gave Maria an unexpectedly sweet and friendly smile, then spoke with Amy for a few minutes.

Rachel steered Nahum close to the women so that she could overhear the conversation. News certainly traveled fast in the West Riding. Miss Brontë was concerned that the Bournes might sell the Bradford Mill. "It will bring bad times again, Mrs. Bourne. A calamity. There will be the men out of work. The women and children hungry as before."

Amy said hoarsely, "No one knows better. But it must be. We owe a debt." She paused. "A debt of honor."

Miss Brontë inclined her neat, austere head. She looked around at the dancers with a wistful expression, then said abruptly, "I must go. My father will wish me to read to him." She bade Amy good-night, then departed.

The dancers had broken into small groups and were roaming the lower floor, most of them having filled their plates with pasties and other food. Nahum offered to fetch Rachel a plate, but the sound of a woman sobbing in the kitchen drew him away from the buffet table. It was Mrs. Hepton.

Amy was there comforting her. "You don't mean that," she scolded. "So stop talking nonsense." She looked around and motioned to Nahum. "You will have to go after Hepton. The man tried to beat his wife, and she is determined to leave him."

"Aye, ma'am. And what do I do with him?"

Amy Bourne shrugged. "He should be remanded into custody. Such aggression cannot be tolerated."

"Beg pardon, ma'am, but Mr. Jason will be out-of-reason cross. He says there's hope in the fellow."

"My son isn't being systematically beaten by that brute."

"I'll go across to the farm."

Mrs. Hepton raised her head, swiped a hand across her tear-streaked face, and glanced at Amy Bourne. "The man's not to the farm. "'E may look to see Hepton by the village path. Off to the Black Bull, he was, for more to drink."

"Yes, go to the village," Mrs. Bourne agreed. "Perhaps one of the men at the Black Bull will help you."

Nahum hesitated. "If Mister Jason comes home while I'm away, would you be good enough to tell him it was your order, ma'am? Him being Hepton's champion, and that."

Mrs. Bourne smiled grimly. "Very well. I'll relieve you of my son's wrath."

While they had been arguing, Cecily Debenham, arriving appropriately late in the evening, was exchanging superficial greetings with guests who sat on the stairs eating their late supper before departing. It was hard to guess who disliked Cecily more—Rachel or Amy. She was dressed gorgeously for the occasion, and accompanied by her doting father. Mr. Wentworth helped Dilys remove Cecily's fur-trimmed cloak, revealing an elaborate purple gown hung with jet beads—a tribute to her mourning, Rachel thought cynically. But all in all, the golden-haired beauty was as coldly dazzling as ever.

Mrs. Bourne put out both hands as if to stop the unwanted guests from entering the drawing room. But there were too many witnesses, guests in cloaks and shawls ready to leave, the younger guests still eating, and other curious eyes staring from doorways and the long main hall. Rachel shared Amy's passion to be rid of Cecily, but she understood the consequences of such rudeness. Whatever details of Maria's early trouble had not been known before would certainly be spread to the winds if they made a scene with the widow now.

"Dear ma'am," Cecily gushed, "do forgive us for what can only be regarded by you as an intrusion. My dearest papa thought, in the most cowardly way—excuse me, Papa—that we should let things simply take their course, but I said, 'No, Papa. I am a firm believer in honesty above all else. I abhor even the shadow of deception.' My visit has to do with dear Maria. Is she about?"

"Maria is otherwise occupied. As you see, Mrs. Debenham, we are entertaining. The annual Revels, you know. I am afraid you would be better off to follow your father's advice, cowardly though it may be."

As if signaled, Nahum Cload pushed his way through the crowded hall. "Do you need me, ma'am?"

"No," she said shortly and added for the benefit of her other guests, "Go and find Hepton. He seems to be rampaging over the moor."

"Aye, ma'am." He went out the front door without giving any indication that he saw the new arrivals.

Cecily looked after him, her flawless cheeks reddening. Mr. Wentworth fussed around apologetically, rubbing his palms. "I wonder, ma'am, if I might trouble you for a drop of something warm. A rumfustian, perhaps. Or brandy. Or even Madeira."

His polite and commonplace request shook Rachel to her senses. She hurriedly found him a glass and poured some wine while Maria asked Rachel sharply, "What the devil does that creature want with us?"

Rachel forced a smile. "A mere glass of something warm."

"Well, I for one have no intention of receiving them." Nevertheless, she lingered near the side table with its collection of filled glasses and pewter mugs.

Rachel wondered uneasily if she was contemplating a glass herself, but Maria drummed her fingers, studied Rachel's face, and said with justifiable annoyance, "I am drinking only cider tonight, so you may relax your vigil. . . . Why on earth are they here? I don't like that woman's smug look."

Meanwhile, Mrs. Bourne turned from her unwanted guests to accept the thanks and holiday wishes of several families who were leaving. Mr. Wentworth drank his wine, settling in a tall-backed chair with a sigh of pleasure. It looked very much as though he intended to stay for a pleasant hour. "Excellent," he murmured of the wine and reached for Rachel's arm, patting the taffeta sleeve. "Such a devoted little wife, it is!"

Flashing a false smile, she moved out of his reach and was soon busy helping Dilys send off happy guests into a cold, crisp night, where stars dotted the eastern sky.

Deeply aware of the Wentworths waiting in the house, Rachel returned, relieved to see that Cecily had asked for her cloak. Mr. Wentworth was accepting another glass of Madeira from Dilys. His pleasant round face beamed. Mrs. Bourne, having apparently resigned herself to the man's presence, sat with great dignity in a hard-backed settle, sipping a tiny glass of port. Maria made her way over to the group, obviously sensing a confrontation of some sort. She pretended to watch the musicians picking up their property, but it seemed to Rachel that she was tensely awaiting whatever "scrupulously honest" communication Cecily had to offer.

The widow made a little gesture like a prayer, with both hands clasped, but her radiant face contradicted the pious gesture. "I felt that it would really be too cruel—and I am never *consciously* cruel to my fellow man—if you were forced to hear the truth from some wretched gossip determined only to cause you pain."

Rachel, guessing immediately what the secret was, despised the woman for her theatrics. But it was Amy who topped Cecily of her grandest scene yet. She waved away the suspense with a fine show of impatience. "Surely you have not come such a distance merely for the purpose of announcing your betrothal."

Cecily was shaken and speechless, but Mr. Wentworth, truly impressed, burst out, "Good God, but news travels fast! How might you have known, madame?"

"Edward Culhane is a dear and valued friend," she remarked, rather cleverly, Rachel thought. "It is understandable that he would wish to impart such fine news."

It was all a lie, but it gave Maria a chance to recover, and it nearly crushed all of Cecily Debenham's malicious pleasure.

"He told you? He was expressly warned—I mean to say, how could he? We had agreed!"

"But he is such an old friend, and I daresay he wished to confide in us, to seek our advice, in a manner of speaking."

Rachel wanted to applaud this remarkable improvisation. Whatever it had done to mar Cecily's opinion of her betrothed, the news of Edward's indiscretion certainly lowered his standing in his prospective father-in-law's eyes. "What damned—pardon, ladies, but there is no other word for it—damned effrontery, to ask your opinion of his proposal to my daughter!"

"They are all cut from the same cloth," Maria put in unexpectedly, with a show of teeth. "Little men, all of them. Little and unworthy."

Outraged, Cecily rose suddenly and wrapped her cloak around her. She was joined by her father, still puffing with indignation. They passed into the entry hall, more or less ushered out by the three Bourne women.

But Cecily was determined to save face. In the open doorway she offered one last parting word to Maria. "I would certainly not put Edward Culhane into a class with your precious Everett Hinton. Mr. Hinton may have been a fine London dandy but he abandoned you in a most ungentlemanly manner. Edward, as we both know, would never do such a thing. And then, to sneak away and let Lord Branscomb send Jason to that odious prison! No, indeed. My Edward is vastly superior to that scoundrel."

She and her father marched out over the cobblestones to their team, leaving the three women staring speechlessly out into the cold brilliant night.

TWENTY-ONE

Maria spoke first. "A bitch in a kennel is worth a hundred of that one."

Her mother grimaced as she closed the door. "Maria, such language does not suit you." She moved through the hall, then groped for the newel post as if she had lost all strength. Nobody looked at Rachel.

She stood near the door, fingering the heavy lace curtain, looking out at the snow-dappled landscape. For at least a full minute she had stood there with her head spinning. Her thoughts assaulted her, one after another.

It was all amazing coincidence. Who would have thought Maria's seducer had the same name as Rachel's father? And the next coincidence—her father *was* quite a lad with the ladies. He had returned to Yorkshire on Tory business many times in the mid-thirties. He must have broken many hearts. Maria's seducer was married, a gentleman who treated her abominably.

Physically Everett Hinton was very like Edward Culhane in so many ways. She had noticed it herself. And Maria admitted that she had been drawn to the same type both times.

And as she realized there was no hope of a mistake, the horror grew. Endless, tangled pictures, memories flashed through her brain. The night at the Italian Opera when Jason's indifference to her suddenly changed after they were properly introduced. It was not Rachel Etheredge who interested him but Rachel Hinton, daughter of the man who had destroyed him and his family. It was not love but hatred and revenge that drove him into their marriage.

She remembered the endless tricks that disturbed her so much, her appearing and disappearing handkerchief at Scarborough, the check to Madame Bertrand for the lease of the Paris flat, the accusation that she had written a ten-thousand-franc check instead of the one thousand due Madame Bertrand. It had all been part of Jason's revenge, to confuse her, make her suffer that uneasiness.

And lastly, she wondered if the words Jason had used to belittle their marriage, his referral to it as "medieval," had been one more function of that revenge.

Rachel straightened to her full height and walked toward the stairs. Amy Bourne stood in her way. "Rachel, we must talk."

Rachel moved her arm aside, firmly but without violence. "There is only one thing I can do, Mrs. Bourne. I must leave this place." She went around her mother-in-law and up the stairs. She heard Maria's call, tentative, almost afraid. "Rachel?" followed by her mother's tired voice: "It was inevitable. Someone was bound to mention the name."

"But why. . . ?" Maria's voice faded to a tense whisper.

Rachel went into the big bedchamber and closed the door. She looked through the floor of the big clothespress, cleared away shoes and boots, and found one of her small valises. As she pulled the valise out, one of Jason's boots fell into her arms. She found herself embracing the boot while her head buzzed with fear and disbelief. She searched her memory and found many clues.

His sleeplessness at night. When she saw him at the window across the room he had looked haunted, sad. Obviously, he regretted what he was determined to do. Revenge must be a saddening task. How much easier to walk away from an enemy, begin a new life with no regrets or bitter debts to repay.

But, of course, Jason had ten years to plan his revenge. Ten ghastly years.

And how could her gentle father have committed such crimes, first against sixteen-year-old Maria, then, apparently maneuvering with a Tory aristocrat, to destroy Maria's brother? She set the boot back in the clothespress.

How do I know it is all true? If Jason tried to kill Father, and perhaps that Lord Branscomb, why would he not be condemned? As for Maria, I saw how desperately she pursued Edward Culhane. Was it possible, even probable, that she led Father on?

Disgusting. A vile excuse. Rachel hardly recognized herself in this woman who made excuses for a man like her father. She had always known he was a rake and a seducer. An adulterer killed in the act of adultery. Perhaps Nicolette had known about his adventures in Yorkshire. It may have explained why she pressed so urgently for her daughter to accept the Etheredge name.

The greatest hurt was the knowledge of the hatred that Jason and his family must feel for her. They despised her, as she would despise anyone who belonged to a family that so terribly hurt her and those she loved.

I must go, she told herself. She could never face them again as a member of the family, or as a guest. She recalled Maria's desperate cries of hatred, in London and then in Paris: "You fool. You are such a stupid fool!"

Amy Bourne's antagonism, too, was clear. It was only natural for Jason's mother and sister to involve themselves in his personal revenge. Jason himself had mentioned "owing" something to old friends. . . . He had come to pay them back.

She knew Jason regretted the necessity of his revenge. She knew he had probably come to love her a little. He was too fine a man to have remained so bitter toward Edward Hinton's child. She believed that he meant to make amends. He was honest about selling the Bradford Mill and making up the sums in other ways. But all that had nothing to do with love. It was impossible that he could *love* Edward Hinton's daughter.

She shoved a nightrobe, a shift, and a pair of stockings into the valise and considered her dress. Not really suitable for travel. She pulled it off her body, first the basque, then the heavy skirts, then the white silk underblouse. She tore away the many silk-covered buttons of the basque. They showered the old, worn carpet. Within minutes she had changed to a heavy grosgrain travel dress, jacket, and travel cloak. Her deep-blue silk travel bonnet was somewhere in the clothespress. She was still searching for it when someone knocked on the door.

She stiffened with nervousness and a growing dread. She did not answer. She prayed they would go away.

The blue silk bonnet was at the very back of the high shelf in the clothespress and she stood on tiptoe to reach it. While she struggled to touch the elegant, if battered, black bandbox, the hall door opened and Maria stuck her head in. "Rachel? Please let me talk to you."

Every kind word from Maria was like a drop of acid, stinging and wounding her. Maria closed the door carefully. She was more nervous than usual. "What a dreadful Christmas Eve!" An attempt at a smile flickered across her face and died away. "That Hepton woman wants Mother to take her to her sister's in Keighley. At this hour, can you imagine? Why doesn't she manage her own affairs and leave us to ours?"

Rachel said quietly, "I am going to Keighley—or somewhere—myself. And tonight."

"Rachel, don't. Wait for Jason. Hear the whole story from him. Give him a chance to explain."

Rachel stopped reaching for the bandbox long enough to remark with quiet awe, "How you must hate me!"

To her surprise Maria blinked and waved away imaginary cobwebs. "But that's over and done. I feel sorry for you now. I do realize you had nothing to do with Edward's betrayal of me. Jason made me see it, too. *He loves you so much.* You can't imagine how much. Please let him try and tell you how it was."

Rachel touched her slightly stiffened arm. "It isn't Edward Culhane. It is Everett Hinton. And what he did to you that I can't forget. And if I can't forget, how can you? He wronged you so deeply."

Maria shrugged. "Something happens when you fall in love again. The first love begins to fade. The pain eases. I lived with all that bitterness too long. I wish I hadn't. Don't go, Rachel. Wait for Jason."

Without looking into the mirror, Rachel slapped her bonnet

on her head and tied the grosgrain ribbons at the side of her chin. Maria watched her helplessly. "If you could hear how Jason talks to me! He said only last Sunday after church that it had been what he called 'an abomination,' treating you that way."

"What are you talking about?"

"When you and Jason used to quarrel it would trigger his obsession with the revenge. He must have thought of nothing but that revenge all the time he was in prison. Rachel, they locked him up in such hideous places." She shuddered. Then with a last hope of persuasion, she moved to cut Rachel off from the door. "He didn't intend to kill your father or Lord Branscomb but he'd just found me in the street. He was almost insane with rage."

"I can well understand. I would have been outraged, too." Rachel stopped to ask curiously, "Did Mrs. Debenham defend him at the time?"

"It was Cecily Wentworth's contempt for me that broke off the betrothal before Jason was arrested that night. He brought me to the Wentworth house. The incident with Lord Branscomb came later. Jason had struck your father, and Lord Branscomb charged him with murderous assault."

"And the assault was really because of you?"

"It had nothing to do with politics," Maria repeated impatiently. "Everett was married and didn't want a scandal, and Jason would never involve my name."

"It might have saved Jason from prison if the real facts were known."

Maria nodded. "I know that now; so you see, we all commit terrible acts, sometimes unconsciously. Rachel, do you understand what I am saying?"

"Yes, I do," she admitted sadly. "The one good thing that came of this wretched business was that I think we could have been friends, if only others had not made it impossible."

In the doorway she heard Maria's last plea, "Don't do this, Rachel. Not tonight."

Rachel closed the door gently, carrying her valise. The upper floor was empty and dark, but there were lights somewhere downstairs. She contemplated walking across the moor trail to the village. Those open spaces held less horror for her now that they might be a means of escape. But on the village path she was sure to meet Revels guests. If she could only take another direction!

On the lower floor she encountered Amy, dressed to go out in the cold December night. She had wrapped herself in an ancient homespun cloak and wore boots, which were revealed below her dark skirts when she moved. She had completely changed from the brown silk Revels gown.

Startled, Rachel asked, "Are you going out?"

Mrs. Bourne said grimly, "I was, but it appears that one hot posset has sent Mrs. Hepton off to sleep. I have put her into the room back of the service quarters. At all events, it stopped her demands to be taken to her sister's place. She will stay the night here." She looked Rachel over, showing neither surprise nor pleasure, simply the well-bred indifference she had always shown. "You have made your own decision, I see. Forgive me if I say, you are being perhaps too hasty."

"I must go." Then she asked after some thought, "Where are you taking Mrs. Hepton? Are you walking?"

"I am—or was—taking the gig and our mare, Blinker. Mrs. Hepton didn't want to chance meeting my son or her drunken husband on the way to the village."

It was too much to hope for. Rachel ventured hesitantly, "Is there some way I could take the cart to Keighley?"

Amy Bourne was abrupt and superior. "I intended to go over the Withins Rise. I'm afraid that would be long and tedious for a person unfamiliar with the trail."

All the same, Rachel thought the woman's expression had softened a trifle. It was the moment to throw all the dice, discover whether the woman would help her or not. "You were prepared to go to Keighley tonight. Could you possibly take me in place of Mrs. Hepton?"

Amy Bourne looked down at her own heavy travel clothing. "I am certainly not ready to sleep. Cecily Wentworth has remedied that matter for all of us. But frankly, I will not be sorry to see you gone, though I would have preferred a more civilized hour."

Rachel said, "I understand. I never knew the truth before. Is there somewhere we may rest briefly in Keighley, before you return to the Hall? And before I take the railway cars to London?"

"Mrs. Hepton's sister has lodgings there. I think I might get there and return if I had something to warm me first. A cup of hot tea perhaps." She smiled for the first time. "With a spoonful of brandy. Yes. I might. Would you care to join me?"

"Thank you. I would like that very much. I want to get as far as possible before Jason comes home. I'm sure you understand."

Jason's mother agreed. "He can be persuasive. But he was always weak. Like his father. Easily swayed by his affections. It was I who had to stand as the rod and staff of the family, as you have seen. Come. There must still be water on the hob. Hepton's wife drank her share of the liquor but there might be a little left. I do not believe in cosseting myself with strong spirits."

In the kitchen she set about making tea, while Rachel, for want of something to occupy her nervous hands, threw the last of Mrs. Hepton's now-cold "posset" in the slop jar. The hot water was soon ready, and Mrs. Bourne poured two mugs of tea, dosing them with brandy from a bottle in which only the dregs remained.

As they sipped the steaming brew, they heard neighing protests from the road in front of the house. Mrs. Bourne gasped. "Blinker! I left her in harness. I meant to get Mrs. Hepton and hurry out. Poor animal!" She hurried out to soothe the fretting mare.

The tea warmed Rachel, but it was bitter and strong. She poured most of it into the slop jar before she got up to follow Amy outside.

She was holding a storm lantern, which shone on the two-wheeled gig. Harnessed to it, the vigorous young mare was stamping impatiently on the frozen ground. Amy hung the lantern with its metal protectors on the side of the gig. As Rachel got into the cart, she noted the bright patch of stars toward the east and was relieved that it looked better than the westerly direction, where the night was gray-white with a promise of fresh snow.

"I want to get back by midnight if I can," Amy said, taking up the reins.

"Will that be possible?"

"I think it is important that I be home when Jason returns." There was no sound in the snowy stillness except the clip-clop of the mare along one of the narrow wheel ruts. Rachel felt the sickening finality of Amy Bourne's words. She could almost hear Jason's Amy telling him in her calm way, "It is for the best. She never belonged here. She was Everett Hinton's daughter, after all."

Amy indicated a turn along the light reins, and the mare obediently trotted off the narrow road and onto the snow-covered, rising moorland. The gig jumped about as the two big wheels carved new ruts in the thin layer of snow. The mare had better luck. One or two other horses had gone before her for some distance over the undulating ground that began its climb shortly after.

Amy Bourne's hand trembled on the reins as she yawned and apologized. "Perhaps I am not quite so wide awake as I thought."

Her yawn was contagious. Rachel found herself sleepy. "It is very likely the brandy." But she thought it was also the after-effect of her shock. They plodded along at a much slower pace as the climb began. The patch of stars overhead became gradually shadowed by clouds as the great western blanket of sky that promised snow moved eastward toward them. There was an insidious dry cold to the night air. It crept around them so deceptively Rachel was hardly aware of it until she found herself stomping her feet, still in their thin evening pumps.

"Is there any danger in this cold? Do people get lost and freeze to death?"

"Outlanders are forever getting lost. Strangers from outside the Riding. But freezing to death is exceedingly uncommon. You need not be so frightened."

The contempt was unmasked.

"I am not frightened," Rachel insisted. "Only curious."

She settled back again, lulled by the stillness and the somnolence that began to creep over her. She opened her eyes minutes later. They were moving upward through a powdery snowfall toward the crouching dark farm buildings she had seen so often from Bourne Hall.

"Go back to sleep," Amy urged, her own voice surprisingly animated. "When you wake up we may be in sight of our destination."

No talk of her own sleepiness now. Amy Bourne was very much in her element.

Rachel thought, *I must remember that she is my enemy and was my enemy when I was ten years old.* She also remembered the strong tea with the spoonful of brandy. She wondered what else may have been in that tea. How fortunate that she hadn't drunk it all! As her suspicions grew, it occurred to Rachel to play along with Mrs. Bourne's game. If it came to physical combat, she was reasonably sure she would be the stronger woman. Life and heat returned to her limbs, as she considered the prospect of danger.

She yawned exaggeratedly and sighed, huddling in her cloak. "Darling . . ." she murmured like one in a dream.

As she had guessed, Amy was disconcerted by the endearment. "Sleep on, girl. We are nearly there."

"Where. . . ?"

But Amy did not answer, merely clucked to the horse. Soon they stopped abruptly.

Rachel opened one eye. They had pulled up opposite the first of several small shacks attached to the main, low-roofed farmhouse of Withins. From a lesser distance the structure appeared far smaller and yet more sinister through the falling snow.

"Asleep?"

"Um," Rachel said.

"Sleep on, girl."

Mrs. Bourne got down from the gig and stood beside the mare for a minute in the snow. Then she went around to the other side. Why had she released the mare from the shafts? Obviously she intended to abandon Rachel, but was she planning on making her own way on foot?

Yawning and confused, Rachel climbed down over the wheel. Suddenly Amy gave Blinker a hard swat across the flank. "Go home, Blinker! Home!"

The mare, finding herself free of the harness, plodded around in a circle until Amy urged her on, and she headed back down the narrow path.

TWENTY-TWO

Rachel had no doubt she could follow the mare's path down the slope and across the moors, but she wanted to be quite certain she read Amy Bourne's plan correctly. The main door of the farmhouse appeared to be securely locked. Rachel watched Amy fumbling with a lock on one of the farm's outbuildings. It seemed the whole structure would tumble down upon her under the strain. The broken roof was piled high with snow and the windblown debris of autumn. Snowy leaves, juniper, and dirt showered her. The wood squeaked in protest.

Rachel, fighting back grogginess, watched all this with a vague fascination. She had never consciously met anyone who was willing to commit murder for revenge or for money. She rubbed her hands under her cloak and steeled herself against the creeping terror she felt.

"Come," Amy Bourne said in her quiet way. "I'll help you. It will be warmer over there."

Rachel played the part expected of her, weakly leaning against the big wheel of the gig. She stepped into a snowdrift with her ridiculous and inadequate shoes, almost losing her balance. She reached for Amy, who kept tight hold of her wrist. Wondering how she hoped to explain this sinister business, Rachel protested feebly, "Jason will never forgive you. You will be found out."

Amy Bourne's grim smile looked hellish in the light from the flickering lantern beside her. "I think not. He protected me when those prying friends of yours questioned the letters."

In this desolate freezing place at the top of the world the warm glow of new life came to Rachel. She almost forgot to play her role of the easy victim. "But Jason is protected by law. You aren't. You could go to prison for the rest of your life, for stealing from me."

"And you think my boy would see that happen? Never. Come along. I have things to do. I must stop the Bradford sale. You are making this unnecessarily painful for yourself."

"But I don't want to die," Rachel pleaded, marveling at her own cunning.

"You are dead already. There was enough laudanum in that tea to put you under the sod in minutes."

Good God, how lucky that she hadn't finished the mug! "You are going to leave me in the snow to die?"

"It's you who are callous. The sale of our mill would turn out hundreds of workers and their families to starve. Just so you might live above the rest in your fine London palace. My son swore the Hintons would pay. But he is weak, like his father. He destroyed all your plans to ruin you. Love! Bah! Lust is more like it."

Rachel braced herself. Even her snow-covered feet became warm with the surge of triumph. Jason loved her, and he had loved her throughout most of their marriage. The knowledge gave her strength. "I won't go any farther. Why do you want me by that shed?"

"You will sleep here, at the door. Soft. Sheltered. You see? But alas! The shed collapsed. Everyone knows it is liable to go at any time. Children are always warned. And you were trapped, poor thing!"

Amy reached for her. Rachel felt one last surge of energy, and pushed Amy against the ancient and warped door. The wood screeched again. Amy had been knocked, breathless and stunned. Her back supported the trembling wall.

"So that is the way of it?" Her face was ashen. She looked dead, except for her thin mouth, which seemed to move, though no sound came out. She left the wall, hurling herself at Rachel, who leaped aside as the wooden timbers of the wall fell outward, showering the area with wood and thatch and great billowing clouds of snow.

The wall of the little farm building itself, with part of the timbers left standing, fell across the gig, overturning the lantern. In seconds the wet thatch began to smoke. Fire from the oil inside the lantern ignited the dry splinters of wooden beams that had held up the shed.

Digging herself out of the snow, shivering, her teeth chattering, Rachel found a handful of fleece in her fingers. The shed must have been used for a sheepshearing at one time. She got to her feet, stamped on a wooden plank to restore circulation, and swung around in a panic. She had only screamed once, when the wall fell outward upon Mrs. Bourne. Screaming was pointless. Who would hear her up here so far from any human being?

She stumbled through the snow to the splintered boards that covered Amy. Somewhere underneath, at one end of the wall, a fire was nibbling away, while the snow fell gently over the scene.

She felt around the edges of the splintered boards trying to get a hold on them. Her chief regret at this moment was that in her hurry to leave Bourne Hall she had forgotten her gloves. Her fingers were paralyzed with cold. She shifted one leg under the edge of the wall to use as a jack. Thus she raised the planks.

Amy groaned faintly. Her head was free after Rachel threw aside two boards and quantities of new-fallen snow. One of Amy's hands fluttered at the splintering edge of the wooden blanket that covered her. Rachel got behind her, feeling her own hips and legs sink into the snow as she tried to get a grip on Amy's shoulders. She struggled for several minutes, trying vainly to drag the woman out.

By this time Rachel's own skirts were weighed down with snow and ice. She gave up trying to shake them free. She began to talk to Amy, shouting first, then speaking naturally, saying anything that came to her mind. "Come now! Get up. You said you hated me. Show me. Jason is coming. Raise your head. Speak! Hate me. You want to kill me? Try. Wake up. Wake!"

Shaking, pulling, wedging her shoulder under the boards, did no good. She hated and feared the woman but she couldn't let Jason's mother die. Amy stopped struggling. Her face and one free hand lay limp in the snow.

Rachel got up, stretched, tasted blood on her lips, and struggled through the falling snow toward the trail by which they had come. The wheel tracks had already disappeared, but down in the valley, before the last climb began, she made out a glorious sight. Lights flickered and swayed. Lanterns. Carried by men on the Withins trail.

Rachel raised her arms, waved, and screamed until she was hoarse. Her voice seemed to disappear into the night, muffled by the snow. She made her way back to Amy. The smouldering fire had caught the far end of the timbers, and despite the snow, it seemed to be creeping inexorably along one splintered board toward the woman's fallen body.

Rachel tried once more to move her, but she seemed to be made of lead. Desperate to do something, she attempted to smother the fire with snow. Smoke filled the air. Rachel felt around for the lamp. In the debris of the gig the metal-protected lantern still survived. She lit the wick again by the flames and struggled through the snow to what remained of the trail made by Blinker. She waved the lantern wildly in the air.

Below, much nearer, someone flashed a lantern in response. Then other lanterns were raised. To Rachel it seemed a miracle. She began to scream again. It was only then that she realized two men on horseback were plowing up the western slope. She raised the lantern in their direction.

"Hurry! Hurry!"

By the time she got back to Mrs. Bourne, the fire had sputtered out and only the acrid smoke remained, curling toward the injured woman. Rachel wedged herself under the edge of the boards again, getting between Amy and the smoke, but the woman remained still. Not knowing what else to do, Rachel slapped Amy's face. "Wake up."

The crunching noise grew louder, changing to the sound of hooves plowing through the drifted snow. She called, "This way. Help us."

One of the men swung off his mount. The other man took

both reins, and Rachel looked up to see Jason's dark figure running toward her.

"Here!" Rachel cried.

"Sweetheart! My God! You're half-frozen."

He pulled Rachel up against his body, holding her so tightly she gasped. "Your mother needs you. I can't get her out."

He called over her head, "Hold Rachel close, Hepton. Her skirts are all ice. Her feet are freezing."

She found herself lifted up into Big Hepton's arms like a doll, still protesting. But she also had time to think: *This man isn't drunk at all. He never was. It was all part of her scheme to separate us from rescue. . . . And that rescue could have saved her from being crushed there in the snow!*

By the flare of the approaching lanterns she could see Jason set his shoulder under the remaining portion of the wall while Nahum pulled Amy out. The two men worked frantically, rubbing and massaging her limbs while the other searchers gathered around. It was Nahum who shook his head first and placed his hand over Jason's. "Not a mite of use, sir. She's gone."

Jason called to one of the watchers, a rugged sheep farmer, who fell on his knees in the snow and massaged Amy's hands between his own great palms. In the flare of the lanterns Rachel could see Jason's grim face as he and Nahum uncovered his mother's cloak. It was sticky with her blood, across her breast and stomach. She had been crushed to death.

"We'll be makin' a bed-like, out of yon boards," one of the men volunteered, "to carry the lady down."

Jason nodded. His mouth was set and his face looked unusually pale, but there were no tears. He got up. "Hepton, I'll take my wife now."

There was considerable muttering and discussion among the men as they made a stretcher.

"A daft thing for Amy Bourne to do. Her that knows this country. Where'd she hope to go? And taking an outlander, too. She weren't thinkin' proper," one of the men protested.

"Nahum, throw me one of the blankets." Jason wrapped it around Rachel's body, enveloping carefully her soggy feet and ice-encrusted skirts. Nahum took a second blanket and tucked it over Amy Bourne.

It's over, Rachel thought. She had done what she could, but the danger was gone. The danger and the bitterness and the awful, haunting thought that she was not loved. . . .

She felt wildly exhilarated, anxious to ask questions. She marveled at how easily Jason carried her, and that even after this occurrence, he could put her cold cheek against his and murmur, "I almost lost you, sweetheart."

"I'm fine. Truly I am. It's odd. I feel quite drunk."

"It is the reaction. . . . Hepton, when I mount, hand her to me."

A minute or two later she was perched high on one of the Bourne farm animals, and warm, though soggy, in her husband's arms.

"Did Blinker get home?"

"She did. Maria found her. Maria was on her way up here. She climbed on Blinker's bare back and caught us as we came galloping over the moor from Haworth."

Somewhat subdued, Rachel asked after a hesitation, "Maria suspected?" Before he could answer she whispered urgently, "Remember, I was determined to meet you. I set off and your mother tried to warn me. I didn't harness Blinker properly, and the mare broke away. We tried to take shelter and the shed fell on us."

Jason's mouth remained firm and a muscle in his cheek stiffened. Then, with a weariness that made her long to comfort him, he said, "They are not fools. They will guess."

"Not if we stand by the . . . truth."

"Sweetheart, Maria and I both guessed the truth the minute we knew she had gone with you. If I had lost you . . ."

"You didn't. Jason, we must think about the people at the mills, and what Bourne ownership means to them and their families. She was right about that, you know. All my life I've taken everything and given nothing. But I can change."

He held her painfully close. "I don't want you to change, and I especially don't want you to become a copy of my mother. I knew a long time ago what a disastrous thing we had set out to do. I told her so. But she was sick with hate. Occasionally, in prison, the warders gave me a letter. It was all I read for those ten years. Bitterness and hate. I've done with all that."

He started to say something more, choked on the snow that

powdered his face, and she had a terrible urge to laugh. He said finally, "The Bradford Mill is sold. Or will be, within the week."

"No. I don't want that." She struggled in his arms, disturbing the horse and nearly upsetting herself. "I know about the letters. And I don't want you to sell the Bradford Mill. Your mother was right about that, too."

With his head bent over hers and his dark eyes fixed on her she felt as if he could read her soul. That would never do. She didn't want him to know the extent of Amy Bourne's insane plot. It would serve no purpose and he would carry the dreadful knowledge to his grave.

She raised her head. She could see a light in the single window of a sheep farm across the moor to the west. They were approaching Bourne Hall on the Haworth road. She began, "Jason?"

"Yes, sweetheart."

"So many odd things happened to me. Forgetting. Mixing up addresses. And they always happened after you had heard from home."

He avoided her eyes. He was watching the four men carrying Amy Bourne on the improvised litter. She realized suddenly the extent of the woman's influence over her son.

"I heard you arguing with Amy one day," she continued. "You said she was not to mistreat or hurt someone. It was someone she hated. I thought you were talking about Mrs. Debenham."

He was completely taken by surprise. "My God! Cecily? A shallow creature without a single redeeming feature. Rather like your friend Culhane."

"I wouldn't go that far." Poor Reverend Culhane! But it revealed a strong jealousy in Jason and she liked that part.

"At least, you rescued me from that wretched tavern in Paris the night I went there by mistake."

"I would never let you get far from me. I'm too possessive of my treasures."

They had reached the low stone wall of Bourne Hall. Maria was standing out on the cobblestones between the door and the road. She still had on the gown she had worn at the Revels. She looked chilled and white. Recognizing Jason, she ran out in the frozen wagon ruts of the road and reached for the reins. "Are they safe?"

Rachel said sternly, "Let me down."

Maria squeezed her hand. "Heaven be praised for that! I was out of my senses, thinking—everything."

Jason lifted Rachel down and dismounted. "Mother is dead."

Maria brushed past them, looking up the road. "Was she violent? What did she do?"

Jason started to speak. "It seems clear. She tried to—"

Rachel cut in. "Maria, your mother tried to persuade me to return. There was an accident at the Withins farm. She was crushed by a wall that collapsed."

Maria looked doubtfully from Rachel to Jason. He shrugged. Maria pushed past him and ran along the road to the men bearing the litter.

"You must stay here and see to things," Rachel told Jason. "I'll go in where it is warm. Join me when you can, darling. And ask Maria if she will come."

"Sweetheart." He kissed the tip of her nose and sent her into the house. She looked back from the doorway in time to see Jason's quick stride bring him to Maria's side. He put an arm around her, and they walked on into the darkness together. Rachel felt her heart responding with love and sympathy for them both.

Dilys and Finbar stood in the entry hall, gaping at her. In Finbar's eyes, curiously enough, there were unshed tears. He looked very old.

Now that the worst was over, Rachel found herself barely able to climb the stairs. The big, comfortable room she shared with Jason had never looked so warm and inviting. This was the heart of what she knew now as home. Trailing the blanket and her soggy skirts, she dragged herself to the comfortable chair she always thought of as Jason's.

She stripped off her cloak absently, then the skirt of her gown, thinking of what was happening on the ground floor of the house. She could imagine Jason's and Maria's anguish. Amy's body would be brought to lie in her own house. Tomorrow the wake would follow. Then the Yorkshire arvals. There would be much drinking and a somewhat festive air.

She undressed to the skin, wishing she had ordered up a bath.

She ached in every bone. The bad things, the dreaded things, were over, and now she ached. She felt faint and unsure of herself. Had she misinterpreted Jason's reaction to her safety, or Maria's feelings?

She would have welcomed Brigitte's ministrations tonight. Her hands shook so much she found it difficult to get into fresh petticoats and a shift and warm robe. Afterward, she curled up on the carpet in front of the fire, hugging her knees, and waited.

Voices shifted from the ground floor of the house to the outside and were gone. A horse neighed. Wagon wheels shrieked. The neighbors were returning to their farms.

The door opened and Maria stuck her head in. Her hair was still damp with snow and her eyes were red-rimmed. Rachel stared at her tensely. Maria's severe features softened. "Feeling better?"

"Yes, thank you. . . . Maria, how did you suspect I was in trouble?"

She hesitated, then burst out, "That tiresome Mrs. Hepton. She never expected to go to Keighley. I asked her after I heard Mother leave with you. It's my opinion the woman likes to paint Hepton worse than he is."

Rachel agreed. "I've always suspected it."

Maria's sudden smile lighted her worn features. "Then I'll say good-night."

"Good-night, dear."

Maria nodded and, leaving the door ajar, went back to her room.

Rachel had almost dozed off, when Jason came in. She heard his step in the hall. He still wore his wet boots, but he was peeling off his best greatcoat. He dropped the coat on the floor in a heap as he saw Rachel. She held her arms out to him, too tired even to rise from the floor.

There was no need. He moved slowly at first, perhaps unsure of her reactions, but he could not mistake the message of her welcoming arms. He reached down for her.

She complained, "You're soaking wet."

"So I am," he murmured huskily.

"Hold me closer. I'll warm you."

The low-burning fire in the grate threw its steady heat into the room, but they were not aware of it.

Outstanding Bestsellers!

FREE!!
BOOKS BY MAIL
CATALOGUE

BOOKS BY MAIL will share with you our current bestselling books as well as hard to find specialty titles in areas that will match your interests. You will be updated on what's new in books at no cost to you. Just fill in the coupon below and discover the convenience of having books delivered to your home.
PLEASE ADD $1.00 TO COVER THE COST OF POSTAGE & HANDLING.

BOOKS BY MAIL

320 Steelcase Road E.,
Markham, Ontario L3R 2M1

In the U.S. –
210 5th Ave., 7th Floor
New York, N.Y., 10010

Please send Books By Mail catalogue to:

Name_____
           (please print)

Address_____

City_____

Prov._____ Postal Code _____

(BBM1)